Turn Back
TIME

What Reviewers Say About Radcly*f*fe's Books

"…well-plotted…lovely romance…I couldn't turn the pages fast enough!"—**Ann Bannon**, author of *The Beebo Brinker Chronicles*

"The author's brisk mix of political intrigue, fast-paced action, and frequent interludes of lesbian sex and love…in *Honor Reclaimed*… sure does make for great escapist reading."—**Richard Labonte**, Q Syndicate

"If you're looking for a well-written police procedural make sure you get a copy of *Shield of Justice*. Most assuredly worth it."—**Lynne Jamneck**, author of *Down the Rabbit Hole* and reviewer for The L Life

"Radclyffe has once again pulled together all the ingredients of a genuine page-turner, this time adding some new spices into the mix. Whatever one's personal take on the subject matter, *Shadowland* is sure to please—in part because Radclyffe never loses sight of the fact that she is telling a love story, and a compelling one at that."—**Cameron Abbott**, author of *To The Edge* and *An Inexpressible State of Grace*

"*Stolen Moments*…edited by Radclyffe & Stacia Seaman…is a collection of steamy stories about women who just couldn't wait. It's sex when desire overrides reason, and it's incredibly hot!"—**Suzanne Corson**, *On Our Backs*

"With ample angst, realistic and exciting medical emergencies, winsome secondary characters, and a sprinkling of humor, *Fated Love* turns out to be a terrific romance. It's one of the best I have read in the last three years. Run—do not walk—right out and get this one. You'll be hooked by yet another of Radclyffe's wonderful stories. Highly recommended."—Author **Lori L. Lake**, *Midwest Book Review*

"Radclyffe, through her moving text…in *Innocent Hearts*…illustrates that our struggles for acceptance of women loving women is as old as time - only the setting changes. The romance is sweet, sensual, and touching."—**Kathi Isserman**, reviewer for *Just About Write*

Turn Back TIME

by

RADCLY*f*FE

2006

TURN BACK TIME

ISBN 1-933110-34-1

This Trade Paperback Original Is Published By
Bold Strokes Books, Inc.,
New York, USA

First Printing: March 2006

Credits
Editors: Ruth Sternglantz and Stacia Seaman
Production Design: Stacia Seaman
Cover Design By Sheri (GRAPHICARTIST2020@HOTMAIL.COM)

By the Author

Romances

Safe Harbor
Beyond the Breakwater
Innocent Hearts
Love's Melody Lost
Love's Tender Warriors
Tomorrow's Promise

Passion's Bright Fury
Love's Masquerade
shadowland
Fated Love
Distant Shores, Silent Thunder
Turn Back Time

Honor Series

Above All, Honor
Honor Bound
Love & Honor
Honor Guards
Honor Reclaimed

Justice Series

A Matter of Trust (prequel)
Shield of Justice
In Pursuit of Justice
Justice in the Shadows
Justice Served

Change Of Pace: *Erotic Interludes*
(A Short Story Collection)
Stolen Moments: *Erotic Interludes 2*
Stacia Seaman and Radclyffe, eds.

Acknowledgments

This story is a love story. At its heart, it's the story of two women's discovery of their love for one another. It's also the story of love between friends and the love for one's calling. Despite the fact that it is based upon some of my own personal experiences, this is Pearce and Wynter's story, not mine.

Many of the medical scenes are drawn from my experiences during surgical training. The hospital complex has changed a great deal in the last three decades, but I bet that little room with the cases of dusty medical texts and cracked leather sofas is still there, bypassed by the new construction and long forgotten. No one in this work is intended to represent any individual, living or dead, although Pearce and Wynter are as real as any people I've ever known. I've walked in their shoes, or they in mine, and the distinction is of no consequence.

I thank my teachers at the Hospital of the University of Pennsylvania and, most importantly, my fellow residents, for providing me with the finest surgical training possible anywhere in the world. I thank Lee for understanding that it is possible to love two things with equal passion, and that it was time for me to give to writing and publishing the attention and commitment that I had given to medicine. *Amo te.*

Radclyffe 2006

Dedication

For Lee
Past, Present, and Future

CHAPTER ONE

The instant Wynter Kline ducked through the archway into Perelman Quadrangle she was accosted by a wall of sound so overwhelming she nearly turned around and left. The block-wide flagstone square, flanked on all sides by the Collegiate Gothic and High Victorian brick buildings that typified the University of Pennsylvania, was jammed with three hundred fourth-year medical students. With music, beer, and convivial shouts, the members of the graduating classes from Philadelphia's four medical schools boisterously celebrated the most important event of their professional careers to date. Match Day was the long-awaited day when a computer program—having factored the variables of student rankings, interview results, and residency choices into a complex formula—ultimately assigned each fourth-year medical student from every medical school in the United States to a single residency position. At least 95 percent of the fourth-year students matched, and the other 5 percent were left to scramble madly for the final unfilled positions or go without a job after years of grueling study.

Early May evenings were still a little cool, and Wynter wore a pale yellow cotton sweater over a white Oxford shirt, khaki chinos, and docksiders. *Terminally preppy*, she'd often been told. It wasn't so much a style statement as how she felt most comfortable, so she generally ignored the good-natured, and sometimes *not* so genial, comments of her family and friends. She definitely wasn't in the mood for a party and hadn't bothered to change after a day spent on the wards. In fact, she barely felt as if she belonged with the revelers. Before she could dwell on the odd sense of detachment that had befallen her the moment she'd been handed the envelope containing her match results, the jostling, shouting mass of students magically shifted out of her way. Now that she could see more than the back of the neck of the person in front of her, she made out at least a half dozen kegs of beer, all tapped and dispensing foamy brew nonstop, and twice as many catering tables set end to end and littered with half-empty bottles of liquor and soda. Somewhere, a rock band competed with the human voices through speakers that must have been fifteen feet tall, if the blaring decibels that beat against her tympanic membranes were any indication. Everyone was celebrating, or drowning their sorrows.

Wynter didn't yet know which fate awaited her—joy or anguish. The envelope that held the key to her future, or at least the next five years of her life, was tucked into her back pocket. She was on the verge of escaping, having decided that she would rather not share this moment with hundreds of others. Particularly when she expected to be disappointed.

"Hey!" A wiry African American man a dozen years older than her own twenty-three pushed his way to her side. "You made it. I thought you were going to bail."

"Rounds ran late, and then two packed subway cars passed me by." Wynter smiled at Ken Meru. It seemed like only days, and not three years, since they had first introduced themselves over the white plastic–shrouded form of their cadaver. Although they had initially had little in common other than their desire to be physicians, the many Saturday afternoons they had spent alone in the eerie lab, bent over the desiccated, foul-smelling remnants of what had once undoubtedly been a vital human body, surrounded by death as they struggled to understand the mysteries of life, had forged the bonds of true friendship. Wynter squeezed his arm and forced excitement into her voice. "So? Tell me. What did you get?"

"Anesthesia."

"Just like you wanted." She threw her arms around his slim shoulders and kissed his cheek. "That's terrific. I'm so happy for you. Where?"

His smile, already brilliant, widened, and with shy pleasure, he tilted his head toward the towering buildings visible above the campus Commons. "Right here."

Wynter struggled not to let him see her reaction, which was a mixture of jealousy and disappointment. He'd gotten one of the best positions available in a highly competitive field. *His* dreams were about to come true. But it wasn't Ken's fault that she hadn't been able to pursue her dream with the same freedom that he had. She was truly happy for him, but her heart hurt. She forced a smile. "University Hospital. That's…that's the best news, Ken. What did your wife say?"

Ken laughed. "Mina said I better not stay too late. She wants to take me out to dinner."

"Then you should probably get going, buster." Wynter frowned and tapped her Seiko. "It's already after seven."

"I will. I will. But what about you?" He turned sideways, pressing close to allow a gaggle of excited students to shoulder past. "Did you get surgery?"

"I don't know."

"What do you mean?"

Wynter shrugged sheepishly. "I haven't looked yet."

"What? What are you waiting for?"

You wouldn't understand if I told you. I don't understand it myself. She was saved from answering when Ken's cell phone rang. He pulled it off his belt and pressed it to his ear, shouting hello. A moment later he closed the phone and bent close to her.

"I have to go. Mina got a babysitter and says I'm to come home right now."

"Then you'd better go. Another month and you won't have that many nights to spend with her."

"Call me," Ken said as he eased away. "Call me tomorrow and tell me what you got."

She nodded, realizing as she lost sight of him that she was surrounded by strangers. She didn't know the students from the other schools and had rarely socialized with those from her own. She'd been part of the accelerated combined BS/MD program at Penn State and had begun her clinical rotation at Jefferson Medical College off-cycle with the other students. Unlike her classmates, she'd preferred to study in her Center City high-rise apartment and not the medical school library. During her clinical years, she spent her days in the hospital, took night call every third or fourth night, and had rarely repeated a rotation with the same group of students. She had acquaintances but few friends, at least not in the medical community. Now with Ken gone, she had no reason to stay. *I shouldn't have come. I'm not even a part of this.*

Suddenly angry, she turned abruptly, intent on leaving. Her head snapped back as her chin slammed into the face of a dark-haired woman, and when her vision cleared, she found herself staring into stunned charcoal eyes. At almost five-eight, Wynter was used to being taller than most women, and she was as much surprised by the fact that she was looking up as she was by the sudden pain in her jaw. "God. Sorry."

"Ow! *Christ.*" Pearce Rifkin brushed a finger over her bruised lip. It came away streaked with blood. "Score one for your team."

"Oh no." Wynter reached out automatically. "You split your lip."

Pearce caught Wynter's wrist and held her hand away from her face. "It's okay. Forget it."

Pearce surveyed her assailant intently. She didn't know her, because she was certain she would have remembered had they met. An inch or so shorter, wavy shoulder-length reddish brown hair generously streaked with gold highlights, and sapphire blue eyes. With her fresh features and clear complexion, she was a walking J. Crew ad. "You're going to have a hematoma on your chin."

"Feels like it," Wynter agreed, fingering the already palpable lump. "We both need ice."

Pearce grinned, then winced. "Lucky for us there's about a ton of it here." She held out her hand. "Come on. Follow me."

Wynter stared at the outstretched hand. The fingers were long, capable looking. A broad hand, strong. It suited the woman, whose athletic build was obvious beneath her tight navy T-shirt and low-slung faded jeans. Her collar-length black hair, carelessly cut and verging on shaggy, framed a bold, angular face. She looked more like a college jock or one of the gathering's bartenders than a soon-to-be doctor. Wynter took the hand, and warm fingers closed around her own. Then, she was tugged none too gently into the crowd. In order to avoid playing human bumper cars with those being forced out of her path, she pressed against the back of the woman leading the way.

"What's your name?" she shouted.

The dark head half turned in her direction. "Pearce. You?"

"Wynter."

"Stay close, Wynter." Pearce clasped Wynter's hand more tightly and pulled it around her middle, drawing Wynter near as she faced forward and kept shoving. "Wouldn't want to lose you."

Wynter felt firm muscles rippling beneath her palm as Pearce twisted and turned and forged ahead. She was equally conscious of her own abdomen pressed to Pearce's backside. It was oddly intimate, and wholly unlike her. She was neither impulsive nor prone to letting others take charge. But here she was, being led—no, *dragged*—along by a stranger. She hadn't felt like her usual self-sufficient self for far longer than she wanted to admit, so she told herself that was the reason she didn't resist. Plus, she was curious. Curious about the woman who so confidently cut a swath for them as if she owned the Commons.

"Hey, Pearce," a man called out. "You're bleeding."

"No shit," Pearce called back. "Brilliant. You must almost be a doctor."

Raucous laughter followed them, until Wynter jerked Pearce to a stop. "Hey! Hold on a minute and turn around."

Surprised by the strength in the arm encircling her waist and the command in the smooth voice at her ear, Pearce halted and angled around in the crowd. "What?"

"Did you ever think to ask if I wanted to go where you're going?"

"Nope. I'm a take-charge kinda person."

"Well, so am I." Wynter extracted her hand from Pearce's grip and studied her lip. "And he's right. You're bleeding pretty briskly. Do you have a handkerchief?"

Pearce laughed. "Come on. Do *you*?"

Wynter smiled and shook her head, then tapped a young blond woman in a scrub suit on the shoulder. "Can I have that napkin, please?" She pointed to the paper square beneath the woman's plastic cup.

"Huh?" The blond gave them a curious look, her eyes widening as she focused on Pearce's face. "Oh, Pearce. Baby. Look at you. What happened?"

"She hit me," Pearce stated matter-of-factly, nodding toward Wynter.

"Now wait a minute," Wynter protested as she watched the blond's expression change from surprise to…jealousy. *Jealousy?* Wynter took a good look at Pearce—at the way she tilted her hips forward suggestively while smiling at the blond, the way her eyes unconsciously flickered over the woman's mouth, at the lazy grin. She'd seen that look before—on men. *Oh. So that's the way it is.*

The blond visibly bristled. "What do you mean, she *hit* you."

Wynter edged away. *Time to get out of the line of fire.*

Laughing, Pearce reached out and reclaimed Wynter's hand. "It was an accident, Tammy." She took the napkin and dabbed at her face, then looked at Wynter and indicated her lip. "Better?"

Wynter assessed the damage, ignoring the other woman. "It's slowing down, but you still need ice. It's probably a branch of the labial artery."

"Yeah, probably. Come on, almost there." Pearce was about to turn away when Tammy grasped her arm.

"Where did you match?" Tammy asked, adding almost petulantly, "As if I didn't know."

"University," Pearce replied, her eyes narrowing dangerously. Then she pointedly slipped her fingers through Wynter's and pulled her against her side. "Let's go."

Wynter couldn't move away as the crowd automatically shifted to fill the slightest available space. "Look, I have to—"

"You're not going anywhere fast," Pearce said, "and your face is swelling."

"Fine. Go."

It took another five minutes of determined effort, but eventually they reached the tables where the drinks were being dispensed. Huge coolers lined the sidewalk. Pearce collected two plastic cupfuls of ice and handed one to Wynter. "Better hold one of these cubes against your chin. You're getting a pretty good bruise."

Experimentally, Wynter worked her jaw from side to side, noting the tightness just in front of her ears. She sighed. "It looks like I'm going to be wearing my bite block for a week or so too."

"TMJ?" Pearce wrapped the napkin around an ice cube and held it against her lip.

"Yes, but not too bad. Just every once in a while my jaw reminds me that I landed on my face too many times when I was a kid."

"Climbing trees?" Somehow Pearce couldn't see Wynter playing contact sports. She looked more like the tennis type. A good workout in a country club where you didn't get dirty, barely worked up a sweat, and had lunch in an air-conditioned restaurant after your set was finished. She knew, because it had been her mother's favorite pastime.

Wynter laughed, thinking of how much she had wished for tennis courts and a chance to play when she'd been young. "No, ice skating. I started when I was two, and I can't tell you how many times I landed on my face while trying to do triple axels."

"Olympic aspirations, huh?" Pearce could see her on a rink, a trainer nearby, choreographed music coming through the speakers. *Yeah. That fits.*

Though Pearce's tone was teasing, for some reason, Wynter didn't mind. She shook her head. "Nope. Always wanted to be a doctor. You?"

"Yeah. Pretty much always." Something dark passed through Pearce's eyes, making them even darker, nearly black, and then was gone. She glanced at her free hand, which was streaked with dried blood. "I should go wash this off."

Wynter recognized when a subject was off-limits. "I'll go with you. I want to get a look at your lip once you get it cleaned up. You might need stitches."

"I don't think so."

"Well, we'll decide after we see it."

Pearce grinned, ignoring the pain in her lip. She wasn't used to letting anyone else call the shots. It was neither her nature nor the reputation she had acquired in the last four years. And because of who she was, others expected her to lead. It was refreshing to find someone who didn't seem to care who she was. "Okay, Doc, whatever you say."

"Very good," Wynter said with an approving laugh. "But since you seem to be good at it, I'll let you navigate."

Once more, Pearce clasped Wynter's hand in a motion so natural, Wynter barely gave it a thought. They stayed close to the buildings, skirting the crowds, until they reached Houston Hall. When they slipped inside the student center, the noise level mercifully fell.

"Oh, thank God," Wynter murmured. "I might actually be able to think in a minute." She glanced around the high-ceilinged room with its ornate carved pillars and marble floors. "These old buildings are amazing."

"Where did you go to school?" Pearce asked.

"Jefferson."

"Ha. We're rivals."

Wynter stopped, extricated her hand from Pearce's grasp, and regarded her appraisingly. "Penn?"

"Uh-huh."

The two medical schools, a mere twenty blocks apart, had sustained a rivalry since the eighteenth century. Over the decades, the competition had become more theoretical than real, but the students of each still claimed superiority.

"Well, then you better let *me* decide how bad the problem is," Wynter said with utter sincerity.

"I might," Pearce allowed, "if I didn't care what my lip looked like when it was healed."

They regarded one another, eyes locked in challenge, until their smiles broke simultaneously and they laughed.

"Let's go upstairs," Pearce suggested. "The bathrooms down here are going to be too crowded." After years on campus, she knew the out-of-the-way restrooms that were never occupied, and quickly guided Wynter through the twisting hallways and up a wide flight of stone stairs. "Here we go."

Pearce pushed the door open and held it for Wynter, who preceded her inside. There were three stalls, all empty. Wynter ran cold water in one of the sinks and pulled paper towels from the dispenser. She soaked several, folded them, and motioned for Pearce to lean over the sink. "I guess I don't have to tell you this is going to sting."

"I can do it."

"I'm sure. But this way I can see what I need to see before you stir up the bleeding again."

Pearce quirked an eyebrow. "You don't have much faith in my skill."

"Well, considering where you trained…" Wynter carefully loosened the crusted blood below the pink surface of Pearce's lip. "Damn. This goes right through the vermilion border, Pearce. You probably *should* get stitches."

"Let's get a look." Pearce leaned toward the mirror and squinted. "It's not too deep. A Steri-Strip will probably take care of it."

"And if it doesn't, you're going to have a very noticeable scar because of the color mismatch," Wynter said pointedly.

"Jeez, you sound like a surgeon."

"I hope so. That's the plan."

"Really? Where are you going?" It was the most common question of the day, but for Pearce, the day had held little excitement. She knew where she was going. She'd always known where she was going. Suddenly, she was much more interested in where *Wynter* would be going.

Embarrassed, Wynter sighed. "Actually…I don't know."

"Oh. Shit. Sorry. Look," Pearce said hastily, "maybe I can help out. You know, with finding places that still have openings."

Wynter frowned, trying to make sense of Pearce's offer. Then, suddenly, she understood what she was saying. "Oh, no. It's not that I didn't match. Oh well—*maybe* I didn't match, but…I just haven't looked yet."

"You're kidding. You got your envelope three hours ago, and you haven't looked yet? Why?"

Because I know it's not going to say what I want it to say. Wynter didn't want to admit the truth, especially not to this woman, and struggled for an explanation. "I was tied up on rounds. I didn't get a chance."

Unexpectedly bothered by Wynter's obvious discomfort, Pearce didn't push for further explanation. "Do you have the envelope with you?"

"Right here." Wynter patted her back pocket.

"Well, come on. Let's see it."

For the first time, Wynter actually wanted to know, and she wanted Pearce to be the one who shared the moment with her. It didn't make any sense, but she felt it all the same. With a deep breath, she pulled the envelope from her pocket and opened it in one unhesitant motion. She slid out the card, and then without looking at it, passed it to Pearce.

Pearce looked down, read the words, and hid the swift stab of disappointment. "Surgery. Yale–New Haven." She met Wynter's eyes. "Good place. Congratulations."

"Yes," Wynter said, not surprised. Her tone was flat. "Thanks."

"Well. Let's see to the rest of you."

"What?" Wynter asked, still trying to decipher the odd expression on Pearce's face. For an instant, she'd looked sad.

Pearce handed the card back and cupped Wynter's jaw with both hands. She saw Wynter's eyes widen in surprise. "Open," she said, placing her thumbs over each temporomandibular joint. "Slowly, but go as far as you can."

Wynter was aware of a rush of butterflies in the pit of her stomach and her face flushing. Pearce's hands were not only strong, but gentle. They stood so close that their thighs brushed.

"Feels okay," Wynter murmured as Pearce carefully circled the joints. *Feels...wonderful.*

Pearce slid her fingers along the border of Wynter's jaw and over her chin. "Sore?"

Wynter shook her head. She couldn't feel her chin. All she could feel was the heat of Pearce's skin. She was breathing fast. So was Pearce. Pearce's eyes had gotten impossibly dark, so dark that the pupils blended with the surrounding irises, creating midnight pools that Wynter was absolutely certain she could drown in.

"Pearce," Wynter whispered. Whatever was happening, she couldn't let it. But as she slipped further into Pearce's eyes, she couldn't recall why not. She forced herself to focus. "Don't."

"Hmm?" Pearce lowered her head, intent on capturing the hint of spice that was Wynter's scent. She slid her hand around the back of Wynter's neck as she very lightly kissed the tip of her chin where the bruise shadowed it. Her lips tingled and she tightened deep inside. "Better?"

"Much," Wynter said teasingly, hoping to make light of the moment.

"It gets better," Pearce said, her lids half closed, her mouth closing in on Wynter's.

"I...Pearce...wait..." Wynter's cell phone rang, impossibly loud, and she jumped. She fumbled for it, unable to look away. Pearce's mouth was an inch from hers when she whispered, "Hello?" She listened, staring at the pounding carotid in Pearce's throat. "I thought you weren't coming. Okay. Fine. I'm in the bathroom. I'll be right out." She closed the phone. Her voice was thick. "I have to go."

"Why?" Pearce kept her hand on the back of Wynter's neck and caressed her softly, tangling her fingers in Wynter's hair. She knew what she saw in Wynter's eyes. She'd seen it before, but it had never stirred her quite like this. "Got a date?"

"No," Wynter said as she gently backed away, escaping Pearce's grip, if not her spell. "It's my husband."

Standing absolutely still, Pearce said nothing as Wynter stepped around her and hurried out. When the door swung closed, leaving her alone, Pearce bent down and retrieved the forgotten white card. Wynter must have dropped it. She ran her thumb over the type, then slid the card into her breast pocket.

Goodbye, Wynter Kline.

Chapter Two

Four Years Later

Just as Pearce pulled her robin's-egg blue 1967 Thunderbird convertible into the parking garage on South Street next to the University Museum, her beeper went off.

"Shit," she muttered as she tilted the small plastic rectangle to check the readout. Five a.m. and the chaos was starting already. The number, however, wasn't one of the nurses' stations in the twelve-story Rhoads Pavilion, which housed most of the surgical patients. It was the chairman's office. And at that hour of the morning, it wasn't his secretary calling. It was him. "Fuck."

She pulled the classic car into the angled slot in the far corner of the first floor next to the security guard's tiny booth. It was a reserved space and one for which she paid premium rates, but she wasn't about to let some idiot dent the vehicle that she had spent countless hours restoring. She knew all the guards would keep an eye on it. She tipped them every month in thanks. "Hey, Charlie," she called as she climbed out.

"Good morning, Doctor," the pencil-thin retired cop said. He wore his security guard uniform with the same pride with which he had worn the Philadelphia Police blues for thirty years. "Might better have left the baby home today. The news is calling for rain later. Could be snow if it gets a little colder."

"I'll leave the car here until spring, then," Pearce yelled as she jogged toward the street. Her cell phone wouldn't work in the parking garage. And it wouldn't matter to her if it rained or snowed, because she was on call for the next twenty-four hours and would not be leaving the hospital for at least thirty. "You take good care of my girl, now."

Charlie laughed and sketched a salute as she disappeared up the ramp.

Once on the sidewalk, she thumbed the speed dial and punched in the number. When it was answered by the voice she anticipated, she said, "Rifkin."

"Would you stop by the office before rounds this morning?"

Although framed as a question, it wasn't a request.

"Yes sir. I'm just outside the hospital."

"Come up now, then."

Pearce didn't have time to reply before the call was cut off. *Fuck.* She ran through the list of patients on the chairman's service, wondering if something had gone wrong that she didn't know about. The junior surgery resident who had been on call the night before knew that he was to advise her of any problem, no matter how small. But other than several routine questions about transfusions and antibiotic coverage, she hadn't gotten any calls of note. Despite the fact that her family home was only forty minutes away in Bryn Mawr and she could easily have had her own wing of the house and all the privacy she required, she lived in an apartment in West Philadelphia so that she could make it to the hospital in less than fifteen minutes. She did not like to be surprised by problems in the morning, and a call at this hour to the chairman's office could only be a problem. *Fuck.*

The elevator was empty when she got in. It stopped at the second floor to admit a bedraggled blond with dark circles under her eyes, a bloodstained Rorschach on the left thigh of her scrub pants, and a crumpled piece of paper in her right hand that she studied as if it were the Holy Grail. Pearce knew it was "the list"—an inventory of all the patients on the service to which the resident was assigned, with coded notations as to each patient's admission date, date of surgery, procedure performed, most recent lab tests, and outstanding test results. The work of the day—or night—centered around the list and, if an attending surgeon were to call for an update on one of their patients, everything the resident needed to know was on that single piece of paper. Even though every resident carried a PDA and there were computers at every nurses' station, the "list" still prevailed as the source of all vital info. Without it, more than one resident had found himself giving incomplete or incorrect information, and in short order, had been looking for a new job. At least once a day, some frantic resident could be seen rushing through the halls asking all and sundry, "Have you seen my list? I lost my list. Has anyone seen my list?"

"Hey, Tam," Pearce said. "How you doing?"

Tammy Reynolds looked up from the page, blinking as if she had awakened from a dream. Then she smiled slowly, some of the fatigue leaving her eyes. "Hey you. I haven't seen you at O'Malley's recently. Have you been hiding, or has someone been monopolizing all your time?"

"Neither. But I'm senior on the chief's service, and it's been busy."

"I know which service you're on." She moved a little closer in the elevator and put her hand on Pearce's waist. She circled her thumb on Pearce's pale green scrub shirt, massaging the muscles underneath. "I pay attention to where *you* are. And you're never too busy when you want something."

Pearce moved back out of touching range, aware that they were slowing for the fifth floor. She didn't want the doors to open and someone to see them. And she didn't want Tammy's attentions. At least, not right at the moment. "I gotta go. Take it easy, okay?"

"Call me. I'm on the onc service this month," Tammy called as Pearce stepped off the elevator. "I could use some of your medicine, baby."

Pearce lifted a hand in a parting wave, grateful that there was no one waiting in the hall who might've heard the comment. She didn't care what her fellow residents knew or thought of her, but she preferred that her private business not become the topic of conversation among the administration. Well, at least not by her own invitation.

She walked along the maroon-carpeted hallway toward the large corner office. The staff surgeons' offices were clustered in one corner of the fifth floor with the surgeons' lounge adjoining them and the operating suites taking up the rest of the floor on the opposite side of the building. This arrangement enabled the surgeons to wait in their offices, working, until their cases were ready to go. Since it was a matter of routine for cases to begin late, it prevented lost time, something that every surgeon loathed. The secretarial spaces, separated from the hallway by waist-high partitions, were all empty. The office doors were closed. The administrative work of the day would not begin until eight thirty, and by that time, most of the surgeons would already be in the OR. She enjoyed the quiet, empty warren, and likened the stillness to the calm before the storm. She glanced at the yellow face of her Luminox sports watch and grimaced. Five fifteen. If this took more than a few minutes, she would be late meeting the other residents, and that was a bad precedent to set. As the most senior resident on the service, she organized the daily work schedule, assigned the more junior residents to assist on cases, and oversaw the night call rotations. She was always on time, if not early, because her behavior set the tone for her service, and she expected everyone to be prompt. She expected a lot of things, and if she didn't get it, there was hell to pay.

She was the ultimate authority over all things resident-related on the chief's service, the busiest of the general surgery services. The only individual in the hospital with more power within the resident hierarchy was the chief surgical resident, and he was in charge of his own service and outpatient clinic—for all practical purposes functioning as a junior attending with only minimal supervision from the attending surgeons.

"I hope this is quick," she muttered as she approached the closed door to the chairman's office. An unassuming plastic nameplate next to the door announced his name. Ambrose P. Rifkin, M.D., Chairman.

She knocked on the door.

"Come in."

His desk was situated in the far corner of the room, angled so that he sat with his back to the two walls of windows, as if the outside world were a distraction or, at the very least, of no interest to him. It also allowed him to look at his visitors with the sun at his back, and in *their* eyes. He knew how to position himself to advantage.

"Pearce," he said, gesturing to the two armchairs in front of his broad walnut desk. The dark furniture and thick area rugs lent the room a traditional air, heavy and rich, and suited his style. Though he was in his mid-fifties, his thick hair was still midnight black, his aquiline features patrician, and his body trim from twice-weekly squash matches. He looked—and was—a commanding presence.

"Sir," she said as she sat. The last time she'd seen him had been the previous afternoon when she'd assisted him on a low anterior colon resection. They'd said nothing to one another during the case, other than when she had provided him with the pertinent patient history and he had asked her to outline the plan for removing the constricting carcinoma that was lying in the patient's pelvis. She'd answered succinctly and accurately. He'd said nothing until an hour and a half later, when he'd stepped back from the table and said, "I have a meeting. Close her up."

He'd left without waiting for her reply. Now, the sound of his modulated baritone brought her back to the moment, and she realized she'd missed the first part of his sentence.

"...resident."

Pearce straightened, her forearms resting on the wooden arms of the chair. She was careful not to grip the armrests and allow him to see that she was nervous. "I'm sorry, sir. I didn't get that."

He frowned, his piercing blue eyes raking over her. "I said, we're adding a new resident."

"In January?" The residency year ran from July to July, and it was very unusual for anyone to start off-cycle. In fact, she couldn't remember ever having seen that happen.

"We've had an empty third-year slot since Elliott decided he couldn't cut it. Now we have a body to fill it. Are you complaining?"

"No, sir, but why is he switching programs in the middle of the year?"

Ambrose Rifkin smiled wryly. "*She.*"

Pearce flushed, knowing that he would enjoy her inadvertent confirmation that surgical residents were usually men. She knew it was his opinion, and that of most of his contemporaries, that they *should* be men. She was one of the few exceptions in the program, and despite the fact that more female surgeons were trained every year, the specialty remained the last bastion of male privilege within medicine. She said nothing, wishing to avoid another trap.

"She's technically a fourth-year, but she missed six months because of some...personal issues. Spent a few months working in an emergency room, apparently." His tone was both dismissive and disdainful. "But she has good credentials, and I know the chairman of her program. He says she has good hands."

Coming from a surgeon, that was the highest compliment another surgeon could receive. It was better to be the most technically proficient than to be the smartest. Brains didn't help much when you were faced with a bleeding vessel and twenty seconds to stop it before the patient bled to death. The only thing that mattered then was the steel in your spine and the skill in your hands.

"When is she starting?"

"She should be here at seven."

"*Today*?"

"Problem, Dr. Rifkin?"

"No sir," Pearce said quickly, reshuffling the day's priorities in her mind. Every night before she left the hospital, she double-checked the surgery schedule to make sure that nothing had been changed without her knowledge. Nothing made a staff surgeon angrier than showing up for a case and discovering there was no resident available to assist him. Unfortunately, sometimes the secretaries canceled or, worse, added cases without informing the resident in charge, and it was the resident who paid for such miscommunication. She'd already assigned today's cases to her team, and she had no one who could orient the newcomer. "Uh, could Connie take care of her this morning, until I'm done with the aneurysm?"

Connie Lang was the department chair's admin, and the go-to person for anything that the residents needed.

"Call Dzubrow and tell him to assist on the aneurysm. Whatever he's doing in the lab can wait."

Pearce bit back a protest. An abdominal aortic aneurysm resection was a major case, and as the senior resident on the service, it was hers. She needed every major case she could get if she wanted the chief surgical resident's position the following year. Henry Dzubrow was her only real competition for the position among the other fourth-year residents, and he was supposed to be spending the next six months working in the shock-trauma lab. It seemed to her, though, that he was showing up in the operating room at every opportunity.

She stood, because she knew if she stayed much longer, she was going to complain about Dzubrow's preferential treatment. And that would surely doom her. A surgery resident did not complain about anything. Period. She could still remember her first day and her father standing in front of the auditorium where the twenty-five new first-year residents sat nervously awaiting his instruction. His expression had been unreadable as his cold blue eyes had swept the room, passing over her face as if she were just one of the indistinguishable bodies. She could remember his words and knew that he'd meant them.

If you're not happy here, all you need to do is come to me and say so. There are fifty people waiting for every one of your positions, and I can guarantee they will be happy to take your place. Never forget that being here is a privilege, not a right. He'd looked over the room one more time, his gaze settling on Pearce just a moment longer, it seemed, than on the others. *Privileges can be lost.*

"What's her name?" Pearce asked.

The chairman looked down at a folder on his desk. "Thompson."

"Okay."

He said nothing, and Pearce left, closing the door behind her without being asked. She took a deep breath and let it out, forcing down her anger and the frustration that always accompanied any kind of interaction with her father. The only time they ever seemed to be comfortable together was in the operating room. She probably should be used to it by now, but she wasn't.

"Fuck."

"Having a rough day already, Pearce?"

Pearce jumped in surprise and spun around. Connie Lang stood behind her balancing two cups of coffee in cardboard containers and a Dunkin' Donuts bag.

"The usual," Pearce said. "You're starting a little early, aren't you?"

Connie nodded toward the closed door. "He's got a budget meeting at six thirty." She smiled, a predatory gleam in her eye. "He knows that the desk jockeys can't think clearly this early in the morning, and he has a much better shot at getting exactly what he wants this way."

"Doesn't he always?"

Wisely, Connie said nothing. "He told you about the new resident?"

Pearce nodded.

"She's downstairs at the admissions desk. I heard her ask for directions to the surgeons' lounge."

"Jesus. Already?"

Connie smiled. "She's eager. Isn't that what you want?"

"Oh, sure. Can't wait." With a sigh, Pearce started toward the elevators. "I better go find her. What does she look like?"

"Just a little bit shorter than you. Nice looking. Shoulder-length hair, a little bit blond, a little bit reddish brown. She's wearing navy scrubs."

"I'll find her," Pearce said, wondering just what Connie meant by nice looking. She was getting tired of dating the usual suspects—nurses and other residents. She didn't date anyone for very long and didn't have much time to look elsewhere for new prospects, so new faces, especially pretty ones, were welcome. *Maybe this won't be so bad after all.*

Chapter Three

Pearce turned the corner toward the elevators and caught sight of a woman in navy blue scrubs at the far end of the corridor heading toward the surgeons' lounge.

"Hey, yo!" She sprinted down the hall. "Are you the new—" She skidded to a halt, her voice trailing off as she looked into the face she had not expected to see again. Wynter's face had lost the soft fullness of youth and taken on the angular lines of full-blown womanhood. She looked tired, but that was to be expected. She looked leaner than Pearce recalled, too, as if she had taken up running in the intervening years. "Are you…Thompson? We met—"

"Yes," Wynter said quickly, not wanting to bring up the specifics of an interaction she still didn't understand. She had expected to run into Pearce at some point, because she remembered Pearce mentioning where she had matched. She just hadn't expected it to be so soon, and not this way. "Pearce, right?"

"That's right," Pearce said, trying to fit the pieces together in her mind. The match card had said Wynter Kline. She knew, because it was still stuck in the corner of the mirror over her dresser. Why she'd never thrown it away, she wasn't certain. *Married name,* Pearce thought with a jolt. *Thompson must be her married name.*

"I, uh…I'm starting today," Wynter said into the silence.

"I know." Pearce tried to hide her shock. It didn't matter who Wynter was. Didn't matter that for just a moment four years ago they'd shared…something. She needed to stay on track, needed to regain control of the situation. "I'm your senior resident, and we've got two minutes to make it to rounds. Follow me." Then Pearce turned and pushed through the fire door into the stairwell at the end of the corridor. Wynter hurried to keep up.

The senior resident? God, we're going to be working together every day for the next four or five months. She could only imagine what Pearce thought of her. She'd practically let Pearce—a total stranger—kiss her, in the bathroom of all places. And then, to make matters worse, she'd just walked out without a word. *Could you have been any more stupid, or more unkind?* She'd thought of those moments often over the years. It was a night she'd regretted ever since, for a multitude of reasons. With a deep breath, Wynter put the memories of that brief interlude out of her mind. That was in the past and had nothing to do with her current situation. There were much more important things to deal with now. "We're on Rifkin's service, right?" Wynter asked of Pearce's back. "The chief's service?"

"Yeah." They reached the bottom of the stairwell, and Pearce shouldered open the door, belatedly holding it for Wynter. Reluctantly, she started her orientation spiel. It was the last thing she wanted to do at any time, but especially not right before rounds when it was going to cost her a great case. "Did Connie give you the breakdown of the services?"

"Not exactly," Wynter said, pulling even with Pearce, who had picked up her pace again. "This all happened kind of fast, and I only interviewed with Dr. Rifkin a couple of days ago. Connie walked me through getting my ID, parking sticker, payroll information, and my employee health physical yesterday afternoon. Then she just told me I'd start on Rifkin's service today and that someone would pick me up at seven."

"Did you meet with any of the residents?"

"No."

Pearce clenched her jaw. It was perfectly within her father's purview as the chairman of the department to hire anyone he wanted, but it was very unusual to interview a new resident without soliciting the input of at least one of the senior residents. He had obviously known for a few days that Wynter would be joining the service, but he hadn't said anything to her. She'd been cut out of the loop, but then, no one ever said the hospital was a democracy.

"You didn't know anything about it, did you?" Wynter said quietly. *No wonder she's peeved.*

"Doesn't make any difference." Pearce stopped and turned to face her. The hospital was waking, and nurses and other personnel hurried through the halls around them, preparing for the shift change. They stood like an island in the sea of white, ignoring the passersby. "We've been down a resident since September—one of the third-year guys decided that he wanted to go into anesthesia. We carry fifty patients on the service and it's every third night."

Wynter blanched. "Every third? That's rough."

Pearce grinned and a feral look came into her dark eyes. "We do things here the way they've been doing it for sixty years or so. We don't cross-cover at night. Every surgical service has its own residents in house. I guess Connie didn't tell you that, huh?"

"I'm sure it never crossed her mind," Wynter said steadily. She'd gotten her balance back. She was being tested, and she didn't intend to show weakness. "And if it had, it wouldn't have made any difference. I was just surprised."

"Yeah, well, like I said. It's not the norm, but it's the way we do it here."

"No problem."

"We make dry rounds every morning in the cafeteria at five thirty. That means you have to see your patients before then. We need a rundown of vital signs, I and Os, updates on lab tests, that kind of thing."

Wynter nodded, mentally doing the math. If she needed to be at the hospital by five, she'd need to be up at four. She could handle it. She had to handle it. She didn't have any choice.

Pearce made a sharp left, and they descended a set of stairs into a basement cafeteria. The round tables in one half of the room were filled with residents and students, most of them in scrubs and white coats. "Let's get some coffee."

"Amen," Wynter murmured.

As they made their way through the cafeteria line, Pearce said, "There are five of us on the service, counting you. Two first-years, a second-year, and me."

"You're acting chief?"

"Yeah."

"The other fourth-years are either in the lab, on the other two general surgical services, or on vascular." Pearce grabbed a bagel and a plastic container of cream cheese, then filled a twenty-ounce Styrofoam cup almost to the brim with coffee. "We only have one chief resident slot. The other fifth-years get farmed out to the affiliate hospitals in the system."

Wynter could tell by the tone of Pearce's voice that anyone who didn't finish their final year of training at the main hospital as the chief surgical resident automatically qualified as a loser in Pearce's mind. She could understand the sentiment. You didn't give up five years of your life to come in second. She'd already lost one year of training because she had to accept a third-year slot or give up surgery. She felt the anger rise and quickly pushed it aside. What was done was done. All she could do now was go forward. "If there's five of us now, why are we taking call every third?"

Pearce handed a ten to the cashier and said, "For both of us."

"You don't have to—"

"Tradition." Pearce looked over her shoulder at Wynter. "Chief buys. And as far as the schedule goes, on this service, you and I back up the first-years—so we're on every third and the second-year fills in the blanks. The chairman doesn't trust the first-years alone with his patients."

Wynter ran the night call schedule in her head. Two first-year residents and a second-year, also technically a junior resident. Then Pearce. It didn't jive. "So who's been backing up the other first-year if you're the only senior resident on the service?"

"Me. We have to stagger the call now so I can cover one of them every other night."

"Every other?" Wynter tried not to sound appalled. Twenty-four hours on, twenty-four off could get old really, really fast. She'd only ever done it for a day or so when another resident had a family emergency or had been too ill to get out of bed. She remembered one of the first rules of surgery she'd been quoted. *The only reason for missing work is a funeral. Your own.* "How long have you been on every other?"

Pearce shrugged. It didn't matter to her if she was officially on call or not. She was always around. She had to be. She knew what she wanted and what it took to get it. "A while."

"Okay." Wynter decided it was not prudent to bring up the newly instituted eighty-hour rule. In theory, house officers—all the residents in any specialty—were prohibited by law from working more than eighty hours in one week, were required to have one day off out of every seven, and were supposed to be allowed to go home after twenty-four hours in a row on call in the hospital. Surgical training programs, however, often interpreted those rules very loosely. The dictum was that surgery could only be learned in the operating room, and if there were cases to be done, the residents needed to be there, no matter what time of the day or night. Residents who questioned their hours often found themselves being assigned to the least interesting cases, or worse, being cut from the program. Pyramid programs like the one at University took more residents during the initial years of training than they could finish, knowing that some would quit or be cut before their fifth and final year. Wynter couldn't afford to lose her position. If she needed to work a hundred hours a week, she would. She'd just have to make some adjustments in her personal life.

"There's the team." Pearce nodded toward a table where three young men waited. "I bring reinforcements, guys," she said as she sat. She did not apologize for being late.

Wynter took the seat between Pearce and a rangy Asian who looked too young to be a doctor. *Must be one of the first-years.* She nodded to each man in turn, fixing a name with a face, as Pearce introduced them in rapid fire sequence. Liu, Kenny, and Bruce. They acknowledged her with a range of grunts and clipped hellos. It wasn't hard to tell which one had been on call the night before, because he was unshaven and he smelled like he could use a shower. It didn't bother her, because she'd gotten used to the familiarity bred by shared stress and the camaraderie that made it tolerable. She was exquisitely aware of Pearce just to her left, radiating energy that warmed her skin. She could still remember how hot Pearce's hands had been. All these years later, the memory burned as brightly as the touch.

"Bring us up to speed, Kenny, and then you can get out of here," Pearce said.

Kenny, despite his weary appearance, shook his head. "I want to stay for that lap chole that Miller is doing. I'm up for the next one, right?"

"There's one on the schedule tomorrow," Pearce replied. "You can have that one. You're supposed to be off at eight. The rest of the day's light. Take advantage of it."

He didn't look happy, but he nodded. He pulled a folded piece of paper from his shirt pocket, unfolded it, and began his morning litany. "1213, Constantine, fem-pop bypass, postop day four. Tmax, 101. Temp 99.9. I pulled his drain and wrote for him to be out of bed to a chair TID."

"Pulses?" Pearce asked, making a note on the clean sheet of paper where she had written the information just relayed to her.

"Plus four in the posterior tib."

Pearce raised her head. "What about the dorsalis pedis?"

"I couldn't feel it."

"It wasn't there or you couldn't feel it?"

Pearce's expression made him squirm. "I…don't know the answer to that."

"Go back and find out. Next."

Wynter leaned close to Pearce. "Got another piece of paper?"

Wordlessly, Pearce slid a second sheet out from beneath her fresh page and passed it to Wynter, who began to make her own list.

It took another twenty minutes to go through the fifty patients on the service, the other two residents chiming in with the information on the patients assigned to them. They finished at six fifteen.

"Liu, you've got the mastectomy at eight with Frankel. Bruce, you're with Weinstein for the amp, and Kenny, you're out of here. Thompson and I will take the floors."

Wynter noted the use of her last name and knew it was a subtle reminder that she was not yet part of the team. She had to earn that right, although none of them would actively exclude her. She simply would be invisible until she had shown that she could do the job and not make more work for them.

"What about the chief's aneurysm?" Liu asked.

Pearce carefully folded her list and slid it into her breast pocket. "Dzubrow will take it."

The three men looked at each other, but no one said anything.

"Okay, hit the floors and get your notes done before the OR. I don't wanna have to clean up behind you."

Wynter waited until the three men gathered their paperwork and cleared their breakfast remnants before she spoke. "I guess I lost you that case, huh?"

"You didn't." Pearce slid her smart phone from the case on the waistband of her scrubs where it kept company with her beeper and the code beeper. The weight of her various electronics pulled her scrubs down over her narrow hips to the point where it seemed like she was about to lose her pants. "Got one?"

Silently, Wynter slid her PDA from her shirt pocket.

"I'll beam you my cell phone, my beeper number, and the other guys' beeper numbers. Connie can get you the departmental numbers that you need to know."

"What's the chief's number?" Wynter asked as they synchronized their data via the infrared beam.

Pearce grinned. She'd expected Wynter to be smart. That had been apparent even as a medical student. The one critical number you always wanted to answer promptly was the chief's. "3336."

"What's yours?"

The second most important number. "7120."

"Then I'm all set," Wynter said with a small smile.

"I guess it's time for the grand tour, then. Let's make rounds, and I'll tell you about the attendings."

"How many are there besides Rifkin?"

"Five, but only two are really busy."

"What about him? Most chairmen don't really do much surgery."

Pearce shook her head. "Not him. He does four or five majors, three days a week."

"Jeez. How?"

"He runs two rooms from eight until finishing Monday, Wednesday, and Friday."

Wynter groaned. "Friday?"

"Yeah. That sucks. Especially if it happens to be your only night off for the whole weekend."

"Two rooms," Wynter noted. "So a senior in both rooms?"

"You got the system down. You and I start and close his cases. He'll bounce back and forth between the two rooms for the major parts. That satisfies the insurance requirements because he's there for the critical part of the case."

Wynter didn't want to ask too many questions too early in the game, but it seemed that Pearce was willing to provide the kind of inside information that was going to make her life a lot easier. So she persisted. "Does he let you do anything?"

"It depends. Are you any good?"

"What do you think?" The question was out before she could stop it, and she wasn't even sure why she'd said it. First days were always tough. And now she was starting all over again in a new place and needing to prove herself yet again. She hadn't expected to see Pearce, not today, and not like this. It rattled her. It rattled her to realize that she'd be seeing Pearce every single day, and every day she'd be wondering if Pearce remembered those few minutes alone when something so intense had passed between them that the rest of the world had simply faded away. She remembered, even though she had no place for the memory.

"Well, you were right about my lip," Pearce said softly.

Wynter studied Pearce's face. A faint white line crossed the junction of the pink and white portions of Pearce's lip, and where the scar had healed unevenly, there was a notch in the border. "I told you you needed stitches."

"Yeah, you did." Pearce suddenly stood. "Let's get going."

"Sure," Wynter said quickly, standing as well.

"Hey, Rifkin," a male voice called. "It's going on seven. Don't you have any work to do?"

Wynter didn't hear the reply over the buzzing in her ears. She stared at Pearce as the pieces fell into place. She saw the nameplate by the chairman's door. Ambrose P. Rifkin, MD. Ambrose *Pearce* Rifkin. "You're related to the chairman?" she said in astonishment.

"He's my father."

"Nice of you to tell me," Wynter snapped, trying to remember if she'd said anything negative about him. "Jesus."

Pearce appraised her coolly. "What difference does it make?"

"It would have been nice to know, that's all."

Pearce leaned close. "Kind of like knowing you have a husband?"

Before Wynter could reply, Pearce turned her back and walked away.

Oh God, Wynter thought, *she hasn't forgiven me*. But then, she hadn't forgiven herself, either.

CHAPTER FOUR

"You don't usually make floor rounds, do you?" Wynter asked as she matched her stride to Pearce's. The attending surgical staff delegated routine daily patient care—changing bandages, removing sutures, ordering lab tests, renewing medications, and dozens of other tasks—to the residents. The most senior resident on each service ensured that the work was carried out by the more junior physicians. Pearce should be exempt from such menial tasks.

"I see every patient on the service every day," Pearce said, "but the juniors do all the scut. I just like to make sure they don't miss anything."

As they hurried along, Wynter tried to set landmarks in her mind so she wouldn't get lost the first time she was alone. The University Hospital was a labyrinth of interconnected buildings that had been erected at various times over the last hundred years, and to the uninitiated, it appeared to be a haphazard jumble of walkways, bridges, and tunnels. Despite having a good sense of direction, she was already a little disoriented.

"Thanks for showing me around." Wynter was starting to huff just a little as Pearce made a sharp right and directed her into yet another dark, narrow stairwell. *I won't gain any weight on this service if this is her normal pace.*

Pearce shrugged, taking the stairs two at a time. "Part of the job."

But it wasn't, Wynter knew. Many other residents wouldn't have bothered, leaving her to fend for herself in a strange place with a heavy load of brand-new patients. Nor would they take the time to double-check on the patients the way Pearce apparently did. Even though

Wynter barely knew the woman, Pearce's professionalism didn't surprise her. She remembered the way Pearce had cradled her face, examining her jaw, her eyes focused but compassionate, her hands—

"Oh!" Wynter exclaimed as she caught the toe of her clog on a tread and plunged headlong toward the railing. She thrust out her arm to break the impact and landed in Pearce's arms instead. They went down in a heap on the stairs.

"Umph," Pearce grunted. "Jesus Christ. What *is* it with you?"

"Believe it or not," Wynter gasped, "I'm usually very coordinated." She took stock of her various body parts, uncomfortably aware of Pearce beneath her, sprawled on her back, Wynter's arms and legs tangled with hers. The pain in her left kneecap did nothing to mitigate the sensation of Pearce's tight, lean thigh between her legs. Pearce's heart hammered against her breast, and warm breath teased her neck. "Sorry. Are you hurt?"

"Hard to tell," Pearce muttered. *All I can feel is you.* She kept her hands carefully at her sides, because any movement at all would only increase the unintentional intimacy of their position. Wynter was soft in all the right places, and every one of them seemed to fit perfectly into Pearce's body, as if the two of them had been carved into mirror images. *It's been too long since I've gotten laid. That's all it is.* "Any chance you can get off me? I'm going to have a permanent groove in my back from this stair."

"Oh God, yes. Sorry." Wynter braced both hands on the next stair, bracketing Pearce's shoulders, and pushed herself up. Unfortunately, the movement lifted her torso but pressed her pelvis even more firmly into Pearce's. She heard a swift intake of breath just as the rush of heat along her spine took her by surprise. "Oh."

"Something hurt?" Pearce asked, managing to keep her voice steady. Two more seconds of this full-body contact and she wasn't going to be able to keep her hands to herself. As it was, her thighs were trembling and her stomach was in knots. "God, you feel good."

"What?" Wynter asked through a haze of unanticipated and inexplicable sensation.

"Hurt," Pearce mumbled, fighting down her arousal. "Anything hurt?"

"Oh, no," Wynter said quickly. *Just the opposite.* She wondered fleetingly if Pearce was always so warm. She could feel the heat radiate from her even through their clothes. Pearce's body was firm, but so unlike the angles and hardness she was used to. But then, it had been so long since she'd been this close to anyone that perhaps her memory was distorted. As carefully as she could, she rolled away until she was lying on her back next to Pearce, staring at the watermarked, yellowing paint of the ceiling. "What's the damage?"

Other than the fact that I'm going to be turned on for hours with no relief in sight? Pearce sat up and rested her elbows on her knees. She rubbed the back of her neck where a muscle had knotted when she'd tensed to keep her head from striking the stairs. Then, she carefully rotated her back from side to side. "Everything seems to be in working order. You?"

"I gave my patella a pretty good crack," Wynter admitted, realizing that Pearce had probably prevented her from sustaining a really serious injury. Gingerly, she extended and flexed her leg. "Thanks."

"Here, let me check it out." Pearce slid down several steps and turned. She bent forward and slipped both hands around Wynter's calf. "Pull your scrubs up so I can see your knee."

"It's okay. Just bruis—"

"Let me decide. We might need to X-ray it."

"Look. We need to make rounds—"

"Jesus," Pearce said irritably, "are you going to argue with everything I say?"

"I'm just trying to save time. We've got patients to see."

"And we will. As soon as I check this out. Now pull up your pants."

Considering the fact that Pearce was standing over her and she had nowhere to go, even if she were able to gracefully extricate herself, Wynter complied. A four-inch abrasion extended over the upper portion of her tibia to her kneecap, which was swollen and discolored. When Pearce instructed her to straighten her leg, she did, watching Pearce's fingers press and probe her knee. Good hands, in every sense of the word. Certain, proficient, and gentle. The dance of flesh over flesh, no matter how innocent, was nevertheless an intimate exchange. She was always aware of the trust bestowed upon her when she examined a patient, and felt it now in Pearce's touch.

"Hurt here?" Pearce asked, palpating first the medial and then the lateral ligaments surrounding the joint.

"No, feels stable. I'm sure it's fine."

Pearce glanced up, her dark brows coming together as she frowned. "You're a lousy patient."

"So I've been told. Can I get up now?"

"Slowly." Pearce straightened and extended her hand. "And don't full weight-bear right away. Put your other hand on my shoulder until you test the knee."

Wynter took Pearce's hand and allowed herself to be guided upward, but she resisted the instruction to lean on Pearce. She'd had quite enough bodily contact for the moment, and she needed to reassert her independence. She'd be damned if she'd let Pearce think she was anything less than capable in all regards. She gradually settled all of her weight onto the injured leg. "All systems go."

"Good." Pearce noticed Wynter's reluctance to touch her and chalked it up to the usual reluctance of straight women to get too close to her, even when they weren't bothered by her being gay. Somehow, they were still uncomfortable. Usually she didn't care, and the ripple of disappointment she felt at Wynter's avoidance was a surprise. She dropped Wynter's hand. "One more flight."

"No problem."

Pearce waited for Wynter to set the pace and followed this time, carefully assessing Wynter's gait. She was pleased to see there was no evidence of a limp. The stairwell led into a short corridor that ended at a plain brown metal door. She nodded when Wynter gave her a questioning look. Wynter hit the door bar and together they stepped into a brightly lit hallway opposite the surgeon's lounge.

Wynter looked around, frowning. "Damn. I could've sworn we'd be on the fourth floor."

Pearce leaned a shoulder against the wall, fiddling with the tie on her scrub pants, rhythmically drawing the string through her fingers. She grinned, enjoying the role of tour guide. She didn't question why. "We were—in the Malone building. Except that the fourth floor of *that* building connects to the *fifth* floor of this one. Don't ask me why."

"You're putting me on, right?"

Slowly, Pearce shook her head.

"Oh, I am in so much trouble."

"No, you're not. It's my job to see that you aren't." Pearce pushed away from the wall and walked a few feet to the elevator. She punched the *up* button. "Usually we walk, but I'll give you a break."

"Don't bother. I can handle the stairs."

"Maybe *I* can't."

Wynter snorted, but smiled. "I feel like I should be drawing a map or dropping breadcrumbs."

"Pay attention, and in a few days, you'll know all the secrets to this place."

"Really?" Wynter watched Pearce's face, searching for some hidden meaning. They'd been alone for close to an hour, but they hadn't really talked about the last time—the *only* time—that they'd been alone together. They should clear the air. She knew they should. But she didn't want to bring it up. She didn't want to know that Pearce had been angry with her all these years. Or perhaps she didn't want to know that Pearce had never thought of her at all.

"It's not all that complicated." Pearce turned away from Wynter's probing gaze. She didn't know what might show in her face, but she didn't want Wynter to think that those few moments years before meant anything now. So many things had happened since then, it might have been another life. She was certainly a different person. The elevator bell rang and saved her from thinking about it any longer. "Let's start at the top."

"Sure."

Several minutes later, they stepped out into a dimly lit corridor, and Pearce pointed. "Two wings on each floor. The lower numbers are to the left, the higher to the right. Main surgical floors are twelve, ten, nine, and eight. Intensive care units are on six."

Wynter groaned. "The ICU is one floor up from the OR? I hate transporting postop patients in the elevator."

"Me too," Pearce agreed. "But there wasn't enough room for them to expand the number of OR suites and still keep the intensive care units on the same floor."

"How many OR rooms?"

"Twelve general surgery, four GYN, four ortho, and a few unassigned."

"Busy."

"Oh yeah." Pearce started down the hallway on their left and indicated the first room. "This is an APR patient—"

"Wait a minute," Wynter said, frowning down at her list. "APR?"

"We tend to identify patients by their attending's initials. This one is Rifkin's."

"The colon resection from yesterday, right?" Wynter asked, still scanning the patient names. "McInerney."

"That's the one. We finished at six last night, routine case. She still has a drain, an NG tube, and an IV."

"Is it weird, working with your father?"

"I wouldn't know," Pearce said flatly. "Rifkin is the chairman. That's the only relationship we have in here."

Wynter was surprised by the absence of anger or much of any emotion at all in Pearce's voice. Nevertheless, she recognized the finality of her tone. She wondered if it was the subject matter or the fact that *she* was asking that bothered Pearce. Either way, she had clearly stepped out of bounds. What was it about Pearce Rifkin that made her forget the rules? "I'm sorry. That was none of my business."

"No problem. I get asked it a lot." Pearce pivoted and walked into the first patient's room.

It took a moment for Wynter to recognize that the discussion was closed. She hastened after Pearce, and for the next fifty minutes they moved from one patient to the next, reviewing chart notes, pulling drains, updating orders, and generally coordinating each patient's care. They didn't speak except to discuss care and treatment plans until everyone on the list had been examined. They worked quickly and efficiently. Comfortably together. Wynter wasn't surprised. From the very first they'd had a natural rhythm, even when they were sparring.

"Ready for another cup of coffee?" Pearce asked as they sat together at the eighth-floor nurses' station finishing the last of their chart notes.

"Oh yeah," Wynter replied. She hadn't had much sleep the night before. The week had been a whirlwind of activity what with packing and moving, worrying about her new position, and trying to anticipate all the difficulties inherent in her new life. She was beat. A sudden thought occurred to her as she and Pearce started down the stairwell yet again. "Am I on call tonight?"

"New residents always take call the first night. You know that."

She did, but she still hadn't planned for it. Foolish.

Pearce put both hands on the push bar of a door that sported a large red sign proclaiming *Fire Door—Do Not Open*. "Let's get some air." She gave it a shove.

"Why not," Wynter said, glancing at the time. She needed to make a phone call.

"Something wrong?" Pearce asked, checking the sky. The rain in the forecast was nowhere in sight. It was thirty degrees outside, a clear, crisp January day. Neither of them wore coats. The street vendors, as usual, were undeterred by the weather. Their carts, pulled into position each day behind trucks and four-wheel-drive vehicles, were lined up in front of the hospital and throughout the entire campus, dispensing every kind of food from hot dogs to hummus.

"No," Wynter said quickly. "Everything's just fine."

"Actually, *I'm* on call tonight." Pearce walked toward the third stainless steel cart in the row. The small glass window was partially closed and steamed from the food warming inside. "But I want you to stay and get used to how the service runs. You'll be on tomorrow night."

"Fine." Wynter had no choice, and it really wasn't an unreasonable request. She'd be expected to shoulder some of the responsibility for running the service as quickly as possible, and in order to do that, she had to be familiar with the procedures and protocols of the new institution. Even had she disagreed, it was Pearce's call. That was the nature of the hierarchy, and she accepted that. Time to claim her place in it. She edged in front of Pearce and ordered. "Two coffees." She glanced at Pearce. "Want anything else? It's on me."

"In that case, I'll take a street dog with chili and mustard."

Wynter winced. "It's ten thirty in the morning."

Pearce grinned. "Then I'll take two."

"You're sick," Wynter muttered and then relayed the order. She paid and collected the brown paper bag, turning to Pearce. "I suppose you want to eat outside?"

"Cold?"

"Not at all."

"Uh-huh, sure. You're shivering from the thrill of it all." Pearce laughed at Wynter's muffled expletive. "Come on, I'll show you my hideaway."

"Is this one of those secrets?" Wynter watched Pearce's expressive eyes turn inward, wondering if she'd once again tread on forbidden territory, but then she saw the smile flicker and flare. The tiny scar did nothing to detract from the lush beauty of Pearce's lips. In fact, the irregularity made her mouth all the more appealing, and Wynter had the sudden urge to touch the less than perfect spot with her fingertip. She tightened her grip on the paper bag, afraid of the impulse. She'd never just wanted to touch someone for no other reason than to feel their skin.

"You never know," Pearce replied, taking one of the coffee cups from Wynter. Her fingers brushed over the top of Wynter's hand. "It might be."

Chapter Five

Wynter groaned as Pearce grasped her elbow lightly and guided her down a narrow alley between two buildings. When Pearce pulled open a nondescript door that led into yet another stairwell, Wynter balked. "You're just doing this to torture me, aren't you?"

Pearce turned innocent eyes to Wynter as she propped the fire door open against her hip. "Doing what?"

"You know very well," Wynter grumbled, edging past her. When her arm brushed across Pearce's chest, she blushed. "How far up are we going this time?"

"Third floor."

"Fine." Wynter started up and did not look back until she reached the third-floor landing. "You just want to make sure I can never find this place again."

"Well, it wouldn't be a hideaway if everyone knew about it," Pearce said reasonably.

They were obviously in one of the older buildings in the complex. The vinyl tiles on the floor were scuffed and gray with age. The overhead fluorescents flickered halfheartedly, as if they might go out at any moment. Abandoned equipment lined the walls, some of a vintage well before Wynter had even contemplated medical school.

"Where are we? This looks like where old EKG machines go to die."

Pearce laughed. "In a way, that's true. It is a graveyard, of sorts, now. This entire building housed Women's Care at one time, with Labor and Delivery on the upper floors, GYN and the outpatient clinics on the lower floors. Then, when the new buildings were built, all of the clinical services moved out. There are just a few leftover administrative offices still here and some lab space that no one uses."

"And we're here…why?" Wynter felt as if she were in a museum, not a hospital. The place had an eerie feel, as if they were in a time warp and at any moment, nurses in starched white dresses and caps would appear, trailing along behind physicians as they made their rounds.

"I told you," Pearce said as she removed a key ring from her back pocket. She unlocked a wooden door whose varnish had started to crack and peel, reached inside with a certainty born of habit, and turned on a light. She stepped aside and gestured into the room. "After you."

Wynter gave Pearce a quizzical glance, but stepped inside. "Oh," she murmured in surprise.

The room was small, perhaps eight by ten, and appeared even smaller due to the bookshelves that lined three walls, and the large dark green leather sofa, matching chair, and wooden desk that crowded together in the center of the room. There were books and journals everywhere, crammed onto the shelves, stacked on the desk, and heaped in untidy piles on the floor around the sofa and chair. She tilted her head to read some of the titles. *Annals of Surgery*, *Journal of OB/GYN*, *Archives of Surgery*, and a half dozen others that she recognized. The books on the shelves were all surgical textbooks, some of them clearly decades old. She turned to Pearce. "What is this place? It looks like an old library."

"It used to be the residents' lounge."

"But it isn't anymore?"

Pearce shook her head. "When they moved all the surgical patients into the pavilions around the corner, this was too far away to be practical. Now, no one but me even remembers it's here."

Wynter sat on the sofa and ran her hand over the soft surface, worn smooth and thin in places from years of use. A green-shaded student's lamp—an original, not a reproduction—sat on the desk. Once again, she felt like she'd stepped back in time. Even though this room was part of an era when she would not have been welcomed as a member of the club, she felt a kinship to those who had come before her. "This place is awesome."

"Yeah." Pearce flopped into the oversized leather chair and swiveled sideways, hanging her legs over one arm and bracing her shoulders against the opposite one. She dug in the paper bag and extracted a wax paper–wrapped hot dog. The roll was orange from the chili sauce that had soaked into it. She took a bite, chewed quickly, and swallowed before lifting it in Wynter's direction. "You sure you don't want one?"

"Not without premedicating with Prilosec first." Wynter sipped her coffee and watched Pearce inhale the hot dog in three bites. Her pleasure was obvious, nearly carnal, and Wynter found herself staring at Pearce's mouth as she licked a drop of mustard from her chin.

"What's the matter?" Pearce asked. "Am I drooling?"

"No," Wynter said quickly, coloring. To cover her embarrassment, she said, "So if this place is such a well-kept secret, how come you know about it?"

"I used to come here when I was a kid."

"A kid? How old?"

Pearce managed to shrug even lying down. "Eight or nine, maybe."

"With your father?"

Pearce swung her legs around and sat up, extracting the second hot dog from thc bag. She kept her head down as she unwrapped it. "Uh-huh. He used to bring me in on the weekends sometimes when he was making rounds. Then, if things got busy, he'd park me over here until he was done."

"Did you mind?"

"Nah. I could always find something to read."

Wynter tried to imagine a young Pearce browsing through the bookshelves or falling asleep on the couch. She wondered if she'd been lonely. "Did you already want to be a doctor by then?"

"Rifkins are always doctors."

"Your grandfather worked on the first heart-lung machine, didn't he?"

"Yes. His lab used to be in the building behind this one. I don't remember him all that well, because he never seemed to make it to any of the family gatherings. Always at the hospital." Pearce rose and paced in the narrow space between the sofa and the bookcases, running her fingers over the dusty spines of the now-historic tomes. She pulled one off the shelf, opened it, and leaned over Wynter's shoulder from behind, holding the book at eye level.

Without thinking, Wynter curved her palm beneath Pearce's hand to steady her grip on the book. Pearce's forearm rested against hers. The name William Ambrose Rifkin was scrawled across the inside of the cover in fading black ink. She took a sharp breath. "I can't believe this book is just sitting in here." She twisted around until she could look into Pearce's face. "Shouldn't it be in a medical museum or something?"

"Like I said, I don't think anyone remembers this room is here. And a lot of my grandfather's papers and notes are archived at the Philadelphia College of Surgeons already. This probably isn't worth all that much." She closed the book, suddenly feeling foolish. She had no idea what had prompted her to bring Wynter to this room, let alone show her some old books that belonged to a man she barely remembered. Abruptly, she reshelved the volume and returned to her chair and her coffee. "I can get you a key if you want."

"Oh, I don't—"

"Never mind. The library's a lot more comfortable." Pearce stood, agitated and restless. "We should probably head over to the OR and make sure everything is running on time."

Wynter rose quickly and intercepted Pearce's flight to the door. "What I *meant* was I don't want to impose on your space. It's obviously special to you."

Pearce's eyes were opaque black disks, revealing nothing. "Sometimes this place"—she swept her arm in a wide arc, indicating the hospital complex, like a small city, and the hundreds of people who worked inside it—"can wear you down. Sometimes you just need a few minutes to regroup. This is a good place for that."

"I appreciate it." Briefly, Wynter trailed her fingertips over the top of Pearce's hand. "I just might take you up on it. Thanks."

"You're welcome." Pearce's eyes cleared and she grinned. "Come on, I'll show you a shortcut to the OR."

Wynter took a deep breath and plunged after her as Pearce bounded out the door. It occurred to her that this hospital was Pearce's own private playground, and she was being introduced to the neighborhood by the kid who ruled it. She realized something else as well. She very much wanted to be worthy of playing on Pearce's team.

"Pearce," Wynter called, "stop for a minute."

"What's the matter?" Pearce said with a laugh, turning to face Wynter but continuing to walk backward down the hall. Somehow, she managed to miss running into the people coming in her direction, or perhaps they simply parted for her like the Red Sea before Moses.

"Tired already?"

"Not on your life, Rifkin," Wynter snapped, yanking her beeper off her pants and peering at it. "What's 5136?"

Pearce's expression immediately grew serious. "The ICU." She was tempted to take the call herself, but Wynter was a senior resident and it was about time they both got a sense of what she could handle. She pointed to a wall phone next to the elevator and leaned against the wall while Wynter dialed.

"Dr. Thompson," Wynter said when a ward clerk answered the phone. She pulled her list from her pocket and anchored the phone between her shoulder and ear while she unfolded it. "I was paged. Uh-huh. Uh-huh. Wait a minute, who…Gilbert, uh-huh…how much fluid?"

Pearce tensed. It was all she could do not to grab the phone and ask the nurse what the problem was, but she forced herself to stand still and just listen. She needed to find out just how far Wynter could be trusted alone.

"No," Wynter said firmly. "Leave the bandage in place, soak it with salinc, and make sure she's had a CBC and electrolytes drawn today. We'll be right there. Oh, and make sure she doesn't eat or drink anything."

"What's up?" Pearce asked as soon as Wynter hung up.

"Mrs. Gilbert complained that she was leaking."

"Leaking. As in…?"

"As in," Wynter informed her as they hurried down the hall, "her gown and bed seemed to be covered with cranberry juice."

"Fuck."

"That was my thought too. She's what, three days post gastric bypass?" Wynter took a look at her list. "Yeah. And her last hemoglobin was 12, so it's not likely she had a big postop hematoma that no one noticed. Too soon for that to drain anyhow."

"I agree," Pearce said darkly. "If she bled after surgery, her blood count would be lower, and even if that were the case and we missed it, it's too soon for a collection of blood to drain. Did they get her out of bed today?"

"I don't know," Wynter said, pushing the button for the elevator. "But apparently, the patient had a coughing episode just before she noticed the leaking."

"Dandy. So what are you thinking?"

They stepped into the elevator and moved to the rear, where Wynter said in a voice too low for the other passengers to hear, "I'm thinking that Mrs. Gilbert has a dehiscence. Aren't you?"

"Yeah, that's exactly what I'm thinking."

"Is she yours?" Wynter asked as they maneuvered their way through the crush of people and into yet another hallway. It was a touchy question, and she half expected Pearce to lose her temper. No one liked to have a complication, especially a surgeon. And a technical complication, one that might have been avoided had the surgeon performed the procedure differently, was the hardest thing for a surgeon to accept or, sometimes, even to admit to. She had a feeling that Pearce did not like to have complications.

"No. Dzubrow…one of the other fourth-years…did it with the chief." There was no satisfaction in her voice. The double doors to the ICU were closed, so she swiped her ID through the card lock and punched in the code. "3442," she said for Wynter's benefit.

"Got it."

The doors swung open and they entered the controlled chaos of the surgical intensive care unit. Twelve beds were lined up along the far wall, separated only by curtains and the minimum amount of room to allow a nurse to move in between them. Tables at the foot of each bed were covered with charts and graphs and lab reports. Flexible plastic tubes connected ventilators to many of the motionless patients in the beds. The lights were too bright, the beeping and clatter of machines too loud, and the atmosphere far too impersonal for the severity of the illnesses housed within.

It looked exactly like every other SICU that Wynter had ever been in. "Which one is she?"

"Bed five."

When they reached the bedside, Pearce leaned over the bed rail and smiled at the anxious woman in the bed. "Hi, Mrs. Gilbert. What's going on?"

"I think I sprang a leak, dear."

"This is Dr. Thompson. She's going to check you out." Pearce eased away from the bed and signaled Wynter to move closer. "See what you think."

Wynter pulled on latex gloves and lifted the sheet. "Mrs. Gilbert, I'm going to remove your dressings so I can get a look at the incision.

Are you having any pain?"

"It's sore. No worse than this morning, though."

"Did this happen while you were coughing?" Wynter lifted one corner of the sterile gauze that covered the midabdominal incision as she talked. A little conversation often helped to distract the patient during the examination.

"Right after that, I think. They told me coughing was good for my lungs. Do you think I shouldn't have done it?"

"No, I think it's important to keep your lungs clear after surgery. You did fine." Wynter had a good idea of what she would find, and she wasn't surprised to see a glistening pink loop of bowel protruding through the central portion of Mrs. Gilbert's abdominal incision. She gently replaced the bandage.

"Dr. Rifkin and I are going to talk for a minute, and then we'll be right back," she said and turned away. She met Pearce's gaze. "Did you see it?"

"Yep. Looks like we're going to have to do a little repair job. I'll call the chief. You get her ready to go."

"Okay." Wynter turned back to explain to Mrs. Gilbert that her incision had partially opened and that they would need to go back to the operating room to reclose it. She didn't tell her any more, because it wouldn't change the procedure to be done and would only frighten her. Although it looked gruesome, it wasn't a serious situation as long as they took care of it before infection set in or the bowel was injured. By the time she had the consent signed, Pearce was finishing on the phone. "Are we all set?"

"Well, the chief is in the middle of the aneurysm, and after that he's got a colon resection waiting."

"She shouldn't sit around here for a few hours," Wynter said quietly.

"That's what I said."

Wynter waited, catching the glint in Pearce's eyes. "And…?"

"Looks like it's you and me, Doc."

Doc. No one else had ever called her that with quite the same mixture of teasing and respect. Wynter smiled. "Well then, let's go do it."

CHAPTER SIX

What have you got?" Ambrose Rifkin asked as he backed through the swinging door of the operating room, his gloved hands held at chest level. He'd shed his gown and used gloves after the last case, but kept his freshly gloved hands uncontaminated before he scrubbed again. It allowed him to cut down his time between cases.

Pearce waited several feet away from the operating table, already gowned and gloved, while Wynter prepped the patient's abdomen with Betadine, taking care to avoid the surface of the exposed loop of bowel with the caustic solution. "Mrs. Gilbert, a sixty-three-year-old female, three days post gastric bypass. She dehisced her wound about forty-five minutes ago."

"Any precipitating event?"

"Probably coughing."

"Huh." He walked to within three feet of the table, took one quick glance at the patient's abdomen, and then swept an eye over the monitors at the head of the table. He nodded to the anesthesiologist. "Everything okay, Jerry?"

"She's fine, Am."

Pearce's father regarded Wynter across the table. "What's your plan here, Dr. Thompson?"

Putting a resident on the spot by asking them to outline a procedure that in all likelihood they would not do was a tried-and-true technique that quickly identified lazy or inferior candidates. It was axiomatic that a resident never came to the operating room without understanding both the problem and the solution, even when they did not expect to be performing the surgery.

Surprised that the chairman even remembered her name, Wynter made a last swipe over the stomach with the prep solution. "We need to extend the incision and do a thorough intra-abdominal washout as well as a visual inspection of the gastric plication." As she stripped off her prep gloves and extended her arms for the sterile gown which the scrub nurse held out to her, she continued, "We ought to culture the wound too."

"What makes you suspect infection?"

The chairman's tone was level, but his inflection suggested that he disagreed with her.

She shrugged, snapping on her sterile gloves. "I don't. But we're here, and it's a simple test to do, and if we miss an early necrotizing fasciitis we're going to look pretty stupid tomorrow."

He laughed. "And we wouldn't want that, would we."

"I don't know about you, sir," Wynter's eyes sparkled above her mask, "but I wouldn't like it."

"Very well, then. Just make sure you use something that's not going to come apart this time."

"I was planning on a nonabsorbable," Wynter said, wisely refraining from pointing out that she had nothing to do with the previous complication. Culpability was not the issue. Correcting the problem was. "O-prolene should be sturdy enough to hold her together."

"Make sure you interrupt the suture every few inches, because I don't want her back here again." As quickly as he had entered, he turned to leave. With his back to the room, he said, "Call me if you have any problems, Dr. Rifkin. I'll be in eight doing the colon."

"Yes sir," Pearce said as the door swung closed behind him. She reached for the sterile sheet that the scrub nurse held out and passed it across the operating table to Wynter, who waited on the opposite side. "You like to live dangerously," she said low enough that the others couldn't hear.

"Why?"

"That remark about infection—you'd probably be safer with him sticking with protocol."

"Thanks for the tip," Wynter said, meaning it. In many ways, residents bonded and protected one another, very much like other closed societies such as the military or police. They covered for each other, and they very rarely laid blame, knowing next time they could be the one whose actions were being scrutinized. "He seemed to take it well enough."

"That's because you're a bit of a cowboy, and he likes that. You wanna be careful, though, because that kind of confidence can backfire if you're wrong."

Wynter snapped the sterile drape down over the patient's feet and picked up the next one that would cover her head. "Well, you should know. You've got hot dog written all over you, and I don't mean with chili and mustard."

"Maybe," Pearce said lightly, "I'm just really good."

"And maybe," Wynter said, "so am I."

"Let's find out."

When they'd finished draping off the sterile field, leaving only a square of abdomen around the open incision exposed, Wynter automatically circled the foot of the table to the left side, to the assistant surgeon's position. When Pearce didn't move out of her way, she stopped in puzzlement. "What?"

"Are you left-handed?" Pearce asked conversationally.

"No."

"Then you ought to be operating from the other side of the table."

Without a word, Wynter headed back to the right side of the table, hiding her surprise. She hadn't expected to be given quite so much responsibility so quickly, but Pearce was letting her act as the primary surgeon. Granted, Pearce was with her and was technically responsible since she was the most senior surgeon in the room, but still, she was turning the case over to Wynter. It was a test, but it was also an honor.

Wynter looked over the raised sheet suspended between two stainless steel poles, which separated the nonsterile area from the sterile operating field, at the anesthesiologist who sat monitoring the patient's vital signs. At one time, when anesthesia was delivered via ether dripped from a can onto a cloth over the patient's face, the divider had been called the ether screen. It still was, although no modern surgeon actually remembered when ether was used. "We're starting."

"She's all yours."

Without looking at Pearce, her attention already focused on the surgical field, Wynter held out her right hand. "Scalpel."

❖

"Nice job," Pearce said as she and Wynter stood side by side in the women's locker room.

"Thanks." Wynter unlocked her locker and opened it, in search of clean scrubs. The case had only taken an hour and a half, but the patient was large, and it had been hard work retracting the thick abdominal wall enough to be certain that their sutures were placed in healthy tissue that would not pull apart yet again. By the time they'd finished, they were both sweating, and when they'd removed their gowns, both their shirts were soaked with sweat. "The second time around is always tough."

"Yeah. But now it's done right."

"For sure." Wynter pulled off her scrub shirt, acutely aware of Pearce standing just a few feet away. Wynter wore a tank top beneath her scrubs because wearing a bra all day was too confining. She was used to changing clothes in front of other women; she had done it thousands of times in the last eight years. She had known that some of those women were gay and it never bothered her. When you lived and worked in such close physical proximity to others for hours on end, you learned to respect personal space. Still, Pearce being this close unsettled her, and she didn't know why. "Thanks for letting me do the case."

"No problem."

Out of the corner of her eye, Wynter saw Pearce strip off her shirt and quickly looked away when she realized that Pearce wore nothing beneath it. The image of toned arms, small smooth breasts, and muscular torso lingered as she stared into her locker. Quickly, she extracted a clean shirt and slipped it over her head. With her face averted, she said, "That was a blast."

"Yeah. It was." Pearce slammed her locker and leaned her shoulder against it. She felt exhilarated, the way she always did after a difficult case went well. In many ways, this one had been routine, because technically it wasn't all that challenging. On the other hand, she'd been under extra pressure because the patient had already sustained a complication, and she wanted to be sure there were no more problems. Plus, the attending had given her full responsibility for the procedure, and that added to both her anxiety and her pleasure.

Wynter leaned her back against her locker, her shoulder a few inches from Pearce's, and pulled her damp hair off her neck, securing it with a simple gold clip. "How did he know exactly the right moment to come back?"

"Beats me." Pearce shook her head. Her father had popped in unexpectedly at the precise moment when they were exploring the abdomen. She didn't know how he did it, but he always seemed to show up for the critical portions of the case. He'd watched for four or five minutes and then left without a word. But his implied approval had been enough to satisfy her. She'd learned over the years that that was the most she would get from him. "No one can ever figure it out, but it always happens just like that. He just *knows* when it's time for him to check up on us."

Wynter wondered what it must be like, having one of the world's premier surgeons for a father and a mentor. Somehow, hearing the controlled nonchalance in Pearce's voice, she sensed it was a burden that Pearce tried to ignore. The shadows in Pearce's eyes suggested a more personal pain that Wynter wanted to reach out and brush away. Unused to the intensity of her response, she forced a casual note into her voice. "What's he like to operate with?"

"He doesn't say much once a case starts. It's all business. He's fast, and he expects you to be."

"Must run in the family," Wynter jested. Pearce had been just as slick as she'd expected her to be. Fast and competent, certain. Almost cocky, but careful too. The perfect combination for a surgeon.

"Look who's talking. They'll start calling you Flash before long."

Wynter grinned, pleased. "You know what they say—there are good fast surgeons and bad fast surgeons, but there are no"—they finished together—"good *slow* surgeons."

They both laughed.

"From the looks of things, you're not going to have to worry about that," Pearce said. She'd been pleased to see how skilled Wynter was in the operating room. It was good to know she wouldn't have to worry about Wynter when she wasn't around, and it just added to Wynter's attractiveness. She was smart and quick and clever. And she had good hands. Pearce's heart started to race, and she swallowed around a sudden surge of desire. *Jesus. This isn't good. I can't keep getting hot every time I'm around her or I'm going to be miserable for the next two years.*

Wynter smiled. She couldn't remember a day of residency that she'd enjoyed so much. Surgery was always a rush, but the pleasure had been heightened by knowing that Pearce thought she had done well. She liked pleasing her. "So, what now?"

Let's go across the street and get a room. All I need is a quick thirty minutes so you can put me out of my misery. It wouldn't be the first time she'd skipped out for a quickie in the middle of the afternoon. The desk clerks at the Penn Tower Hotel directly across the street were discreet and never raised an eyebrow at an early checkout, even when it was only an hour or so after arrival. As long as she had her beeper, she could be back in the hospital within minutes, which was no more than it took to get from one end of the hospital to the other had she been on-site. *Oh yeah, thirty minutes ought to be plenty of time.*

She fell into Wynter's blue eyes and saw them together on the bed, their hands inside the other's scrubs, too eager even to undress. Wynter's skin was soft and firm, her body sleek and strong. They fit together physically the way they had in the operating room, effortlessly, without words. Each knew the other's need, anticipating the next movement, the next touch. From somewhere deep in her unconscious, the memory of Wynter's spicy scent rose to assault her, and her body quickened. "Oh, man," she whispered, her vision wavering. "This is bad."

"What?" Wynter repeated, confused. "Are you okay? You look…I don't know—" She put her hand on Pearce's forehead. "You're warm. You must be dehydrated. It was really hot in there."

Pearce flinched and pulled her head away. "I'm fine." She cleared her throat and forced a smile. "Sorry, just thinking about what we need to do next. First, we'll round up the troops and make sign-out rounds." She was seized with sudden inspiration. Maybe the hotel wasn't out of the question after all. "Then, I'll take you across the street to din—"

"Sorry," Wynter said as her cell phone rang. She looked at the caller ID. "I have to take this. Hang on."

"Sure."

"Hi. Everything okay?" Wynter caught Pearce's arm in one hand as she started to move away, stopping her motion. Then she held up one finger to indicate she would only be a minute. "Listen, I'm going to be later tonight than I thought. I know, I'm sorry. I should've thought. I don't know, probably at least midnight. I know…no, I'm fine." She laughed softly. "You sure? Okay. Thanks." She smiled, listening. "Hey, I owe you…whatever you want. Uh-huh, sure. I'll call you later, then."

As Wynter talked, Pearce tried to ignore the intimacy in her voice. All day, she'd managed to forget that Wynter was straight and married.

They'd worked together so well, and being around her had been so easy, that she'd forgotten how much stood between them. She remained motionless, but inside, she drew away. She'd let her guard down, and that was foolish. She'd made it a point never to get seriously involved with anyone she worked with. Casual suited her just fine—she was too busy for anything else and wasn't looking for complications. Sure, some of the women she'd had flings with had been straight, but that had never mattered—to either of them. With Wynter, it mattered. *Not good. So not good.*

"Sorry, sorry," Wynter said as she terminated her call. "What were you just saying about sign-out rounds?"

Pearce stepped over the low bench that ran down the center of the aisle between the facing rows of lockers, suddenly needing to put distance between herself and Wynter. "Nothing. I'll page the guys and we'll meet in the cafeteria in half an hour."

"How about I get you a Coke, then? We can hang out in the surgeons' lounge until—"

"I'll pass, thanks."

"But I thought—" Wynter looked after her in surprise as Pearce walked out of the locker room without a backward glance. She seemed angry, but Wynter had no clue as to why. The day had seemed to be going so well, and they'd moved like clockwork together in the operating room, each anticipating the other with no need for words. "What the hell?"

Irritated now herself, feeling abandoned even when she knew it was irrational, she yanked her lab coat out of her locker and shoved her arms into the sleeves. She double-checked the breast pocket of her scrub shirt to be sure that she had her list and decided she'd take a quick walk through the wards before the end of the day. *If Pearce is in a mood, fine. Let her be. I couldn't care less.*

Chapter Seven

Yo, Phil. Can I borrow a smoke?" Pearce gave the gray-haired, stocky security guard a light punch in the arm.

He frowned. "You're about hitting your limit this month, Sport. A couple more and you're gonna owe me a pack."

"I'll see that you're appropriately recompensed." She grinned. "You know my credit's good."

"Don't give me that," he said good-naturedly, shaking a filtered Marlboro from the pack he kept out of sight in the desk at his station near the Spruce Street entrance to the hospital. A bank of video monitors lined up behind him on a counter showed real-time images of passersby on the street and visitors and staff making their way through the hallways leading from the auxiliary entrance into the main areas of the hospital. "I've been feeding you these things since you were fifteen, and you haven't paid me back yet."

"Sixteen," Pearce corrected. "And I bet in all these years, it's only added up to a few cartons."

"Let me check my tally," he said, making a show of moving some papers around on his desk.

Pearce laughed, rolling the firm white cylinder between her fingers. "Thanks. You want to key the freight elevator for me?"

"Is there anything else I can do for you, your highness?"

"Coffee?"

"Don't push," he said, wagging a finger at her. He preceded her down a short corridor to the elevator adjacent to the corrugated metal roll-up doors that opened onto a loading dock. He inserted a key from a ring he pulled off his wide leather belt into the control panel and the oversized doors slid open. "Been a while since you took this ride."

"Just looking for a little air," Pearce said, knowing that Phil had caught on years ago that she escaped to the roof when something was bugging her. Phil Matucci had befriended her when she was just a child, allowing her to sit beside him on a tall stool while she waited for her father on endless Saturday afternoons. She'd watched the World Series with him on his tiny portable television, they'd discussed politics when she'd gotten older, and on rare occasions when she'd been more lonely than usual, she'd told him about her dreams. Maybe it was because he had five children of his own that he never seemed to mind her company. He'd chastised her when she'd started to smoke and made a deal with her that if she didn't buy her own, he'd give her one whenever she wanted. She'd broken their agreement on a few occasions when she'd been a teenager, and then felt guilty about it, tossing the illicit packs into the trash so he wouldn't see them.

"Let me know when you come down, so I know you didn't freeze to death up there."

"Thanks," Pearce said quietly. "I will."

The elevator stopped on the top floor, and she went down the hall and out the fire door to the roof. Before the Rhoads Pavilion had been erected with its state-of-the-art heliport, Penn Star—the medical helicopter—had landed here. She crossed to the concrete barricade surrounding the tarmac, hunched down against the wind, and lit the cigarette from a paper matchbook she kept in her back pocket along with other essentials. Taking a deep breath of cold air and smoke, she straightened and looked out over the city. There'd been a time when she'd been too short to see the Schuylkill River that separated West Philadelphia from the downtown area without jumping up and down, her hands pressed to the top of the wall for leverage. Now, she could lean her elbows on it, and she did, contemplating her strange day.

She couldn't figure out why Wynter got under her skin so badly. It had to be more than that Wynter was hot. Instant attraction was nothing new—hell, she got turned on by good-looking women all the time. Sometimes they connected and sometimes they didn't, and either way, it never mattered enough for her to lose sleep over. When she thought back to their encounter that afternoon in the quad on Match Day, she could easily chalk up her reaction to Wynter to the fact that she'd been high on the excitement of the day, knowing that med school was almost over and she was finally about to start the journey she'd been preparing for her entire life—or so it felt. Wynter had literally walked into her, and for a few brief moments, they'd shared a pivotal point in their lives. They'd been alone, and Wynter *was* beautiful, and so damn sexy, and she'd had the overwhelming desire to kiss her. It wouldn't have been the first woman she hadn't known whom she'd kissed.

But she *still* wanted to kiss her.

"Fuck," Pearce muttered, crushing out the cigarette beneath her foot. The wind lashed her shirt around her body as if it were a windsock, plastering it to her chest. Her nipples tensed in the cold beneath the thin cotton. The sensation was too close to sexual, the memory of wanting to feel Wynter's mouth beneath hers still vivid, and she hummed with another swell of desire. *Perfect. I come up here to settle down, and all I do is make it worse than ever. I should've spent the time in my on-call room taking the edge off.*

She wished for another cigarette, but Phil would rag on her if she asked for one.

"I just need to keep my distance until I can find a woman to spend some time with."

Armed with a plan, she headed back to work. That was her panacea—loneliness, arousal, anger—she could lose it all in work.

❖

Wynter noted with satisfaction that she was the first to reach the cafeteria. She couldn't put her finger on exactly why it mattered to her that Pearce was not there first, but it did. She was used to feeling competitive with her fellow residents; it was part of the world she had chosen to inhabit. From the time she had been in high school, she'd understood that if medicine was to be her choice, she would have to be the best at everything she did. Even though the field was not as competitive as it had once been, medical school slots were still at a premium, and once she'd decided on surgery, the field had narrowed even more. There were often hundreds of applicants for a handful of residency positions in the most sought-after programs. It was only because they depended upon one another for mutual survival, banding together against the pressure of long hours and constant stress, that the competition between residents usually remained friendly as opposed to cutthroat. There were exceptions, but she had never had any desire to win at the cost of others. Hers were personal goals. She wanted to be the best, because this was what she had chosen to do with her life and anything less was not acceptable.

She grabbed a cup of coffee and staked out one of the larger tables for their team. As she ran her list again, checking to see that she hadn't overlooked anything during her walk-through, she thought back to the case she had just done with Pearce. It wasn't the most difficult case she'd ever done, or all that unusual. It always felt good to operate—a personal challenge, a problem to solve, a wrong to set right with her own hands. But operating with Pearce had added something special, something she hadn't experienced before. They'd accomplished something together, a mutual victory, and the sharing was…satisfying. She frowned. Satisfying. That wasn't quite right. Exciting? Yes, it seemed so, but that didn't make much sense. She leaned back and closed her eyes, trying to figure out what it was about Pearce that confused her so much.

"Hey," Bruce said, pulling out a chair and dropping into it with a sigh. "What's up?"

"Not much," Wynter said. "We took Mrs. Gilbert back this afternoon. She dehisced."

"No shit. Wow." He made a note on his list of the new OR date. "Did it go okay?"

"Not a hitch."

"I wish I could've been there," he grumbled. "I spent the afternoon holding hooks on that colon."

Wynter suppressed a smile. There was nothing worse for an eager young resident than to be stuck in surgery holding retractors while someone else had all the fun. However, it was a rite of passage, and the junior residents had to first learn to assist on surgeries before they won the right to do the operations themselves. It was a process that took years, not months. "It sucks, I know."

"Tell me about it."

"Tell you about what?" Pearce asked as she settled down across from Wynter. "Problem?"

"Nope," Bruce said quickly. He wasn't going to complain to his chief about anything, especially not when the attending surgeon for whom he'd been holding back the abdominal wall all afternoon had been her father. "Everything's cool."

"Where's Liu?" Pearce felt Wynter's eyes on her, but she kept her gaze on Bruce. She didn't need to look at Wynter to remember the shape of her face or the color of her eyes or the way she tilted her head and looked out from beneath those long honeyed lashes when something amused her. She didn't need to look at her to feel that tug deep in her belly. *Man, I am not looking forward to spending the next six hours or so with her.* She put her mind to the job, hoping to block out Wynter's effect on her. "Page Liu and tell him he's late. If he's not here in five minutes, I'm leaving, and we'll have sign-out rounds in an hour."

Bruce bounded up and practically ran across the room to the wall phone.

"Works every time," Wynter murmured. There was nothing worse than spending an extra hour in the hospital when you didn't have to. The most effective way to make sure that residents showed up where they were supposed to *when* they were supposed to was to punish tardiness by making them wait longer to go home. Unfortunately, the entire team suffered if one member was late, so peer pressure was relentless.

Pearce couldn't help but grin. "Well, I'm not going anywhere tonight. If they wanna hang around, it's fine with me."

Wynter nodded her head toward the far side of the cafeteria. "Here he comes."

Liu looked as if he might hurdle the chairs in his path in his haste to reach them. He slid the last few yards and crashed into a chair. "Sorry. Sorry."

"Six thirty means six thirty," Pearce said flatly.

"I know. I know. I was trying to get that culture report on Hastings, but..." He caught himself as he saw Pearce's eyes narrow. "Won't happen again."

Pearce didn't bother to respond, but focused on Bruce. Never a particularly fit-looking guy, he'd gained a good twenty-five pounds in the last six months. It wasn't uncommon for residents who were deprived of just about every pleasure in life to turn to food, which was always available, as a source of comfort. She controlled her own weight by jogging every morning and lifting several times a week at the university gym. "Let's start at the top."

Bruce pushed up his wire-rimmed glasses and said, "1213. Constantine. Fem-pop bypass..."

Evening rounds took longer than morning report, because all the critical leftover work of the day needed to be discussed and eventually taken care of by the person on call. Even though Liu would also be on call, Pearce, in addition to covering the ICU and the ER for their service, would need to see that everything got done before morning. Everyone made notes. When the last patient had been covered, she put down her pen.

"Okay. Bruce, you're done. Dries at five thirty."

"See ya," Bruce said and within seconds, was gone.

Liu rose and said, "I'm gonna grab something to eat while it's quiet. You want anything?"

Pearce raised an eyebrow in Wynter's direction. Wynter shook her head.

"No, thanks," Pearce said. "I'll check in with you about eleven. Call me if you need me, but remember…To call—"

"Is a sign of weakness," Liu replied, grinning. It was the first thing she'd said to him his first day on the service. It was the first thing that every senior resident said to a first-year resident the first day on any surgical service. It was the great paradox of surgery. Responsibility warred with autonomy, and the need to stand alone in the midst of uncertainty underlay every action.

When he left, Pearce looked across the table at Wynter. "You should probably eat. Things could get busy."

"What about you?"

"I was thinking about street dogs."

Wynter gave her a hard stare. "I don't know you well enough to know if you're kidding, but I'm not going to stand by and watch you take your life in your hands twice in one day. Let's go next door to Children's and get McDonald's."

Children's Hospital was part of the university system and had a self-contained McDonald's on the ground floor. It was always busy, twenty-four hours a day. Against her better judgment, Pearce countered, "What do you say to dinner at the Penn Tower restaurant?"

"It's my first day. I don't want to stretch the rules quite that far," Wynter said quietly.

"You're not on call, I am."

Wynter regarded her steadily, annoyed that she couldn't decipher anything in Pearce's expression. She'd seen those dark eyes hot with desire once, and the answering surge of longing Pearce's gaze had stirred within her had surprised and disconcerted her. She'd written her response off as momentary insanity and chaotic hormones, but now she found the inscrutable coolness even more unsettling. She didn't like that Pearce could shut her out so completely. Her voice betrayed her irritation. "I'm not sure I want to help *you* break the rules either."

"My father is the chief of surgery. Do you think anyone is going to complain if I walk across the street for dinner?"

"I don't believe you. I don't believe you'd take advantage of your father's position for one minute." Wynter leaned forward, resting her forearms on the table, fixing Pearce with a blistering glare. "In fact, I bet you push the envelope just because your father *is* the chief of surgery, and *you* don't want anyone to think you're getting special treatment."

Pearce laughed. "And you base this all on what?"

The sadness in your eyes that you think no one sees. Wynter said nothing, because she had a feeling that Pearce Rifkin did not want anyone to see her vulnerability. And she didn't want to threaten her. More importantly, she didn't want to risk hurting her by bringing up her father. She shrugged. "It's your ass, not mine, if we're in the middle of fettuccine Alfredo and someone calls a code in the SICU."

"Did I mention to you that I ran track in high school?"

"You've never mentioned anything about high school." Wynter couldn't prevent her smile. She could see Pearce's long legs stretching out in an easy gait as she circled the track or loped over a rolling cross-country course. With her muscular upper body, she didn't look like a typical runner, though. "You're pretty built up for track, aren't you?"

"I switched to crew in college."

"So now you're slower."

"You like to push, don't you?" Pearce said with a hint of challenge in her voice. "You wanna come running with me some morning?"

"Any time. I've done some running myself." Wynter didn't feel like mentioning it had been four years since she'd done any serious running, and she wondered if she'd be able to keep up. She wasn't going to show her doubts, though.

"I'll give you a couple of days to get settled in, and then we'll see who can still run." Pearce stood, forgetting her earlier vow to keep her distance. Being around Wynter felt too good to be cautious. Besides, there was nothing wrong with being friendly. "Come on. Let me take you to dinner."

Laughing, Wynter nodded. Pearce was impossible to say no to. "All right, but it's Dutch treat."

"We'll do it your way," Pearce said. "This time."

CHAPTER EIGHT

Should we change?" Wynter asked as she and Pearce left the cafeteria.

"We don't have to. They're used to seeing people in scrubs across the street," Pearce said. "Do you have a blazer or something? That should be good enough."

"I've got something in my locker."

"Let's grab it, then. I'm starving."

Two minutes later, Pearce nodded in silent approval as Wynter pulled on an ocean blue cable knit sweater that was a few shades lighter than her eyes. The sweep of her red-gold hair against the soft blue wool reminded her of a flaming sunset over crystal Caribbean waters. She had an image of Wynter on the beach, small drops of sweat beaded on her skin. She could taste the salt.

"That's perfect."

Wynter gave her a quizzical look, then regarded her favorite, but hardly new, sweater. It wasn't her usual dinner attire, but the compliment pleased her, as did the appreciative expression in Pearce's eyes. Slightly disconcerted by that fact, she said, "What about you?"

"Oh," Pearce said, remembering why they had stopped by the locker room. She dragged her eyes away from Wynter, pulled out her baggy, faded navy and maroon Penn sweatshirt, and shrugged into it. "All set."

The shapeless garment did little to hide her physique and reminded Wynter of the way she'd looked the day they'd met. She said without thinking, "That's pretty perfect too."

Pearce blushed. "Come on, before we get paged for something."

They were both quiet as they hurried outside. As if sensing freedom, they dashed across the street in front of the hospital's main entrance and into the lobby of the hotel. The restaurant was in the rear, and as they crossed the plush carpeted expanse of lobby toward it, the hostess stepped forward from behind her small dais and gave Pearce a welcoming smile.

"Dr. Rifkin," the blond breathed. "How nice to see you. It's been far too long."

"Hi, Talia," Pearce replied. "Can you put us in the corner by the windows for dinner?"

The hostess glanced briefly at Wynter, then seemed to dismiss her. Wynter found the Elle Macpherson look-alike's expression verging on avaricious as her gaze roamed unabashedly over Pearce, and for an instant, Wynter contemplated stepping directly into her line of vision. She was startled by her reaction. She'd seen women look at her husband that way on more than one occasion, and their interest had never bothered her. Irrationally, she found this woman's attention—to another woman, no less—supremely irritating. She held out her hand, diverting the hostess from Pearce. "Hello. I'm Dr. Wynter Thompson."

With a courteous but cool smile, Talia turned toward the dining room. "Very pleased to meet you. Let me show you to your table."

"Come here often?" Wynter said when they were alone.

"Every once in a while," Pearce replied noncommittally, glad to have escaped Talia's scrutiny before Wynter noticed the unwanted attention. She should have realized Talia would not be pleased to see her with another woman, even if it was just for an innocent dinner. She set the menu aside; she knew it by heart. "If you're not a vegetarian, the steak is great. If you are, they really do make a great fettuccine Alfredo."

Wynter laughed. "I'm not a vegetarian, but the pasta sounds good. I'll have it."

"I'll stick to Coke because I'm on call, but you're not. Feel free to try the wine. Their house label isn't bad."

"Coke will be fine for me too." Once they had ordered, Wynter leaned back and regarded Pearce thoughtfully. "You don't mind being a resident, do you?"

"I'll be a lot happier in two years when I can call my own shots," Pearce answered. "But I knew what I was getting into, so, no, I don't mind. Why do you ask?"

"Because you don't seem angry. Most…well maybe not *most,* but many residents at our stage hate the work, or at least hate being on call." She looked around the restaurant, which was upscale for a hotel, probably because of the proximity to the hospital and the fact that many VIP patients' families stayed there. "Take this place. for example. You're on call, but you're about to have a very nice dinner, and it appears that's not unusual. You don't seem to let being a resident cramp your style."

Pearce grinned. "Why suffer when you can be comfortable?"

Wynter laughed. "I agree."

"What about you? Being a resident for you must be a little bit harder."

"Why?" Wynter asked, feeling the slightest bit uneasy.

"Well," Pearce shrugged. "Being married."

There. Finally. Wynter felt an unexpected surge of relief. "I'm divorced."

"Oh."

"Yes." Wynter had no idea why it should be important to her that Pearce know this about her, but it was.

"That helps, then." As if realizing what she'd just said, Pearce gave Wynter a wry smile. "Sorry. I just meant—"

"No need to apologize. I happen to agree with you. It makes quite a few things simpler."

"So I don't need to offer my sympathies?"

"I won't pretend it's been fun, but no condolences required."

"Is that why you're back a year?" When Wynter looked away, Pearce said hastily, "Sorry. None of my bus—"

"No, that's okay," Wynter said with a wan smile. "It's complicated, but that's part of the reason, yes."

"Well, you landed in a good place. Too bad about the extra time, though."

"Thanks," Wynter replied. "It hurts to lose a year, but all things considered…" She held Pearce's gaze. "I'm happy to be here."

"Good," Pearce said, feeling suddenly euphoric. She wished she weren't on call and could order a bottle of good red Bordeaux to celebrate. *Celebrate what? So she's divorced. It doesn't change anything.* But it didn't matter, it just felt good.

"What?" Wynter asked.

"What what?"

Wynter shook her head. "We're having the most bizarre conversation. You just looked…happy, all of a sudden."

"No reason." Fortunately, the waiter approached with their meal at that moment, saving Pearce from any further explanation. "Let's eat while we have the chance."

"Ah yes, another important surgical dictum," Wynter said, forking up a few strands of fettuccine. "See a chair, sit in it. See a bed, lie in it. See food…eat it."

Cutting into her steak with gusto, Pearce said, "And truer words were never spoken."

"God," Wynter said with a moan, "this is great."

"Yeah, it is." And Pearce didn't mean the food.

"So," Wynter said when she slowed down enough for air and conversation, "how many sibs do you have?"

Pearce poised with her fork in midair. "None. What made you think I did?"

From the carefully neutral tone in Pearce's voice, Wynter knew immediately that she'd once again trespassed on forbidden territory with what she had thought was an innocent question. "I didn't, not really. I guess I just assumed…"

"Yes?" Pearce put her fork down, growing very still.

"Oh, I'm making this worse. I'm sorry. I didn't mean to get personal."

"No, go ahead. I want to hear what you have to say."

"Pearce, really…it's not import—"

"It is to me," Pearce said quietly.

Wynter let out a long breath. "Okay, here goes. It's just always seemed to me that doctors, and especially surgeons…often have more than the average number of children. You know—powerful men, the prestige of carrying on the family name, and all that."

"I know." Pearce scraped back her chair and twisted to the side so that she could stretch her legs out. She draped one arm over the back of her chair and gazed past Wynter out the plate glass window to the street where taxis lined up in front of the hospital. "You're right. And you would have been right about us, too, except there was a small problem—Rh incompatibility. The first child, a boy, died as a result of it. Then I came along, and after that, there was one more miscarriage. I think they decided the risk wasn't worth another try."

Wynter closed her eyes for a second. "I am so sorry. I didn't mean to blunder into this."

Pearce shrugged. "It's ancient history now."

She smiled as she spoke, but Wynter saw no warmth in her expression. There was more, much more, she knew, but she couldn't bear to explore areas that obviously hurt Pearce. She wanted to get them back to the lighthearted moments they had shared during dinner. "There are three of us, all girls. My oldest sister is a stay-at-home mom who lives two miles from my parents, and my younger sister is a first-year law student at Temple."

"Here in the city. That must be nice for you." Pearce pushed back at the specter of loneliness and disenchantment that accompanied thoughts of her family. "Are you from around here?"

"Not too far away. My parents have a working dairy farm in Lancaster."

"You're kidding."

Wynter pretended to take offense. "There are still real live farms in this country, you know, Dr. Rifkin."

"Yeah, but you don't strike me as a farmer's daughter."

"Really?" Wynter said playfully, enjoying the light that had returned to Pearce's eyes. "And why is that?"

"Well, for one thing, you're not a wide-eyed and innocent country bumpkin." Pearce narrowed her eyes as if in serious thought. "Well, maybe the country bumpkin part fit—" She ducked, laughing, as Wynter's napkin sailed toward her face. "Hey!"

"I'll admit to being naïve at one point, but believe me, I'm quite worldly now," Wynter said archly. She kept her tone casual, thinking that Pearce had no idea how naïve she had been at one time. Naïve enough to think that she had understood what direction her life would take, and she'd followed that path for far too long before she'd begun to question it.

"Seriously," Pearce said, leaning forward, turning the butter knife on the white linen tablecloth in a slow circle as if it were the hand on a clock, "if you'd told me that you'd grown up on the Upper East Side of Manhattan, the daughter of a family of doctors, with a summer home in the Hamptons, I would have believed you."

"Thank you. I think."

Pearce laughed. "Yeah, maybe that's not such a compliment after all. Listen, do you want cof—" Her beeper sounded, and she rolled her eyes. "I knew we were living on borrowed time." She glanced down and stiffened. "Fuck."

Wynter immediately rose, her voice tight. "The SICU?"

"Almost as bad," Pearce said, standing too as she sorted through her wallet for her credit card. "My father."

"What does he want? It's almost nine o'clock," Wynter said as she and Pearce hurried toward Talia.

"He wants to make rounds." Pearce handed her credit card to the hostess and then punched in the extension on her cell phone. After a second, she said, "Rifkin. Yes sir. Five minutes. See you there." She met Wynter's anxious gaze. "Yep. He wants to see patients."

"Now? Does he usually make rounds this late at night?"

Pearce shrugged. "He makes them whenever he wants to. Sometimes if he's been out of the country and gets in at three in the morning, he'll show up here and want to go around. He calls, we go."

They sprinted across the street, dodging traffic without even giving the taxis, limos, and cars a second glance, then jogged through the fairly deserted lobby to the elevators. They made a quick stop at the locker room to shed their outerwear and grab their lab coats. As they rode the rest of the way to the twelfth floor, Pearce said, "When we get up there, you run the list for him."

Wynter wanted to object. The fastest way to make a bad impression on her very first day was to screw up on attending rounds. She'd taken the extra time to get to know the patients on her walk-through right before sign-out rounds, but there were still fifty new names to assimilate, and many of the cases were complicated. Plus, she didn't know the physical layout all that well. The last thing she wanted to do was lead the chairman of the department into a dead end somewhere. Still, she couldn't object. It was Pearce's call.

"Okay."

They stepped off the elevator and Pearce led the way to the nurses' station. Ambrose Rifkin was already there, studying a lab report. He wore a perfectly pressed, spotless white coat over dark trousers, a white shirt, and a blue tie with thin red stripes. He turned to watch Pearce and Wynter approach, nothing registering in his face. When they were a few feet away, he said, "Everything quiet?"

"So far," Pearce said. "Do you want to see everyone, or just make spot rounds?"

Ambrose shifted his gaze to Wynter. "Since we have a new member of the team, let's see everyone."

Wynter hid her surprise. It would take close to an hour and a half for them to see all fifty patients, but apparently, time of day had no meaning to the chief of surgery. She took out her list and stepped up to his side. "Mr. Pollack is in room 1222. He's four days post abdominal hernia repair and…"

As Wynter and her father started down the hall toward the first patient's room, Pearce detoured to the storage area adjacent to the nurses' station and began gathering the supplies they would need. She automatically sorted through the rows of plastic bins stacked one on top of another from floor to ceiling, grabbing sterile gauze pads, tape, Steri-Strips, suture removal kits, and all the other supplies required for changing bandages and anything else that the attending might want done.

"Who's the new resident?" a female voice said.

Pearce turned slowly and faced the small brunette in the tight black skirt and scoop-necked beige Lycra top. A good deal of her cleavage was showing, and the outfit would undoubtedly fail to pass an "appropriate outfit for work" check, but Andrea Kelly was a ward clerk, and a very good one, and no one was going to complain about her style of dress.

"Don't tell me you don't know," Pearce said teasingly. "You who know all?"

Andrea stepped closer, running her bloodred nail-polished fingertips along the edge of Pearce's lab coat. "I heard there was a new third-year, but no one mentioned that you were going to be escorting her around personally."

"Just doing my job."

Andrea stepped even closer, sliding her hand inside Pearce's coat and around her flank to her ass, which she squeezed. She swiveled her hips as she insinuated herself tightly between Pearce's thighs and looked up through lowered lashes. "I can think of some other work to keep you busy."

Pearce was bombarded by images of Andrea writhing beneath her, her arms and legs wrapped tightly around Pearce's body, her nails digging into Pearce's back as she clawed her way to a screaming climax. The visceral memory, coupled with the pressure of Andrea's body undulating against hers, made Pearce close her eyes with a groan. With her free arm she twisted her fist in Andrea's hair, her mouth against Andrea's ear. "You gotta cut it out, babe. I'm working here."

"That never stopped you before," Andrea gasped, her teeth raking down the side of Pearce's neck.

"I wasn't in the middle of ro—"

"Oh! Sorry," Wynter exclaimed as she pushed through the door and nearly stumbled upon the two women locked in an embrace. "I…I need some four-by-fours."

Pearce backed away from Andrea and indicated the supplies cradled in one arm with a tilt of her head. "I've probably got everything you're looking for right here."

Andrea smirked as she edged around Wynter and disappeared into the hall. "Don't you just always."

"Thanks. We're in 1215," Wynter said curtly as she turned her back and walked out.

Pearce sighed. "Perfect. Just perfect."

CHAPTER NINE

During the rest of rounds, Wynter directed her conversation to the elder Rifkin, speaking to Pearce only when it related to one of the patients. It was after ten p.m. when they were finished, and Ambrose Rifkin left with a short good night.

"You should probably take off too," Pearce said as soon as her father was out of earshot. "You're on call tomorrow."

"Good night, then," Wynter said, starting down the hall.

Pearce debated letting her go. The air had been decidedly chilly for the last hour, and she wasn't in the mood to apologize. Hell, it's not like she had been committing a crime. She had nothing to apologize for. *Fuck.*

Wynter disappeared into the stairwell. Pearce debated for another second and then jogged after her. On the landing, she leaned over the rail and called down, "How're you getting home?"

Startled by the question, Wynter craned her neck to peer up to the floor above. "What?"

"I know you weren't expecting to be on call tonight. Did you drive to work?"

"No. I took the trolley."

"Well," Pearce said as she clambered down the stairs, "you can't ride the trolley home alone at this hour."

Wynter was still too annoyed to be gracious. She'd been embarrassed and uncomfortable walking in on an intimate encounter. "Pearce, I took the trolley the entire time I was in medical school. I'm used to it. I'm only going out to Forty-eighth Street."

"Yeah, but West Philly isn't all that gentrified yet, and it's late." She reached into her back pocket and extracted her keys. "Here. Take my car. I'm not going to be using it."

"I'm not taking your car."

"Look, you'll get home sooner and be well rested for tomorrow. I just wanna make sure you're up to speed so you can carry your share of the work."

"You don't need to worry about *that*." Wynter turned away.

"It's not safe, Wynter, God damn it."

"Then I'll take the security van if it makes you feel better. I'll see you tomorrow." Without looking back, Wynter hurried down the stairwell. Reluctantly, she acknowledged that Pearce's concern was touching, but she was still too disturbed by the unexpectedly erotic image of Pearce with her fingers possessively entwined in another woman's hair. She didn't want to think about her own reaction to the sight. She didn't want to think about Pearce Rifkin at all.

Thirty minutes later, Wynter climbed out of the security van, one of a fleet of vehicles provided by the university to ferry students and employees to off-campus locations, and waved to the driver as he pulled away. She hurried up Cedar Avenue to a Victorian twin in the middle of a block of similar structures and let herself into the kitchen through the side door. The house was dark and she switched on a light over the sink. A chocolate Lab padded into the room and nosed her hand.

"Hey, girl," Wynter murmured, leaning down and patting the dog's head absently. She took a battered white teapot with yellow painted daisies on the side and filled it in the sink, then set it on the stove to boil. She was searching in the unfamiliar cabinets for a mug when a voice behind her caused her to jump.

"Honey, if you wake up the kids, I'm gonna have to shoot you."

Wynter spun around, contrite. "Oh my God. Was I making a lot of noise? I wasn't even thinking about it."

"Well, it sounded like you were putting on an addition to the house," the comfortably round, warmly attractive, and very pregnant African American woman said. She pulled out a chair at the table and settled heavily into it with a grateful sigh. "And if you're making tea, I'll have some."

"I was actually thinking of cocoa," Wynter said, taking down an extra mug.

"Even better."

"How were the kids?"

"Everyone's getting along just fine."

"I'm glad someone is," Wynter muttered.

"I figured you were having a rough first day when you called to say you'd be late. I told you to go into anesthesia if you didn't want to work so hard."

Wynter smiled at Mina Meru. "Tell that to your husband. I'm sure his opinion is very different."

"I keep telling him he should stay at home with these two children if he wants to see hard."

"And here I've added to your burden with mine." Wynter spooned cocoa into the thick ceramic mugs as they talked. "I promise, as soon as I have time to find an apartment, we'll be out of here."

"Don't you worry about little Miss Ronnie. She's the best three-year-old I've ever seen. She keeps up with my four-year-old, and it gives him someone to play with."

"I know, but—"

"I was serious when I said I want you to keep her here during the day even after you get your own place. Preschool is expensive—"

"I can afford it—the one thing I got out of the divorce was good child support."

"But with your schedule being so unpredictable, it's going to be hard to manage just dropping her off and picking her up on time."

"I know. It was easier when I was working shift in the ER." Wynter sat at the heavy wooden table in the old-fashioned eat-in kitchen and leaned her head in her palms. She rubbed her temples and sighed. "My God, Mina. I really appreciate it, but with the new baby coming in a few months, it's going to be a handful."

"You know my mother and sister are in and out of here all day long. That's one of the reasons that Ken wanted to stay here to train, so I'd have more help. One more kid is not going to be a problem."

The kettle whistled and Wynter got up to get it. As she stirred the cocoa, she said, "I would feel a lot better with her here. Before, with two of us, she was only in daycare during the day, but now…" She shook her head. "I don't know how single women do this."

"Well, you haven't been single very long. You'll get the hang of it."

Wynter carried the cocoa to the table and sat down again. "I hadn't planned on getting pregnant until after my residency, and I certainly hadn't planned on raising a child without a husband."

"Things don't always work out the way we plan, honey, that's for sure," Mina said, squeezing Wynter's arm. She sipped her cocoa and regarded Wynter fondly. "If you don't mind me saying, I think you're better off without Dave."

"I don't mind at all. I agree." Wynter closed her eyes and leaned her head back. "Half the time I feel like a huge burden has been lifted off my shoulders, and the other half, I'm downright panicked."

"Well, you don't show it."

"Practice. A surgical residency will do that for you. Never show fear." Wynter sat forward again, frowning into her mug. "I didn't think things could get much tougher than at New Haven, but this place is something else."

"You looked wired when I walked into the kitchen. Somebody giving you a hard time already?"

"No more than I expected." Wynter blew on her cocoa and then took a healthy swallow. "Actually, the residents seem really nice, and that's the most important thing."

"Then what was bothering you so much just now?" Mina reached down and absently petted the dog's head. The Lab thumped down beside her on the floor with a long-suffering dog sigh.

Wynter colored slightly and shook her head. "Oh, it's nothing. It's silly."

"Can't be that much of nothing if it had you slamming cabinet doors in the middle of the night."

"It was just something that happened on rounds tonight." Wynter pushed a hand through her hair, still struggling with the remnants of discomfort. "I walked in on the chief resident in a clinch with one of the ward clerks."

"Is that all!" Mina laughed. "I thought that was standard operating procedure for residents. I told Ken before he started that he'd better keep his hands and all his other parts to himself, or else lose them."

Wynter laughed self-consciously. "You're right. It's not all that unusual. I just didn't expect it—it was embarrassing."

"So this new chief resident of yours. Is he worth a second look?" Mina waggled her eyebrows. "Maybe you should think about taking him on."

"He's a she," Wynter said, feeling herself grow warm.

"Oh, my. That's interesting." Mina studied Wynter over the top of her mug. "And I assume the ward clerk was of the usual female variety?"

"Oh yes, very much so." Wynter's eyes glinted. "She looked like she was about to start taking bites out of Pearce any second."

"Pearce. That's the chief resident with the wandering hands?"

Wynter flashed on Pearce's hand, strong and broad, and the ward clerk's dark black hair tangled between her fingers. Such a beautiful hand, so powerful. She remembered how precisely Pearce's hands had moved in the operating room, deftly teasing at the tissues with her instruments, gently pushing aside vital organs. *Good hands.* Simple words that said everything.

"Wynter, honey? Where did you go?"

Wynter jumped. "Oh. Nowhere. Just tired, I guess. What were we saying?"

"Dr. Hotty Pants. Is that Pearce?"

"Yes. Pearce Rifkin. She's the chairman of surgery's daughter."

"Well, no wonder she doesn't mind having a quickie during rounds. She can probably get away with anything she wants."

"No," Wynter said immediately. "She's not like that at all. She's incredibly focused and very responsible about work. She's not taking advantage of her position."

"Sounds like you like her a little bit."

"I..." Wynter stood and carried her mug to the sink. As she rinsed it out, she said with her back to Mina, "I don't have to like her, I just have to work with her. And I'd rather not walk in on her when she's feeling up some bimbo in the storage closet."

"Uh-huh. I get that." Mina pushed herself up with one hand on the edge of the table and released a soft groan. "Maybe I should let Ken take care of his urges at the hospital. I'm about done with this baby-making business."

Laughing, Wynter turned and rested her hips against the sink. "Oh yeah, I can see that." She reached out for Mina's cup. "Here, let me take that."

"So, is it the extracurricular activities that bother you or that she's gay?" Mina asked casually.

"I don't care that she's gay," Wynter said immediately. She frowned. "Why would you think I would?"

"I didn't. I just wondered."

"I couldn't care less who Pearce Rifkin sleeps with," Wynter said succinctly. "Man, woman, or beast."

Mina laughed. "Well, sometimes they *are* hard to tell apart."

"Oh, who cares who any of them sleep with." Wynter linked her arm through Mina's. "I'm going to go kiss my sleeping fairy princess good night."

"Just be sure you don't wake her up."

"Don't worry, I'll be careful. I have to be up at four and I'm ready to fall into bed."

"Pleasant dreams," Mina said as they parted just outside the kitchen.

Wynter hoped that she didn't dream at all.

❖

Pearce stretched out on the narrow bed in the small windowless on-call room. She'd shed her shoes and arranged her assorted equipment on the tiny bedside stand—beepers, cell phone, wallet, and keys. She folded her arms behind her head and stared at the ceiling. She didn't expect to sleep, because she knew that within a few minutes—or certainly before an hour had passed—the phone would ring. Sometimes it would just be a question about medication or instructions for dressings, and she could take care of it without leaving the room. But her sleep would be interrupted nevertheless, and sometimes the frustration made it not worth going to sleep at all.

Other times, a nurse would call to report a change in a patient's vital signs, and Pearce would need to get up to evaluate the situation. A temperature spike in the middle of the night could signal something as simple as incisional pain preventing the patient from taking a deep breath. Mucus and other secretions eventually accumulated in the lungs and produced a fever. The treatment was simple—voluntary coughing. At other times, however, a sudden fever indicated a severe wound infection or, worst-case scenario, a breakdown in the area of surgical repair. In those instances, a missed diagnosis or delay in treatment for even a few hours could seriously affect the patient's well-being. Those were things she couldn't, or shouldn't, handle over the phone. Some residents tried, because night after night of no sleep and the unrelenting pace made cutting corners look inviting. But for the most part, the residents lived up to their responsibilities, and for Pearce there was never any question. She knew what needed to be done, and she did it.

She willed her body to relax, hoping that if she didn't sleep, at least she could unwind. But she tossed and turned, more keyed up than usual. The day had been a roller-coaster ride of unexpected emotions, starting when she'd first seen Wynter in the hallway. Wynter had been on her mind ever since they had parted, and why she couldn't just shrug off Wynter's anger, she didn't know. Sure, they had a little bit of history, but a lot less than she had with some women she saw every day. A few of the women she'd had short liaisons with made it pretty clear that they'd like to hook up again, but she had no problem sidestepping their attentions. She'd never even kissed Wynter, and she was totally off her stride around her. She made a disgruntled sound and squirmed around, trying to get comfortable.

"Horny," she muttered, but she didn't have the energy or inclination to do anything about it. She'd been keyed up all day, and she doubted it would take more than a minute or two, but somehow she knew that a quick orgasm was not going to settle her disquiet. She rolled onto her side and faced the wall, drawing her knees up and closing her eyes.

She must have drifted, because the soft kiss on her neck was completely unexpected. She hadn't heard anyone come in. Blinking in the dark and trying to clear her fuzzy brain, she rolled onto her back. "Who?"

A warm wet mouth descended onto hers, a soft tongue tracing the outline of her lips. She tasted something sweet. Peppermint, maybe. The curve of full firm breasts pressed against her side and a hand tugged at the tie on her scrub pants. Pearce slapped her hand over the fingers working at her pants.

"Hey. Andrea?"

"You expecting someone else, baby?" Andrea murmured, nipping her way along Pearce's jaw as she pushed her hand inside Pearce's scrubs. "I couldn't wait until I got off work tonight. I am so hot for you."

"How about you slow down a lit—" Pearce gasped as Andrea's fingers dove between her thighs. "Jesus!"

"I knew you'd be wet." Andrea climbed onto the bed, her skirt hiked up to her hips, and threw one leg over Pearce's thighs. She rocked hard against her leg. "I have been dying to do this. Oh, you feel so good."

The shock of the sudden assault on her already overstimulated nerve endings catapulted Pearce's body into overdrive. She wanted Andrea to stop and she wanted to come all at once. Panting, hips heaving, she groaned, "Let up on me for a minute. Just *wait,* will you."

Andrea was moaning, pulling at her, writhing against her, already too far gone for reasoning. Pearce felt teeth against her neck, and before she had time to object or resist, she came in quick sharp spasms. She bit Andrea back, her mouth finding soft flesh, and Andrea screamed out in pleasure. Pearce's mind went blank as another orgasm rocketed through her.

"Oh God, baby," Andrea moaned, licking at the spot she had bruised on Pearce's neck. "I needed that. And I could tell that you did too." She squeezed between Pearce's thighs. "Didn't you."

"Sure," Pearce said tonelessly as Andrea sat up to rearrange her clothes. "That was just what I needed."

"You should change your pants, baby," Andrea said as she stood and fluffed her hair. "I left a wet spot on your leg."

Pearce closed her eyes to the sound of Andrea's laughter fading down the hall. When sleep eluded her, she got up and made her way to the roof. The sky was overcast, the night bitterly cold. The distant echoes of Andrea's attentions still twisted through her, but there was no trace of warmth left by her touch.

CHAPTER TEN

Wynter arrived in the cafeteria the next morning ten minutes before rounds. She was slightly annoyed, but not surprised, to see Pearce there before her, slouched in a chair, a Styrofoam cup of coffee in her hand. She checked the table, half expecting to see evidence of street dog detritus, but there was none. She assumed that the street vendors hadn't warmed the chili yet. She pulled out a chair next to Pearce. "Morning."

"Looks like it," Pearce grunted.

"Rough night?" Wynter sipped her own coffee and glanced at Pearce, then stared at her neck. A quarter-inch bruise marred the pale skin just above her collarbone. It was more than a hickey; it was an intentional bite mark. Someone had meant to mark her, and had succeeded. The idea that someone wanted to possess her that way, and that Pearce had allowed it, offended her. An image of the brunette in the utility room, crawling all over Pearce, flashed through her mind, and she reacted without thinking. "From the looks of things, I guess so."

Pearce frowned at the sarcastic note in Wynter's voice, then saw where her eyes were riveted. She rubbed her neck and felt the tenderness. *Crap.*

"I've got some cosmetics in my locker if you want to cover that up," Wynter said coolly. "Unless you don't mind that everyone knows what you were doing while you were…on call."

"I might have been on call," Pearce said with an edge to her voice, "but what I do while I'm waiting for something to happen is no one's business."

"Has it occurred to you that it sets a lousy precedent for the other residents?"

"You think so?" Pearce leaned forward, her nerves jangling. Despite the fact that no emergencies had arisen after Andrea's middle-of-the-night visit, she hadn't slept. She'd spent an hour on the roof, despite the frigid temperatures, then been propelled inside by the urgent desire to shower. She felt soiled, and wasn't sure why. It wasn't as if she'd never had a tryst in her on-call room before, and she usually enjoyed a woman who took what she wanted, because so did she. Plus, Andrea hadn't done anything she hadn't done half a dozen times in the last year. But for some reason, Pearce was angry. Angry that Andrea thought she could walk in uninvited and find Pearce willing. Angry that she hadn't said no and meant it. Angry that when it was finished, she'd felt nothing. Wynter's criticism now only underscored her own self-loathing, and that was more than she could handle after thirty hours of no sleep. "Has it occurred to you that your job is to take care of patients and not offer your opinions on things that don't concern you?"

Wynter rocked back in her chair, stunned by the cutting tone of Pearce's voice and the flat, hard fury in her eyes. Belatedly, she realized that she was out of line. Pearce was not only her senior, she was a virtual stranger. They'd shared a dinner, but that didn't give her the right to pass judgment. Still, the anger—arising from where, she couldn't be certain—simmered. It was all she could do not to snap back. Instead, she did what she always did when her back was against the wall. She grew very still, damping her emotions with iron control. In a voice that revealed none of her feelings, she said, "I'm quite prepared to take care of my patients. Thank you."

Cursing under her breath, Pearce stood abruptly and walked back to the cafeteria line. When she returned with her second cup of coffee, the other members of the team were present. As she sat, she avoided Wynter's eyes and said curtly, "Let's take it from the top."

In a studied voice, Wynter said, "1222, Arnold. Four days post…"

When they'd finished updating the patients' status, Pearce gave everyone their instructions for the day. "Wynter, you're with the chief on that splenectomy he's doing later this morning."

"Great case," Bruce said enviously.

"Are you leaving?" Wynter asked Pearce as the junior residents left to take care of the work generated during rounds.

"In a while," Pearce said vaguely. By rights, she should be off call now and could go home. *Should* go home. But she very rarely did.

Wynter gave her an appraising glance, but decided not to mention the fact that Pearce looked worn out. As the senior resident had just pointed out quite succinctly, it was none of her business. "I'll see you tomorrow, then."

"Right," Pearce replied, waiting for some indication that Wynter wanted company on the way to the operating room. When Wynter turned and walked away, Pearce shrugged and let her go. Watching her disappear up the stairs, she wondered how they had gone from their friendly and relaxed dinner the night before to this uncomfortable silence. She wondered, too, if she had been a guy whether Wynter would have minded that little scene with Andrea quite so much. She'd never been sensitive about being gay, because she didn't care who had a problem with it. But it saddened her to think that Wynter might. *Fuck.*

With a sigh and a shake of her head, she tossed her empty coffee cup into the trash. She headed toward radiology to check on the X-rays that had not been officially read the night before. She wasn't going home. She would have nothing to do except lie around and think, and that was exactly what she did not want to do.

❖

"What changes can we expect to find in the patient's peripheral blood following this procedure, Dr. Thompson?" Ambrose Rifkin asked Wynter as he made a midline incision in the abdomen of a twenty-three-year-old woman extending from the xiphoid at the lower end of the sternum, curving around the umbilicus, and stopping several inches below.

Wynter hadn't known which case she would be assigned to scrub on when she'd left the hospital the night before. Even though she'd taken a copy of the OR schedule home with her to review the upcoming cases, she had never looked at it. She'd fallen asleep instantly and, despite her plans, slept through the alarm she had set an hour earlier than usual. She had awakened with barely enough time to shower and kiss her daughter goodbye.

Ronnie, wide awake, had greeted her with a smile and upheld arms. Despite the little time she had, Wynter sat on the side of the bed as the three-year-old clambered into her lap. They had an animated conversation about something the child had seen on a video that Mina had apparently played for the kids. Wynter didn't recognize the names or the references, but she nodded excitedly and faked her way through the discourse. She scooped the little girl up and held her close, losing herself for a few moments in the unique smell of childhood, brushing away the sadness that consumed her when she realized how much of her daughter's life she was likely to miss in the next two years.

Now, she scrambled through her memory for the answers to a fairly esoteric question. If the chairman had asked her about the blood supply to the spleen or the differential diagnosis of hemolytic anemia, she might have fared better. However, the adage *Better wrong than uncertain* played through her mind, and she said with conviction, "An elevated white count and megakaryocytosis."

"Hmm. Pack that bleeder off back there, would you please," Rifkin said to Wynter.

As Wynter carefully placed a surgical sponge behind the spleen, she caught movement out of the corner of her eye and saw the OR door open. Pearce walked in. Surprised, Wynter quickly checked the plain-faced wall clock. It was almost 1:00 p.m.—Pearce should've been gone hours ago. Wynter looked back to the surgical field, peripherally aware of Pearce quietly approaching until she stood next to the anesthesiologist and looked over the top of the sterile sheet.

Without taking his eyes off what he was doing, Rifkin said, "What can we do for you, Dr. Rifkin?"

"There's a patient in the emergency room with a dissecting abdominal aneurysm. He needs to come up right away."

The chief continued to work, quickly and precisely. "How big is it?"

"Eleven centimeters. It involves the left common iliac too."

"What's your plan?" Rifkin held out his right hand and requested a vascular clamp. "Satinsky."

"We can open the aneurysm and place the graft in situ, then jump to the femoral on the left," Pearce replied immediately.

Rifkin straightened and looked across the table at Wynter, who raised her head at his movement. "Finish removing this spleen, Dr. Thompson. Dr. Rifkin will lend you a hand."

With that, he stepped back from the table and indicated to the circulating nurse to untie the back of his gown. He stripped it off along with his gloves and tossed the bundle in the direction of the used linen container. It drifted to the floor several feet short of the bin.

For several heartbeats, Wynter was speechless; then she said, "Yes sir," just as Ambrose Rifkin walked out. Wynter quickly moved around to the opposite side of the table where she would have the appropriate view and exposure to complete the procedure. Five minutes later, Pearce stepped up into the first assistant's position.

"Hi," Pearce said.

"Hi," Wynter replied, gently palpating the posterior surface of the spleen. There did not appear to be any unusual adhesions that might tear and lead to hemorrhage. She opened her right hand, palm up, and extended it toward the scrub nurse, who stood so close to her right side that their shoulders brushed. "Metzenbaum scissors, please."

Pearce leaned over and looked into the abdominal cavity. "Man, that really is big."

"Mmm. Could you pull a little harder on that retractor."

"Did he ask you about the peripheral blood tests after splenectomy?"

Wynter's eyes flickered up quickly and then back to the field. "Is that one of the standard questions?"

"Uh-huh."

"Thanks for the heads-up," Wynter muttered.

"How far did you get?" Pearce grinned behind her mask. It was a rite of passage, and although she would ordinarily have warned Wynter about the kinds of questions various attendings asked, everyone got caught on the splenectomy question.

"Leukocytosis and megakaryocytosis."

Pearce whistled softly. "Very good. Did he ask you the follow-up?"

Wynter clipped and then divided the splenic artery and vein. Carefully, she removed the hugely engorged organ. "No. You walked in."

"I saved you, then. He was going to ask you what distinguishes the red cells after splen—"

"Hal Jolle bodies," Wynter said.

Pearce blinked. "Very impressive, Dr. Thompson."

Pleased to hear the surprise and the grudging respect in Pearce's voice, Wynter smiled to herself. She was even more relieved to see that the spleen had come out without inordinate bleeding. Now all she had to do was be sure that all of the major vessels were appropriately tied off, and then they could irrigate the abdomen, wash out any bits of debris, and close.

Forty minutes later Wynter and Pearce rolled the patient's stretcher into the recovery room and turned her care over to the nurses. As they walked back toward the lounge, Wynter said, "What are you still doing here?"

"What do you mean?"

"You're post-call. You're supposed to go home right after rounds in the morning."

For an instant, Pearce was genuinely confused. She never went home during the day, whether she'd been on call the night before or not. "Oh. Things got busy and I lost track of time."

"Uh-huh." Wynter had a feeling that Pearce often *lost track of time* when it suited her to stay at work. She respected her for her ambition, but didn't share her single-mindedness. She had a life outside the hospital, and even though at the moment that consisted primarily of her daughter, that was reason enough to leave when she could. Pearce looked tired, and for a second, Wynter contemplated urging her to leave, but then she decided that what Pearce Rifkin chose to do was none of her business. "Do you think I should go down to the emergency room to see if the chief needs any help?"

"I was just going down to make sure that the patient gets up to the OR before he blows that aneurysm and bleeds to death down there."

Wynter stopped in the middle of the hall and turned into Pearce's path. "I'm on call tonight, and I'm supposed to be the most senior resident in the house today. I'll go down and take care of it."

"Why don't you go check on the boys and make sure things are under control on the floors."

"Pearce," Wynter said quietly. "I know you're the chief, but—"

"That's right, I am," Pearce replied just as quietly.

Wynter flushed, realizing that Pearce's suggestion had not been a request. "Right." She pivoted and started toward the elevators, wondering if she would have any opportunity at all to manage things on her own if Pearce was always around.

"I'll page you when the patient is in the holding area," Pearce called after her. "You can scrub the case."

Convinced that she was never going to understand Pearce Rifkin, Wynter halted once more and looked back. "You sure?"

"Yeah," Pearce said with a grin, wondering why the hell she was giving up a great case. "You take it. I'll just hang around to put out fires until you're free again."

"Okay. Thanks," Wynter said, frowning slightly. She didn't get her, not at all.

❖

Six hours later, Wynter made her way wearily toward the surgeons' lounge, her scrubs soaked with sweat, her body feeling as if she'd spent the day performing manual labor. The case had been difficult, as all major vascular emergencies were. If they could not remove the diseased portion of the patient's aorta and replace it with an artificial graft, the patient would lose his leg or die. It was one of those procedures that needed to be done right the first time, because there were no second chances. Nevertheless, Rifkin had been calm and cool and methodically proficient. He'd even let Wynter perform a portion of the anastomosis, sewing the Gore-Tex graft into the section of diseased artery. It had surprised and thrilled her.

She was halfway to the soda machine in the surgeons' lounge when she realized that the resident sacked out on the couch, whom she had initially ignored since it was such a common sight, was Pearce. They were the only ones in the room. An empty pizza box sat in the middle of the coffee table in front of the sofa where Pearce slept. Wynter was willing to lay odds that had been Pearce's supper.

Pearce lay on her back, one knee slightly bent, an arm dangling half off the edge of the green vinyl sofa. Her face was unlined, youthful, beautiful. Wynter watched the slow, steady rise and fall of her chest, noting the swell of her breasts and the long hollow curve down her abdomen to the jut of hipbone. Her hand was open, supplicant, waiting. Wynter was glad they were alone—she didn't like to think of strangers seeing her this way, so innocent and exposed. She had the urge to cover her, to protect her from prying eyes while she slept.

She debated letting her sleep and then decided that Pearce would want an update on the case. Plus, she really did need to go home. She leaned over the sleeping woman and gently shook her shoulder. "Hey.

Pearce."

Pearce opened her eyes, which were hazy and unfocused. After a few seconds, she smiled. Wynter bent over her, her eyes soft with welcome. It was a wonderful way to wake up. "All done?"

"Yes," Wynter said softly, resisting the urge to brush the damp strands of hair off her cheek. When Pearce sidled over to make room, Wynter sat next to her without thinking, their hips lightly touching. "It went great. Thanks for letting me do it."

"No problem." Pearce stretched lazily, her hips coming off the sofa as she raised her arms over her head and rolled her shoulders. Her scrub shirt had come untucked while she slept and rode up now to expose an expanse of smooth, tanned belly surrounding a tight, shallow navel.

Wynter tracked the path of fabric over flesh and was struck by the unexpected beauty of muscles playing beneath soft skin. She saw bodies every day of her life, clothed and unclothed, in every stage of health and disease, but she couldn't remember ever seeing anything quite so lovely.

Pearce followed Wynter's gaze, and the muscles in her belly twitched as if stroked. In an instant, she was aroused. She searched Wynter's eyes, wondering if she knew what her glance had stirred, hoping that her own hunger did not show. Her voice was hoarse when she said, "I should probably get home."

Abruptly, Wynter stood, backing away as she spoke. "Yes. Everything is quiet here, I take it?"

"As the grave." Pearce swung her legs to the floor and rose. Wynter was already feeding coins into the soda machine with her back turned. "You should get some dinner. You can't afford to lose any more weight."

Wynter turned, her expression questioning. "What do you mean?"

"You look thinner than I remember you. Surgery residencies will either pork you up or cause malnutrition."

"Oh, you mean when we first met?" When Pearce nodded, Wynter smiled. "This is my baseline. I was pregnant then."

Pearce grew suddenly very still. "You've got kids?"

"One. A little girl. She's three."

"Jesus," Pearce whispered. *She's straight and she has a kid. Oh, man. You need to stay far, far away from this one.*

Busy opening her soda, Wynter didn't see the shock on Pearce's face. "So, can I buy you dinner?"

"No, thanks," Pearce said hastily. She gestured toward the wall clock. "It's late. See you tomorrow."

Hurt by the sudden shift in mood, Wynter watched her hurry away, certain she would never figure Pearce out. And just as certain that she didn't care.

CHAPTER ELEVEN

Okay, let's take it from the top," Pearce said, as she did every morning at 5:30 a.m.

"1211, Myzorsky, three days post fem-pop bypass," Wynter began, as *she* had every day for the last month except for the Saturday and Sunday, a week apart, when she had not been on call. She could barely remember a time when she had not been a resident at University Hospital. Spending twelve to twenty-four hours a day immersed in what amounted to a self-contained society with its own particular rules and regulations had inculcated her quickly to the habits and expectations of her fellow residents, the nursing staff, and her attendings. She had a good sense of what everyone wanted—everyone, that was, except Pearce. She studied her senior resident as the other residents began their run-down of the patients assigned to them.

Pearce had dark half-moons smudging each lower lid, as if the delicate, pale skin had been pinched by brutal fingers. Shadows danced in her even darker eyes, whispering of thoughts Wynter could only guess at and tried not to. Since the night she had awakened Pearce in the surgeons' lounge, they'd had no interaction that hadn't been strictly clinically related. Pearce was a fair and highly competent acting chief, and Wynter appreciated how much teaching Pearce provided everyone on the service, including her. But there had been no more offers of dinner, no detours to Pearce's secret hideaways, and no stolen moments to exchange a personal word between cases. As the days passed, Wynter found it more and more difficult to believe that they had shared such an easy connection over dinner the night she had arrived and impossible to accept that there had once been a connection so immediate they had almost kissed. Clearly, whatever had drawn them together in that singular sliver of long-ago time had disappeared with the years. Even as she accepted what she could not deny, this new distance between them made her edgy and short-tempered, which was wholly unlike her.

"Does that meet your approval, Dr. Thompson?" Pearce asked dryly, wondering where Wynter had drifted off to. Her blue eyes were stormy and distant.

"What?" Wynter jumped, aware that she had not been listening. "Sorry?"

"I just said you can take Liu through the hernia this afternoon. Marksburg is a hands-off attending and will probably only stick her head in now and then. Of course, if you're too busy—"

"No! Of course not. That sounds great." She purposely slid her eyes away from Pearce, who was staring at her so intently she feared her thoughts might be visible. She gave the first-year resident, who looked both excited and frightened, an encouraging nod. "That will be fine. Make sure you review the patient's chart before you come to the OR."

"Oh, I will," Liu said. "For sure."

Wynter hid her smile, remembering those first few times she had been given responsibility for performing an operation. It had taken her several years to appreciate that she was not really operating at all, but following the subtle directions of those more experienced as they led her by the hand through the procedure, guiding her movements with small verbal and physical cues. The experienced surgeon could perform most of the operation without her even noticing, so that when it was over, she felt as if she had done the procedure. Eventually, she realized that had she been left to her own devices, she would have foundered in the middle of the case with no idea what to do. But a good teacher left her feeling accomplished rather than lost and inadequate. That caliber of instruction was a balancing act that only the very best could perform. Pearce was that kind of mentor. It was just one of the many things that Wynter admired about the difficult but irrefutably talented chief resident.

Pearce wondered at the small frown line that creased the smooth skin between Wynter's brows. Obviously, something was bothering her.

And that bothered Pearce. That was foolish, and she knew it. Whatever was going on in Wynter's life was no concern of hers as long as it didn't affect her work. She reminded herself of that at least once daily. In recent weeks, Pearce had been very careful not to infringe on personal territory. The day Wynter had arrived she'd been so surprised to see her that she had behaved completely unlike herself. She still felt mildly embarrassed to think that she had taken Wynter to the old residents' lounge, as if she were a kid showing off her favorite rock collection to an adult she wanted to impress.

"Everybody knows what to do." Impatient with her own wandering thoughts, Pearce collected her paperwork and stood. "So let's get to work."

Pearce detoured to the cafeteria counter for a cup of coffee that she didn't really want so that Wynter and the other residents could get ahead of her as they dispersed for work rounds. As she held down the lever to refill her cup from the stainless steel urn, she felt a not-so-subtle brush of fingers over her ass. She didn't have to look to know who it was.

"Not here," she murmured.

"Where have you been?" Andrea said in a low throaty voice. She moved closer and skimmed her hand inside Pearce's lab coat, playing her nails up and down Pearce's thigh.

Pearce took a sharp breath and drew back. "Busy."

"So busy you don't get horny anymore?"

"Look," Pearce said, sliding away even though her coffee cup was only half full. "I gotta be in the OR in a few minutes. I'll catch you later."

Andrea wet her lips with the tip of her tongue, a moist pink flicker of invitation. "Next time, I'll take care of *you* first."

Skip Ronito, a resident in Pearce's year, snickered as he passed with a breakfast tray laden with bacon, eggs, and a six-inch stack of toast. When Pearce followed him to the checkout line, he muttered, "Hey, Rifkin, if you don't have time for her, I'll take your place. Just thinking about her gives me a boner."

"Now *there's* a news flash," Pearce said. "Be my guest."

He looked at her quizzically. "You really don't care?"

"What Andrea does is none of my business."

"Does she…you know…swing both ways?"

Pearce shrugged but she definitely doubted it. "Ask her."

"Yeah, maybe," Skip said, glancing over his shoulder. Andrea looked past him as if he were invisible, her gaze riveted on Pearce. "Yeah," he added with a sigh, "right."

"Here," Pearce said, dropping a dollar on his tray. "Get my coffee, will you?"

Not waiting for an answer, she edged around him and beat a hasty retreat before Andrea could catch up to her and make another offer that didn't interest her any longer.

❖

"Whoa, whoa. Slow down," Wynter said sharply. "That thing you're about to cut is the spermatic cord, and I don't think this guy would like it very much if you chopped it in half."

Liu looked where Wynter pointed, now clearly able to discern the round tubular structure as large as his little finger. "I don't know how I missed that."

"Well, how many times've you seen it in a living person?"

"This is the first time."

"That's how you missed it. So be careful and *look* before you cut. It's good to be fast. It's bad to be sloppy."

Liu nodded earnestly and resumed dissecting the filmy hernia sac from the surrounding muscles and fascia in the groin of the twenty-five-year-old weightlifter. Wynter heard a small snort of disgust and looked over the top of the ether screen at her friend Ken, who was managing the anesthesia for the procedure. He rolled his eyes at her and she grinned behind her mask. Because anesthesia had a shorter training period than surgery, Ken was in his final year of training. He had seen hundreds of surgery residents come and go, and like most anesthesia residents, shared a mostly good-natured rivalry with his surgery counterparts over who had the ultimate authority in the operating room. All surgeons felt that the operating room was their kingdom and often opined on the fine points of appropriate anesthesia management. The anesthesiologists invariably took offense and often vented their frustrations by heckling or deriding the hapless junior surgery residents.

"You're doing fine, Liu," Wynter said, ignoring Ken's grumbling about the longest hernia repair on record. "There…right there. See that little pink half-moon? Poking out right next to the vas? That's a loop of bowel. Do *not* cut it."

"Okay, okay," Lu muttered, sweating as if he were defusing a ten-megaton bomb without a shield.

From just behind her right ear, Wynter heard a soft, sensuous voice ask, "Having fun?"

She didn't look around, but her pulse sped up and her stomach tightened. Keeping her voice cool and professional, she said, "We just isolated the hernia sac and are about to tie it off. It's small."

"Good," Pearce said, moving closer so that she could see over Wynter's shoulder. Careful not to overbalance and push Wynter into the field, she rested her fingertips on Wynter's back to steady herself. Since nothing *behind* a surgeon was sterile, she didn't risk contaminating anything. She watched the first-year resident work for a few moments, automatically following his progress as all of her senses became absorbed by impressions of Wynter—the slight sheen of sweat on the back of her neck, the movement of firm muscles as she reached for instruments, the scent of her skin like the flowers that ringed Pearce's grandmother's porch, their petals heavy with early-morning rain—sweet and fresh and rich. Unconsciously, Pearce swept her fingers in a slow rhythmic arc along the curve of Wynter's shoulder blade. "Looks great."

"Yes." Wynter imagined she could feel Pearce's breath against her skin, although she knew that Pearce's mask prevented that. With effort, she cleared her mind of the feel of Pearce's hands on her back, the gentle pressure along her body that she knew came from Pearce's breasts and thighs just touching hers as the other woman leaned over her shoulder. Carefully, she massaged the adventurous loop of small intestine back into the abdominal cavity where it belonged. Holding the bowel firmly out of the way, she directed, "Now put your suture just above my fingers. You want to be careful…Ow…*ow*, damn it…damn!"

"You get stuck?" Pearce asked briskly as Wynter reflexively jerked away from the table and slammed into her. She was already reaching for the bottle of alcohol from beneath the metal prep cart as Wynter swore again and jerked off her glove. Blood streamed from the pulp of her index finger onto the floor. "Here, hold out your hand."

"God, that hurts," Wynter said, gritting her teeth as she squeezed her finger to force the blood from the puncture site. At the same time,

Pearce doused it with alcohol, adding to the pain but making her feel better, at least psychologically. She looked back at the operating table, where Liu was watching her with wide, panicked eyes. "It's okay. Just put a moist sponge on the field. I'll be back in a second."

Pearce grasped Wynter's hand when she tried to pull away, ignoring the blood that dripped into her palm. "Wait a minute while I pour some Betadine on it."

"Now I have to rescrub," Wynter protested halfheartedly. "And you're getting blood on you."

"I'm not worried." Pearce grabbed several gauze pads from a nearby stack and pressed them to Wynter's finger. "Looks deep."

"Deep enough," Wynter muttered, fighting a wave of nausea. Surgical needles were razor-sharp, heavy steel. The puncture had struck bone.

"What's the story on your patient?" Pearce asked, dabbing at the still-bleeding site. She had an insane urge to kiss it. *Like her chin.* She chased the image away. "Anything we should worry about?"

"No. No history of drug abuse. No transfusions. Straight, as far as we know. Mr. Joe College." Wynter shook her head. "It's no big deal."

Pearce met Wynter's eyes. They both knew that needle sticks were par for the course in the operating room. Everyone got stuck at least once a month. Fortunately, the needles used for suturing were not hollow, so they were far less likely to transfer contagious viruses than syringe needles. Despite the deadly threat of HIV, the possibility of hepatitis was much more likely and often as debilitating. "After the case, stop by employee health and get baseline bloods drawn. I'll order an HIV and hepatitis screen on this guy just to be sure."

"It's not really necessary. I'm sure he's clea—"

"I'm sure too. But let's be safe. Get the baseline titers drawn."

Wynter sighed and nodded assent, realizing that Pearce was right, even though it was a nuisance. Now she'd have to have follow-up bloods drawn at six weeks and six months. They'd come back negative. She was sure of it. She glanced down and saw that Pearce's fingers shook as they cupped her hand. She'd never seen Pearce tremble the slightest bit, even after thirty-six hours of no sleep and gallons of coffee. Suddenly hyperaware of Pearce's touch, she pulled her hand away as her stomach cartwheeled. "I need to finish this case."

"Right," Pearce said hoarsely. "Go ahead and scrub. I'll watch Junior until you get back."

Wynter hurried out, anxious to complete the surgery and even more anxious to reclaim some semblance of control. Pearce had a way of making her do things she didn't want to do. She'd spent almost seven years with a man who'd manipulated and cajoled her into making choices she didn't want to make. Now, when she thought she'd left all that behind, it seemed that Pearce had only to ask and she was willing to comply. It was maddening and more than a little frightening.

When Wynter returned, ready to don new gloves and a clean gown, Pearce was leaning against the anesthesia machine, laughing at something Ken had just said. As Wynter stepped up to the table, Pearce said, "You okay?"

"Fine. Just a little bit swollen."

"I know how much that can hurt. If you want me to scrub the rest of the case—"

"Oh sure," Ken interjected teasingly, "I bet she's just trying to get out of moving furniture tomorrow. Seems like a cheap trick to me."

Pearce raised a questioning brow.

"Go ahead, Liu," Wynter said, redirecting the resident to the case. "Put that suture in before the wound heals by itself…and try to miss my finger this time."

"I'm sorry. I'm sorry."

"Don't be sorry. Just don't do it again." Wynter kept her tone light, but all business. Once the resident had safely placed the first suture, she glanced at Pearce. "I'm moving tomorrow."

For a second, Pearce had a vision of Wynter sharing an apartment with some unknown man. Sharing the moments of her day, her bed, her life. She searched for words and couldn't find any.

Wynter, her attention back on the field, continued, "My daughter and I've been staying with Ken and his wife since I moved here. I just got a sublet in the other half of their Victorian for six months. It's perfect while I look for a permanent place."

"That's good," Pearce finally managed.

"Yeah," Ken said. "We're glad she's not going far. You're welcome to come and help move furniture tomorrow, Pearce."

Neither Pearce nor Wynter said anything.

Ken continued, oblivious to the silence. "We're having pizza and beer after."

Pearce spoke before she could change her mind. "I never pass up free beer. I'll be there."

"Don't break that when you tie it down," Wynter instructed, suddenly looking forward to the next day's labor. Moving hadn't been her choice as to how to spend her first full weekend off, but now, it didn't seem quite so bad.

CHAPTER TWELVE

"You don't have to do this, you know," Wynter said when Pearce entered the locker room the next morning. She tucked in her blouse and tossed her scrubs into the nearby laundry basket.

"Hey, I already signed on for the detail." Pearce banged open the steel door of her locker and draped her white coat over the metal hook. Then she stripped off her scrub top and exchanged it for a navy blue rugby shirt. "When is everyone getting together?"

"About eleven. That gives those of us who were on call last night time to go home and get cleaned up." Wynter resisted the urge to look down as Pearce stepped out of her pants and tugged on threadbare 501s. While Pearce buttoned up, Wynter shrugged into her knee-length woolen coat and eyed the brown leather bomber jacket that Pearce tugged out of her locker. "Don't you freeze in that?"

"This?" Pearce said, pulling on the jacket. "No way. It's the real deal. My grandfather was a Navy flight surgeon."

Wynter smoothed her hand down the sleeve, amazed at the suppleness of the leather. Pearce looked young and tough and outrageously attractive in it. Fleetingly, Wynter wondered just when it was that she'd begun to think of women that way, but she quickly pushed the question aside. "It's beautiful."

"Thanks." Pearce held her breath, watching Wynter's face soften with pleasure. At that moment, she'd have given anything she had if only that look were for her. Warning bells clanged, and she reminded herself why she wasn't going down that road. "It keeps me warm."

Wynter lifted her eyes to Pearce's, her fingers still resting on the jacket. "I bet it does."

"See you in a little while," Pearce murmured, sidestepping over the bench and out of touching range.

"Come hungry," Wynter called after her.

"Count on it." Pearce laughed as she shouldered out the door. *That's my problem.*

❖

"Who are you waiting for?" Mina asked.

"No one," Wynter said.

"You've been watching that clock like an expectant father. So don't tell me no one."

Wynter blushed. "I was just checking…" She saw Mina's eyes narrow the way they did when one of the kids was telling a particularly clumsy fib. She sighed. "My senior resident is supposed to come over to help out. That's all."

"Dr. Hotty Pants?"

"Shh," Wynter admonished, stifling a laugh. "Someone will hear you."

"All the men are in the living room plotting strategy. You'd think they were going to war and not unloading a truck full of furniture. Speaking of which, they're late."

"When have you ever known a delivery service to be on time? Everything about this move happened so quickly, I'm just grateful I don't have to leave everything in storage for the next year."

Ken walked into the kitchen and threw an arm around Mina's shoulders. "The truck is just pulling up out front. Is your sister with the kids?"

"They're all tucked away upstairs with Chloe and a roomful of toys. If anyone wants me, I'll be next door in Wynter's new kitchen telling her where to put everything. I just adore organizing kitchens."

"Yeah, and just about everything else," Ken said good-naturedly. He kissed Mina and hurried outside to continue his supervisory role.

Wynter looked after him fondly. "I don't know what I'd do without you and all the rest of your family. I—"

"Just hush up. You and Ronnie *are* family. Now let's get going before those men put everything in the wrong place."

They made it as far as the front porch before Mina stopped so abruptly that Wynter nearly ran into her. The eighteen-foot delivery truck had backed up onto the sidewalk, and its tailgate now rested on the wooden steps that led up to the wide front porch of the other half of the Victorian twin. A small cluster of people congregated by the open truck bed, most of them gesticulating and talking at once. One person stood apart observing the conclave, legs spread and arms folded, sporting an amused expression.

"Well doesn't she make an interesting picture," Mina said softly. "Would that be your Dr. Hotty Pants?"

"Mina," Wynter hissed, "for God's sake…she'll *hear*."

"Ooh, she's a real looker. I bet plenty of men have been brokenhearted to find out she plays for the other team."

Pearce glanced up to the porch idly, then fixed on Wynter and waved. "Hey."

"Hey." Wynter waved back, unable to put the image of Pearce—in low-slung black jeans, scuffed brown boots worn down at the heels, and olive-green army jacket with faded patches where the insignia had once been—together with a man. It didn't seem right. "You think? She doesn't seem like the type guys would go for."

"It's not what she's wearing, honey, it's her face. She's beautiful—and I bet she's got a body to match under that bad-boy get up."

"She does. And I think she looks great exactly the way she is," Wynter said. Pearce was just Pearce. An attractive, desirable woman where everything fit just the way it should. Her looks, her brains, her spirit. Her charm. *Oh my God. What am I thinking.*

"Did I say she didn't?" Mina gave her a look, then ambled over to the porch rail and called down. "You sure you want to get mixed up with these crazy men, honey?"

"I figure someone needs to keep them out of trouble," Pearce called back.

Mina laughed. "Well, good luck. You'll need it."

Wynter joined Pearce on the sidewalk while Mina headed for Wynter's new house. "You made it."

"Just in time, it looks like."

"I'm going to direct traffic inside. If you get tired, don't feel you need to stay—"

"Are you kidding? These are a bunch of anesthesiologists and internists, for crying out loud. They'll quit a long time before me." She scanned the porch, looking for the glimpse of Wynter's life that she didn't know. "Where's your daughter?"

"Upstairs with Mina's sister and Ken and Mina's kids. I'll introduce you later—if you want."

"Sure. I'd like that." She turned when Ken called her name. "Time for me to flex my muscles."

Impulsively, Wynter grasped her arm. "Be careful, okay?"

Pearce laughed. "No sweat. I'll see you later."

Wynter sidled around the tailgate and joined Mina inside. The three-story Victorian, renovated by a recent owner, featured a clerestory ceiling in the rear of the first floor that opened all the way to the third. The hardwood floors gleamed. The kitchen had been modernized as well, and although she rarely had time, she looked forward to the opportunity to cook. Decks opened off the kitchen as well as off the master bedroom on the third floor. Although the backyard was postage-stamp sized, she contemplated yet again getting a puppy for Ronnie. The problem was that when the sublet was over and she moved to a permanent location where Mina and her extended family were unavailable to help with child care, a dog would be out of the question.

"What are you thinking about so hard?" Mina pointed several men who had boxes marked *kitchen* in their arms toward the rear, calling after them, "And don't drop them on the floor when you put them down."

"Ronnie keeps asking for a puppy. She's a good age for it, but I just don't see how I can handle taking care of one."

"Our kids want another one too. Maybe we could work out joint custody," Mina suggested. "Our yards are side by side, and if we put a gate in the fence, we can share the whole space."

Wynter shook her head. "It's going to be hard enough as it is for her not to be with you and the kids every day once we get a permanent place. I don't want to add a puppy to everything else she's going to miss."

Mina pursed her lips as if to disagree but merely said, "We'll see."

For the next hour and a half, Wynter directed the half dozen men carrying boxes of books, furniture, and suitcases to various parts of the house. One of the last items off the truck was a tiger oak rolltop desk that she'd inherited from her grandmother. It was huge, heavy, and cumbersome, but she loved it and had carted it all over the country.

"Where to?" Pearce asked as she balanced one rear corner of the desk on her knee at the foot of the second-floor staircase. Ken had the front and another anesthesia resident, Tommy Argyle, had the opposite back corner.

"The middle room on the second floor. On the wall opposite the fireplace."

"It's going to be a tight corner up here," Ken called down.

"We might have to lift it up over the banister," Pearce said. She glanced at Tommy. "Think you can handle it?"

"Huh. With one arm tied behind my back."

Wynter rested a hand on Pearce's shoulder and said quietly, "Do you compete with everyone about everything?"

"It's no fun otherwise." Pearce craned her neck and called up to Ken, "Let's get this done. I smell pizza."

Wynter turned, and sure enough, the pizza delivery man stood behind her in the middle of the living room with eight large pizza boxes cradled in his arms. "Back here in the kitchen. I'll show you."

Wynter and Mina were setting out paper plates, napkins, and bottles of soda and beer when a crash sounded from above followed closely by a chorus of shouts. Wynter ran ahead of Mina and started up thc stairs two at a time. Ken came racing down and nearly collided with her.

"Ice. We need some ice," Ken said urgently.

"What happened?" Wynter, a sick feeling in her stomach, searched the landing above but saw no one.

"Tommy dropped the damn thing."

"Is he hurt?"

"He's fine, but Pearce got her hand caught—"

"Oh God. Pearce." Wynter pushed around Ken and ran upstairs. The men huddled around a figure on the floor. The desk sat on its side nearby. She pushed at the nearest figure. "Move. Move out of the way."

Pearce slumped on the floor, one arm cradled across her chest, her head leaning back against the wall. Her face was ashen. Wynter dropped to her knees beside her. "Let me see."

"Give me a minute," Pearce whispered.

Wynter could hear the pain in her voice and it tore at her. She was used to seeing people in pain from far greater injuries, but she felt exactly the way she did when Ronnie hurt herself. She wanted to absorb the pain, take it away at all costs. So she did exactly what she did when Ronnie was hurt. She put her arm around Pearce's shoulders and drew her close. "Let me see, honey. It's okay."

Eyes still closed, Pearce buried her cheek against Wynter's chest, trying to lose herself in the scent of petals and raindrops and long ago joy. "Hurts. Hurts like a mother."

"I know. I know it does." Wynter pillowed Pearce's head between her breasts, rocking her softly. Then she kissed the top of her head and stroked her sweaty cheek. "Are you bleeding?"

"Don't know. Don't think so."

Wynter felt a rush of relief. Her stomach was twisted into knots, her chest so tight she could barely breathe. "Do you think you can let me look now?"

"Couldn't have been my foot," Pearce said, her voice stronger. "Had to be my goddamn hand."

"Pearce," Wynter said more firmly, her own strength returning along with Pearce's. "Let's see what we're dealing with."

With a soft groan, Pearce sat forward, still half in Wynter's lap. She lifted her left hand, gently supporting it with her right. It was already twice its normal size, the knuckles scraped and swollen.

"Range your fingers for me…slowly," Wynter instructed quietly, one hand on the back of Pearce's neck, lightly caressing her.

Even though the pain threatened to overpower her, Pearce managed to extend her fingers nearly completely, but she could not make a fist. There was too much swelling. "I don't think anything's broken."

Wynter laughed softly. "Thank you Dr. X-ray Eyes. That's so helpful."

Ken clambered up the stairs, shouting, "I've got the ice."

"Good. Give it to me." Wynter reached behind her without taking her eyes off Pearce's hand and set the plastic bag of ice on the floor by her feet.

"Is it bad?" Ken asked anxiously. "Should we take her to the ER?"

Wynter felt Pearce tense. "No. We're okay. I'll be down in a minute."

Ken rocked back and forth uncertainly for a minute, and then when ignored, crept away.

"I'm going to palpate it," Wynter said.

Wincing, Pearce gently probed the base of each finger. "I don't feel anything."

"Just let me confirm." Gently, Wynter repeated the action, searching for point tenderness that would indicate a fracture. On close examination, Pearce's fingers did not appear deviated, and there was no apparent deformity of the hand. The marked swelling and rapidly discoloring skin made it difficult to examine her critically, however. "We've got to X-ray this."

"Let's ice it first and see what it looks like in a few hours. The last thing I want to do is sit in the emergency room for half the day." What Pearce didn't say was that if she showed up in the emergency room, someone would call her father within two minutes. She didn't want him involved. She didn't want to hear him tell her that she shouldn't have been doing anything to endanger her hands. Every time she worked on her car, she heard his voice admonishing her. She could just imagine what he'd say about her moving furniture.

"I'll call ahead and let them know we're coming," Wynter said. "I'm sure they'll get you right in—"

"*No*," Pearce said fiercely.

Wynter recognized the fear beneath the stubbornness, and because she couldn't imagine Pearce being afraid of anything, she relented. After a final gentle caress down Pearce's neck and over her shoulders, she retrieved the ice pack and held it out. "We'll wait until tonight. If it's worse, we're going."

Pearce carefully placed the ice pack on the palm of her hand and leaned back against the wall. She regarded Wynter through eyes dull with pain. "You've been waiting for this moment, haven't you?"

"What are you talking about?"

"For me to be helpless so that you could take charge."

Wynter laughed. "Oh, if I had wanted to take charge, I already would have." She brushed the damp midnight strands off Pearce's forehead. "And if I had wanted you helpless, I probably could've managed that without the desk."

Despite the relentless, thundering pain in her arm, Pearce was aware of her body quickening. She knew that Wynter didn't mean what she had said *that* way, but her body would do what her body would do. She stretched her legs restlessly, trying to lessen the sudden tightness in her thighs. "Pretty confident."

"You just noticed?"

Pearce grinned and closed her eyes with a sigh. "No. I noticed."

Wynter wanted to tell everyone in the house to clear out. She wanted to take Pearce to her bedroom, where she didn't even have a bed, and tuck her in. She wanted to watch her sleep and guard her while she did. She wanted to take away her pain. She *wanted* to kiss her and make her feel better—make herself feel…something. Something she couldn't even name.

Instead, she got unsteadily to her feet, her legs weak with the force of her unexpected desires. "I'm going to get you a soda. Can you eat anything?"

Pearce shook her head. "Not yet. But I could use something to drink and a half bottle of aspirin."

"Coming right up."

Ken and the others waited in a nervous clump at the bottom of the stairs. Tommy stood next to him looking miserable.

"Is it bad?" Ken repeated anxiously.

"I can't tell. It's pretty swollen."

"Oh man," Tommy moaned. "Jesus, if it's broken her old man is going to take me out and kick my ass into the river."

"If it's broken…" Wynter said tightly, wanting to say that Rifkin wouldn't have to kick Tommy's ass because *she* would, "it will heal, and it will be fine. *She'll* be fine." She walked away from them, determined that it would be so. She didn't intend to let anything hurt Pearce.

Chapter Thirteen

Do you think we should wake her up?" Mina asked Wynter, who leaned in the doorway between the dining room and the living room watching Pearce.

Wynter shook her head. "It's her hand, not her head. We don't have to wake her up for neurochecks."

"She sure sleeps like someone knocked her out."

Although Wynter's books and personal articles were still in boxes stacked about the room, the living room furniture was at least accessible, and she had insisted that Pearce stretch out in the leather recliner and rest. The men had consumed the pizza and quickly disappeared. While Ken and Mina fed the kids next door, Wynter had curled up on the sofa next to Pearce to read a book. Now, four hours later, Mina was back, the sun had gone down, and Pearce had not stirred.

"She works too hard," Wynter murmured, trying to recall the last time she had seen Pearce leave the hospital before midnight. *Just like her father.*

"I'm awake." Pearce, her long legs spread on the raised foot support, shifted in the chair and opened her eyes. "Stop talking about me."

"Well, there goes all the fun," Mina said, starting toward the front door. "I'll see about getting the Wild Bunch settled in for the night. Chloe's probably ready to go home."

"I'll give you a hand in a minute," Wynter called.

"I've got it all under control—you'll just mess up my system. You look after the patient here."

Laughing, Wynter edged around boxes and settled on the corner of the coffee table nearest Pearce. "How do you feel?"

"A little fuzzy. What exactly did you give me?" she asked suspiciously.

"Three aspirin and ten milligrams of Valium. I thought the muscle relaxation might help with the pain."

"Jesus," Pearce muttered. "Leave it to a surgeon to just take over. Don't mind me, I'm only the patient."

"It's standard procedure to sedate a trauma patient," Wynter said, looking not the least bit contrite. "No one's allergic to Valium. And admit it—you feel better, don't you?"

Pearce rolled her head back and forth. The sick headache was gone. Then she glanced down to her lap where her hand rested on the soggy ice pack wrapped in a towel. Experimentally, she flexed her fingers. "It's easing up."

"Let me see."

Wynter cradled Pearce's injured hand in both of hers. She felt the pulses, examined the scrapes, probed gently. "It's definitely not worse."

"I said that." Pearce wasn't even thinking about the pain. She was studying Wynter's face as she bent her head over Pearce's injured hand. Pearce wanted to run her fingers through Wynter's hair. She wanted to trace her fingers along the edge of Wynter's jaw as she had that one time years before. She wanted to close her eyes, believing that she would awaken to the smile in Wynter's eyes. "I should get home."

Wynter straightened, carefully releasing Pearce's hand. She wanted Pearce to stay so that she could check her hand throughout the evening and just…watch her. Watch her sleep, watch her laugh, watch her stretch her long body in that lazy animal way she had. "I'll drive you. Where is your car parked?"

"I walked."

"You live near here?" Wynter had not expected that the chief of surgery's daughter would live in the off-campus student enclave. University City was an eclectic mixture of beautiful old homes that had been converted into student apartments, gentrified sections cheek by jowl with blocks where it wasn't safe to leave any items in a parked car. It was convenient to the hospitals and campus and cheap by comparison to many other areas, but not the first choice of those with enough money to live in Center City apartments with all the amenities and close to the night life. Many of the residents like Ken and Mina lived there, and Wynter needed an apartment with proximity to the hospital so that she could minimize her time away from Ronnie. Adding an hour-a-day commute to her already overburdened schedule was simply not acceptable.

"About five blocks," Pearce said. "A ten-minute walk."

"I'll walk you home, then."

Pearce grinned. "Do you think I need an escort?"

"No," Wynter said with exaggerated emphasis. "I think you've taken a muscle relaxant and the effects have not worn off. You have a badly injured hand. And you shouldn't be walking around at night alone when you're incapable of protecting yourself if you have to."

"I'll be fine." To prove it, Pearce kicked the foot extension down and stood. She swayed, instantly dizzy.

"God, you're stubborn," Wynter snapped as she jumped up and wrapped an arm around Pearce's waist. When Pearce sagged against her, Wynter knew she must really be feeling ill. "You don't have to prove anything to me. I already know how tough you are."

"Not trying to prove anything," Pearce muttered, desperately willing her head to stop spinning.

Yes, you are, if you know it or not. Wynter rubbed her palm in circles in the center of Pearce's back, supporting her until she saw the vacant expression on Pearce's face disappear and her usual focus return. "Okay now?"

Pearce, embarrassed by her weakness but enjoying the contact with Wynter, settled her arm around Wynter's shoulders and squeezed. "Yeah. Thanks."

"Let me go next door and tell Ronnie I'm going out for a while, and then we'll get you home. I'll just be a minute."

"You're going to introduce us, remember?"

"You sure? We can do it some other time when you're feeling better."

Pearce shrugged. She liked the idea of there being another time, but she didn't want to wait. *She* might not have anything else in her life except work and her car, but Wynter did, and she wanted to know something about it. "No, come on. I'll go over with you."

"All right," Wynter relented dubiously, "but take it easy, okay?"

Pearce looked down at her hand. It was discolored and raw, the knuckles crusted where the skin had been crushed between the desk and the banister. Just remembering it made her queasy. "You don't think this will scare her, do you?"

"Ronnie understands about owies, she just doesn't appreciate that some could be much worse than others. She won't be frightened because she's used to bumps and bruises."

"Some fucking owie," Pearce muttered.

"Come on, Chief," Wynter said, squeezing Pearce's good hand. "Let me take you over to meet my little angel."

The little angel, looking cuddly and sweet in soft flannel jammies covered with Scooby-Doo and friends, was in the midst of demolishing a fort, which she and Mina's son Winston had built out of blocks, by crashing a red fire truck into it and screaming *boom* each time more blocks scattered across the floor. Plastic action figures that had been perched atop the blocks flew willy-nilly through the air. Winston, his face set in studied concentration, carefully picked up each fallen body and placed it into a white plastic ambulance.

Pearce stood in a doorway observing the carnage, thinking that the beautiful child with the red-blond hair might very well be angelic under other circumstances. At the moment she looked like a little terror. "They make a good pair," she whispered to Wynter, who stood beside her looking amused. "Ronnie runs them down and he resuscitates them."

Laughing, Wynter picked her way across the toy-littered floor and squatted down by the absorbed children. After a few whispered words to her daughter, she stood, Ronnie in her arms, and crossed back to Pearce. "Honey, this is my friend Pearce. We work together at the hospital."

Ronnie studied Pearce solemnly, her enormous blue eyes the exact color of Wynter's. Then with a squeak, she buried her face in her mother's neck.

"Oops," Pearce said.

Wynter rubbed Ronnie's back and rocked from side to side in a motion that was second nature to her. She shook her head. "It's just the age. Nothing personal."

"If you say so."

"Let me get her settled and then we can go."

"You sure? Because I can—"

"Stop," Wynter said firmly and returned Ronnie to the play area. Within seconds, the two children were once more absorbed in their demolition activities.

As they walked outside, Pearce said, "She's gorgeous. She looks just like you."

"Thank you." The sidewalks were dry, but snow banks lined the walkways, remnants of the last storm. In the dark, with only the street lights for illumination, everything looked clean and oddly peaceful. Wynter took a deep breath of the cold night air and felt good all over. She did not have to work the next day, her child seemed to be settling into their new living circumstances well with the help of Ken and Mina's extended family support structure, and she was walking with a person whose company she enjoyed. An attractive, intriguing person. A woman. A woman who occupied far more of her thoughts than any person in recent memory. She was going to have to think about that soon, but right now, she just wanted to be happy. "She's a really solid little kid."

"Uh…what about her father?"

Wynter looked straight ahead, her expression remote. "What about him?"

"Does he…you know…get to have her part of the time?" Pearce unzipped her army jacket halfway and slid her left hand inside against her body, letting the material form a makeshift sling. The cold was making her hand ache.

"Is your hand okay?"

"I know it's there."

"I want to take another look at it when we get to your place."

"It's just around the corner." Pearce recognized evasion. She was an expert at it. "Ronnie's father?"

"I have primary custody. He gets unlimited visitation—which he apparently has no desire for." Wynter pushed her gloved hands into the pockets of her coat. "He also has a new wife and an infant. He started *that* family before our divorce. I haven't seen or heard from him in six months."

"Fucker," Pearce said vehemently.

"Yes."

"I can't imagine anyone looking at another woman when they had you."

Wynter blinked, speechless, and tried to remember when anyone had ever said anything as nice to her before. And the funny thing was, Pearce hadn't said it to get anything from her. Not a date, not a kiss, not a promise of anything at all. In fact, she'd said it in an angry tone as if deeply affronted by the very thought. "Thank you."

Pearce whipped her head around and frowned at Wynter. "He was obviously a jerk."

"He was," Wynter agreed. "I feel stupid for not realizing it sooner. He wanted a stay-at-home wife, but I never saw that, even when he tried to talk me out of surgery."

"But you were married when you were a medical student. He must've realized you weren't going to be that kind of wife." Pearce stopped in front of what had once been a huge single-family home. It was set back from the street with a slate sidewalk that bisected the front lawn. Four mailboxes were lined up on the wall next to the double wooden front doors. "I'm in here."

"We met when we were freshmen in the combined BS/MD program. I don't think either one of us realized what medicine was going to be like—we were only eighteen years old. We got married in med school before I'd even had a surgery rotation. My choosing surgery was our first big issue, because he wanted a family right away and my residency was going to be a problem. My hours weren't conducive to easy child care."

"And what about him? Couldn't he have helped out there?"

"He's an orthopedic surgery resident at Yale. That's why I ranked Yale surgery first—he already had a promise of a spot outside the match, and obviously, I had to go where he was going." She tried to keep the bitterness from her voice. She'd followed him to Yale, even though it wasn't where she wanted to train. Her fault. She'd ignored all the signs that they were a bad match until it was far too late.

"You should have dumped him then."

Wynter smiled wryly. "Probably. But I was pregnant. I didn't mean to be—but the Pill never agreed with me and he hated condoms and sometimes—" She colored and looked away, realizing how pathetic she must sound to Pearce. "I made some stupid choices."

"Maybe, maybe not. But you have the little angel to show for it," Pearce said quietly, gratified to see Wynter's smile deepen to one of pleasure. "Look, do you want to come in for a minute?"

"I'd like to see your hand again."

"Come on, then." Pearce led the way up the sidewalk and unlocked the front door. She stepped into a small granite-tiled foyer with beaten tin wainscoting painted eggshell white. When Wynter followed her in, she felt the press of Wynter's body close against her side. She never wanted to move. She wanted to stay in that warm secluded space where they had nowhere to go except up against one another. She wanted Wynter to hold her injured hand again, to cradle it against her breast, to ease the pain with the force of her caring. She couldn't think of anything except Wynter and the smell of her hair and the soothing tones of her voice, and she fumbled for the doorknob on the interior door with its leaded glass windows. Her voice sounded hoarse to her own ears. "One flight up."

"Okay," Wynter said softly.

Pearce led the way up the wide curved wooden staircase to the central hallway on the second floor. She unlocked a door on the right side that opened into what once had been a formal sitting room. It was now her bedroom, living room, and study all rolled into one. A dark burgundy sofa bed sat in front of the bay windows, facing into the room. A stone fireplace was centered on the opposite wall, a desk next to it, and an archway beyond that led into a small kitchen. A dresser stood in the far corner of the room next to another door that undoubtedly led to the bathroom. There were books and journals everywhere, and the room reminded Wynter of the abandoned residents' lounge in the hospital. It was definitely Pearce.

"I like your place," Wynter said.

Pearce was busy making space on the sofa, awkwardly stacking textbooks and stapled articles into piles on either side with one hand. "I don't get many visitors."

Wynter wondered whether Pearce brought women here. Dates or…whatever. The thought unsettled her, because it was so unlike her to even go there, let alone to have the quick surge of jealousy that accompanied the visions. "That's okay. Don't fuss."

"I have…" Pearce ran a hand through her hair, looking flummoxed. "I don't know what I have. Beer for sure. Maybe a bottle of wine somewhere. Hot chocolate?"

"You have hot chocolate?" Wynter asked with pleasure.

Pearce grinned. "Yup. It's a weakness of mine."

"Mine too."

Relieved to have something to do, Pearce indicated the sofa. "Sit down. I'll have it in a minute. I like mine with warm milk. Is that okay?"

"It's perfect, but let me help. You're one-handed, remember?"

The kitchen, although tiny, was impeccably clean. Probably, Wynter surmised, due to the fact that Pearce obviously didn't cook. The refrigerator held a container of milk, a pizza box on the bottom shelf, a six-pack of beer, some cheese, and a half dozen eggs. While Pearce got mugs and cocoa, Wynter warmed the milk. "How long have you had this place?"

"Since I was a medical student."

"You didn't live at home?"

Pearce carefully placed the mugs on a metal tray with a Coca-Cola sign painted in the center. She didn't look at Wynter when she answered. "No. I haven't lived at home since I was seventeen."

Wynter leaned one shoulder against the refrigerator, watching the shadows flicker over Pearce's face. "Did your father and your grandfather go to Penn too?"

"Yup. And my great grandfather, and my great great grandfather."

"Did you ever think about going somewhere else?"

"No."

"It must've been tough."

Pearce pointed to the refrigerator. "I should make another ice pack."

"I'll get it." Wynter opened the freezer door and jiggled the ice tray to free it from the accumulated frost. Pearce was very adept at deflecting the conversation away from the personal. At least *her* personal life. Wynter realized she'd shared more with Pearce in a few brief conversations than with anyone other than Mina. Pearce had a way of listening that made her feel heard. "That's quite a legacy to live up to. Did it bother you?"

"I always knew what I would be. I always knew where I would end up." Pearce spoke quietly as she searched in a cabinet for a dish towel. "It never occurred to me that there was any other choice."

Wynter turned with the ice cube tray between her fingers, trying not to freeze her hands. She held it out. "Are you happy with the way things turned out?"

Pearce settled the tray onto the palm of her uninjured hand, studying the orderly alignment of the rectangular cubes. “I don’t know. I’ve never stopped long enough to think about it.” She looked into Wynter’s eyes. “How about you?”

“I’m pretty happy with where things are right at this minute.” Wynter smiled. Standing in Pearce’s kitchen with the smell of cocoa in the air, she realized just exactly how much she meant that.

CHAPTER FOURTEEN

Oh, God," Wynter murmured, stretching her stocking feet toward the fireplace. "If I stay a minute longer, I'm not going to be able to get up and go home."

Pearce turned her head lazily on the sofa, her heavy white mug of hot chocolate balanced on her knee. She had forgotten to drink it as they had talked about medical school and Wynter's residency at Yale, sharing the many experiences they had in common. They had not mentioned Wynter's ex-husband again, although Wynter spoke often and freely about Ronnie. Pearce found she could easily discount the shadow of a husband if she didn't think about it too hard. She could sometimes even forget that Wynter was very likely to have another husband before very long. She was too beautiful and bright and dynamic to be without a partner. But those were thoughts for lonely nights when she stared into the fireplace and saw only dying embers, not the promise of light and warmth. Tonight, Wynter was beside her, and nothing had ever felt quite so right. "I'll walk you home."

"I believe I see a pattern forming here." Wynter tipped her cup and drank the last of the bittersweet chocolate. "No. We already established that you shouldn't be wandering around by yourself."

"I'm fine now. The Valium has worn off, and"—she held up her hand—"this feels a lot better."

"What are you going to do if you have to operate tomorrow?" Wynter tucked her feet up under her on the sofa and studied Pearce, who lounged a foot away on the opposite end, her head tipped back against the sofa, her back relaxed into the curve of the cushions, her legs splayed. So comfortable in her own body. So apparently unaware of how beautiful she was.

"I'm backup call. Hopefully it will be quiet. If not, I'll get a glove on somehow and fake it with my good hand. I'd only need to scrub to second assist anyhow."

"Pearce," Wynter said with real worry. "It will kill you to scrub with those open wounds. Your hand will be a bloody mess before you're done."

"I'll use one of the scrubless chemical disinfectants." She grinned at Wynter's groan. "Okay, so it'll still sting like a mother, but I won't tear anything open with a brush. I'll survive. Besides, chances are I'll get a few phone calls during the day and nothing else, so I won't even need to go in. How 'bout you? What are your plans for tomorrow?"

"You know that you're an expert at changing the subject?"

Pearce frowned in confusion. "What do you mean?"

Wynter leaned toward her and rested her fingertips on Pearce's knee. She tapped for emphasis as she spoke. "Whenever we talk about you, if it gets the least bit confrontational, you change the subject. Or if we're sharing secrets, you manage to turn everything back on me. You know more about me than my mother at this point. And I don't know anything about you."

"Okay," Pearce said with a hint of challenge in her voice. "Ask me something."

"It doesn't work that way," Wynter said in exasperation. "It's not about twenty questions. It's about…it's about…" She stopped, uncertain *what* it was about. She'd never been bothered when her other friends had been overly private. She'd never wanted to know everything about one of them. What made them happy. What made them sad. What they dreamed about. She had no idea why it annoyed her that Pearce would not easily disclose those things to her. "Never mind."

"You know things about me too," Pearce said quietly. "Secret things."

"Really? What?"

Pearce tapped the back of Wynter's hand where it now rested on her thigh. "You know about my secret room. You know about the hot chocolate. You know about…" She searched her mind frantically and then looked into Wynter's inquisitive eyes, knowing that she had told Wynter her story in fragments over dinner the night Wynter had arrived, in the abandoned residents' lounge, in the operating room as they teased and bantered, and this evening, as they talked in desultory tones about growing up with the knowledge they would always be doctors, and nothing else. "You know that I am everything my family expected me to be…except a son."

Wynter's lips parted in stunned surprise. "You can't mean that."

"You've seen him with me. I'm the only heir." She tried to put words to what she had always known but never wanted to face. From the time he had first taken her with him on rounds, she had understood that that place—those buildings, those people, that world—was her destiny. She would be what he expected, because that's why she had been born. "I'm his legacy. That's what he sees when he looks at me."

"Are you doing what *you* want to do with your life?"

"I don't know. I never had any reason to think about it." Pearce rolled her shoulders and forced a smile. "It doesn't matter now. It works for me."

Wynter didn't question that statement. It wasn't her place to second-guess what made Pearce happy. "What are your plans? After you finish?"

Pearce watched the flames lick at the center of a thick log, destroying it from the heart out, weakening it until only a shell remained around a crumbling black core. "I'll do a vascular or CT fellowship somewhere, then move into an academic position. I'll earn my stripes, and eventually I'll come back here. And I'll take my father's place."

"Is that what he did?"

"No, he's always been here. But there won't be room for me here for a while. Things have changed enough that he won't be able to push for me to succeed him unless I've got the credentials to support it. To do that, I'll have to break ground elsewhere."

"There aren't very many female chairs of surgery," Wynter said, stating what they both knew. It was still very rare for a woman to head the most powerful division in the hospital hierarchy, and the competition for the coveted position was fierce. Pearce would have to devote every waking moment for years before she might obtain the reluctant respect and support of her colleagues.

Pearce grinned, a hard, feral grin. "None of it's a cakewalk, is it?"

"No," Wynter admitted, thinking that there were easier paths to take. Paths that would allow Pearce some kind of life, some kind of happiness. "Is it what you want?"

"Sure." Abruptly, Pearce stood. "I'll walk you halfway home."

"I want to check your hand tomorrow. Remember that you agreed if it wasn't better you'd get an X-ray."

"If it's not better, I'll—"

"No. No deals."

Pearce started to protest, then sighed. "Okay. Come by whenever you're free. I don't have any plans."

"All right," Wynter said, watching as the large log split in half. The pieces dropped to either side of the dancing ring of flames and lay smoldering alone on the edges of the fire. The blaze was so beautiful as it consumed itself. And so sad.

❖

"And then the Little Prince…" Wynter carefully closed the book and leaned over her sleeping daughter to rest it on the windowsill. Ronnie lay curled up against her side, sleeping the dreamless sleep of the innocents. She'd awakened when Wynter had kissed her upon returning home, and had insisted on a story. Wynter leaned down and kissed her forehead once more, then eased out from under the covers and tucked her child in securely. A Mickey Mouse night-light by the bed guided her through the small room to the door that connected to hers. She left Ronnie's door slightly ajar and turned on the standing lamp just inside her own bedroom.

With a sigh, she contemplated her empty double bed and the prospect of reading until she fell asleep. That usually took under five minutes. Tonight, however, she was restless and had a feeling that it would take more than a few chapters of Elizabeth George to wash away the residual tensions of the day. The move, Pearce's accident, the storm of emotions that her conversation with Pearce about her marriage had brought up for her had left her feeling wired.

A glass of wine might help.

As she passed Ken and Mina's bedroom, she saw that the door was open. Mina always slept with the door open when Ken was on call, as if to maintain contact with the other sleeping members of the house when the bed beside her was empty. The blue-gray light of the television seeped into the hallway. The sound was muted, but she could hear laughter. Probably Letterman. She tapped lightly on the door and pushed it open an inch. "Mina?"

"You're up late," Mina called.

"It's only midnight."

"And you're usually asleep before dinner's over. Come on in."

"I was going to get some wine. Can I bring you anything?"

"Popcorn. Make it two bags. And a Dr Pepper."

"Coming right up."

Ten minutes later, Wynter returned with a tray laden with snacks and drinks and a bottle of wine under one arm. "I'm going to miss this when I'm living next door."

"Well, you're not going to be over there for at least a week until we get you unpacked and settled. And then you're only going to be next door, which means we can still have slumber parties." Mina patted the bed beside her. "Come get under the covers and bring all that good stuff with you."

Wynter set the tray down on the bedside table, put the bottle on the floor, and dug through the closet where she knew Mina kept the extra pillows. She grabbed one, then returned to the bed and kicked off the moccasins she wore around the house. She tossed the pillow onto Ken's side of the bed, placed the tray carefully in the center, and climbed under the down comforter. With a sigh, she poured a glass of wine, balanced the wineglass on her stomach, and leaned back into the pillows. "I feel guilty about being happy that Ken's not here tonight."

"No reason to. He gets me two out of every three nights." Mina turned down the sound on the television until it was only background noise. Reaching for the popcorn, she said, "Something wrong?"

Wynter sipped her wine. "No, not really. Just—I don't know, sometimes I'm so busy trying to get through every day that I never really stop to think what I'm doing."

"You've been going pretty much full speed ahead since you were a medical student. Feeling a little burned out?"

"I don't know. I don't think so. I really like the work. I'm no more tired now than I ever used to be. In fact, it's a lot easier than it was when Ronnie was three months old and never slept through the night."

"You had Dave around then," Mina said carefully.

"Oh yeah, and he was so much help." Wynter snorted and downed half the wine in her glass. She leaned over the side of the bed and found the bottle, replenished her wine, and took another swallow. Then, remembering her vow not to be bitter about what she couldn't change, and not to forget that she had had some part in the decisions that had led her into a life she had not wanted, she amended, "All right, he was good with Ronnie in the beginning. And that did make a difference."

"I wasn't talking about child care. I was talking about him warming your bed."

"I'm not talking about sex."

"Maybe that's because you haven't had any for a while."

Wynter laughed and nearly upset her wine. "I don't have time to get a haircut, let alone find the time or privacy to have sex."

"Don't tell me there aren't some likely candidates at that hospital that you couldn't drag off into some empty room for twenty minutes."

"Oh, please. That's just what I need. To get the reputation for being an easy lay."

"Well, would you rather get the reputation of being an Ice Queen and scare all the likely takers away?"

"I'd like," Wynter said with feigned dignity, "to get the reputation of being an unassailably professional physician."

"Oh, bull. You just haven't seen anyone you want to get into the sack."

Wynter had to admit that that was true. Even well before her divorce, she and Dave had not been sleeping with one another. It had taken her a while to realize that he was home less and less, even more absent than a busy residency would require, and after she had become suspicious, she hadn't wanted to sleep with him when he *was* home. When he didn't challenge their sudden abstinence, she had finally put all the pieces together. She had asked a few friends who were nurses at the hospital what they knew, and they had reluctantly admitted that it was common knowledge that he was involved with a senior medical student. She'd met him at the door after he'd been out all night with another "emergency," demanded his keys, and told him to pack a suitcase and get out. That had been over a year ago, and with her life in total disorder since, sex had disappeared from her radar.

"I'm not looking for a bedmate."

"All right," Mina acquiesced cheerfully, "then what do you think it is that's gotten you out of sorts?"

"I'm not out of sorts. I'm just…restless."

"Restless. Restless like you want to take a trip?"

"No."

"Restless like…you hate your job and want to do something else with your life?"

"No."

"Restless like you need an emergency vacation from the kids?"

"No. Mina—"

"Restless like—"

"Stop!" Wynter pleaded. "Just forget I said anything."

"You know I can't. It's gonna bother me so much that I won't be able to sleep."

"Liar."

"Are you going to eat that popcorn?"

"No, go ahead."

"So," Mina observed, tearing into the second bag, "maybe it's got something to do with Pearce."

A rush of heat started at Wynter's toes and climbed to the top of her head. "What are you talking about?"

"Maybe she's making you uneasy."

Wynter's throat was so dry she could barely speak. "What…why do you say that?"

"Because she's got the hots for you."

Wynter shivered as if the wind had suddenly blown through the room, carrying slivers of ice that pricked at her skin. "That's ridiculous."

Mina laughed. "Oh, honey. You do need a vacation if you can't recognize when someone is looking at you like they want to lick every little drop of sweat from your—"

"Pearce is a lesbian. She's not going to be looking at me that way."

"Last time I looked, you were female."

"That's different. I'm not even her type."

"How do you know that?"

"Because I've seen the kind of women she goes for, and believe me…This is ridiculous. What difference does it make what kind of woman Pearce Rifkin is attracted to? It wouldn't be me."

"You sound like that might bother you," Mina said with a gentle question in her voice.

"That's not what I meant. I just meant…" Wynter had no idea what she meant. She emptied her wineglass in a long swallow and gathered the remnants of their late-night snack. "I promised Ronnie she could help me make pancakes tomorrow morning. Which means she's going to be up at five a.m. We'd better get some sleep."

"You can snuggle up right here," Mina said. "You know I don't snore."

"Thanks," Wynter said, leaning over to give Mina a quick hug. "I'd better bunk in next to her so that I can divert her if she decides to go exploring when she wakes up."

"Well, if you want company, I'm here."

"I appreciate it. Night." Wynter made her way through the silent house to the kitchen. As she methodically rinsed the wineglass, put the bottle in the recycler, and tied up a bag of trash, she kept thinking about what Mina had said. That Pearce had looked at her with desire. It shouldn't have meant anything to her, no more than if a man she was not attracted to had made an overture. But Pearce wasn't a man, and the only thing she knew for certain was that she liked the way Pearce looked at her.

CHAPTER FIFTEEN

Pearce watched the fire die. The room grew steadily darker and a numbing chill settled upon her. Finally, she roused herself enough to stand up and squint at the Seth Thomas clock on the mantel, one of the few keepsakes she had wanted from her grandmother's home after her death. She could have had anything she wanted from the Main Line estate, but the only other things she'd taken were the photograph albums. When she was young, she and her grandmother had spent hours poring through the albums that had seemed enormous to her then. They had been filled with treasures—photographs of her grandmother when she was a child Pearce's age, images of old-fashioned cars and young men and women dressed in 1920s clothes, mementos of her grandmother and grandfather's courtship, and faded pictures of her grandfather in uniform from World War II. She loved to look at the hospital tents and jeeps with white crosses painted on the side, imagining herself in one of those field hospitals under a sweltering sun with the backdrop of aircraft and mortars for company while she performed life-saving surgery. Each photograph had been a story, and she had always loved her grandmother's stories, no matter how many times she heard them. Now she kept the albums in a sealed plastic container on the top shelf of her closet, where they would be safe.

The clock chimed once, twelve thirty. She slid the key beside it off the mantel, carefully opened the hinged faceplate, and wound the springs for the hands and the gong. It was a seven-day clock, and every Saturday night she wound it, just as she had seen her grandmother do throughout the years of her youth. It was a ritual that reminded her of the best years of her life. She closed the clock and repositioned it in its place in the center of the mantel. Then she flicked on a wall switch that lit the chandelier in the center of the room and crossed to the bathroom, where she turned on the shower and efficiently stripped off her clothes while waiting for the water to heat. She let the warm water sluice over her injured hand while lathering her hair with the other. She didn't linger in the soothing spray. She had places to go.

❖

"Hey, Rifkin," Mark Perlman called to her. "How about a game of pool?"

Perlman was a second-year surgery resident, and his first rotation upon arriving at Penn had been on service with Pearce. He'd been green and arrogant, a rich boy from Brown who still wore Ralph Lauren polo shirts and fabric belts with ducks on them. Six weeks into his residency he had called her in the middle of the night on the verge of a nervous breakdown, literally weeping because he never got home before ten at night and didn't have time to work out and how was he supposed to study when he didn't have time to sleep? He had said he was going to walk out of the hospital and never come back.

She'd debated telling him to switch to anesthesia or, better yet, internal medicine, but she considered maybe it wasn't his fault that no one had prepared him for what a surgical residency was really going to be like. She'd gone to the hospital, helped him finish his night work, and pretty much held his hand for the next six weeks. He'd adjusted, like most did, and now his arrogance was tempered with a little humility. And Pearce had earned his undying gratitude.

"Maybe later," Pearce replied, lifting her glass and indicating her beer. She didn't want to call attention to her hand by trying to play pool, and she doubted that she would be able to shoot with her usual proficiency. It was a rare night that she didn't win twenty bucks if she was playing seriously. "I just got here."

Here was O'Malley's, the neighborhood bar two blocks from the hospital and across from the high-rise dorms. Students, residents, and nurses congregated there after work during the week and most weekend nights. She usually made it by a couple of times a week, especially when, like tonight, she wanted casual company and a diversion from the relentless pace of her life. And, she admitted, she'd been too content just relaxing with Wynter to face her empty apartment quite so soon.

"If you change your mind, look me up," Mark said exuberantly. "I feel like winning a few rounds tonight."

Pearce laughed and leaned back against the bar. "Still dreaming, I see."

"Maybe. And maybe not." The thin, sandy-haired man, whom most women considered very handsome with his sharply carved features and brilliant blue eyes, sidled closer to Pearce. "So what's the inside story on the new resident on your service?"

"Story?" Pearce sipped her beer, her fingers tightening around the handle of the glass mug.

"You know—with Thompson. First I heard she's married, but then one of the nurses told me she's divorced."

"Do I look like I'm the newsroom?"

"I just figured you'd know. A couple guys already tried to feel her out, but she kind of blew them off. So I thought I'd give her a—"

"Look," Pearce said so abruptly Mark jumped, "she's a surgery resident. What more do you need to know? She probably doesn't have time for a social life. Go sniff around one of the nurses."

"Some of us don't have your luck," he said good-naturedly.

"Maybe if you tried not to drool quite so much, you'd get somewhere." Pearce wanted him off the subject of Wynter. She'd seen the attention Wynter got from the male residents when they all hung out together in the surgeons' lounge between cases. If they weren't blatantly staring at her, they were striking up a conversation. Circling her, like a pack of dogs around a new bitch in the park. Feeling her out, trying to get a sense of whether she was interested. Pearce hadn't seen any sign of Wynter returning the interest, but she wasn't entirely certain she would recognize the subtle signs between women and men. It wasn't something she usually paid any attention to. Most of the time the men's attention to Wynter made her so antsy, she had to leave the room. She kept having fantasies of stuffing their heads in the freezer.

"Can I ask you something?" Mark asked.

Pearce regarded him suspiciously. He swayed, even though he had an elbow on the bar, and his gestures were expansive, as if he were an actor on a stage playing to the audience seated in the back row of the balcony. He'd clearly had one too many beers. "Are you driving somewhere tonight?"

"Nah. I'm staying at José's over at Forty-second and Spruce."

Pearce made a mental note to make sure that José, another resident, was actually riding herd on Mark. "Where are your car keys?"

"He took him…them." Mark smiled beneficently and bumped Pearce's shoulder. "How did you know you were…you know."

"You mean, like, gay?" Pearce stared at him in astonishment. All the guys pretty much knew her story, because she was certain it was one of the first things they told the new residents when they started. The fact that the chairman's daughter was a fellow resident and a lesbian was too good a topic of conversation not to share. But it was rare for one of them to really ask her about it, other than the occasional joke or innuendo.

"Yeah. That."

"When did *you* first start thinking about girls like they were different than boys?"

Mark's brow creased as he considered the question. "I don't know. When I was six, maybe?"

"Me too."

"No shit." Mark grinned. "Cool."

"Yeah." Pearce didn't see any point in disillusioning him. Instead, when Mark ambled away in search of more loquacious company, she watched the crowd, listening to the sound level increase as the night wore on and the liquor flowed. She was nursing her second beer when Tammy walked in. The small, tight-bodied blond cut a path straight through the crowd toward her.

"Hey there," Tammy said, turning sideways against the bar so her inside thigh slipped behind Pearce's leg.

"You're kind of late getting started, aren't you?" Pearce said, aware of Tammy's crotch pressed against her hip.

"Oh no. I've been partying, but it broke up early. We ran out of coke."

Pearce glanced around quickly, but it was already going on two and everyone was pretty well lubricated. No one was listening to their conversation. "You might not want to advertise that." She took a closer look at Tammy's face and saw the pinpoint pupils and the flush that suffused her neck. "How much have you been doing?"

"Enough to get me really jazzed." Tammy snaked a hand around Pearce's leg and cupped her crotch. She squeezed, her thumb working the lower edge of Pearce's fly over her clit. "I'm so horny."

"Chee-rist," Pearce muttered, slamming her beer down on the bar. She peeled Tammy's fingers from between her legs and kept a grip on her wrist to prevent another grope. "Who did you come with?"

"Alice. I think. Or maybe she left before we got here. We hit a few other places on the way."

Pearce started off into the crowd, Tammy in tow. "We're getting out of here."

"That's exactly what I was hoping."

"José," Pearce called in passing.

"Yo."

"Watch Perlman."

"Yo, boss."

Pearce flagged a cab and they piled into the backseat. She would have walked had she been alone, but there was no way that Tammy was going to make it on foot. As it was, Pearce had all she could do to keep Tammy's hands out of her pants and her tongue out of her mouth. She kept up a steady defense all the way back to her apartment. She tossed the amused cabbie a ten when he pulled up in front of her apartment. "Thanks."

She pulled Tammy out of the backseat.

"Good luck," the cabbie called.

Pearce could hear him laughing as she slammed the door. She took Tammy's hand again. "Come on. Let's get inside."

Tammy continued her assault all the way upstairs, and when Pearce finally managed to get her apartment door open, Tammy picked up the pace. The instant Pearce closed the door, she was on her, her hands in Pearce's hair, her teeth on Pearce's neck. She thrust her pelvis between Pearce's legs, grinding into her, her breath rasping. "I'm so hot. Mmm, I'm gonna come so hard for you."

"Tam, let's take this over to the couch," Pearce said, jerking her neck out of range and twisting away. She could feel Tammy's pulse hammering beneath her fingers as she continued to hold her wrist. She was willing to bet her blood pressure was through the roof, and the last thing she wanted was to precipitate a confrontation. What Tammy needed was to settle down, not get more excited. "Come on."

"Oh yeah. Better over there. Come on, baby. Hurry." Tammy rushed to the sofa and, the instant they were seated, threw her leg over Pearce's and half climbed into her lap. "Play with my nipples, baby. I love it when you do that."

"Let's go slow. There's no rush," Pearce said soothingly, easing Tammy down beside her and turning so they faced one another. She kissed her gently. "That's nice. Nice and easy."

"I don't wanna go easy," Tammy protested, her hand on her own breast, tugging feverishly. "I wanna fuck. I wanna fuck so bad."

"In a little while." Pearce had seen Tammy like this before—it was one of the reasons they were no longer going out together. Pearce wasn't into drugs, and although she didn't mind when others indulged in a little recreational use, Tammy had been getting in deeper and deeper, and nothing Pearce said could stop her. She knew what Tammy would do when she was like this. She leaned over and pulled a light cotton blanket from the shelf underneath the coffee table and stood up, handing the blanket to Tammy. "I gotta take a shower, baby. Take your clothes off and cover up. I'll be right back."

"You don't need a shower. You're just fine. You always taste so good." Tammy was frantically peeling down her jeans. "Don't go anywhere."

"Get undressed. I'll be right back." Pearce disappeared into the bathroom and locked the door. Despite the excuse to escape, she really did need a shower to get rid of the scent of the bar and the sweat she'd worked up keeping Tammy at bay. She washed her hair again, thinking that she'd had two women who'd been more than willing to hop into bed in the last month, and this time, she hadn't even been tempted. Tammy was a skilled lover when she wasn't coked out of her mind, and even high, she'd always managed to satisfy. Tonight, Pearce hadn't felt anything except concern and sadness.

When she judged enough time had gone by, she emerged in the robe she kept behind the bathroom door. Tammy was stretched out on the sofa, her body forming a soft curve under the blanket, her head pillowed on her bent arm. Pearce crossed to her and knelt on the floor by her head.

"You shouldn't have left me, baby," Tammy said drowsily, her expression lax, her eyes dazed. "I couldn't wait for you."

Pearce stroked her hair, having counted on this happening. "You feel a little better?"

"Mmm. It was nice and hard." Tammy clasped Pearce's hand. "Do me again?"

"Aren't you sleepy?"

"Feel kind of wrecked. Came forever."

Pearce leaned down and kissed her forehead. "Close your eyes for a while, then."

Tammy rubbed her cheek against the back of Pearce's hand and moaned softly. "You'll stay?"

"Right here."

"All night?"

"Uh-huh."

"Pro…mise?"

"Promise."

Pearce waited until Tammy's breathing grew quiet and her grip on Pearce's fingers loosened. Then she carefully rose and settled on the far end of the couch. Wondering how she had ever been satisfied with these frantic couplings and hasty affairs, she leaned her head back, closed her eyes, and willed sleep to come.

CHAPTER SIXTEEN

Ronnie, honey, don't put that in Winston's hair," Wynter said as she diverted her daughter's spoon. "Here, you two drop these berries in the batter and then you can both stir."

Winston and Ronnie, both still in pajamas, stood on adjoining chairs with a huge bowl of batter between them. As usual, Winston took the task extremely seriously, carefully stirring in the fruit, while Ronnie preferred to use the food ingredients as missiles. Both had red and yellow striped dishtowels loosely tied around their necks as makeshift bibs. Ken and Mina's seven-year-old daughter Janie sat on the opposite side of the table, out of Ronnie's range, playing with a Game Boy.

From the doorway, Mina, in her favorite pink chenille robe and slippers, laughed. "Oh, I can see that reinforcements are needed here."

Wynter smiled gratefully. "Good morning. You're just in time."

"I'm not so sure about that. I can see from the looks of the floor just how *well* things have been going." Mina skirted around the droplets of batter and crushed blueberries on her way to the stove. "You supervise the rest of the prep, and I'll cook. Just give me plenty of room."

"You sure? We were going to bring you a tray in bed."

"I'm not going to lie in bed when everyone else is having so much fun. Besides, it looks like you made enough batter for three families. We'll have pancakes for days." She pursed her lips. "Why don't you call Pearce and ask her to come over. We might as well be neighborly, now that we know she lives so close. Besides, it's the least we can do with her getting all banged up helping with the move yesterday."

Wynter felt her face flush. She'd just been thinking that she'd walk over to Pearce's as soon as breakfast was over and she'd cleaned up.

She was looking forward to seeing her away from the hospital. When Pearce wasn't working, she was easy to be around—far more relaxed and surprisingly tender. "I don't have her home phone number."

Mina put her hand on her hip and regarded Wynter skeptically. "Now I *know* you can call the page operator and they'll put you through. All you have to do is say you're one of the residents. Ken does it all the time."

"She's probably busy."

"At seven thirty?"

"Sleeping, then."

"A surgery resident? You all get up early."

Wynter indicated her baggy Yale sweatpants and mismatched T-shirt. "Besides, I'm not dressed."

"We're talking breakfast, not…" Mina narrowed her eyes even further. "Go call her, and then take a quick shower. I'll watch this crew."

"Mina," Wynter said with a sigh.

"Go."

"All right." Admitting defeat and not really minding, Wynter headed for the wall phone by the kitchen door. It took her several minutes to reach the hospital page operator, but once she explained that she was a doctor and wanted to be put through to Dr. Pearce Rifkin, carefully emphasizing the *Pearce*, she was immediately connected. The phone was answered on the first ring.

"Rifkin."

"Pearce? It's Wynter."

"Hey," Pearce replied, obviously surprised.

"I hope I didn't wake you."

"No."

"I know it's short notice, but we're making breakfast over here, and I thought…we thought…Mina and I thought…" Wynter caught Mina staring at her out of the corner of her eye and added hastily, "Why don't you come over? We've got lots. And good coffee."

There was a long silence before Pearce replied, her voice pitched low.

"Thanks. I'd like to, but I—"

Wynter heard someone call Pearce's name. A female someone. "Oh. I'm sorry, I didn't mean to…look, I'm sorry. I'll talk to you—"

"Would fifteen minutes be too late?" Pearce said quickly.

"Uh, no. It would be fine. Are you sure?"

"I'll be there."

Wynter hung up the phone and stood with her hand on the receiver, trying to sort out the awkward conversation. Obviously, Pearce had had someone there. Some woman. Some woman who had spent the night. "She must have them taking numbers."

"Them who?" Mina asked.

"Oh," Wynter said, giving a little jump. "What? Nothing. I'm going to run and take a shower. Will you be okay for ten minutes?"

"Go. Go." Mina made shooing motions. "I think I can manage."

"You don't have to hold her, you know," Wynter said, snatching up Pearce's coffee cup just before Ronnie, who was sitting on Pearce's lap, careened her Batmobile into it.

"She's okay." After Pearce had gotten over the shock of having the child climb into her lap and settle in for the duration of breakfast, she was glad to have the warm, sweet-smelling bundle of babbling energy to keep her mind off how good Wynter looked in a pair of tight-fitting blue jeans and a mint green crew-neck sweater. Surgical scrubs had a way of making everyone look asexual, but this outfit left no doubt as to what a great body Wynter had. Pearce tried not to stare, but as long as her heart was beating it would be difficult not to look now and then.

"Did you get enough to eat?" Mina asked.

"I'm stuffed," Pearce said. "It was great. Thanks."

Mina looked from Pearce to Wynter, then pushed up from the table. "I'll make a deal with you two. You walk down to the store and get me a gallon of Rocky Road, and I'll clear the kitchen. Oh, and take little Ms. Tornado with you."

"I'll get your ice cream," Wynter said quickly. "I'm sure Pearce has things to d—"

"Not really," Pearce said quickly. "I've got my beeper, and if I get called, well—I get called. Otherwise, I'm free."

Wynter wondered about whoever was in Pearce's apartment, if she was still there. Maybe she was snuggled in, taking a nap after a long night of…activity. Pearce certainly didn't look as if she'd slept.

She looked like she did after being up all night in the OR. The same shadows and slightly haunted look. Wynter tried not to stare at the pale expanse of skin above the collar of Pearce's blue button-down shirt, but she couldn't resist looking for bite marks. Nor could she deny her relief when she didn't see any. Of course, it could be that this one just wasn't a biter. Or maybe she liked to bite somewhere else. Maybe just above the top of those low-slung black jeans. Wynter shook her head, knowing that she was on the verge of making herself crazy with ridiculous thoughts.

"Something wrong?" Pearce said quietly.

"No. Nothing."

"Would you rather it be just you and…" She nodded her head toward Ronnie.

Wynter smiled. "No. Let's go. It'll be fun to take a walk. I just need a few minutes to get her ready."

"Okay. I'll give Mina a hand."

"You don't have to. You can wait in the living room. Read the newspaper."

Pearce stood, swinging Ronnie up under her good arm as she did so, making her squeal. When she set her down, Ronnie tried to drive the Batmobile up her leg. "Whoa!" Pearce diverted the car before it scored a direct hit. "Go ahead. Mina and I will be fine."

"Five minutes," Wynter said, corralling Ronnie and whisking her away.

Grinning after them, Pearce turned to find Mina staring at her speculatively. She waited, but when Mina said nothing, she asked, "What can I do?"

"Bring me those plates and I'll get the dishwasher loaded."

"Got it."

"Wynter tells me you're her senior resident."

"Technically," Pearce said as she handed off the first stack of dishes. "We're actually the same year, but…well, I guess you know Wynter got a bit behind because of…that business at Yale."

"Mmm-hmm," Mina said noncommittally. "Ken thought about surgery—for about two days."

"Then he saw the light?"

"Then I informed him that he had a choice—more children or surgery."

Pearce glanced at Mina's prominent belly and laughed. "Easy choice."

"Not everyone thinks so." She turned away from the sink and regarded Pearce with a friendly smile. "How about you? Are children in your future?"

"I'm not married."

"That's not a prerequisite."

"I'm also gay."

"That's not a disqualification."

"Ever considered becoming a lawyer?"

Mina chuckled. "I've given it some thought, when the kids are big enough to stay in school all day. And there's no law against not wanting kids, you know."

Pearce stacked another armload of dishes next to the sink. "I didn't say that. Being a surgery resident makes it pretty much impossible."

"It sure makes it difficult, I agree. More so than for most residents."

"Wynter obviously does a good job of it."

"I do a good job of what?" Wynter said, leading Ronnie by the hand. In her red snowsuit, Ronnie looked like a fireplug with feet.

"Everything," Mina said fondly and turned back to the sink.

Pleased to be rescued from the odd conversation, Pearce grabbed her bomber jacket off the coat tree by the back door. "All set?"

"We're ready."

Outside, they walked side by side with Ronnie between them. She immediately took each of their hands and alternated between running until their arms were outstretched and then picking her feet up and swinging back.

"She'll do this until you're worn out," Wynter warned.

"Me? Not a chance."

"Uh-huh. I still want to get a good look at your hand. I noticed you kept it out of sight during breakfast."

"It's okay." When Wynter gave her a hard stare, Pearce amended, "All right. It's much better."

"Will you be able to operate tomorrow?"

"I'll probably beg off doing anything in the OR until Tuesday."

"Won't your father notice?"

"You can take his cases. He'll just think I'm being generous."

"You *are* generous with the cases."

Pearce shrugged, but she was pleased. "Thanks. And thanks for the breakfast. It beats the…heck…out of Pop-Tarts."

"Oh, you're welcome. I'm sorry it was such short notice. I know you had company." Wynter blushed, having said more than she intended. "I mean—"

"I couldn't sleep so I went out for a while after you left."

"Uh-huh." Wynter knew she should tell Pearce that she didn't need to explain, but she said nothing.

"I ran into one of the OB-GYN residents at O'Malley's, and she was a little under the weather," Pearce said, wanting Wynter to know it wasn't what she thought. If she thought anything about it at all. Mindful of Ronnie, Pearce said circumspectly, "I couldn't send her home alone, and it was already so late, it just made more sense to bring her to my place."

"Of course." Wynter knew it shouldn't make one iota of difference to her what the reasons for Pearce having a woman in her apartment overnight might be. But she was unreasonably glad.

"I was going to call and explain, tell you to come by later, after she left."

Wynter smiled. "Well, it doesn't matter now. I'll look at your hand when we get back, before you go inside."

"Jeez, you're relentless."

"What did you expect? I'm a surgeon."

Pearce laughed. When Ronnie started making car noises—at least that's what Pearce *thought* she was doing—she had a sudden idea. "Look, do you have a few extra minutes?"

"Sure. It's my day off. Why?"

"There's something I want to show you. Ronnie will like it."

Wynter gave her a perplexed look but nodded. "Okay."

They continued a few blocks in silence, and when they passed in front of Pearce's apartment, Wynter refused to think about Pearce's *company*.

"It's right here," Pearce said, leading the way down a narrow driveway toward a garage at the rear of a lot two houses away from her building. The white concrete structure with the black tar roof had double wooden doors and small round windows above each one. An industrial-scale lock secured the metal clasps, holding them closed. Pearce pulled her key ring from her jacket pocket. "It stays pretty warm in here, but I have a kerosene heater if you're cold."

"Is this yours?" Wynter asked curiously.

"I rent it."

Pearce pulled open the doors and reached inside for the light switch. Unzipping her jacket, she watched Wynter gaze curiously around. Pearce's Thunderbird occupied nearly half the space. The frame of a '65 Corvair stood on cinder blocks next to it. Workbenches covered with neat rows of tools lined one wall, and an air compressor, jack, and other automotive equipment stood on the floor.

"I take it this is what you do with your spare time," Wynter said, not surprised to see that the space had a certain order and precision, not unlike an operating room.

"It's relaxing." Pearce squatted down next to Ronnie. "These are my cars. They're just like yours, only a little bit bigger."

"Mine," Ronnie announced, pointing to a shelf that ran above the workbench filled with classic car models.

Laughing, Pearce picked her up and carried her to the side of the room. "Which one?"

Wynter joined them. "She probably means all of them."

Pearce took down the replica of her Thunderbird. "You like this one?"

"Pearce," Wynter warned, but it was too late. Ronnie immediately grasped the car and held it tightly.

"Mine."

"Ronnie, honey, that's—"

"She can have it." Pearce leaned against the workbench, holding Ronnie loosely while the child waved her new possession in the air. "I can replace it."

Wynter turned away, feigning interest in the cars, which she knew absolutely nothing about. Pearce had such an easy way with her daughter, and Ronnie looked so sweetly happy that it hurt. It hurt because it should have been Dave holding Ronnie and making her laugh, and she didn't want it to be him. Realizing that only made her own unexpected sense of joy even more confusing. Her throat was tight, and she hoped her voice would sound normal. "You're careful, aren't you? Working in here alone?"

Pearce walked up beside her and put Ronnie down. The child sat at her feet and began to drive the car over the concrete. "I've been doing this since I was just a kid. I'm very careful."

"Did your father teach you?"

"Hell no," Pearce said with a bitter laugh. She glanced down at Ronnie. "Sorry."

"It's all right."

"My grandfather—my mother's father. I spent every weekend with my mother's parents, and some nights during the week too, if my father was working and my mother was busy."

"What does your mother do?"

"She was a microbiologist. She taught at Bryn Mawr."

Wynter heard the careful phrasing and saw the pain in Pearce's eyes. "I'm sorry."

"Hey, careful, you," Pearce said, quickly stepping sideways to block Ronnie's path before she could bump her head on the undercarriage of the elevated Corvair. Then she met Wynter's sympathetic smile. "Thanks."

"How old were you when it happened?"

"Nine."

Wynter reached for Pearce's hand. She squeezed it and didn't let go.

Pearce resisted the urge to thread her fingers through Wynter's. Her hand was so warm. So soft. The garage suddenly felt hot and close. She dropped Wynter's hand and stepped away. "I guess we should go get that ice cream for Mina."

"Yes." Wynter shivered, although she hadn't unzipped her parka, and she wasn't cold.

CHAPTER SEVENTEEN

"Did you have a good walk?" Mina asked when Wynter joined her in the living room. She'd changed into a loose denim jumper and tie-dyed T-shirt but still wore her fuzzy pink slippers and was ensconced in a rocker surrounded by the Sunday papers.

"It was nice," Wynter said, leaving the door to the adjoining family room open so she could keep an eye on the children, all of whom were sprawled on the rug with their toys and games. "Do you want your ice cream?"

"In a little while." Mina nodded toward the overstuffed chair next to her. "Sit down and enjoy the fire."

Wynter settled back with a sigh and propped her feet on a footstool. "Is Ken home?"

"Taking a nap. He said he was up all night."

Wynter made a sympathetic sound. "I'm not so sure it's a good thing I have two days off in a row. It makes me realize how abnormal my life is."

"Looked pretty normal this morning," Mina said. "Family breakfast, friendly company, nice quiet walk."

Wynter smiled, thinking just how right that had felt. Spending time with Ronnie. Being with Pearce. *Pearce.* She had no idea how Pearce had become part of her life outside of the hospital, but she was glad. The last month had brought so many changes, sometimes she felt as if she couldn't keep up. "I just wish there were more mornings like this."

"It won't be forever. You're more than halfway done."

"I know," Wynter said, staring at the ceiling. "It was just so nice to take Ronnie out and spend an hour just having fun."

"You were gone for a while. I was starting to worry."

"Sorry. Pearce took us by her garage where she restores old cars. Ronnie loved the place."

"If it had anything to do with cars, she would."

Wynter laughed. "I think I'm raising an auto mechanic."

"Well, maybe it's hereditary. That's a lot like surgery."

"If I had the energy, I'd throw a pillow at you."

Mina reached for the cup of tea resting on the reading table beside her. "Pearce was good with her."

"She was great."

"So you all had fun."

"Yes." Wynter felt a ripple of apprehension for which she had no explanation. Almost every minute they'd spent together had been effortless and enjoyable. They'd conversed easily about Pearce's cars and Wynter's family. She'd told Pearce about growing up on a farm, and how shocked her parents had been when she'd said she wanted to be a doctor. Neither was a college graduate, and in their small community, many of the young people still married and settled down within walking distance of their parents. Even the ones who went away to college frequently returned, preferring the quieter life they had grown up with.

Ronnie seemed taken with Pearce. Although Ronnie rarely stopped babbling, she and Pearce seemed able to communicate even without words. Everything had been perfect, and yet the closer they had drawn to Pearce's apartment on the return trip, the less they'd talked and the more heavy the silence had become.

They'd climbed the front porch and stood facing one another, Ronnie between them, one of her small mittened hands on each of their thighs. Their breath hung like mist, an uninvited guest. Wynter had the urge to brush it away, as if it prevented her from seeing Pearce clearly.

"Let me check your hand," she said.

Pearce glanced up at the porch ceiling, as if she could see through the structure. "I'd ask you up, but…"

"No problem." Wynter tried to sound nonchalant, but she knew her words had come out harshly. She smiled to take the sting away. "Let me see your hand. Please."

Without another word, Pearce pulled her ungloved hand from her jacket pocket and held it out, fingers splayed. She slowly made a fist and opened it again. Wynter pulled off her own gloves and stuffed them into her pockets. She kept Ronnie trapped between her knees so she could use both hands to examine Pearce's. She repeated the procedure from the day before, gently probing, flexing and extending each finger, and studying the scrapes and bruises. Finally she was satisfied. "It's still very swollen, but better."

"It'll be okay." Pearce withdrew her hand from Wynter's grip. "You should get going. It's freezing out here. Have a good one—I'll see you tomorrow."

As Pearce turned toward her front door, keys in hand, Wynter blurted, "What about you? What are you going to do today?"

Pearce gave her an inscrutable look over her shoulder. "I'm going in to make rounds, see what's going on. If I'm lucky, a good case will come in." Pearce glanced down at Ronnie and smiled. "Bye, kiddo."

Ronnie waved her new car and giggled. "Bye, kiddo."

Replaying the scene in her head, Wynter continued to stare at the ceiling. She still couldn't figure out what bothered her. She knew that someone waited for Pearce upstairs, but that didn't have anything to do with her.

"You look kind of lost, honey," Mina said. "Something wrong?"

"No, not really." Wynter frowned. "I guess I just don't know what to do with myself. Too much time on my hands. If you don't mind watching Ronnie, I'll go next door and do some unpacking."

"Want some company? I'll be over as soon as Ken wakes up. He can watch the kids."

"Sure," Wynter said, wondering what Pearce was doing and wondering why she couldn't get her out of her mind. "Company would be great."

❖

"Where did you go?" Tammy asked petulantly the minute Pearce walked into her apartment.

"Just for a walk. How are you doing?"

Tammy sat up, the blanket falling to her waist. She was nude. "I'm still a little wasted. What time is it?"

"Just after eleven. Are you working today?"

"I'm the night float. I don't have to be in until eight."

Pearce hung her jacket over the back of her desk chair. "You want something to eat?"

"Are you on the menu?"

"Not at the moment." Pearce went into the kitchen to investigate the food situation. Knowing what Tammy was like under these circumstances, eggs would probably do. She opened the cabinet above the sink and was in the process of taking down a bowl when Tammy's arms came around her from behind. Carefully, she set the dish on the counter, ignoring the play of Tammy's fingers over her abdomen. Without turning around, she said, "Why don't you take a shower? I'll leave some of my sweats for you in the bathroom and by the time you're done, I'll have breakfast ready."

Tammy adroitly opened the button on Pearce's fly with one hand and pulled her shirt loose with the other. "You know I'd rather fuck first and eat later."

Pearce caught both wrists and stopped Tammy's errant explorations. "Cut it out, Tam. You need something to eat, and I'm not in the mood."

Tammy stepped back as Pearce turned around. She stared, mouth agape. "You're not kidding, are you?"

Pearce shook her head.

"Since when aren't you interested in sex?"

"Since right now." Pearce leaned against the counter, wincing when she tried to curl the fingers of her left hand around the edge of the counter.

"What the hell did you do?" Tammy reached for Pearce's hand. "Jesus. You really did a number on this."

"I jammed it up yesterday."

"How?"

"Just helping someone move." The last thing Pearce wanted to do was discuss Wynter with anyone, but definitely not anyone from the hospital. And not one of the women she used to sleep with. She wasn't exactly sure why, because Wynter was just a friend. A fellow resident. That's all. But she just didn't want to talk about her.

"Helping someone move." Tammy enunciated each word as if it were a foreign language. "Let me see if I get this right. Pearce Rifkin, the senior surgery resident who never does anything except work and screw, spent her day off helping someone move."

"Come on," Pearce said, grinning despite herself. "I do more than that. I read a book sometimes. I've even been known to watch a movie."

"When?"

"Once. Look, aren't you cold?" It was hard not to look at Tammy's naked body, especially when her nipples were puckered and hard. She had a beautiful body, muscular and compact, her narrow waist leading to subtly curved hips and smooth thighs. Pearce recalled vividly what that firm, smooth flesh felt like in her hands. "Besides, you're not legal, looking like that."

"It's about time you noticed." Tammy slid her arms around Pearce's waist and pressed against her. "Now, where were we before you lost your mind?"

"Tam," Pearce said, embracing her gently and kissing the top of her head. "I really don't want to. It's got nothing to do with you. I've just got…" *Wynter. I've got Wynter on my mind. Jesus Christ. What am I doing?*

Tammy tilted her chin up, studying Pearce's face. "You okay?"

"Yeah. Sure." Tammy's nipples were firm against her chest, Tammy's body warm in her arms. One kiss was all it would take. One kiss and she could lose herself the way she always had in the sounds and sensation of passion. For a few minutes, an hour, there would be no expectations other than pleasure, no goals other than satisfaction. She could be no one—or anyone—whomever she chose. No legacy, no promises. Just the moment burning bright, and then gone. She eased out of Tammy's grip, resting her hands on Tammy shoulders. "I gotta get over to the hospital."

"I don't care if you're seeing someone else," Tammy said, her tone surprisingly serious.

Pearce's heart began to pound. "I'm not seeing anyone at all."

"You're lying. To me. Or yourself. But I can see it in your eyes. Somebody's got ahold of you deep inside."

"No," Pearce said hoarsely.

Tammy ran her fingers down the center of Pearce's chest, then put both hands on her waist and stood on her tiptoes to kiss Pearce hard. Even when Pearce didn't respond, she kept her mouth against Pearce's for a long moment, as if imprinting the taste of her. Then she let go.

"You don't have the slightest idea what a woman can do to your heart. You're in trouble, baby."

Pearce didn't argue.

❖

Wynter hit the knee switch to turn on the water at the scrub sink next to Pearce's. It was the first time she'd had a chance to talk to her in over thirty-six hours. Monday had been the day from hell. They had just begun dry rounds at five thirty in the morning when Pearce had been STAT paged to the emergency room. The entire team had been racing down to the ER when Wynter had been STAT paged to the SICU. It had been nonstop surgery and emergencies the rest of the day, and the only time she'd seen Pearce had been at sign-out rounds that evening, which were truncated because there were three scheduled cases still to be done. Those cases had been bumped from the OR schedule during the day to accommodate the emergencies, and the attendings were insisting that they be done that night so as not to back up the next day's cases. The entire service had worked until midnight, even the residents who hadn't been on call. Now it was a new day, and it looked like it might be more of the same. "How does your hand feel?"

Pearce glanced around, but the adjoining scrub sinks were empty for the moment. "It hurts like a son of a bitch. I didn't want to operate yesterday, but it held up okay. I was too busy to notice that it hurt."

"It still looks swollen."

"It looks worse than it feels today. Really."

Wynter smiled. "Good."

"You're post call, Wynter. You need to go home. Why are you scrubbing?"

"Because we've got three rooms running, the first-year is taking McMurtry on rounds, and we need someone free to do floor work."

Pearce shook her head. "Anderson can start that mastectomy by herself. When Liu is done with rounds, he can scrub in and help her out. Go home."

It annoyed Wynter that she could only see Pearce's eyes above the surgical mask, and they were flat black disks, completely devoid of emotion. "*You* wouldn't go home."

"That's different."

"And why would that be?"

"Because I'm the chief, and I don't have a kid waiting for me."

"You can't be serious," Wynter said, her voice laced with acid. "Are you suddenly going to become a jerk because you know about Ronnie? Like all the male residents and attendings who think that women shouldn't go into surgery because they should be home raising children?"

"What I think," Pearce said, her voice still steady and calm, "is that you were on call last night, and you're supposed to be going home this morning. You should take advantage of that and do whatever you might like to do with your time off."

"You *are* being a jerk. You never tell the guys to go home."

Pearce stepped on the kick bucket and threw her scrub brush into it. "Maybe I would if they had anything to go home to."

"I'm not leaving."

"Suit yourself." Pearce turned and started for room seven and the carotid endarterectomy that awaited her, not even certain why she was pissed. Wynter looked beat, and it bothered her.

"Pearce," Wynter called.

Pearce turned around, one eyebrow raised in question.

"Thanks."

"For what?" She walked back and leaned one hip against the scrub sink, her hands held out in front of her, the water dripping from her elbows onto the floor.

"For thinking about me…and about Ronnie. I appreciate it. But that's my responsibility."

Pearce blew out a breath, making her mask puff out like a tiny sail in a brisk breeze. When she breathed in, it molded itself to the contours of her lower face. "You're right. It's none of my business. Did you get any sleep last night?"

"A few hours."

"Will you go home after this case?"

"Yes."

"Okay."

Wynter moved closer, keeping her voice low when several residents stepped up to the scrub sinks adjacent to theirs. "My sister called me last night. Rose—the one who goes to law school at Temple."

"Uh-huh? Something wrong?"

"No," Wynter said quickly. "She and her boyfriend are going to the TLA on Friday night to hear Patti Smith. Friends of theirs were going with them, but they can't make it. So Rose is giving me the other tickets."

"That's cool."

"So I was wondering…you want to come with us?"

"Me?" Pearce couldn't hide her surprise.

"Yes. Do you like rock?"

"I like Patti Smith. You sure? I mean…don't you want to ask…" She couldn't bring herself to say, *Don't you want to ask a guy to go with you?* because she didn't want to think about that reality. Stupid, she knew. But if she didn't think about it, maybe it wouldn't happen. At least not for a while.

"No," Wynter said firmly, as if she had heard the rest of Pearce's question. "I want to go with you. Okay?"

This time, Pearce's eyes sparkled, reflecting her smile. "Yeah. Okay."

CHAPTER EIGHTEEN

Thursday was turning out to be a repeat of Monday. They'd barely finished morning rounds when Wynter was paged to the ER to see a patient with a cold foot. Sure enough, the sixty-eight-year-old diabetic, a feisty, birdlike man who watched everything she did with bright, blinking eyes, had a pale, numb, pulseless right foot. The STAT arteriogram she ordered revealed occlusion of the superficial femoral artery just above the knee with minimal collateral flow.

"You've got a blockage in the main artery that goes to your foot, Mr. Samuels," Wynter explained. "You're going to need an operation to remove it. You might also need to have a bypass or some other kind of graft to help widen that area so it doesn't get blocked again."

"Will it work?"

"Most of the time it does. Sometimes the artery will go into spasm and clot off or little bits of debris from the inside can float downstream and cause problems in your toes, but—"

"What happens if you don't fix it?" he asked impatiently, waving one hand as if chasing away flies.

"You're going to lose your foot."

"Well then, why don't you get started?"

"Yes sir. I'll do that." With a small smile, she picked up the wall phone and asked for Margaret Chung, the vascular surgeon, to be paged. Dr. Chung was a young surgeon who allowed the residents a fair amount of autonomy. She answered within five minutes, and Wynter explained the situation.

"Is Rifkin still on service?" Margaret Chung asked.

"Yes."

"Call her and tell her to give you a hand until I get there. Some tractor trailer dumped a load of hams on 95, and I'm going to be about forty-five more minutes."

"Will do. Thanks." Wynter redialed and asked the operator to find Pearce. Then she advised the patient of the plans. "Is there someone you want me to call?"

"You can call my daughter when you're done fixing things."

"She might want to be here before you go to surgery."

He shook his head. "She'll just fuss and worry. Worse, she'll probably cry."

"Well, it's a daughter's prerogative to cry over her father if she wants to. Would you rather she fuss a little bit before surgery, or fuss a *lot* afterward because we didn't call her?"

"You think that's the way it will be?"

Wynter laughed. "Oh, I can guarantee it."

With a long-suffering sigh, he relented. "Well then, go ahead and call her. But if she doesn't want to come in right away, that's just fine."

"Yes sir. I'll tell her that."

Wynter found his contact information on the chart, asked the operator for the outside number, and was listening to the phone ring when Pearce pulled the curtain aside and stepped in.

"What's up?" Pearce asked.

Wynter covered the receiver and said hurriedly, "This is Mr. Samuels. His arteriogram is on the board over there. He's got an acute occlusion of the right superficial femoral and a badly ischemic foot.... Hello? Mrs. Rice?"

"Huh." Pearce looked at the films and then walked to the side of the stretcher. She held out her hand. "How are you doing? I'm Dr. Rifkin. I need to take a look at your foot."

"Why not? Everyone else down here has."

Pearce grinned. "Yeah, but we're the only ones who count."

Mr. Samuels eyed her guardedly. "Don't they have any men doctors anymore?"

"There are a few around. We let them in when we can't find enough good women." As Mr. Samuels snorted and tried unsuccessfully to hide a laugh, Pearce lifted the sheet and placed her hand lightly on the top of Mr. Samuels's foot. It had the consistency and temperature of refrigerated chicken. "How long has it been like this, sir?"

"Since right after supper last night."

She looked up and met his eyes. "Your foot's in a bit of trouble here. You know that you need surgery, right?"

"The other doctor there explained it to me. You two planning on doing something about it?"

"We're going to take you up to the operating room and get things started. By then, Dr. Chung will be here. She's the vascular surgeon who will be in charge. Are you okay with that?"

"Have you ever done this before?"

"A few times." Pearce still held his gaze.

"You think you can be done before lunch? That one," he said, gesturing to Wynter who had hung up the phone and now stood with her arms folded, watching the conversation, "said I can't have anything to eat or drink."

"She's right. I can't promise you lunch, but you should be able to have dinner. Did you take any insulin this morning?"

"No."

"All right. We'll give you some sugar through the intravenous line while you're sleeping and insulin when you need it." She looked over her shoulder at Wynter. "Do we have labs and a consent?"

"We're just waiting on his CBC. I'll get his consent now. Then we're good to go."

"I'll meet you upstairs." Pearce patted Mr. Samuels's thigh. "See you later."

"See you, Doc." He leaned back and closed his eyes. "Did you talk to my daughter?"

"She's on her way."

"Good."

Three hours later, Wynter carefully rotated the tiny bulldog clamps that occluded the femoral vessel on either side of the opening they had made to remove the embolus. Then they had widened the narrowed area by meticulously suturing in a dime-sized vein patch. She studied the sutures she had just placed under Pearce's supervision. Dr. Chung had scrubbed out after Pearce had completed the first half of the anastomosis, leaving them to finish up.

"It looks pretty good, don't you think?" Wynter said.

"It's a thing of beauty," Pearce agreed. "Now let's see if it works." She raised her voice and angled her head over the top of the ether screen. "We're going to take the clamps off now. You might see a little dip in his blood pressure."

"Go for it. He's stable," the anesthesiologist said.

"Okay," Pearce said to Wynter. "Let's see if your stitches will hold."

Carefully, Wynter released first the distal clamp to allow outflow and then the proximal one to allow the full force of the arterial pressure to stress the area of her repair. At first, thin rivulets of blood seeped between her sutures, but as her heart rate escalated into the stratosphere, the leakage quickly stopped. The artery danced in the depth of the wound as if resurrected. Not yet ready to celebrate, she said, "Can someone feel under the drapes and see if he's got pulses in his foot?"

"Stop worrying," Pearce whispered too softly for anyone else to hear. "It's perfect. You did a great job."

The circulating nurse called, "Plus four pedal and PT pulses. And his foot's warm."

Wynter looked across the table into Pearce's eyes. They were alight with pleasure, and—she couldn't be certain, but she thought—pride. "Fucking A."

"You got that right," Pearce said with a laugh. She glanced at the clock. "I've gotta go scrub on that hemicolectomy with the chief. You okay here?"

"I'm fine, but you're post call. Shouldn't you go ho—"

"Nice job, Doc." Pearce turned from the table, stripped off her gloves and gown, and was gone before Wynter could lecture her about never going home.

❖

Three and a half hours later, Pearce rolled her patient into the recovery room. She carried the chart to the counter at the nurses' station to write the postop orders. Ten stretchers with barely a foot between them lined the opposite wall, one nurse for every two postoperative patients. X-ray technicians trundled through with their heavy portable machines, shooting postoperative films. Lab techs swarmed around the beds collecting blood samples, and EKG and respiratory techs jockeyed for space around the patients, who were dwarfed by the plethora of monitoring devices and equipment.

Pearce was used to blocking out the cacophony of sound and the buzz of activity, so she wasn't aware of anyone nearby until her father spoke.

"I'd like to speak with you outside in the hall, Doctor."

Pearce finished writing the order she was working on and looked up. "Of course. I'll just be another minute with this."

Ambrose Rifkin, who somehow managed to look commanding even in rumpled scrubs, nodded. A minute later, Pearce joined him just outside the intensive care unit. Neither of them spoke until they walked to the far end of the corridor out of earshot and sight of visitors. If patients' family members saw them, they were likely to be accosted with questions. It was only natural that family members thought that the physicians' only concern was for their loved ones and that physicians were always available to discuss their care. It made accomplishing the work of the day difficult, however, unless one rationed one's time carefully.

"I'd like to speak with you about Dr. Thompson," Ambrose Rifkin said.

Pearce's stomach instantly tightened. "What about her?" She knew she sounded defensive, but she couldn't help it. Her immediate instinct was to protect Wynter.

"I need to know what your—"

"Look. She's an excellent resident. She's smart, she's got great hands, she's good with the pa—"

"If I may finish."

Pearce flushed. "Sorry."

"You've worked with her more than anyone else. What's your opinion?"

For a second, Pearce was confused. Somehow, she had expected him to confront her about something else. Something personal. But then, why would he? "My opinion?"

Ambrose studied her with a sharp, appraising expression. "You seemed to have quite a few of them just a moment ago."

"Oh. You mean what kind of a resident is she. She's great." Pearce repeated her previous assessment, trying to sound as objective as possible. "Why?"

"In confidence," he said, "I just learned that the Residency Review Committee has approved us for an additional slot. We can finish one more resident beginning next year. I intend to speak to Thompson this afternoon about moving her up a year so we won't lose that advantage."

"That's great," Pearce said immediately.

"You do realize that means more competition for the chief surgical resident slot."

Pearce smiled grimly. "I'm not worried."

Her father did not smile, but his eyes flashed with what Pearce hoped was pride.

"Your confidence is apparent. We'll see if it's warranted."

"Yes, we will," Pearce whispered as he turned and walked away.

❖

Wynter left Ambrose Rifkin's office at 6:45 p.m. She was on call, and she needed to get dinner before the cafeteria closed or else she'd be relegated to eating vending-machine food until midnight dinner. Her stomach rumbled, reminding her that she hadn't had lunch. But as hungry as she was, the only thing she wanted was to find someone to share her excitement with. Suddenly, she wasn't looking at almost three more years before she finished, she was only looking at eighteen months. It felt like she'd been given a reprieve from a life sentence with no possibility of parole. She hurried toward the surgeons' lounge, and then, heart sinking, she realized there was no reason to rush. The only person she wanted to celebrate with was Pearce, and Pearce would have left hours ago.

As she slowed and turned the corner, she saw a familiar figure leaning against the wall just outside the women's locker room. Her heart leapt. "Pearce!"

Pearce grinned. She'd been waiting, hoping that she'd catch Wynter after the meeting. "You look hap—" She stopped when Wynter raced toward her. As if she had done it a thousand times, Pearce opened her arms and Wynter flew into them. Lifting Wynter's feet a few inches off the ground, Pearce held her around the waist and spun her in a half circle. When she set her down, they were both laughing, their bodies pressed together and arms entwined.

"I guess you saw the chief, huh?" Pearce said. "Congratulations."

"You knew?" Wynter said in astonishment.

"Just a little while ago. I didn't want to spoil it for you."

"Isn't it great?"

"Terrific." Pearce gave her a squeeze. "I'm really glad."

"You're okay with it?" Wynter asked softly. "I mean, we'll be in the same year now."

Several residents passed by, but Pearce never even gave them a glance. Wynter was still holding on to her, their bodies pressed together, their foreheads nearly touching. She marveled at what happiness did to Wynter's eyes, making their blue irises blaze with an untamed excitement that captivated her more deeply than any lust she might have encountered in another woman's gaze. Wynter's pure and simple joy gave her more pleasure than anything she'd ever known. She wanted to kiss her. She wanted to breathe in her pleasure and ride her wild joy. She wanted to be the source of that happiness every bit as fervently as she wanted to taste it.

"Oh, baby, of course I'm okay with it," Pearce murmured. "You deserve it."

Wynter's lips parted and she stared into Pearce's eyes. Then she whispered gently, "Thank you," and eased away until their embrace broke. She felt Pearce's arms drop from around her waist and saw Pearce's expression shutter closed, but not before she had seen what was in her eyes. In the few seconds before Pearce brought her iron will to bear, Wynter had caught a glimpse of the same naked craving she had seen there once so long ago. But this time, the desire had been far more intense. This time, Pearce wasn't a stranger who took her by surprise and whisked her away to an isolated corner to sweetly seduce her with a moment of respite and escape from a life that suddenly seemed unbearably foreign. This was a woman she knew and respected and cared for. And she understood in that instant, more clearly than she ever had before, that Pearce was a woman for whom it was natural to desire the touch of another woman. She felt it in the fine trembling of Pearce's body and witnessed it in the arousal that had fleetingly escaped the mask Pearce usually wore. Wynter knew that she had finally seen Pearce Rifkin.

"I haven't had anything to eat for hours," Wynter said quietly. "Can I treat you to dinner across the street? I think it's my turn."

"I…uh…" Pearce was a bit dazed. She'd come close to crossing a line, and she wasn't even certain why she hadn't. She'd been with women since she was seventeen years old, and some of them had been straight and a few had been married. She didn't have any political or philosophical objections to it. Her body couldn't help responding to

Wynter, and she sensed—as she had the very first time they'd met—that if she pushed just a little bit, Wynter would be willing. But she just couldn't do it. She drew a ragged breath. "Thanks. I…I think I'll take a rain check. I've still got a few patients to see."

Wynter hid her disappointment behind a smile. "And you're still post call, and you still should be going home."

"I will. Promise." Pearce started walking backward, putting some much-needed distance between them. "I'm just going to check a few X-rays and I'll be gone."

"Don't forget about the TLA tomorrow night," Wynter said.

Pearce hesitated, knowing now was the time to break the spell before Wynter's hold on her grew any stronger. She hadn't been able to think of anything else all week except Friday night and being with Wynter, and being around Wynter was beginning to hurt. *Idiot*, she muttered.

"What did you say?" Wynter called.

"I said…" Pearce took a deep breath. "Don't worry. I'll be there."

CHAPTER NINETEEN

Wynter tilted the cream-colored silk lampshade rimmed with fringe the color of warm caramel toward the broad, bevel-edged mirror above her bedroom dresser. Both items had been in her family for generations, and she'd come to love them even though the lamp didn't provide much light, having been designed for an era when a muted glow that softened the features was desirable. Squinting, she assessed the damage wrought by the previous sleepless night on call. Judiciously applied makeup had covered the worst of the fatigue lines and blunted the obvious shadows beneath her eyes. She'd had a nap when Ronnie had finally tired in the midafternoon, and they'd both fallen asleep while she'd been reading *Charlie and the Chocolate Factory*.

"I don't know, honey," she murmured to Ronnie, who sat in the middle of the floor intently covering pages of her coloring book in bright primary colors. "Clinique might not be enough tonight."

Ronnie held up a Jackson Pollack reproduction with exuberant pride.

"Beautiful!" Wynter proclaimed. "Maybe I should try crayons instead of blush. Maybe then I won't resemble the walking dead."

She jumped when a voice behind her said, "*Maybe* you should stay home and get some sleep."

Wynter turned, a hand on her hip, and gave Mina an arch look. "You're the one who's always telling me I should get out more."

"And it's true, but I didn't mean after you'd been up for thirty-six hours." She dangled the house keys in her right hand. "You didn't answer your bell, so I let myself in." She indicated the mug in her hand.

"Then I made tea."

"Sorry. We were taking a bath."

Mina sniffed and murmured appreciatively. "I just love the smell of baby powder."

Wynter laughed. "I actually feel fine. I slept some this afternoon. Besides, I've been looking forward to this all week. There's no way I'm not going."

"You look nice," Mina observed as she took in Wynter's brown leather pants, matching boots, and forest green silk blouse. Small square emerald earrings set in gold glinted through the strands of her red-blond hair, which she wore loose and down to her shoulders.

"Thanks."

Mina turned at the sound of a shout from below. "That's Ken. The kids were getting ready to watch a movie, and they're probably getting impatient."

"Stay there, I'll bring Ronnie down." Wynter collected Ronnie and her coloring books and led her by the hand from the room. A few minutes later, she returned. "Thanks for watching her tonight. You've got her all week and then—"

"Kids are like dogs," Mina said. "After two, what's one more? You might as well let her sleep the night and just come over in the morning to get her. If you don't sleep in, you can have breakfast with us."

"That sounds great." Wynter made a few final adjustments to her hair.

"So," Mina said as she made her way around a pile of unpacked boxes to the bed and lowered herself with a sigh. "Is this a date?"

Wynter grew still. "I'm going with Pearce."

"I know that, but that's not what I asked."

"We're friends."

"Uh-huh." Mina sipped her tea. "Do you remember when you and Ken were medical students, and we invited you over to dinner for the first time?"

Wynter smiled. "Yes."

"That was my idea."

"That was really nice of you."

"Not really."

Wynter studied Mina curiously. "What do you mean?"

"I wanted to get a look at you. You were Ken's study partner, and he spent hours with you every day—more than he spent with me. He talked about you all the time. I wanted to see if you were competition."

"Me?" Wynter's eyes went wide. "You're serious?"

"Of course I'm serious. Men and women don't usually form simple friendships, not if they're both straight. The sex thing gets in the way." Mina set her tea aside as the sentence hung in the air.

Shocked, Wynter protested, "But I *never*…Ken never once—"

Mina laughed and held up her hand. "I know that *now.* But I didn't know that *then.* I wanted to see if there was a situation brewing that I needed to take care of."

"Is there a reason you're telling me this story now?"

"Pearce is a lesbian, sweetie. You might be thinking of her just as a friend, but chances are she's not thinking about you in the same way. If you went out on a Friday night with a single man, you'd at least be thinking about it being a date—or that *he* might consider it one, wouldn't you?"

"Well, yes. Probably." Wynter remembered the look in Pearce's eyes the previous evening. She remembered how easily their bodies had fit together. How naturally. "What are you saying, Mina?"

"Pearce is probably thinking the same thing, or at least wondering. So sooner or later, you're going to have to be clear with her."

Wynter picked up a small glass prism and turned it between her fingers, studying it as if there were secrets hidden within the rainbows trapped inside. At length she looked up to find Mina watching her. "I almost kissed her once."

Wynter had rarely seen Mina surprised by anything, but the expression on her face now was one of total incredulity. Finally Mina managed an intelligible word.

"When?"

"Match Day."

"Almost four years ago?" Mina shouted.

Wynter nodded.

"And you're just telling me about it now? If I thought I could catch you, I'd get up and thrash your butt."

"You couldn't catch me even when you're not pregnant."

"Don't you try me." Mina crossed her arms beneath her full breasts. "Why didn't you tell me?"

Wynter set the prism carefully back on her dresser. "It was all over in a few minutes. A few minutes that I couldn't even explain myself. I just didn't want to ruin them by trying to." She lifted her hands and let them fall helplessly. "We met by accident, and it was as if there was a connection between us that had always been there. Being with her felt totally…right."

"What about now?"

"It still does."

The doorbell rang.

"That will be Pearce," Wynter said.

"We're not done with this," Mina warned.

"I know," Wynter said softly. She grabbed her full-length dark brown leather coat from the back of a nearby chair, hurried to Mina, and kissed her cheek. "Good night."

"Have fun, sweetie."

Wynter smiled gratefully. "Thanks."

Once downstairs, Wynter rushed to the front door, gathering her keys and wallet from the sideboard in passing. She felt irrationally happy, excited, as if the evening held endless possibility. All she knew for certain was that she was going out with Pearce, and she was going to have fun. She was going to listen to Patti Smith rage, and feel her blood stir, and not think about a single thing that life demanded of her. She pulled open the door and instantly forgot everything she had just been so sure of.

Pearce wore black. Tight black jeans, heavy black motorcycle boots, a black T-shirt, and a black motorcycle jacket cut in at the waist and wide at the shoulders that accentuated her powerful build. Her thick black hair was slicked back, her high cheekbones knife-edged above an angular jaw. This was not the Pearce Rifkin she was used to. This woman exuded something exotic and dangerous and alluring.

"Hi," Wynter said, feeling suddenly bereft of normal speech.

Pearce smiled. "Hi." She reached out and fingered the blond strands that were trapped between the collar of the leather coat and Wynter's throat. "Your hair looks nice down like this."

"Thanks." Wynter's vision narrowed until all she saw was Pearce's face. Then just her mouth, lips parted and intoxicatingly full.

Neither woman moved. The very tips of Pearce's fingers rested against the pulse that beat erratically in Wynter's neck. Wynter leaned ever so subtly into her caress.

Pearce traced her thumb along the edge of Wynter's jaw and let her eyes drift downward, taking in the leather duster, the long legs sleekly encased in softer sheaths of leather, the hint of green silk calling to her like a cool mountain glade on a hot summer day. She'd barely slept the night before, the memory of Wynter in her arms tormenting her all night long.

Mina came up behind Wynter, her gaze traveling between them. "If you all don't want those tickets, Ken and I will take them, and you two can stay here and babysit."

"Not a chance," Wynter said, her eyes never leaving Pearce's face.

Pearce smiled and gently moved her hand away. She looked past Wynter. "Hi. How are you doing?"

"Other than the fact that I'm getting too big to get out of my own way, I'm just fine. Now, if you two could move along, I'll close up over here and go find out what trouble my husband has gotten himself into with those children."

"All set?" Pearce asked, unable to keep her eyes from Wynter's face for long. Looking at her was the only thing that eased the ache that had set up permanent residence in the center of her chest.

Wynter put her hands in her pockets before she touched Pearce somewhere, *anywhere*. And she couldn't. Not when there was so much she didn't understand. She cared about Pearce too much for that. "Yes. I'm ready."

"My car's around the corner."

Wynter followed Pearce down the stairs, Mina's question resounding in her mind. *Is this a date?* Of course it wasn't. Was it?

❖

"There they are," Wynter said, pointing into the crowd that milled around on the sidewalk in front of the Theater of the Living Arts on South Street.

Pearce looked where Wynter pointed and saw a woman who had to be Wynter's sister Rose, since she looked like her carbon copy, only slightly shorter. Rose was glued to the front of a surprisingly scruffy guy in a black leather jacket that looked very much like Pearce's. He had a diamond stud in his left ear and blue jeans that were torn out in the ass. Rose had her arms around his waist, both hands stuffed into his back pockets, and was squeezing said ass. "Tell me he's a law student too."

Wynter laughed. "He's a drug counselor when he isn't playing bass in a rock band."

"Interesting combination."

"Apparently it's working for them. Come on," Wynter said, grabbing Pearce's hand. "Let me introduce you."

If Rose was surprised by Pearce's presence, she didn't show it. She smiled and extracted one hand from her companion's jeans and held it out. "Hi. I'm Rosie, and this is Wayne."

"Nice to meet you. I'm Pearce."

"Good to see you," Wayne said in a surprisingly mellow baritone.

Further conversation was curtailed as the doors opened and the crowd surged forward. Pearce and Wynter fell in behind Rose and Wayne in the haphazard line. Wynter held tightly to Pearce's hand, and in a few minutes the crowd had poured itself into the theater, from which all the seats had been removed on the main level. It was standing room only in the dark, warm space. Staircases on either side led to a balcony area where a few tables stood along the railing, but most of the area on that level was filled with people standing as well.

"It's really jammed," Wynter shouted above the din.

"We're going to go upstairs," Rose said, struggling for balance when someone unintentionally bumped her hip in passing. "We'll meet you after, if we don't see you up there."

"Okay." Wynter looked at Pearce. "Upstairs or down?"

"Your call," Pearce replied, automatically sliding her arm around Wynter's waist and pulling her close as two men with plastic cups of beer sidled past them.

"What do you say we stake out a place on the stairs?"

Pearce nodded as Rose and Wayne disappeared. "We'd better move fast."

Plenty of people had the same idea, but luckily they found two open steps halfway up along the wall. Pearce claimed the upper one and Wynter wedged in on the one just below her, leaving barely enough room for people to pass next to them. They shed their jackets and stashed them against the wall by their feet. The security staff, men and women in black T-shirts and jeans who shouted into walkie-talkies as they pushed through the throng, looked the other way despite the fact that standing on the stairs was in violation of code. The entire theater was wall-to-wall people by the time the warm-up band bounded onto the stage.

Wynter, her back lightly cushioned against Pearce's chest, tilted her head back against Pearce's shoulder. "You okay?"

"Terrific." Pearce steadied herself with a hand on either side of Wynter's hips when another person crowded onto the stair just behind her. As soon as she regained her balance, she quickly moved her hands. "Sorry."

"No need to be." Wynter's face was very close to Pearce's. As the band started to play, she said, "I'm really glad you came tonight."

"Me too," Pearce shouted before all conversation became impossible.

Waitstaff, against all odds, managed to snake their way through the packed room holding aloft circular trays laden with bottles of beer. Pearce snagged two, tossing what she hoped was a ten onto the tray before passing a bottle to Wynter. Unlike most openers, the first band was better than good, and forty-five minutes later the crowd was primed for the main attraction. When Patti Smith hit the stage growling, lean and hungry in leather pants and a faded Dylan T-shirt, the room was seething with the contagious energy of sex and booze and rebellion.

Wynter rocked against Pearce as she clapped and stomped, her body hot against Pearce's chest and stomach. The sounds were primal, the words prophetic, and Pearce was on fire. By the time Patti screamed that desire was the hunger, Wynter's hips pressed and rolled between Pearce's legs so hard that her mind filled with the red haze of arousal. She had no conscious awareness of sliding her arms around Wynter's waist or of Wynter clasping her hands and tightening the embrace. When Patti proclaimed that the night was made for lovers, Pearce buried her face in the curve of Wynter's neck and breathed her scent, her mouth open against sweat-dampened skin. Moaning softly, she surrendered to sensation, content to have just this small, sweet surcease. But it was Wynter who wanted more.

At the first touch of Pearce's mouth against her neck, Wynter turned molten inside. Patti roared, the crowd raged, and Wynter soared to a place she'd never been. She arched her back and, without a single thought, pivoted and wrapped her arms around Pearce's neck. She fisted her hands in Pearce's hair and feasted on her mouth as if she'd been starving for years.

Pearce kissed her back, unable to do anything else. She'd wanted this for weeks. Wynter's mouth was hot, soft, and demanding at the same time. Wynter's tongue raced over the inside of her lips, and her stomach twisted with urgency. When she heard Wynter groan and felt the telltale rocking of Wynter's hips, some part of her mind separated itself from her wildly demanding body. She found herself looking down at them as if from a great distance, saw Wynter carried away on a wave of abandon, and she suddenly knew she had to stop. *She* had to stop it, because she understood the consequences.

"Hey," Pearce gasped, turning her head away from the kiss and brushing her lips over Wynter's ear. "I'm losing my grip here."

"Oh God, me too," Wynter moaned, nipping lightly at Pearce's neck. "I've been wanting to do that since Match Day."

Pearce fished in her pockets for her keys, and pressed them into Wynter's hand. "Take my car home. I need to take a walk."

Uncertain, Wynter searched her face. "Why? What is it?"

"This isn't Match Day anymore." Already slipping into the crowd, Pearce shook her head. "I gotta go, Wynter."

Wynter leaned back against the wall and closed her eyes. Her body was in turmoil, her mind incapable of rational thought, but somewhere, deep inside, she knew Pearce was right.

Chapter Twenty

Pearce cut across the small lobby, ignoring the curious stares of the staff, and shouldered through the door. She carried her jacket hooked over her shoulder, not slowing for even an extra second to shrug it on. The heat from the simmering crowd and the unrelenting arousal chased her, propelling her as if she were besieged. It was nearly 11:00 p.m., and the biting cold never even registered in her mind as she strode west, forcing her way through the teeming streets. Even now, in the dead of winter, the nightlife pulsed along the twelve-block stretch of South Street extending from Penn's Landing on the Delaware River. Boutiques, bars, tattoo parlors, and fast food kiosks jammed every available inch of real estate. Packs of teenagers jostled and preened, taking their first steps in the age-old mating rituals. Curious out-of-towners gawked and the locals strolled. And Pearce ran.

She had only one goal in mind, and that was to put distance between herself and Wynter. She needed some space to resurrect her shattered defenses. She'd known that going out with Wynter tonight was a risk. She'd known for days, weeks in fact, that she'd been pretending. Pretending that her attraction was controllable, her desire containable, and most dangerously of all, that Wynter was available. But she hadn't had the strength to walk away, and now she had to run. She wondered how far and how long it would take to run from the memory of Wynter's hungry kisses, the firm hot pressure of her body, the small sounds of pleasure that had cut through her with the deadly precision of surgical steel. Farther than she had yet, she knew that.

She weaved unseeing through the oncoming Friday night crowds, barely aware of crossing the streets with or without the lights. Her thin shirt stuck to her chest, drenched with the sweat of desire and despair. She almost expected it to be blood.

The University Hospital was thirty blocks west, and she covered the distance in just over thirty minutes, arriving weak-limbed and panting. She fumbled for ID in her wallet, although it wasn't necessary. All the guards knew her. If the two at the main entrance were surprised by her appearance, they didn't show it. She went directly to the elevators and rode up to the locker room. It was empty, as it usually was in the middle of the night. The residents were either busy on the floors or operating, and the only OR personnel around were occupied with the nonstop flow of emergency cases. Pearce opened her locker with trembling hands and methodically stripped off her boots and clothes. She pulled on clean, soft scrubs, stepped into her shabby, blood-spattered clogs, and went in search of forgetting.

Her first stop was the ER, where she perused the whiteboard that covered one wall. It was divided into a series of rows and columns with the cubicle numbers on the left-hand side, followed by the patient name, attending ER physician, and a shorthand chief complaint. She studied the list. Back pain, cough, earache, painful urination, abdominal pain. Abdominal pain. Bingo.

"Hey, Henry," Pearce said when she found the ER attending putting on a cast in the treatment room. "What's the story with the abdominal pain?"

The heavyset African American didn't even look around as he smoothly rolled the three-inch strip of plaster of paris around the soft padding he had applied to an elderly woman's wrist. "Sixteen-year-old basketball player who said he thought he pulled a groin muscle during practice two days ago, but today he lost his appetite and spiked a temp."

"White count?"

"22,000."

"Ouch. X-rays?"

Henry Watson straightened with a grimace but smiled at the white-haired woman in the wheelchair. "All done. How does it feel?"

"Much better. How long will I have to wear this thing?"

"That's going to be up to your orthopedic doctor," he said, "but I imagine about six weeks."

"Oh my. That's going to make it difficult to shovel if it snows again."

He pressed his lips firmly together, apparently trying not to laugh, and nodded seriously. "You might need help with that." He patted her shoulder and motioned to Pearce to follow him back into the hall. When they moved a few feet down the corridor, he said, "I hope *I'm* worrying about shoveling when I'm eighty-seven."

"Yeah. Me too."

"So what are you doing down here? I called for a surgery consult, but I didn't expect to see you."

Pearce shrugged. "I happened to be in the neighborhood."

"Uh-huh. Well, while you're passing through, why don't you go lay your sainted hands on that boy's belly so I can get him out of here. We're backed up until next week."

"I'll take care of it."

Henry grunted his thanks and walked away, and Pearce went in search of the chart. When she found it, she skimmed it quickly to make sure there wasn't anything else she needed to know and then went to see the patient. She introduced herself to Rodney Owens and explained that she wanted to take a look at his abdomen.

All one hundred ninety pounds of Rodney Owens turned bright red as he clutched the thin hospital sheet to his chest. "I don't think there's anything wrong with my stomach."

"Really? Your chart says you came in complaining of abdominal pain."

"It's not exactly my abdomen. It's more…like…lower."

"Lower. Lower like in your groin?"

He nodded vigorously. "Yes. My groin. That's it."

Pearce leaned her hip against the side of the stretcher and tucked the chart under her arm. "Groin as in the inside of your leg or groin as in your testicles?"

"Those," he said faintly.

"Ever had any problem there before? Like a hernia?"

He shook his head.

"Any recent trauma? Maybe during the workout a few days ago?"

Another headshake.

"Swelling?"

"No," he whispered.

"So is it one or both that hurt?"

"Just the right one."

"Okay. Let's have a look at your belly first."

Rodney let go of the sheet, and Pearce pulled it down to his hips. She lifted the stethoscope that was draped over the blood pressure apparatus and put it on the upper left quadrant of his abdomen, then moved it until she had covered the entire surface.

"Quiet in there," she said as she tossed the stethoscope onto the counter. "I'm going to press, and you tell me if it hurts. Okay?"

"Okay."

She followed the path she had previously traced with the stethoscope, probing deeply and letting go rapidly. Rodney showed no evidence of direct or rebound pain until she reached the right lower quadrant, where she felt an infinitesimal tightening of his muscles. She looked up. "Does it hurt here?"

"Just a little."

She didn't feel a discrete mass, but there was a suggestion of fullness in that area. "I'm going to take a quick look at your groin just to make sure there's no problem. If anything hurts, tell me."

Rodney stared resolutely at the ceiling while she palpated each testicle.

"Doesn't seem to be any problem here." She pulled the sheet up and turned to wash her hands. "Are your parents here?"

"Just my mom. I think she went to get a soda. What's wrong with me, do you think?"

"I think you've got appendicitis."

"Then why does it hurt…you know."

"Probably because your appendix is irritating the structures on the inside of your abdomen, some of which lead down to that area. We call it referred pain."

"So I'm going to need an operation?"

"I think so. But it won't be a big deal, and you'll be as good as new in a week or so." Pearce dried her hands and tossed the paper towel into the wastebasket. "I'm going to go find your mom, and then I'll be back."

Thirty minutes later she was wheeling Rodney to the operating room, doing what she did best, and hoping that the challenge of fishing Rodney's appendix out through the laparoscope would be enough to keep her mind off Wynter. She hurt down deep, a little bit like Rodney, but her referred pain struck straight to the heart.

❖

"God, wasn't that fabulous," Rose crowed when Wynter finally found her and Wayne in the lobby.

"It was great," Wynter agreed.

Rose looked around. "Where's Pearce?"

"She had to leave." Wynter tried to sound nonchalant, but she could tell by the expression on her sister's face that she had failed. When, murmuring something to Wayne, Rose took her by the arm and dragged her a few steps away, Wynter steeled herself. The last thing she wanted to do was talk when her mind was a jumble of questions and her body felt like it belonged to someone else. She'd never reacted to anyone that way before. She didn't want to talk or think until she recognized herself. Maybe then she could make sense of what she'd done.

"What's going on?" Rose asked.

"Nothing. Really. Pearce just needed to leave. I have her car, so I'm fine. You two go on home."

Rose pulled Wynter farther into the corner out of the way of people streaming toward the doors. "Did you have a fight?"

"No."

"You work with her, right? I wasn't paying all that much attention when you said you were bringing a friend."

"Look, Rosie—"

"So why are you so upset if nothing happened?"

"Can we talk about this some other time? I'm really beat. I worked all night last night, and now—"

Rose folded her arms and looked as if she were settling in for a siege. "I *never* see you, and you're always too busy to talk on the phone. You and Dave get divorced, and then you show up here two months ago without even telling me you're coming. We get together for the first time in forever and you go from being on top of the world to looking like…" Rose squinted and peered into Wynter's eyes. "You look like you're going to cry. Jeez, what did she do to you?"

Wynter's throat burned and she was terrified that she *would* cry. She never cried. "She didn't do anything. But I think I might've done something stupid."

"Like what? God, you didn't do drugs or anything did you?"

"No, nothing like that," Wynter said, her voice edging upward toward what she feared might become an hysterical laugh. "I'm a mess. I kissed her. She was upset."

"You kissed Pearce? As in a serious kiss kiss?"

Wynter nodded.

"Is she gay?"

Wynter nodded again, but she was thinking about the kiss. About the way Pearce's body had tightened against hers, about the scrape of teeth over her lips and the hungry plunge of tongues, about the possessive hands that had cupped her butt and tugged her close. She shut her eyes, hoping it would stop her head from swimming.

"Holy. Holy holy holy. So what…are *you* gay?"

Wynter opened her eyes. "I haven't thought past her. I can't seem to think about anything *except* her."

"Jeez, Wynter. Maybe you should."

"Yes," Wynter said wearily. "Maybe I should."

Rosie made Wynter's excuses to Wayne, and Wynter walked to the car, hoping against hope that she would see Pearce somewhere along the way—tucked into a doorway, her ankles crossed and that grin on her face that was an irresistible combination of amusement and cocky self-assurance, or leaning against the Thunderbird, waiting as she had been just the previous evening. Thirty-six hours that felt like forever. Her life was divided into thirty-six-hour segments, it seemed, a repetitive cycle from which she could not shift back into the routine that most of the world followed. She'd never been able to explain her work, or what it demanded of her, to anyone who hadn't experienced it. Now, that sense of alienation extended to the very core of her. She could say the words. *I kissed her.* It was simple enough. She even knew why. She'd done it because every atom in her body had been drawn to Pearce from the instant they'd met.

There was no one waiting at the Thunderbird except a couple of young men who stood on the sidewalk admiring its sleek lines and dazzling chrome.

"Yo, lady," one of them said. "Some fine ride."

Wynter unlocked the driver's door. "It is, isn't it."

"Your old man do the restoration?"

"Not exactly." Wynter slid in and took a few seconds to acquaint herself with the gauges and gears. Fortunately, she wasn't intimidated by anything mechanical, and although she hadn't driven anything quite like this before, she knew that she could. She pulled out carefully at the first sign of a break in the traffic that crawled down the two-lane, one-way thoroughfare and quickly headed for one of the less populated streets to return to West Philadelphia. She didn't want anything to happen to this car.

Once she felt comfortable, she fished around in the deep pocket of her leather coat and found her cell phone. She had Pearce's cell programmed in, just as she had the numbers of all the other residents on the service, and they had hers. She tried the number, her heart hammering. When she got voicemail, she didn't leave a message. What could she say? What had she intended to say if Pearce had answered? *I'm sorry, I didn't mean to kiss you?* No, because that wasn't true. She hadn't thought about it, she hadn't made a conscious decision to do it, but she'd meant it.

She disconnected and pushed one on the speed dial for the most important number in her life, the hospital operator. When the call was answered, she identified herself and asked to be put through to Dr. Pearce Rifkin's home number.

"I can do that, Doctor, but Dr. Rifkin is here in the hospital. Would you like me to page her for you?"

"Yes, please," Wynter said. She wasn't surprised, now that she thought about it. Pearce rarely spent any time at home even when she wasn't on call. She felt a surge of irrational relief that Pearce hadn't gone to O'Malley's or some other place looking for a diversion, then laughed at her own self-deception. Pearce could find all the company she needed in the hospital if she wanted it.

As if to prove the point, a woman came on the line. A woman who wasn't Pearce.

"Are you paging Dr. Rifkin?" the woman asked imperiously.

Wynter tried desperately to place the voice. She thought she would recognize Tammy's, because they ran into each other a fair amount in the OR lounge. Andrea she wasn't too sure of. She snapped, "Yes I am. This is Dr. Thompson."

"Dr. Rifkin is scrubbed in the OR. Would you like to leave a message?"

"No. Thanks." Wynter disconnected and put the phone back in her pocket.

She rubbed her eyes, feeling them burn with frustration and fatigue. Whatever she was going to say, she had to say in person. Pearce deserved that.

CHAPTER TWENTY-ONE

Wynter slept fitfully. The new house was too quiet with Ronnie gone. With just the two of them now, Wynter kept both of their bedroom doors open to monitor the small sounds her daughter made in the night. The bedroom was hot, stuffy, and she irritably kicked off the covers in a light doze. Her skin burned, despite the damp film of stress sweat. She was used to this anxious half sleep from being on call, when every night resembled this one; but usually when she was home, she slept like the dead. Tonight, her mind wouldn't stop racing, replaying every minute of the evening until she was once again in Pearce's arms, their mouths and bodies cleaved. Each time she relived the memory she grew aroused, her thighs tight and her stomach twisting with need.

At 5:00 a.m. she finally got up, showered, and went next door to Mina and Ken's. She let herself in and crept quietly up the stairs to the room where Ronnie slept with Winston when she stayed overnight. When Wynter peeked in the room, she saw what she expected: Ronnie was awake, carrying on an earnest and animated one-sided conversation with a stuffed rabbit. Winston, apparently used to Ronnie's early-morning monologues, slept on. Stepping carefully over toys, Wynter scooped Ronnie up and tiptoed out. She left a quick note in the kitchen for Mina, writing one-handed while she balanced Ronnie on her opposite hip.

On the short trip home, she said, "How would you like to go out to the diner with Mommy for breakfast, honey?"

Ronnie and the rabbit thought it was a great idea. Thirty minutes later, with Ronnie washed and dressed and carrying Mr. Bunny, Wynter buckled her into the child seat in the rear of her Volvo wagon and headed for the Melrose Diner in South Philly. Open twenty-four hours a day, seven days a week, it was a perfect place for a fast meal and a chance to think. Unfortunately, by the time she returned home an hour and a half later, her stomach was full but her head was no clearer.

She took Ronnie inside and settled her on the bed with her favorite books and toys while she curled up next to her with a newspaper. It was all for show, because she couldn't concentrate on anything. Fortunately, Ronnie required little in the way of focused conversation. When her cell phone rang Wynter snatched it up, trying not to be disappointed when she recognized the number.

"Hi, Mina," she said.

"I take it that really *was* you who kidnapped our little darling before sunrise this morning."

Wynter couldn't help smiling. "Guilty. Are you interested in the ransom demands?"

"Of course. How much are you going to pay me to take her back?"

"I don't think I've got enough saved." At that moment, Ronnie crawled into her lap and closed her eyes. "However, right this minute, she does resemble an angel. Maybe we could negotiate price."

"Must be nap time."

"You've got it." Wynter nuzzled the top of Ronnie's head, soothed by the smell of Johnson's Baby Shampoo and innocence.

"How come you didn't stay for breakfast?"

"It was early. I knew we'd just wake up the whole house."

"Did you eat?"

"We went to the Melrose."

There was a moment of silence. "The Melrose. On a Saturday morning."

"Uh-huh."

"Something happen I should know about?"

"How do you do that?" Wynter closed her eyes and stroked her daughter's soft hair.

"Doctors, especially surgeons and anesthesiologists, are creatures of habit. You have very few and very predictable responses to stress. Ken eats ice cream out of the carton by the gallon and forgets about sex. You go to the Melrose and brood."

"Ken really forgets about sex?"

"Get Ronnie settled. I'm coming over."

Wynter was in the kitchen making tea when Mina arrived. She looked over her shoulder and said, "Do you want some toast?"

"I'm fine. So tell me what happened, and don't dance around."

"We went to the concert," Wynter said as she carried two mugs of tea to the table. "It was wild. I don't know if it was that place or the music or the fact that I haven't been out on a date in years, but I…" She stopped and stared at Mina. *A date.* "Well. I guess that answers your question from last night."

Mina sipped her tea and said nothing.

"I felt so good. A little bit crazy. She put her arms around me and every nerve in my body fired at once." She smiled, remembering how alive she'd felt. "I turned and kissed her. I couldn't seem to get enough of her." Her voice drifted off as she tried to recognize herself in that kiss and failed. Confused, she met Mina's warm, kind gaze. "I think I scared her. She left in a hurry, and I haven't talked to her since."

"Were you scared?"

"Scared." Wynter tried the word on for size, then shook her head. "No. No, I wasn't. Or uneasy or embarrassed. I was just…nuts for her."

Mina drummed her fingers lightly on the tabletop, a slight frown of concentration breaking the smooth contours of her forehead. "It's funny, the things we don't know about our friends. I've known you, what? Going on eight years, maybe?"

Wynter nodded and pushed her tea aside. Her stomach had tied itself into a knot.

"Have you ever been with a woman before?" Mina asked.

"No," Wynter said softly.

"Ever wanted to?"

"If you'd asked me three months ago, I would have said no." Wynter looked at Mina, but her gaze was unfocused as she searched the past. "I always had a lot of friends growing up. Our community was small and pretty tight. All the kids hung out together in one big social group all the way through high school, boys and girls both. We didn't pair off the way a lot of kids seem to do. I thought of boys as friends first, I guess, and boyfriends second. Naturally, I was closer to my girl friends."

"So you never had any indication that maybe you liked girls as more than friends?"

"No," Wynter said, but she sounded uncertain.

"What?"

"I told you about Match Day. I bumped into Pearce," Wynter smiled, "literally. She looked a little younger and tougher then. Still just as beautiful as she is now, though. I just kind of got lost in her." She looked at Mina and shook her head, unable to find the words to describe what she felt. "I just wanted *to be* with her. When she started to kiss me that day, I wanted that more than I'd ever wanted anything in my life. It made no sense, and I never even questioned it."

"What happened?"

Wynter snorted. "Dave called at the critical moment. And I suddenly realized that I was about to kiss a woman who happened to be a total stranger. I left her there, and I didn't see her again until a couple of months ago."

"But you thought about her."

"Yes."

"That way."

"Yes. Sometimes. For just a second, and then I'd brush it away." Wynter sighed. "I was pregnant when I met her, Dave and I were ready to move to Yale and start our residencies, and I thought it was just a fluke. Just a moment of perfect insanity."

"Like last night."

Wynter shook her head. "No. Last night was a thousand times better."

Mina laughed. "Woo-ie, you *are* in a bad way."

"This is serious, Mina. Pearce was really upset. She walked out of the concert in the middle of the night, left her car, and went to the hospital."

"She's probably scared right down to the tips of those big black sexy boots of hers."

Wynter frowned. "Why?"

"Oh come on, sweetie. You're a divorced mother, straight as far as everyone including you can tell. She probably thinks you're just… playing—you know, experimenting."

Wynter rose quickly and strode to the sink, dashing the now-tepid tea into the drain so forcefully it splashed out. "That's ridiculous. I would never do that."

"Well, she probably doesn't know that."

"Well, she should."

"Honey," Mina said, rising slowly, "you might have to do some explaining. Because I'll tell you one thing. She's got a serious case for you."

Her heart racing, Wynter asked softly, "You think?"

"I know. It's written all over that beautiful face of hers."

❖

As soon as Mina left, Wynter retrieved her phone from the bedroom, called the page operator, and asked for Pearce.

"I'm sorry, Dr. Rifkin has signed out for the day."

"Sorry, didn't I say *Pearce* Rifkin? She's on call for the chief's service," Wynter said, knowing Pearce's schedule as intimately as she knew her own.

"Just a moment."

Wynter tuned out the background chatter of the page operators, four women who occupied a glassed-in booth on the first floor opposite the admissions office. Most of them looked like they'd been with the hospital since the first brick was laid, and they knew every person on staff by name. She was certain they could tell stories that would top the *New York Times* Bestseller List for years.

"Dr. Rifkin is not on call today. Dr. Dzubrow is covering for Rifkin's service."

Wynter frowned. She was certain Pearce was scheduled to be in-house today. "Can you page her to—"

"She left word that she would be off beeper for the entire day. Do you want to leave a message in case she calls in?"

"No," Wynter said slowly. "Thanks."

She closed her phone and stared at nothing, wondering what to do. One thing was certain, she'd go crazy if she had to sit around all day wondering where Pearce was and what she was doing, and with whom. She glanced at the leather coat she'd dropped over the rocker next to her bed, then idly scanned the dresser where her wallet and keys and… Pearce's keys…lay jumbled together. She opened her phone again.

"Mina? I'm sorry. Do you think I can bring Ronnie over for an hour after she wakes up?"

"Chloe is coming by with her kids, so we might as well make it a party. Bring her by whenever."

Just after noon, Wynter walked down the narrow driveway toward the garage where Pearce kept her vehicles. Both doors were open, and somewhere in the cavernous space, Patti Smith wailed about the night.

Wynter unzipped her parka and removed it when she stepped inside. The CD was so loud that Pearce couldn't have heard her coming even if she hadn't been almost entirely underneath the body of the Corvair. All that was visible were the bottoms of her blue jeans and the soles of her scuffed workboots. Wynter knelt down, contemplating how to announce herself without startling Pearce. As if sensing her presence, Pearce shifted one booted foot to the concrete floor and propelled the dolly on which she'd been lying out from underneath the car. Wordlessly, Pearce turned down the portable CD player by feel, then lay on her back on the wooden slab looking up at Wynter, who leaned over her from two feet away. A smudge of grease streaked Pearce's cheek just below her left eye, and there was a small scrape on her chin. She wore no jacket, only a stained gray T-shirt that had pulled free from her jeans.

They stared at one another until Wynter reached down and wiped the grease away with her thumb. Then she brushed Pearce's chin adjacent to the scrape. "Didn't anyone ever tell you that you shouldn't lead with your chin?"

"You should see the other guy."

"I parked your car across from your house."

"Thanks."

"I can't stay very long. Mina's got Ronnie, and I need to spend time with her on my day off."

Pearce sat up and straddled the dolly, her legs kicked out in front of her, her hands resting between her parted thighs. "Good. I understand."

Wynter knelt on the cold hard floor and framed Pearce's face with both hands. "I don't think you do. I don't know that I do. But we need to talk about last night."

"Wynter," Pearce said quietly, remaining still although her every instinct screamed to get up and back away. Or finish what they'd started the night before. "You're a great person. Terrific. But we can't…get involved."

"Why is that?"

The muscles in Pearce's belly quivered, a rush of heat raced along her spine, and everything she had figured out in the last six hours as she'd welded and winched and created order out of disorder began to slip away. Every reason why that kiss had been a mistake seemed negotiable now that Wynter was here and she could see her eyes and hear her voice and feel the warmth of her hands. "Too complicated," she finally managed to rasp.

"I agree with you there," Wynter said gently. She leaned forward and lightly kissed Pearce on the mouth, then drew back. "Just checking."

"Checking what?" Pearce's chest rose and fell as if she had been running for miles.

"To see if kissing you still made me want to climb inside your skin." Wynter drew her fingers over Pearce's mouth. "It does."

"Jesus, Wynter." Pearce closed her eyes. "You're straight. You've got a kid. We're both residents, and it would take about three days before everyone knew we were fucking. I don't have time for a relationship. I don't even *want* a relationship." She opened her eyes. "And I'm done sleeping with women who are sleeping with men."

Wynter leaned back on her heels and rested her hands on her thighs. She held Pearce's gaze and said very clearly, "The last one is easy. I'm not sleeping with anyone at all." She took a deep breath. "The other ones are a little more problematic, except for Ronnie. She's a given. I don't know if I want a relationship either. I don't know if I'm straight. I don't know if I'm not. As to who knows what about anything we're doing, I don't care." She pressed her hands harder against her thighs to hide their trembling. "Your turn."

"No strings. No promises. We see what happens." Pearce reached behind her, found the body of the car, and used it to push herself up. She rested her backside against it, because her legs were shaking. "That's all I've got to offer."

Wynter stood, took a step forward, and pressed full length against Pearce. She put her arms around her neck as she had the night before and kissed her. Unlike the night before, she took her time, starting with a light play of the tip of her tongue over the surface of Pearce's lower lip. When she felt Pearce's arms come around her, she slicked her tongue inside just a fraction—in and out again—forcing Pearce to chase the kiss, to follow with her tongue. They teased and tangoed, back and forth, deepening the kiss until they were both moaning. Finally, Wynter braced her hands against Pearce's shoulders and pushed away, panting.

"No strings. No promises. We see what happens." She turned and retrieved her jacket from the floor. "Come to dinner tonight. Seven o'clock."

Then she walked away.

CHAPTER TWENTY-TWO

Pearce waited until Wynter reached the end of the driveway and disappeared from sight before slumping to the floor, her back against the side panel of her Corvair. She sat with her legs straight in front of her, her hands in her lap, her head back, eyes closed. Her lips tingled. Her face was hot, the thermal imprints of Wynter's hands branded in her skin. One breath. Two. She still couldn't get enough air. Her stomach was tense, her chest constricted.

Wynter had taken her by surprise the night before. Pearce knew that she'd invited the kiss with her unconscious embrace, but she hadn't been prepared for the intensity of Wynter's reaction, or her own response. Wynter's mouth, her hands, had been insistent, taunting and sweet and unapologetic. Pearce was used to women who made their needs clear, and usually she had no problem giving them what they wanted, taking her own pleasure in the process. Last night, her instantaneous and uncontrollable arousal had disassembled her. She'd craved Wynter's touch with the desperation of a drowning woman clawing her way toward the ocean's surface. She felt the same way now, and it scared her in more ways than she could count.

All her life she'd had one goal—to fulfill her father's expectations. His requisites had never been spelled out for her, because they'd never needed to be. From the time she was aware of herself in the world, she'd understood her heritage and her destiny. Nowhere in the design had there been room for anything other than ambition and accomplishment. No blueprint for love, no roadmap for a relationship, no outline for life other than a professional one. She did have the model of her parents' marriage, which appeared to be have been one of mutual convenience and polite propriety, absent of passion or real companionship. She'd learned her lessons well.

The superficial liaisons she'd allowed herself satisfied her needs and never interfered with her aspirations. In less than five months, she'd be the chief surgical resident at one of the premier institutions in the country and on her way to achieving everything she'd set out to accomplish. Everything that was expected of her. Everything that she wanted. Success was within sight.

She opened her eyes to the empty garage, seeking the familiar to remind her of who she was. But she could still see Wynter's face. Still hear her voice. Still *feel* her. And that was not part of the plan.

No strings. No promises.

Whatever it took, that's the way it had to be, because there was no room in her life for complications or diversions. And if she doubted that, she had only to remind herself that Wynter was very likely to wake up some morning and realize that she'd let her body overrule her senses. And then she'd be gone.

"Just let it play out and don't take it too seriously," she muttered as she pushed herself to her feet. Satisfied that she had things under control, she ignored the thrum of excitement that lingered in the pit of her stomach. Dinner was just dinner. Everyone had to eat.

❖

The phone rang just as Wynter was sliding a roast into the oven. She caught it on the fourth ring. "Hello?"

"Hey, whatcha doing?"

She smiled at the sound of her sister's voice. "Cooking dinner."

"What's the Little Princess doing?"

"You're the only one who calls her that, which just proves you haven't been doing enough babysitting."

Rosie laughed. "I hear you."

"At the moment, she's trying to push SpaghettiOs onto her fingers. She thinks they're rings."

"Oh, that sounds so cute."

Wynter glanced over at Ronnie, who had spaghetti sauce in her hair, on her face, and all over the kitchen table as far as her arms could reach. She smiled. "Pretty much. Oh, wait—you should say hi." She held the phone for Ronnie. "It's Aunt Rosie, honey." Ronnie made excited conversation for sixty seconds and then lapsed into silence. Wynter took over again. "So, what's up?"

"That's what I was calling to ask you. What's happening with Pearce?"

"We talked."

"And?"

"She's coming to dinner tonight."

"Your idea?"

"Uh-huh."

"Do you have ulterior motives?"

Wynter ran water in the sink to wash potatoes and carrots. "Such as what?"

"You know *what* what. You already kissed her. Are you planning on doing more?"

"I don't know. Maybe. We agreed to see what happens."

Rosie snorted. "Oh please. That's what everyone says when what they really mean is, let's hop into bed at the first opportunity."

"Is that right?"

"Yes, it is, and you're only hedging because Pearce isn't a guy."

"Don't you think that makes sense?"

"I don't know. Does it? You've already kissed her. That kinda cancels out the guy thing, don't you think?"

Wynter moved Ronnie's empty dinner plate out of reach and draped a damp dish towel over her daughter's hands. As she methodically wiped each finger, she said, "I'm attracted to her. I don't know what that means beyond that fact. Maybe nothing will happen."

"What about last night, then?"

"I hadn't planned it. I just...did it without thinking."

"You're not usually impulsive."

"No. I'm not. I've never had a chance to be."

"What if it turns out you're gay?"

"Is this really why you called?" Wynter picked Ronnie up, cradling the portable phone against her shoulder. "Come on, honey. Bath time."

"I guess," Rosie said after a pause. "I mean, I just never suspected... you never said anything like maybe you were."

"I haven't been keeping secrets, Rosie," Wynter said, hearing the hurt in her voice. "I would've told you."

"Honest?"

Wynter smiled. "Honest. I never thought about it. I was in school, then I was married, then the residency started. Then it all went to hell. My life was either too busy or too crazy to think about much of anything."

"Your life's still pretty crazy, you know."

"I know. She's just coming for dinner."

"Uh-huh. Yeah. Sure."

"Would it bother you?" Wynter sat Ronnie on the closed toilet seat, handed her a bath toy to keep her occupied, and knelt to untie her sneakers. "If it turns out that maybe I am?"

"Would it bother you?"

"I don't think so. Mom and Dad pretty much raised us to believe that people's private lives are private." Wynter tugged off Ronnie's corduroy overalls. "I'm not naïve enough to think it would be easy, but that's never stopped me. You didn't answer my question."

"You know, we never got to talk very much after you went away to school, and I only saw you and Dave a few times a year at holidays. But you never looked particularly happy to me."

"It wasn't all his fault," Wynter admitted, pulling Ronnie's T-shirt off over her head. "He's a horse's a—" she glanced at Ronnie, "behind, but I wasn't paying very much attention to what I needed or wanted."

"You looked happier last night than I can remember since high school."

"I was."

"So why would it bother me?"

Wynter closed her eyes and took a deep breath. "Thanks."

"I love you. I gotta go study. Wayne's got a gig tonight, and I promised I'd be there."

"Have fun."

"You'll tell me when something happens, right?"

"*If* something happens."

"Uh-huh."

"I love you too. Go study." Wynter set the phone aside and cuddled her daughter. "Ready for a bath with Ducky?"

Ronnie nodded yes, accompanied by quacking sounds for emphasis.

❖

As Pearce climbed the steps to Wynter's new home, it occurred to her that she had never had a dinner invitation like this before. She didn't date. She had neither the time nor the inclination. Most of the time she fell into bed with someone she bumped into at O'Malley's or crossed paths with in the middle of the night in the hospital. She didn't take women to the movies, she didn't go with them to concerts, and she didn't spend Saturday nights in their homes. But here she was. She shook her head, wondering exactly how Wynter managed to get her to do things she'd never done before. Deciding there was no point in trying to figure out why everything had always been different with Wynter, she rang the bell.

A minute later, Wynter answered, a scrubbed and pajamaed Ronnie in her arms. "Hi. I was just putting her to bed. Come on in. I'll just be a minute."

"Hi." Pearce noted that Wynter looked just as good in her casual jeans, sneakers, and red open-collared shirt as she had in leather the night before. Realizing she was staring, Pearce held out a bottle of wine. "A housewarming present."

"Thank you." Wynter held the door wide. "Do you remember where the kitchen is?"

Pearce nodded, adding a bit shyly, "And something for Ronnie." She passed the box containing Bob the Builder's Wooden Race Track set into Ronnie's outstretched arms. "Here you go, kiddo."

"Oh," Wynter said with a laugh. "You're in trouble now. She'll never go to bed."

"I suppose it's too late to take it back."

"Way way too late." Wynter leaned forward and kissed Pearce's cheek. "That was sweet."

Pearce wondered if Wynter could tell that the slightest touch from her made Pearce vibrate like a tuning fork snapped against the side of a table. She was surprised the air around her wasn't moving. "It's just a little thing."

"Would you mind very much setting it up for her while I put the last few touches on dinner?" Wynter smiled sheepishly. "I know it's probably not what you had in mind for the evening, but—"

"It'll be fun," Pearce said quickly. "Besides, I wanna see how it goes together."

Laughing, feeling ridiculously happy, Wynter said, "Let's go upstairs."

❖

Fifteen minutes later, Wynter walked down the second-floor hallway to Ronnie's room, listening to her daughter's delighted laughter. She stopped in the bedroom doorway to take in the scene. A wooden racetrack in a figure eight sat in the middle of the floor surrounded by half-constructed houses. Pearce lay on her side on one side of the track with Ronnie on the other. Each held a wooden racecar that they propelled more or less around the track. Ronnie seemed to delight in trying to drive hers into Pearce's. After a particularly resounding crash, Pearce made sounds resembling an explosion and fell over onto her back. Ronnie clapped.

Pearce turned her head, saw Wynter, and grinned. "She's tough."

"I should've warned you." Wynter took in Pearce's form as she sprawled unselfconsciously on the floor. She wore the same black boots as the night before, this time with blue jeans and a plain white T-shirt. The jeans, cinched with a wide black leather belt, rode low on her hips, and Wynter could imagine fitting her body into the vee of Pearce's thighs and the shallow plane of her stomach. Wynter's gaze traveled up to Pearce's face, and when their eyes met, she had to look away as a wave of heat passed through her. "Let me put her to bed."

Pearce got to her feet. "Should I wait downstairs?"

"Probably," Wynter murmured as she lifted Ronnie. "You're too much of a distraction."

"Oh yeah?" Pearce ran a fingertip down the outside of Wynter's arm. She'd seen the appreciative look in Wynter's eyes, and it'd gotten her stirred up. It didn't take any more than that from her. Just a look. Not even a touch. She felt a pulse beat between her thighs. "Is that a problem?"

"Yes," Wynter whispered. "Go away now."

Pearce laughed and touched Ronnie's hair. "Night, kiddo."

Ronnie grinned. "Night, kiddo."

When Wynter came downstairs, Pearce was waiting in the living room. She leaned against the sofa, her ankles and arms crossed, a lazy smile on her face. "Everything okay?"

"No," Wynter said, crossing the room to her. "I forgot something."

"What?" Pearce asked nonchalantly, even though the heat in Wynter's eyes had ignited the fire in her belly that always seemed to simmer when she was anywhere near Wynter. This time, she was more than ready for Wynter to put it out.

"This." Wynter put both hands on Pearce's arms and pulled them down to her sides, then leaned into her and kissed her. It was just as she remembered it, only better. Pearce's body was just as hot, just as tightly coiled, but this time, Pearce kissed her back with a ferocity that took her breath away. Pearce's arms came around her hard, and Wynter felt hands cup her ass, felt a hard thigh thrust between her legs. Then she was spinning, and *she* was against the sofa and Pearce's mouth was on her neck. She arched her back. "Oh God."

"I love the way you smell," Pearce groaned, licking the undersurface of Wynter's jaw. "And taste." She pulled the shirt from the back of Wynter's jeans and slid her hand underneath. "Oh man, your skin's so hot." She caught an earlobe in her teeth and tugged at it. "I want you so bad. Jesus, Wynter." She raked her teeth down Wynter's neck, then licked the faint red mark she'd left behind. "Tell me what you want."

"Pearce." Wynter held her tightly, feeling her tremble, knowing she was holding back. "Pearce." She pressed her mouth to Pearce's ear. "I want you too. I do." She twisted her fingers into Pearce's hair and turned her head until she could find her mouth. She ran her tongue over Pearce's lips, thrust into her mouth, nipped at her jaw. She finally pulled back, gasping. "Oh, I do. Can we just…wait. Just go a little slower?"

Pearce pressed her forehead to Wynter's shoulder, forcing herself to breathe, trying to clear her head, struggling to tamp down the terrible yearning. "Okay. Okay." She shuddered. "Okay."

"God, you're so sexy," Wynter moaned, still holding Pearce close. She nestled her cheek on Pearce's shoulder. "Now I really need that distraction. Can I interest you in dinner?"

Pearce laughed shakily. "As opposed to hot monkey sex with you?"

"Uh-huh."

Pearce kissed Wynter's forehead and stroked her cheek with trembling fingers. "Sure. I'd like that."

Wynter leaned back, her eyes heavy-lidded and hazy with lingering arousal. "You're not mad?"

"No," Pearce whispered. She cupped Wynter's chin, then kissed her eyelids and finally her mouth. "No. There's no hurry."

"I'm not so sure. I feel as if something might explode," Wynter confided as Pearce moved away. She caught Pearce's hand, unwilling to let her go very far.

Pearce grinned. "I hope so."

Wynter laughed and tugged Pearce toward the kitchen. "Come on. I slaved over this, so I expect you to make appropriate sounds of gratitude."

"Considering it's the first meal that a woman has ever cooked for me, I'll probably get on my knees in thanks."

Wynter arched an eyebrow. "That could be interesting."

Pearce stopped abruptly and pulled her into her arms again. She brushed the rim of Wynter's ear with her tongue until she felt Wynter shudder. "Careful. Don't tease if you want me to go slow."

Wynter's breath came in shallow gasps. "Can't I have both?"

"You can have anything you want," Pearce murmured, her mouth against Wynter's neck. In some part of her mind, beyond the madness of desire, she feared that might be true.

CHAPTER TWENTY-THREE

Can I help with something?" Pearce stood next to the kitchen table watching Wynter toss a salad, feeling helpless and inadequate. She hadn't been kidding when she'd said that a woman had never cooked dinner for her before—not counting her mother, who had cooked but usually left it to the housekeeper, or her grandmother. Somehow, it didn't seem right for Wynter to be doing all the work.

"You can open that bottle of wine you brought," Wynter said as she peered into the oven. "This roast looks done. There's a corkscrew in the drawer on the far left of the counter. I hope you're hungry."

"Starving."

Wynter closed the oven door and turned slowly. "If we're going to get through dinner, you can't speak to me in that tone of voice."

The corner of Pearce's mouth quirked upward. "What tone?"

"That smoky, hungry, sexy tone. It goes right through me."

Every muscle in Pearce's body twitched. "Then stop saying things like that. It makes me want to jump you."

Wynter smiled a satisfied smile. "Fair is fair." She pointed toward the counter. "Corkscrew."

Pearce did as directed. She'd never met a woman who could control her so easily with just a smile. She'd been with beautiful women, smart women, sexy women, hot demanding avaricious women, but she'd never been anywhere near a woman who could turn her upside down with a glance. Hell, not even a glance, a single word. "This is crazy."

"What?"

"Nothing. Glasses?"

"Um…water glasses will have to do. I haven't found the wineglasses yet."

"Hell, I'd drink this out of a jelly glass."

"Don't laugh—it might come to that." Wynter placed the serving platter in the center of the table. She'd set two places adjacent to one another at one end, and although she couldn't find her good dishes, she had found the candles. She lit them with a flourish. "There."

"It looks great." Pearce put the wine bottle down on the table and slid her arms around Wynter's waist from behind and hugged her gently. She rubbed her cheek against Wynter's hair. "Thank you."

Wynter leaned back and folded her arms over Pearce's, closing her eyes. Pearce's breath was warm against her cheek, her body solid and strong. She felt arousal awaken from the restless slumber to which she had remanded it a short time before and welcomed the resurgence of excitement. She loved the way Pearce made her feel. Desired and desirable. Alive.

She turned her head and kissed the corner of Pearce's mouth. "I should also mention you're not allowed to touch me until after dinner."

"It's hard not to." Pearce turned Wynter around and kissed her on the mouth. She played her hands over Wynter's shoulders, stroked down her arms, and then settled them on her waist. She kissed her slowly, deeply, enjoying the taste and heat of her mouth. She kept her touch light, her body still, not pressing for more than the kiss. When she drew back, Wynter's eyes were cloudy, her neck flushed. "You're very beautiful."

Wynter drew a shuddering breath and placed her hands flat against Pearce's chest, her fingertips resting on her collarbones. "When you say it like that, I believe it."

"Wynter," Pearce murmured. She forced herself to take a step backward, still holding Wynter, but at arm's length—out of kissing range. "We should have dinner."

Despite a surge of disappointment, Wynter nodded, knowing it was what she had asked for. At the moment she couldn't quite remember why. And God, it was hard to think of anything except the heat in Pearce's eyes, the magic in her hands. "Can I just tell you how much I love it when you touch me?"

"No," Pearce said fiercely. "I'm dying here, give me a break."

"Try to hang on," Wynter lifted Pearce's hand from her waist and kissed her knuckles, which still showed signs of bruises, "and I'll try to be good."

Pearce tapped Wynter's chin with her finger. "You could start by trying not to torment me."

Wynter nipped at the end of Pearce's finger. "But I love to watch your eyes get all dark and—"

"Damn it, Wynter. Stop."

Laughing, Wynter moved away and gestured to the chairs. "Sit down. Let's eat this if we're not going to do anything else."

Shaking her head, Pearce settled beside Wynter. "I really am hungry."

"Good," Wynter said as she dished out the food.

Because they were used to eating together at the hospital, they fell into easy conversation about their cases and the upcoming rotations and other residents. Before Pearce realized it, she had cleaned her plate twice. She leaned back from the table with a groan. "God, that was great."

"You're certainly easy to please," Wynter remarked, pleased herself at Pearce's obvious enjoyment. She couldn't remember when doing something so simple for someone else had given her such satisfaction. When she saw the grin tug at the corner of Pearce's mouth, she held up her hand. "Don't start."

"You might regret saying that," Pearce said playfully, catching Wynter's hand. Their fingers entwined and she did not let go. "One of these days when you're crazy for me."

"Pretty sure of yourself."

Pearce looked down at their clasped hands resting on the tabletop. It looked and felt so natural to be connected to Wynter this way, and at the same time, it was wholly foreign to her. Nothing that had transpired between them was new—she'd kissed women whom she'd known far less well than Wynter, and she'd had quick sexual encounters in dark corners and a few other semipublic places. But she'd never felt the urge to run the way she had last night. She looked up and met Wynter's worried gaze and smiled wryly. "I'm sorry I took off on you last night."

"Why did you?"

"Jesus," Pearce sighed. "Aren't you supposed to say 'That's okay, I understand' or something else like that to let me off the hook?"

"Probably. And I would, if it really didn't matter. But it does, and I want to know."

Pearce stretched her legs out under the table and leaned back in the chair, keeping hold of Wynter's hand. With her free hand she fiddled aimlessly with her silverware. "Ten more seconds of kissing you like that—or of you kissing me, rather—and I'd've been fucking you up against the wall. Right there in the middle of that crowd."

"Assuming I would've let you," Wynter said, her voice husky and low.

"Wouldn't you?" There was neither triumph nor self-satisfaction in Pearce's voice, only a quiet certainty.

"Probably. I wanted you so much I wasn't thinking of anything else." Wynter laughed self-consciously. "I don't usually go quite that far in public places."

"No, I didn't think so." Pearce squeezed Wynter's hand. "I don't usually lose it like that, either."

Wynter heard the lingering desire in Pearce's voice, but also the regret, and that frightened her. She couldn't read Pearce well enough to know exactly what bothered her, but she didn't want anything about what they shared to hurt her. "Should I apologize for kissing you like that?"

"Jesus, no." Pearce turned Wynter's hand over between her own and kissed her palm before looking into her eyes. "Did I embarrass you with your sister?"

"No," Wynter said, smiling. "She's dying of curiosity, but she'll live."

Pearce's brows knit together. "Curiosity." Then came understanding, and she blushed. "You mean…she wants details?"

"Of course. That's what girls do when there's a new hotty on the horizon." Wynter couldn't help but laugh at Pearce's obvious discomfort. It made her all the more charming. "She called this afternoon to give me the third degree."

"Is she upset about you being interested in a woman?"

There, Wynter thought, *finally.* She edged her chair around the table until she was sitting side by side with Pearce. Turning, she placed her free hand on Pearce's thigh. "She was surprised. Not upset. Pretty much like me."

"She might change her mind when she's had time to think about it."

"Pearce, my sister never really liked Dave, but she never said a word against him until she found out he was fooling around. Then she was all for flying up to New Haven and cutting his balls off."

"Good for her."

Wynter smiled. "She's not going to have a problem with me seeing you."

"What about the rest of your family?"

"You mean my parents?"

Pearce nodded.

"We're Quakers. Personal choice and individual freedoms are very important to us. My parents will support whatever choices I make."

"Sometimes people aren't so liberal when it's close to home."

"I know." Wynter caught a flash of some distant pain in Pearce's eyes. Knowing that Pearce's mother had died when Pearce was still a child, she realized it had to have been her father who'd put that sorrow there. She rubbed her hand up and down Pearce's thigh in unconscious comfort. She was venturing into dangerous territory, considering that Ambrose Rifkin was her boss, and discussing him, even when it was personal like this, was probably not the wisest thing to do. But she didn't care. She only cared about Pearce. "What happened?"

Pearce jerked, startled from the unintended memory. "Let's just say it wasn't a smooth ride for a while."

"Your father was unhappy when he found out you were gay?"

"He ignored it at first. I think he thought it would pass."

"How old were you when he found out?"

"Sixteen."

"When did *you* know?" Wynter wondered what was wrong with *her* that she'd never even had an inkling that she could be attracted to another woman. Was she really that out of touch?

"I started to think about it when I was twelve or thirteen, and by the time I was fifteen, I knew for sure. One of the nice things about going to a girls' prep is there's a lot of girls around." Pearce grinned.

"Oh, I bet you were dangerous then." Wynter leaned forward and brushed a kiss over Pearce's lips. "I bet you broke a lot of hearts."

The kiss was light, gentle, and Pearce felt its sweetness all the way through to her heart. Wynter had a way of making her feel so many things—poignant pleasure, wild passion, aching need. How could that be? How could one woman do that so effortlessly? When had anyone touched her that way?

"Not so very many," she murmured. She didn't want to revisit the past. She wanted to feel what only Wynter had ever made her feel. She slipped an arm behind Wynter's back and tugged her over into her lap. The slat-backed wooden chair creaked.

"Hey," Wynter protested with a laugh. "We're going to end up on the floor."

"I'll catch you if we do."

"Promises, promises." But she wound her arms around Pearce's neck and kissed her again. Kissing her was a banquet of delight, a feast that satisfied her in her deepest reaches while whetting her appetite for more. She cupped her hand on Pearce's throat as she slid her mouth over Pearce's lips, loving the slick heat and the racing pulse beneath her fingertips, glorying in Pearce's excitement. She felt heady with power and kissed her harder, probing, reaching inside until she drew forth a groan. "I could kiss you forever," she gasped.

"I might go up in flames," Pearce moaned, slipping both hands beneath Wynter's shirt and onto her bare back. She smoothed her hands up and down Wynter's spine, allowing herself that much and no more. She didn't dare do anything else, because she knew she would never be able to stop. When Wynter shifted to straddle her on the chair, Pearce forced herself to keep her hands on Wynter's back, even though Wynter's breasts were so close, her nipples tight against the stretched cotton fabric. Wynter seemed to feel no such constraints, caressing Pearce's neck, her shoulders, her chest. When her fingers skimmed Pearce's nipples, Pearce jerked in the chair, her head falling back. "Don't."

"Why?" Wynter whispered, rocking in Pearce's lap, sucking the soft flesh at the base of her throat. "Why?"

"Can't stop again," Pearce groaned. She caught Wynter's hands and pulled them from her breasts. "I want you too much."

"No," Wynter said fiercely, pulling Pearce's hands to her own breasts and pressing them there. "Not too much. Never too much. Touch me."

Pearce felt Wynter's nipples harden against her palms, sensed her breasts grow firm with arousal, heard the need in her voice. She couldn't remember why she should hesitate. Wynter wanted her to touch her, and she ached to do it. She'd never hesitated before to take and give pleasure. She squeezed gently and Wynter moaned her name. That sweet sound broke her resolve. She *would* have what she'd hungered for all these weeks. Tightening her hold, she stood, fastening her mouth to Wynter's neck as Wynter's legs came automatically around her hips.

She bit down gently until Wynter whimpered. She wanted to lay her down on the kitchen table and take her right there. She could feel the fire between Wynter's legs through their clothes. She knew she could have her. One touch and Wynter would surrender. Right here. Right now.

She pressed her mouth to Wynter's ear. "I won't make love to you like this. I want to make you come slowly the first time."

Wynter worried she might come just thinking about it. She'd never been so aroused in her life. She dug her fingers into Pearce's shoulders. She wanted to scream, but could barely speak. "If you don't put your hands on me soon, I think I might die."

"Can we go upstairs?"

"Yes. Yes." Wynter feared in another minute she wouldn't be able to stand. "God, yes. Please. Now."

"What about Ronnie?"

"What?" Wynter asked almost desperately, struggling to make sense of Pearce's questions. "She sleeps soundly. She'll be fine."

Pearce covered Wynter's mouth in an urgent kiss, needing the taste of her to carry her until she could have more. Then she gently eased her down, keeping one arm around her waist. "Please, will you take me to your bed?"

Wynter stroked her cheek, wondering why she felt tears threatening. She'd never felt anything as right as when she said, "Oh, yes. Yes, I will."

CHAPTER TWENTY-FOUR

The upstairs hallway was dark. Wynter and Pearce moved quietly with just the night-light in Ronnie's room to guide them. Wynter led the way, holding Pearce's hand. Out of habit, she paused in the doorway to Ronnie's room and listened for her soft, regular breathing. After a second, she continued on, aware of Pearce just behind her, sensing the air around them scintillate with excitement. When she reached her bedroom, she pressed the dimmer switch and turned the light down until there was just enough illumination to maneuver by. She tugged Pearce over the threshold and quietly closed the door.

"What if she gets up?" Pearce murmured.

Wynter pointed to the small receiver on her bedside table. "We'll hear her."

"Handy." Pearce pulled Wynter close and kissed her neck. She ran her hands rhythmically up and down Wynter's back, their bodies melding as they swayed together in the near dark. "Sure about this?"

"Yes." Wynter gripped Pearce's T-shirt and pulled it out of her jeans, then snaked her hands underneath. As she danced her fingers over Pearce's stomach, she confessed, "I haven't used the child monitor in over a year, but I hooked it up after I saw you this morning. Just in case I needed to close the door."

Pearce hissed in her breath at Wynter's caress. "Pretty sure of yourself."

Wynter laughed and skimmed the undersurface of Pearce's breasts with trembling fingers. "Just hopeful. God, can I touch you soon?"

"Oh man," Pearce groaned. "Anything you want."

"Oh," Wynter breathed out, "I like the sound of that."

"Yeah?" Pearce claimed Wynter's mouth again, walking her backward toward the bed while exploring the warm recesses with her tongue. Then, as quickly as she had claimed the kiss, she broke away. At Wynter's muffled cry of protest, Pearce whispered, "No hurry, remember?" She thought back to *her* first time, and how the memory stayed with her always. But she'd been a teenager then, all raging hormones and desperate desire. Everything had been miraculous and mind blowing and she couldn't touch everywhere fast enough. She and her girlfriend had fumbled and groped and crashed into orgasm almost by accident. This would be different. This would be her gift, to Wynter and to herself. "Watch."

"Wha—" The word died on Wynter's tongue as Pearce gripped the bottom of her T-shirt and stripped it off along with everything beneath, baring her upper body. Her breasts glistened in the half-light, lifting and falling with her rapid breathing, nipples tight and beckoning. "Oh my God."

Pearce fingered the waistband of her jeans, watching Wynter's face, pacing herself until any hint of shyness or discomfort in Wynter's expression was eclipsed by desire. She unbuttoned her fly, one slow *snick* at a time. When Wynter stretched out a tentative hand toward her breasts, she shook her head. "Not yet. Not until we're both naked. And I'm going to undress you next, so it will be a while."

"Just looking at you is making me nuts." Wynter drew a ragged breath. "I'm going to fly apart."

"No," Pearce said tenderly. "You won't. Promise." She pushed her jeans down, kicked off her boots, and stepped free of the tangle. If Wynter was like her, it would be easier to touch than to be touched, and she wanted this to be easy for her. For this time to be a wonderful memory. She reached for Wynter's hands and drew them to her breasts. She shuddered, unprepared for her own response. At the first touch she closed her eyes and bit back a groan. When Wynter flicked her thumbs over her nipples, her knees nearly gave way. "Christ."

"You like that?" Wynter murmured thickly, entranced by the incredible softness, the unbelievable firmness, the enchantment of caressing her this way. She wanted to make her groan again. She wanted to make her scream; she wanted to do things for which she had no words. She captured both nipples and squeezed, laughing softly when Pearce jerked and grabbed her hands away. "You like it, don't you?"

"Too much," Pearce gasped. "Makes me want to come."

Wynter's eyes widened. "Could you?"

"Not usually, but you do…unexpected…things to me." Pearce held Wynter's hands away from her body, not daring to be touched again so soon. She'd felt the first twitches of orgasm shimmer down her thighs. "But you're getting way ahead of me. Let me undress you."

"Yes. Please."

Slowly, carefully, Pearce opened each button on Wynter's shirt. When she parted the fabric a few inches and skimmed her fingertips just inside over the rise of Wynter's breasts, Wynter rested both hands on Pearce's forearms as if to steady herself. Pearce dipped her head and kissed between Wynter's breasts. "Your skin's so soft, so beautiful." She fanned her fingers lower, just grazing the tips of Wynter's nipples, eliciting a quiet whimper. When she cradled the soft weight of each breast in her palms and closed her fingers gently, Wynter sagged against her, her forehead on Pearce's shoulder.

"I don't think I can go this slow," Wynter gasped.

"Yes, you can." Pearce kissed her forehead. "I need you slow. Please."

Wordlessly, Wynter nodded, bracing herself with her hands on Pearce's shoulders. She wanted Pearce to have whatever she needed. No matter what it took to bring her pleasure, she wanted to give it. "When can I touch you?"

"Soon." Pearce knelt and opened Wynter's jeans. With her hands curled around the waistband, she pulled them down below Wynter's hips, exposing her smooth abdomen and the top of each thigh. Encircling Wynter's hips to support her weight, she kissed her stomach.

"Oh!" Wynter's thighs trembled, and she clamped both hands onto Pearce's shoulders. She gripped harder as her knees threatened to buckle. When Pearce kissed her lower, brushing her lips just above the delta between her thighs, she insinuated the fingers of one hand into Pearce's hair and stroked the back of her neck. When the barest hint of Pearce's breath blew over her hypersensitive flesh, she moved Pearce's face away.

Pearce looked up, a gentle question in her eyes. "Wynter?"

"I won't be able to stand it." Wynter caressed her cheek. "I'm afraid you'll make me come right away."

"It's all right?"

Wynter laughed shakily. "Oh God, yes. But not yet."

"Sorry." Pearce nestled her cheek against Wynter's stomach and closed her eyes, breathing Wynter's scent, waiting until her own restless need settled and she could start again.

"Not sorry," Wynter said thickly. "Never be sorry for wanting me." She tilted Pearce's face up to hers and waited until Pearce opened her eyes. "Finish undressing me. I want to lie down with you and feel you everywhere against me."

Tenderly, Pearce drew Wynter's jeans down her legs and helped her out of her sneakers and clothing. Then she stood, amazed at her own weak legs, and using just the tips of her fingers, skimmed off Wynter's blouse. When she'd finished, an inch of space separated their bodies. She lowered her gaze, heart pounding. Looking at Wynter's body was like cresting a mountain and coming upon a vista that stretched until forever—incomprehensively beautiful, indescribably exquisite. Her vision blurred as a swell of desire rose so swiftly she lost her breath. She pulled Wynter to her and held her tightly, moaning as Wynter's body met hers for the first time with no barrier between them. She ached and exalted at the pleasure.

"Your skin is on fire," Wynter marveled as she slid her palms down Pearce's back. "Am I doing that to you?"

Pearce laughed unsteadily. "Oh yeah. I'm just about gone here."

"Oh, I love the way you feel." Wynter spun Pearce in a half turn and pulled her down to the bed. They landed facing one another, arms and legs entwined. She drew her thigh up until it was tight between Pearce's legs. When she felt the hot sheen of Pearce's arousal against her skin, she arched her back and cried out in surprise and wonder. "Oh my God. Oh my God. I never…" She framed Pearce's face. "Is that for me?"

"Unh, unh…" Pearce could barely think. The slide of Wynter's skin over her hot and ready flesh was driving her too high too fast. She swore and flipped Wynter onto her back, easing away from the exquisite pressure. Her stomach tightened almost painfully and she groaned. "Damn it."

"What?" Wynter crooned, nuzzling Pearce's neck. "Hmm, what?" But she knew. She'd felt the swift pulse of Pearce's heart beating against her leg. She loved the way it felt. She loved knowing that Pearce trembled with desire for her. For *her.* "I want to make you come."

"Any more of that and you will." Pearce gritted her teeth and forced herself to breathe past the need to surrender.

"Why are you holding back?" Wynter rolled her hips beneath Pearce's and kissed her neck, tangling her hands in her hair. She slid her mouth along the edge of Pearce's jaw and tugged at her lower lip with her teeth. "I can feel how close you are. It makes me crazy."

Pearce's arms shook with the effort of supporting herself. "It's your first time," she gasped. "I want it to be special."

"Oh, honey," Wynter murmured, "*you* make it special. It's you. Don't you know that?" She caressed her hand down the center of Pearce's back and pushed her leg between Pearce's thighs again, urging Pearce to ride out her passion. She pressed her mouth against Pearce's ear. "Come on me. I know you need to. Please. Let me feel you come on me."

With a hoarse cry, Pearce buried her face in Wynter's neck and let herself fall over the edge. She lost her breath, she lost control, she lost her mind. She shuddered and heard herself crying out and couldn't stop. And while she shivered helplessly, Wynter cradled her in her arms and stroked her through the storm. When she finally could speak, she mumbled, "That was an accident."

Wynter laughed and held her fiercely. "Oh, I've never known anything so amazing as that."

Pearce eased onto her side and stared at Wynter through the receding mists of nearly unbearable pleasure. "It wasn't what I planned."

Wynter kissed her. "You aren't what I planned either."

"You mind?" Pearce slipped her hand between their bodies and circled her palm down the center of Wynter's abdomen. She felt the muscles beneath her fingers tense and twitch and saw Wynter's lips part on a gasp.

"Not the tiniest bit. Pearce…"

Pearce heard the urgency in Wynter's voice as her fingertips brushed through moist curls. "Keep your eyes open."

Wynter caught her lower lip between her teeth. She held on to the steady, tender passion in Pearce's eyes as her body tightened. At the first gentle stroke of Pearce's finger over her clitoris, she arched her back and moaned helplessly.

"Wynter," Pearce said soothingly. "Wynter. Not yet. Not yet, baby."

"Oh, I have to."

"I know. I know." Pearce kissed her softly. "Soon. I promise." As she spoke, she slid her fingers lower, gently curling upward and inside.

"Oh. My. God."

Pearce smiled and pressed deeper. "Ready?"

Wynter clutched Pearce's shoulders, unable to speak. She nodded, her hips rocking on Pearce's hand.

"Don't close your eyes," Pearce whispered as she began to thrust, watching Wynter's face, slowing down when she saw Wynter about to come, speeding up to push her to the edge again. She paced her, pushed her, teased her closer and closer until Wynter was pleading and shaking and blind with pleasure and then, with one deep thrust, brought her over.

❖

Wynter awoke with her head on Pearce's shoulder. She sensed from the darkness outside the windows that it was deep in the night. She lay for a few minutes just listening to Pearce breathe, feeling her heart beat beneath her cheek. It had been many months since she had slept with anyone beside her, and she had never awakened in the arms of a woman. Her hand rested beneath Pearce's breast and their thighs were entwined. Pearce's body was hot.

Her own felt languid and supremely satisfied. Her stomach and thighs were heavy with the aftermath of her orgasm. She remembered Pearce trembling in her arms and crying out at the peak of her passion, and she felt herself quicken. She wanted her again. She understood for the first time in her life how sex could be addicting. She'd never felt anything as exciting, as euphoric, as the sweet satisfaction of knowing she had been the cause of Pearce's pleasure. She moaned softly and involuntarily pressed her hips against Pearce.

"You okay?" Pearce murmured, slowly drawing strands of Wynter's silky hair through her fingers.

"Oh, I'm so so *so* good." She kissed the side of Pearce's breast and ran her hand down Pearce's body. She caressed her stomach and the tops of her thighs, then cupped her lightly between her legs.

"Wynter. What are you doing?" Pearce groaned.

Wynter leaned up on her elbow and kissed the tip of Pearce's chin. "I want to feel you come again. You're so amazing when you do."

"Oh, Jesus," Pearce gasped as Wynter's fingers closed around her. "Easy. God."

Wynter gently bit the tip of Pearce's shoulder and stroked. "Too hard?"

"No. Oh man. Wynter." Pearce's legs stiffened, and she lifted her hips into Wynter's palm. "Don't stop."

"Mmm. I don't plan to." Wynter stroked faster. "Are you going to come for me?"

"Want…me to?"

"Oh yes." Wynter bore down when she felt Pearce grow harder. "Oh yes. You're there, aren't you? Going to come, come for me—"

"Yes." Pearce closed her eyes and clamped her jaws down on a scream. "Yes."

Wynter watched the orgasm wash over Pearce's face, scarcely breathing. When Pearce finally sagged back to the bed, Wynter sighed and curled up against her again, holding her hand still until Pearce stopped throbbing.

When Pearce's breathing grew even once more, Wynter said, "Do you how many women I've examined in my career?"

"Hundreds, probably," Pearce said drowsily.

"At least. And I have never imagined, never conceived, of a woman as beautiful as you."

Pearce roused herself enough to turn on her side so she could see Wynter's face. "No one has ever done to me what you do to me."

"Oh," Wynter murmured, tracing Pearce's lower lip with her fingertip. "Oh, I like that."

"Yeah, me too." She kissed the tip of Wynter's chin, then her mouth. "You feel okay about everything?"

Wynter smiled. "You mean what we just did?"

Solemnly, Pearce nodded, her eyes dark with worry.

"If I didn't have to go to work in the morning, I would keep you in this bed for the next twenty-four hours and make love until we both disintegrated."

"Can I have a rain check?"

"Deal."

Sighing with relief and pleasant fatigue, Pearce drew Wynter's head down to her shoulder. "No more tonight, then. You need some rest."

"Will you stay?"

Pearce rarely spent the night in anyone's bed. She held Wynter tighter. "I'll be here when you wake up."

Chapter Twenty-five

"Wynter," Pearce whispered urgently, shaking Wynter's shoulder. "Wynter!"

"Mmm?"

"Wake up."

Wynter burrowed deeper into the curve of Pearce's shoulder. Somewhere in her consciousness she registered that it was too early to be awake. Typical of those whose lives revolved around tight schedules, she rarely needed a watch or an alarm clock. Her body knew when it was time to get up, and it wasn't. Half asleep, she kissed the warm, soft skin beneath her lips. *Nice.*

"She's awake. You have to do something."

"Who?"

"*Ronnie.*"

Wynter opened one eye and squinted at the bedside clock. It was a quarter to five. "Isn't it Sunday?" she muttered.

"Yes. What—"

"Mmph." Wynter closed her eye. It was Sunday. They didn't make dry rounds until seven thirty on Sunday. Sighing, she molded her body more closely to Pearce's and went back to sleep. Almost.

"Wynter," Pearce repeated, a desperate edge creeping into her voice.

Wynter opened both eyes. "What's the matter, honey?"

"Ronnie is talking or something. Isn't that supposed to wake you up?"

A steady stream of happy, staticky chatter came through the monitor and finally penetrated Wynter's foggy brain. Smiling, she levered herself on top of Pearce and settled comfortably into a new position with one leg between Pearce's and her head pillowed on Pearce's shoulder. Her voice still thick with sleep, she said, "That's her 'I'm awake and playing with my stuffed animals' sound. She's not ready to get up yet."

"Are you sure?"

"Mmm-hmm. Lots of practice."

"Should I go?"

Suddenly much more awake, Wynter raised her head. "Why?"

"Won't she think it's strange that I'm here?"

"She's three, Pearce. She doesn't think that way." Wynter blinked, trying to focus. They'd gone to sleep with the light on in the bathroom behind the partially closed door. Even in the dim light, she could see the concern in Pearce's eyes. "What are you worried about?"

"Nothing."

"Bull. What?"

"She's really cute. I like her."

Wynter pushed up further on one elbow, completely awake. She was used to going from deep sleep to full wakefulness within a matter of seconds, especially when she sensed something serious was going on. Pearce's body was one tense knot beneath her. "But…"

"No buts. I…" Pearce hesitated, thinking it unwise to mention that she almost never woke up in a woman's bed, and never with one who had a little chatterbox wired into the room. "I just don't know very much about kids."

"And…" Wynter clasped Pearce's chin and shook gently. "God, getting information out of you is like breaking into Fort Knox. You can't think that Ronnie seeing me being affectionate with a woman is going to traumatize her?"

"No, but I didn't want her to, you know…get used to seeing me here or anything."

A cool wind blew through Wynter's heart. "In case you're just passing through."

"Fuck," Pearce muttered, feeling Wynter pull away. She caught her with an arm around her shoulders and rolled them over until she was on top, looking down into Wynter's face. "I don't know exactly what I mean, Wynter, okay? I've never been with anyone like you."

Wynter took a deep breath. "I'm sorry." She traced her fingertips over Pearce's eyebrows, then down the side of her face and across her mouth. "Ronnie's fine, but your thinking about her—that means a lot to me. Thank you."

"Yes, but—"

"Hey, we said we'd see what happens. So, one day at a time, right?" Wynter tried to sound as if the uncertainty of that didn't bother her. It shouldn't. She knew that. But knowing was different than feeling. And right now, what she felt was how good the weight of Pearce's body felt on hers. Of how comfortable it had been awakening in her arms. Of how incredibly natural it felt to touch her and be touched by her. Of how damn right everything about last night had seemed. Like stop-action images flickering on a screen, she saw Pearce kneeling with her face pressed against her stomach, remembered the heat of Pearce's skin and the aching pleasure of being filled by her, felt Pearce come beneath her fingertips. Arousal shimmered through her, and she was instantly wet. She closed her eyes and closed her mouth over Pearce's.

Pearce shuddered, ambushed by a flood of feeling. Wynter had a way of doing that to her. Catching her completely unawares, even when they stood face-to-face. It was as if she were a house standing empty, waiting to be filled, and Wynter had just stepped through the door unannounced and populated her barren spaces with touches of home. Groaning, Pearce filled her hands with Wynter's hair and opened her mouth to the demanding heat of Wynter's tongue. Her body throbbed, full and ripe to bursting. Lost in the kiss, she was dimly aware of Wynter's hand thrust between them, reaching down to cup her. She pulled back, rasping, "No."

"Why?" Wynter demanded restlessly, her legs twining around Pearce's. "Let me. *Let me.* I know you're wet."

"Jesus," Pearce muttered, sliding rapidly down the length of Wynter's body until she was nestled between her legs. "I'm done waiting for this."

Wynter raised herself on both elbows and looked down at Pearce through heavy-lidded eyes. "You have control issues."

"No, I don't." Pearce grinned and lightly kissed Wynter's sex. "Not when I'm in charge."

"Do that again," Wynter said, her voice catching in her throat.

Pearce's eyes darkened, and she did, more slowly this time, letting her mouth linger just a whisper above Wynter's center. She blew gently, her own sex pulsing as she heard Wynter's swift gasp.

"You told me to watch. Last night." Wynter's voice was dreamy, but her hips rose insistently. "Go ahead. Let me see."

Groaning, Pearce took her fully into her mouth. Gently, she sucked and teased until Wynter's clitoris turned to rock beneath her tongue, and then she grew still, looking up into Wynter's face. Lips parted, breasts heaving, Wynter was a study in need, her expression half pleasure, half pain. Pearce swept a hand up the center of Wynter's abdomen and closed around her breast. When she squeezed, Wynter's entire body shook.

"Pearce." Wynter sounded as if each word were wrenched from the deepest part of her being. "I'm going to come soon."

Pearce licked her once and grew still.

"Again." Wynter made a sound that was half laugh, half whimper. "There. Almost. There."

Pearce did it again and Wynter's head fell back, a strangled sound escaping her. Pearce wanted to keep her there, teetering on the brink while she drank in her beauty. But she couldn't stop herself from drowning in her, and she slipped her fingers inside as she closed her lips around Wynter's clitoris. Wynter came on the first stroke, whispering Pearce's name as her arms gave out and she fell backward, hips thrashing.

"Pearce," Wynter gasped, one hand flailing ineffectively at Pearce's shoulder. "Come up here. Hurry."

Instantly concerned, Pearce pushed herself up and lay on her side, her head propped on her elbow. "What's the matter?"

Wynter turned her head on the pillow, the only body part she could control. "We've got about two minutes."

Pearce stared at the monitor, listening to Ronnie and realizing that the word *mommy* was now frequently interspersed with the happy chortles. Fuck.

"Do you need to come?" Wynter said weakly.

"No," Pearce lied bravely. It wouldn't be the first time she'd finished off in the shower when time was short.

Wynter smiled, her eyes still lazy. "Liar."

Pearce grinned.

"Do it here, not in the shower."

"Oh man," Pearce muttered, her stomach instantly in knots. Her hips twitched before she could stop it and she knew from Wynter's expression that she'd felt it.

"For me," Wynter murmured.

Pearce kissed her and slipped her fingers between her legs, knowing that she'd be gone in a few strokes. She sucked on Wynter's lower lip as the pressure grew in the pit of her stomach. Groaning, she squeezed and circled the spot that always made her come. She was getting close. Her legs tensed. She opened her eyes and saw Wynter's rapt expression. She whispered, "Coming."

"Mmm, yes." Wynter kissed her and she exploded.

A few minutes later, Pearce opened her eyes and stared at the ceiling. Next to the bed, the monitor carried the sounds of Wynter and Ronnie's excited conversation to her. She pictured them together and wondered what she was doing in Wynter's life. Just passing through, Wynter had said. She rolled on her side, straining to make out the words of mother and child. Real people with real feelings. Wynter deserved more than a casual encounter. They both deserved more than Pearce had to offer.

Pearce closed her eyes and listened to their voices, wanting just a few more moments of simple happiness.

❖

"Here you go," Wynter said, settling Ronnie into one of the booster seats at Mina's kitchen table next to the other children. She put the backpack with Ronnie's favorite toys, coloring books, and trucks on the floor. "I should be back in the morning tomorrow unless there's a heavy OR schedule. I'll call you."

"That's fine," Mina said automatically.

Wynter kissed Mina's cheek. "Thanks. Bye."

Mina glanced at the clock, then at Wynter. "You're early and you're leaving without breakfast?"

"I've got a few things to do before I leave for work."

"Uh-huh." Mina narrowed her eyes. "Nice try." She poured milk into three cereal bowls and set them in front of the kids. "Give."

Wynter moved closer to Mina where she stood by the sink and lowered her voice. "I have company."

"Company." Mina's voice rose with interest. "You don't say. And just who might that be?"

"Look, I'll tell you all about it—"

"You just bet you will. But for now, I want the name."

Wynter blushed. "Pearce."

Mina's expression grew serious. "All-night kind of company?"

"Yes."

"And everything's all right?"

"Everything's great." Wynter knew she was grinning like an idiot, but she couldn't stop.

"I wasn't asking about *that*, but I'm certainly glad to hear it," Mina said with arch playfulness. "Call me later when you get a break."

"I'm really okay. She's wonderful." Wynter clasped Mina's hand. "You don't have to worry about me."

"You know I'd be doing the same thing if she were some stud muffin, so don't try to make more out of it than it is. Call me later."

Wynter nodded. "I will. Promise."

Smiling, Mina watched Wynter hurry away, thinking that there wasn't all that much difference between players of the male and female varieties—the game still seemed to be the same.

❖

"Hey," Wynter said, leaning down to kiss Pearce on the mouth. "Time to wake up."

Pearce opened her eyes, blinked once, then caught Wynter around the waist and pulled her down onto the bed. "I'm awake."

Laughing, Wynter got a hand between them and pushed Pearce away. "I'm dressed, and you need a shower, and we have to be at the hospital in forty-five minutes."

"Where's Ronnie?"

"Next door having breakfast."

Pearce frowned. "How did I miss that?"

Wynter grinned and tapped Pearce's chin. "I guess someone did you in last night."

"Oh yeah?" Pearce growled and flipped Wynter over onto her back. Then she straddled her hips and pinned her wrists to the bed. "Says who?"

Wynter looked up, stunned. It was the first time she'd seen Pearce nude in full light. Her hands and mouth and body knew the softness, the curves and planes, of Pearce's form. They were indelibly marked on her consciousness. But now she could see the delicate arch of her collarbones, the teasing sway of her breasts, and the tight inviting curve of her abdomen as it swept down to the bend in her thighs. Trembling, she touched the pale white line in the center of Pearce's lower lip. "It's a good thing I ran into you. Without this tiny scar, I'd worry that you weren't human. You're almost too beautiful to look at."

Shaking her head, Pearce leaned down and kissed Wynter on the mouth, then the angle of her jaw, then her neck. "Should I worry that your judgment seems to be impaired, considering that you're on call for my service today?"

"I should've kissed you four years ago."

Pearce released Wynter's hands and pulled her up until they sat facing one another, her hips between Wynter's spread legs, her knees bent over Wynter's thighs. She clasped her lightly around the waist. "Why?"

"Because I wanted to. Because I wanted you."

"Did you ever think you were—"

"No," Wynter said with a sigh, resting her cheek on Pearce's shoulder, her hands on Pearce's thighs. "And I don't know why, except by the time I had a chance to think about the fact that my life wasn't going the way I wanted it to go, I was already married. And when I saw you that first time, Ronnie was coming."

"Just because you slept with me last night doesn't mean you're—"

"Don't." Wynter lifted her head. "Don't try to convince me that what I'm feeling is an accident."

Pearce swept her fingers through Wynter's hair, then lifted it as it flowed over the back of her hand and kissed Wynter's neck just above the angle of her shoulder. "I wasn't trying to. But it's a big change."

"Not a change. A discovery." Wynter clasped the back of Pearce's neck, pressing Pearce's mouth harder against her skin. "I love your mouth on me. I love your hands on me. I love your hands *inside* of me." She moaned as Pearce's teeth closed on the muscle in her neck. "What do you think that says about me?" She squeezed Pearce's neck harder and whispered, "Suck me."

Gasping at the small point of pain, Wynter dropped her head back, urging Pearce on. "I love the way you get wet for me. I love how hard your nipples are when you're excited. I love feeling you come when I touch you. When *I* touch you." She moaned. "God, that feels so good."

Pearce pulled away, her chest heaving. "Fuck. You make me so crazy, I don't know what I'm doing half the time." Tenderly, she kissed the mark she had left. "Sorry."

"I'm just sorry we don't have time for more." Wynter kissed her hungrily, thrusting her tongue into Pearce's mouth, then pulling away just as abruptly. "I want you so much right now."

"We can't go back," Pearce said, running her thumb over Wynter's mouth. "And we can't make up for lost time overnight." She grinned. "I'm not entirely certain I can even walk."

Wynter smiled, her lips full and flushed with arousal. "Good." With a sudden powerful thrust of her hips, she dislodged Pearce, who landed on her back on the bed with a surprised grunt. "Go shower. If we're late for rounds, the senior resident will be pissed."

"Tease!" Pearce made a grab for her. "The senior resident's already pissed."

Laughing, Wynter rolled off the bed and danced out of reach. "Then I guess it's a good thing you can't run."

CHAPTER TWENTY-SIX

Pearce carried her coffee to the round table in the far corner of the cafeteria where Wynter waited with Bruce, who had been on call Saturday night. Wynter looked up and smiled at her, and Pearce felt a flutter in her chest. She grinned, her eyes traveling from Wynter's face down her body. She frowned when she saw the bruise low on Wynter's neck, exposed by the vee of her scrub shirt. She raised her eyebrows and tugged at her own shirt, mimicking covering part of her throat. Wynter blushed and adjusted hers. Remembering exactly how that bruise had gotten there, Pearce had to admit to a small surge of pleasure. As she sat down, she saw Bruce staring at her with a pensive expression on his face. She met his eyes and held them until he looked away. Then she took her list from her shirt pocket, unfolded it carefully, and set it in front of her. "Okay. From the top."

After they'd run the list of patients and Bruce had left for home, she and Wynter were the only ones remaining at the table. "Tired?"

"A little." Wynter smiled. "Good tired."

"Hopefully today will be slow and you'll have a chance to catch a little sleep."

"Are there any admissions this afternoon?" In recent years, insurance companies had revamped their reimbursement scale to force physicians to bring patients into the hospital on the day of surgery rather than admitting them the afternoon before and keeping them overnight prior to their procedures. When previously there had been a dozen or more patients admitted to the hospital in the afternoon for surgery the next day, now there often were none.

"We're still expecting the transfer from Harrisburg that was supposed to come in yesterday morning. If the bed situation has eased up, she'll probably show up this afternoon."

"The one with the leaking anastomosis?"

"Right."

Wynter looked down at her list. "She's coming to your father, right?"

Pearce nodded.

"Do you think he'll want to operate tonight?"

"It depends on how she looks." Pearce finished her coffee and rolled the cup between her palms. "He's got five cases scheduled for tomorrow. If it looks like she's going to need to go, he'll do it tonight so as not to back up tomorrow. If she looks like she'll hold off a couple of days, he might wait until Tuesday."

"If her surgery was six days ago and they think she's leaking, she's not going to hold for another couple of days. I'll get another CAT scan as soon as she arrives and get started on the preop tests."

"Page me when she comes in."

"It's not necessary. You're off today and—"

"She's a new admission to the service. I have to see her." Pearce set her cup down. "You can call him with your assessment. I won't get in your way over it."

"I know," Wynter said gently. "I just thought I could give you a break."

"It's okay. I feel fine."

"I guess you're used to all-night recreational activities," Wynter said with the barest hint of sarcasm. She couldn't help thinking of the appreciative looks cast in Pearce's direction by more than one woman.

Pearce studied Wynter, her expression placid. "It's probably good that we're sitting in the cafeteria on opposite sides of the table. Otherwise, I'd be tempted to kiss you. You're very sexy when you're jealous."

"I'm not jealous!"

Pearce grinned.

"I'm *not*." Annoyed because it was true and Pearce had noticed, Wynter retorted without thinking, "I suppose you think I've never stayed up all night screwing before?" The instant she said it, she regretted it, especially when she saw Pearce's eyes darken and her jaw set hard. "Pearce—"

"I'll be on my beeper if you need me." Pearce pushed her chair back and stood.

"Please don't go. I'm sorry. That was thoughtless."

"No, I'm sure it's true. I do know where babies come from."

"Damn it," Wynter seethed, looking around the room, aware of their fellow residents everywhere. She couldn't chase her without creating a scene. "Please. Five minutes."

Pearce wanted to walk away. Wynter was like no woman in her experience. She was used to wild sex with wild women who were unfettered or, at the very least, unconcerned about their attachments. She'd never been jealous of who else they were sleeping with and definitely had never cared about anyone in their past. Since the moment she'd learned that Wynter was married, she'd steadfastly refused to think about it. Now that she'd touched her, held her, made love to her, thinking about her being with someone else incensed her. She knew it was crazy, and she couldn't stop. She took a breath. "Look. It's okay. You don't have anything to explain to me."

"If you don't sit down, everyone in this room is going to hear that you're the best lay I've ever had."

"Uh…" Pearce coughed and her mind went blank. She did the only thing possible. She pulled out the chair and sat back down.

Wynter leaned forward, her eyes fierce. "Do you remember what I said to you this morning? About how I felt when you touched me? When I touched you?"

Pearce swallowed. Her head was buzzing. "Wynter—"

"Be quiet and listen. I can't think of any way to say this that doesn't sound like a cliché, but it's true. I've never been so *present*, so much myself, as I was with you last night. That means everything to me."

Me too. Pearce knew it, and she had no idea what to do with that fact. She shook her head, barely recognizing herself. "You must think I'm nuts, going off about something that's already over."

Wynter smiled. "No, not really. I think you're sexy when you're jealous."

"Ha." Pearce felt the tightness in her chest ease. *That means everything to me.* She'd been told some pretty outrageous things by more than a few women after a night of passion, but nothing anyone else had ever said to her had made her feel quite so good. "So how about I drop by later on today, see the new admission, and take you to din—"

"Damn," Wynter muttered as she looked down at the readout on her beeper. She looked up as Pearce's beeper went off and when she saw the grim set of her face, she knew. "The chief?"

"Yeah." Pearce stood. "You too?"

Wynter nodded. "You don't think—"

"There's no way he'd know, and even if he did, as long as it didn't interfere with work, it wouldn't be a problem." She smiled and wished she could take Wynter's hand. "Come on. Let's go see what he wants."

Taking a breath to settle herself, Wynter nodded. "Aye aye, Chief." At Pearce's grin, she added, "And don't get too used to that."

❖

The surgery offices were deserted at 8:00 a.m. on Sunday. The door to Ambrose Rifkin's personal office stood open beyond the large partitioned area where his secretary usually protected his domain. Despite the open door, Pearce knocked.

"Come."

Ambrose Rifkin, dressed in scrubs, reclined behind his desk with his leather chair tilted back and a file folder balanced on his knee. Despite his casual demeanor, neither Pearce nor Wynter spoke until he finished making a note in the margin of one of the chart pages, closed the folder, and dropped it onto his desk. He sat forward and looked from one to the other.

"Please sit down."

Pearce and Wynter took the adjoining chairs in front of his desk.

"I just spoke to Tom Larson in Harrisburg. The patient's on her way and should be here within the hour. Let's get her directly to CAT scan from the ER. The OR is standing by."

"I could've taken care of that, sir," Pearce said quietly.

"I was here." His tone of voice implied that Pearce should have been as well.

She said nothing.

He leaned back slightly and regarded Wynter. In a conversational tone of voice, he said, "Fifty years ago, there were very few general surgical subspecialties. At the time, Isaac Rifkin was the chairman of surgery, and one morning he assembled his senior residents in his office." He glanced at a framed photo on the far wall that showed six men in white lab coats standing in front of one of the older buildings in the hospital complex.

Wynter followed his gaze. She didn't recognize any of them.

"He had evaluated his people, and he not only recognized their talents, but he predicted the future of surgery. He sent one to France to study with a noted cranial-facial surgeon. That resident would return and become the first chief of plastic surgery. He sent another to St. Louis to work with a very gifted general surgeon whose practice was all pediatric in nature. That resident would return to establish the Children's Hospital. He named another to train in vascular surgery, another in cancer, and so on." He moved his hand across his blotter, as if indicating the world beneath his fingertips, and then he looked at Wynter. "Tom Larson tells me that his chief resident just took six months' leave for…health reasons. The slot is open, and he doesn't have anyone experienced enough to fill it."

Wynter's stomach clutched and her heart raced wildly in her chest. She tried to keep her expression neutral, but she couldn't prevent her hands from fisting around the wooden arms of the chair. She'd heard of residents being sent to other programs with no choice in the matter.

"It's an excellent opportunity for the kind of experience a resident needs to move into an academic position." He studied her. "I'd like you to go."

"For how…" Her voice cracked and she cleared her throat. "For how long, sir?"

"Six months. Then we'll reevaluate the situation."

Wynter was aware of Pearce shifting ever so slightly in the chair beside her. "Thank you, Dr. Rifkin. I'm honored. Truly. I'm afraid I can't do that."

The room was very quiet. Ambrose Rifkin's face remained composed; his eyes, not quite as dark as Pearce's but just as sharp, moved slowly over Wynter's face.

"Why would that be?"

"I have a daughter, and there's no way I could arrange for child care up there in a reasonable amount of time. We just moved here, and I've barely gotten her settled."

"You're divorced, aren't you?"

Wynter felt her face go hot, but she held his gaze. "Yes."

"But you have a workable arrangement here for the child?"

"Yes," Wynter said quickly. "The wife of one of the anesthesia residents…" She realized he wouldn't be interested in the details. "A very good one, sir."

"And she's how old?"

"She's three." Wynter couldn't help but smile.

"Three. Well, I can't imagine that your being absent for that period of time would make all that much difference, since you have established a good child-care situation here."

Wynter heard Pearce's sharp intake of breath, but she was too busy trying to understand what Ambrose Rifkin had just said. Then a wave of heat followed by a sudden chill passed through her. "You mean leave her here while I go there?"

"Yes."

"Sir," Pearce began, her voice tight. "I don't think—"

"I'm sorry," Wynter said calmly. "That won't be possible."

Ambrose Rifkin appeared unperturbed, as if Wynter had not just told him no. "Since she's not in school, or—"

"Sir, I wouldn't care how old she was or what the situation. I'm not leaving her for six months. It's difficult enough as it is with the amount of time I have to spend away."

"I see. And what are your plans for the future, Dr. Thompson?"

"I've always planned on a subspecialty in breast surgery. I'll be looking for a fellowship after I finish general surgery."

"That's a nice field for a woman," Ambrose Rifkin said with just the slightest hint of condescension. "Not particularly demanding and very little emergency work."

Wynter said nothing. He was right, insofar as his assessment had gone. A practice limited to surgical treatment of breast disease was usually a Monday-through-Friday, seven-to-five kind of job, and it would allow her time to spend with her daughter. It was also a critical facet of women's health care, and she'd always been drawn to that. Oncologic surgery was on the forefront of medical science, and she had no doubt that she would be challenged as well as rewarded by her choice. There was no point in mentioning any of those things, because for a man like Ambrose Rifkin, the rewards would be far too meager to satisfy.

"Starting tomorrow, Dr. Thompson," Ambrose Rifkin said, "I'm moving you to the vascular service as the acting chief."

"Yes sir," Wynter said. It was not a particularly welcome transfer, but it wasn't horrible. Vascular surgery was technically challenging and interesting. She'd miss working so closely with Pearce, but she'd also have more responsibility. It was all part of the game.

"I've decided to bring Dr. Dzubrow out of the lab," the chairman said, turning his attention to Pearce, who sat rigidly upright. "He'll take over as acting chief on my service. That will free you up to go to Harrisburg. Tonight."

❖

Wynter and Pearce did not speak as they walked side by side to the women's locker room. Once inside, Pearce went directly to her locker and opened it. She pulled out a handful of scrubs and piled them on the bench. She reached back inside for her lab coat, and then pulled her arm out abruptly and slammed the door so violently that the entire row of metal lockers shook.

"Fuck." Pearce leaned her back against her locker and closed her eyes.

Wynter sat down on the bench and placed her hand gently on the pile of scrubs, wishing it were Pearce she was touching. "What's going on?"

"I don't know. You heard him. I'm getting farmed out and he's moving Dzubrow in."

"Is it my fault? Because I said I wouldn't go?"

Pearce opened her eyes and gazed down at Wynter. Slowly, she shook her head. "No. I don't think so. That took balls, by the way."

Wynter grimaced. "No, it didn't. It didn't take anything at all. There's no way I'd leave her."

"He could probably get rid of you for that."

"Maybe. It wouldn't matter. It wouldn't change my mind."

"Really?"

"Really," Wynter said quietly. It had just begun to hit her that within a matter of hours, Pearce would be gone. For weeks and months and most probably, forever. Life would carry on much as it had before their brief interlude. The sadness was swift and aching. She stood. "It doesn't mean you won't get the chief resident's job next year."

"Maybe," Pearce sighed. "Maybe not. He's grooming Dzubrow for something."

"Can you talk to him? Tell him you don't want to go?"

Pearce laughed hollowly. "Sure I can. If I want to finish up with the crappiest rotations and no shot at all of ever getting an academic job." She tried to focus on what she needed to do to keep her career on track, but all she could think was that she was going to have to walk out the door and get into her car and drive away. That she wouldn't be able to take Wynter to dinner that night, or breakfast the next morning, or spend another night in her bed—perhaps ever. She couldn't think about that now. She didn't have the luxury to worry about her personal life. She sighed and opened her locker again. As she drew out her lab coat, she said, "If I'd known this was going to happen, I wouldn't have come over last night. I'm sorry."

"Time has never been on our side."

"No," Pearce said. She pulled a key off her key ring and held it out. "Here. To the old resident's room. Look after…it…for me."

"I will." Wynter's throat ached as she rose and kissed Pearce on the cheek. "Drive carefully."

"Yeah. I will." Pearce watched Wynter turn and leave. She ignored the pain in her chest. Loss was nothing new, and she should know by now not to let anyone in deep enough to miss. She shrugged into her leather jacket, palmed her keys, and grabbed her scrubs. Time to move on.

Chapter Twenty-seven

Wynter came instantly awake at the sound of the door opening. The small, windowless room was completely dark, without even a digital clock to cut the blackness.

"Occupied," she called out irritably. She'd never understand why huge academic institutions couldn't afford decent on-call rooms, but she'd never run across one yet. Whenever she'd had a rotation in a small community hospital, the residents were treated infinitely better. She'd had one rotation where she received three meals a day for free, and there'd even been a television in her *private* on-call room. Amazing. At the University Hospital, however, that was not the case. Everyone vied for limited sleeping space, and even though she'd heard rumors that new on-call rooms were planned for the next addition to the megalithic complex, she'd believe it when she slept in one.

"It's me," Pearce whispered as she closed the door and flipped the lock.

"Pearce?" Wynter bolted upright. "What time is it?"

"Quarter after one."

Wynter snapped on the bedside table lamp and checked her beeper to make sure it was working. When she saw that it was, she put it down and swung her legs over the side of the narrow bed. She pushed both hands through her hair and then dropped her hands to her sides, curling her fingers around the thin mattress. She looked up at Pearce, who still stood just inside the door. She was in jeans, her black boots, and a black fisherman's sweater. She held her leather jacket in her fist. "What are you doing here?"

Pearce shrugged. "I don't know."

"You're supposed to be in Harrisburg in about six hours."

"I know."

"Are you still going?"

"Yes."

"Take off your clothes and come to bed." Wynter snapped off the light.

Pearce kicked off her boots, unsnapped her jeans and pushed them off, and added her sweater to the pile. Although the room was dark once again, Wynter's figure was imprinted on the backs of her eyelids in a blaze of yellow light. She made her way to the narrow hospital-issue bed and put one hand down, finding the sheets pulled back in welcome. She sat down and slid under, turning on her side to face Wynter. She stretched out her arm, found Wynter's bare shoulder, and pulled her close.

Wynter nestled her cheek against Pearce's chest and wrapped an arm around her waist. The bed was narrow for one, dangerously so for two, and she slid her thigh between Pearce's as much to anchor them as to be close to her.

"Is it okay if we don't make love?" Pearce murmured. She smoothed her lips over Wynter's forehead. She'd been in her car and had gotten as far as Doylestown before turning back. She hadn't felt such a chasm of despair since her grandmother had died, and her only thought as the miles stretched away behind her had been of lying in Wynter's arms that morning and how good it had felt. Even as she'd made an illegal U-turn across the median, she'd refused to question her actions. She knew any answers she might find would only frighten her. She closed her eyes and tightened her hold, waiting for Wynter to ask.

"This is fine just like this," Wynter whispered. She kissed the hollow at the base of Pearce's throat and rubbed her face against Pearce's skin. She loved Pearce's smell, windblown and untamed. She was aware of desire, the steady pulse of flesh seeking flesh, but she could enjoy the wanting without craving satisfaction. For the moment. She kissed Pearce's throat again, then the underside of her jaw. "Are you all right?"

"Pissed." Pearce stroked Wynter's shoulders and down her arm, slowly smoothing her fingers up and down, reveling in the softness of her skin and the steel beneath it.

"Mmm. Me too." Wynter sighed. "I know you have to go, but I want you to be angry that we're being separated. I guess I…I'll miss you."

Pearce gave a small groan and buried her face in Wynter's hair. "Yeah. I know."

"But I'll probably see you when you get a weekend off, right?" Wynter tried to sound upbeat, but they both knew how hard it would be to coordinate their schedules, especially long distance. "We're supposed to go running, remember."

"Sure." Pearce knew that now was the time to call things off, and if she'd just kept driving, it wouldn't even have been an issue. No complications. They'd agreed. They'd had a night together. A great night, sure. A night like none she could ever remember. But it was just a night, like so many nights before. A few hours of frantic connection, of desperate joining, of grateful respite from loneliness. So why wasn't that enough? "I expect you'll be seeing other people."

Seeing other people. Wynter knew what the words meant, she just hadn't considered them in relationship to herself for quite some time. Even after her divorce, the last thing she'd wanted to do was create any more chaos in her life by getting involved with someone. She'd had to take time off from the surgery residency in the midst of the divorce because moving out, arranging child care, and dealing with all the legal issues was too much for her to handle and still work the way she needed to. Getting the temporary emergency room position had been a godsend. She'd been able to work and had gotten paid. That was all she had wanted. Now she had an excellent residency position, a new home, and a great environment for her daughter. This was not the time to upset the hard-won balance in her life.

"I don't know," Wynter said. "I'm not sure I want to."

"But if you do," Pearce forced herself to say. "You know, you should."

Wynter doubted it would be long before Pearce sought company, and she could hardly ask her not to. From everything she had witnessed, let alone what she had heard, she knew that Pearce was no stranger to casual encounters. She smoothed her hand between Pearce's breasts, a movement so new to her, and yet completely familiar. Without knowing completely *how* she knew, she was aware that she wouldn't be with a man. Ever again. "Yes. All right."

Pearce closed her eyes tightly. That was right. That was best. Then why did that empty space inside of her come roaring back again?

"Pearce?"

"Yeah?"

"Why did you come back here tonight?"

There it was again. The question she didn't want to ask. The answer she didn't want to face because it left her not knowing what her next step would be. "I didn't want to say goodbye."

Wynter kissed the spot beneath Pearce's breast where her heart tapped out a strong, sharp rhythm. "Good. Neither do I."

"Where does that leave us?"

"I don't know, but I feel better than I did when I left you this morning."

"Doesn't take much to make you happy," Pearce murmured, sifting her fingers through Wynter's hair.

Wynter laughed softly. "That's what you think."

Pearce tilted Wynter's chin up and kissed her slowly, a lingering, searching kiss that would not soon be forgotten.

"Good start," Wynter murmured. "Now go to sleep. You have to drive soon."

Pearce closed her eyes, but she didn't sleep. She had only a few more hours with Wynter, fleeting time too precious to lose.

❖

At nine thirty the next morning, Wynter shuffled to her front door, opened it a crack, and said, "Go away."

"You think I don't know when you come home?"

"Mina," Wynter said with as much patience as she could muster, bracing her knee against the door as Mina pushed from the other side, "I'm going to bed now. Ronnie will be home in five hours, and I'm going to have to play mommy."

"You can go to sleep just as soon as we have our little talk."

"Later," Wynter said, trying to close the door. She looked down and saw Mina's foot, encased in her substantial snow boot, blocking the way. "Mina…"

"This is the first time in six weeks you haven't stopped over to chat when you came home. What's going on?"

"Just tired." Despite her desperate need to be alone, Wynter opened the door. "Come inside. It's freezing out."

Mina forged ahead like a great ship steaming into port, and she didn't stop until she was well into the living room, where she removed her woolen coat and draped it over the back of the couch. "Let's go upstairs and put you to bed. We can talk there."

Wordlessly, Wynter trudged upstairs. In sweats and a T-shirt, she crawled under the covers and curled up on her side. When Mina came in, she eased over enough so that Mina could sit beside her, several pillows propped behind the small of her back.

"Thank God this child will be out of here in a few weeks. There's not enough room inside my body for it and all of my other parts." Mina struggled to turn enough to see Wynter's face. "You've been crying."

"I pity your children. I really do. They'll never have any secrets."

Mina smiled and petted Wynter's hair. "Now is it work or your personal life?"

"Both." Wynter sighed, then went on to explain about Ambrose Rifkin's plan to send her to an outside rotation and the fact that she'd refused and been transferred to another service instead.

"He sounds like a charmer."

"Unfortunately, he's a brilliant surgeon and I can learn a lot from him."

"Doesn't mean he's not a...SOB."

"True."

"Somehow, I can see that little power play making you *mad*, but not causing any tears. What else?"

Wynter bunched her pillow into a fat misshapen ball and wrapped her arms around it. Her arms felt empty without Pearce, and it frightened her that she could feel that way after only holding her a few times. "He sent Pearce instead. She's gone."

"For how long?"

Wynter shrugged. "Six months at least. It might as well be six years."

"Honey," Mina said gently, "are you serious about this girl?"

"Serious? Serious how?" Wynter rolled onto her back and stared at the ceiling. She didn't see the spiderweb of fine cracks. She saw Pearce's face above her, intense, fiercely focused, wildly passionate. "I had the most incredible night of my life with her."

"That's saying something," Mina agreed. "Are we just talking sex here? Because I think that's reproducible given the right circumstances, no matter what kind of parts someone brings to the table."

"No, it isn't." Wynter rolled over again and propped her chin in her hand. "It goes both ways, making love. It's not just how much pleasure someone brings you when they touch you, but how good you feel when you touch them back. Touching her was the most amazing thing I've ever experienced. And it had *everything* to do with the parts." Wynter smiled faintly. "Especially when they're hers. She's so beautiful."

"Do you think you'd feel that way with another woman? Or is it just her?"

"It's her. Everything about her." Wynter shrugged. "And part of that is that she's a woman. I never knew I wanted that, needed that, until I touched her. Now I know."

"And you're okay with that?"

"It feels too good not to be."

"Right," Mina said, dusting her hands together as if one problem had been solved. "So we've established that you've now gone over to the dark side." She smiled when Wynter laughed. "Now explain to me why, assuming that Pearce has any kind of brain in her head at all—which from meeting her, I'd say she does—she would agree to just up and leave."

"She doesn't have any choice."

"Everyone always has a choice. You didn't go."

"That's different," Wynter said. "If he'd fired me for refusing to go, I probably could've won if I'd contested it. It would have been ugly, but I probably would've won. And even if I hadn't, I was willing to take that chance."

"You're willing to give up your career?"

"For Ronnie? Of course." Wynter shook her head. "I can see where you're trying to take this argument. You *should* go to law school. But Ronnie is a child, *my* child, and she didn't choose to have a mother who's a surgeon. I can't make her pay any more than she already does for my choices. Things are different with Pearce."

"What would've happened if she'd said no? He's her father. Wouldn't he make exceptions for her?"

Wynter snorted. "I don't think so. From what I can see, he's never made any exceptions for her. Quite the opposite. The expectations placed on her are enormous."

"Well, what could he do?"

"First of all, you don't say no to the chairman if you have any desire to get a good fellowship or a top faculty appointment. The right connections can make or break a career, and Ambrose Rifkin can pretty much place residents wherever he wants."

"Why would he try to make life difficult for his daughter? I don't get it."

"I'm not so sure it's about making life difficult for *her*. I think it's about paving the way for this other resident. He probably figures Pearce is the easier person to place because she's so damn good." Wynter gave an aggravated sigh. "And who cares what she has to suffer through to get there."

"There's something very wrong with a process that makes you think it's all right for someone to treat anyone, let alone their own child, this way. Why aren't the both of you fighting mad?"

"We're mad," Wynter said quietly. "But I don't see a way out right now."

"So just what do you plan to do? Forget about her? Wait to see if she turns up again in a few months and still wants to play house?"

"That's not very likely. By the time she comes back, we'll probably be in different places again." Wynter closed her eyes, suddenly more weary than tired. She knew that neither she nor Pearce had very much control over their lives at this point and that any kind of relationship during training was fraught with difficulty and usually didn't last. She'd had a wonderful awakening, a brilliant night of discovery with a tender, passionate, wildly beautiful woman. That experience alone should be enough to make her happy and, in all likelihood, would have to be enough. She knew it. She'd been telling herself that since the first time she'd said goodbye to Pearce the day before. Nevertheless, she clenched her fists and said, "I don't know what I'm going to do, but I don't plan on waiting another four years to feel something like this again."

"Even if you have to find it with someone other than her?"

Wynter said nothing, wondering how that could ever be possible.

CHAPTER TWENTY-EIGHT

Wynter popped the top on a can of Diet Coke and dropped onto the cracked dark green vinyl sofa pushed against one wall in the surgeons' lounge. It was flanked by a battered refrigerator at one end and a large, square end table at the other. A phone and a pile of last year's magazines covered the table's surface. She pushed some of the clutter aside and, after draining half the soda, put down the can. Closing her eyes, she let her head fall back, wishing she could go to sleep. Unfortunately, she was only halfway through her night on call, and if the first six hours had been any indication, it was going to be brutal. Immediately after evening sign-out rounds, she'd gotten a call from one of the intensive care nurses reporting that the patient in whom they'd corrected a carotid blockage the previous morning could no longer recall his name and had one-sided weakness. She'd known immediately that the area of surgical repair was blocked, and that if it were not treated immediately the patient would have a full-blown stroke. As she'd hurried to the ICU, she'd paged the attending, and within an hour, they were in the operating room. No sooner had they finished that case then the trauma fellow had called about a twenty-year-old drug dealer who had ended up on the wrong end of a machete. In addition to several stab wounds to the chest, he had also sustained a complete transection of his brachial artery and was in danger of losing his hand.

She'd learned long ago that the only way to get through a night like this was not to think about the time or how tired she was or all the things she had left to do. When she heard footsteps and then felt someone settle onto the other end of the sofa, she didn't bother to look over. Five more minutes. She'd give herself five more minutes to rest, and then she'd get up and check the arteriograms that had been finished late in the day.

"Heard anything from Pearce?" Tammy asked, heaving her feet, clogs and all, up onto the coffee table.

"No." Wynter didn't open her eyes. Even though she didn't want to, she heard herself say, "Have you?"

"*I* didn't even know she was gone until yesterday." Tammy's usual undertone of petulance and annoyance was absent. "This sucks."

"Yes," Wynter agreed, finally opening her eyes. Tammy looked as tired as Wynter felt. It'd been almost three days since Pearce had left. Wynter kept hoping that Pearce would call, despite the fact that she didn't really expect her to. Pearce would be busy getting adjusted to a new hospital, a new group of residents. And in all likelihood, they'd put her on call immediately. Besides, what was there to say? That was the most frustrating part of all. They both understood what was required of them. They both accepted that their life would not be their own for years. Still, being powerless did not sit well. "Sucks big-time."

"Plus Dzubrow is a real pain in the ass," Tammy muttered.

Although Wynter tended to agree with Tammy from what she had seen of him, she made no comment. It was prudent not to openly criticize other residents. She never knew when she might find herself working closely on the same service with one of them.

"Bruce says he's hogging all the good cases," Tammy went on. "Pearce didn't need to steal cases. She already knows what she's doing."

"He's probably just trying to get back into the swing of things after coming out of the lab," Wynter suggested mildly.

Tammy gave her a look. "He was never *in* the swing of things. I heard him tell one of the other guys that he's got an offer from the NIH, and that's why Rifkin brought him out of the lab early. He's always been a lab rat. I don't even know why he wanted to be a surgeon."

What Tammy said made sense. It would explain the sudden shift in the residents between services, and why Pearce had been farmed out. Ambrose Rifkin was priming Dzubrow for the chief resident's position, which would bolster his credentials at the NIH. She wondered if Pearce knew. Surely she must suspect, and although Wynter knew Pearce would never admit it, it must hurt. "God damn it."

She hadn't even realized she'd cursed aloud until Tammy laughed. Wynter smiled wryly and said, "Nothing lasts forever—even pain."

"It just feels like it does," Tammy said with a sigh. "If you hear from her, tell her I…we miss her."

"Sure." Wynter wondered why Tammy thought *she* would be the one to hear, but she nodded. *Tell her I miss her.* She was too tired to be jealous. Almost too tired to miss Pearce. Almost.

By six o'clock in the morning she was functioning on autopilot. She'd never gotten to bed, never closed her eyes again after the few minutes in the lounge with Tammy. It was just one of those nights where the emergency cases and traumas never stopped coming, and all she could do was forget that anything else in the world existed except the next crisis. The hospital was the universe, the operating room her only reality. When her beeper went off just as she reached the coffee in the cafeteria line, she contemplated tossing it into the trash. She glanced at the readout and saw that it was the page operator, which usually meant an outside call. Heart racing, thinking that Mina was calling about a problem with Ronnie, she left her tray on the track in front of the commercial coffee urns and hurried to the nearest phone.

"Dr. Thompson," she said briskly when the operator answered.

"I've got an outside call for you, Doctor. Hold please."

Wynter heard a series of clicks. Then her heart leapt again at the sound of the rich, slightly husky voice.

"Wynter?"

"Pearce?"

"I thought I'd try to catch you before the OR."

Wynter turned her back to the cafeteria and leaned against the wall, much more awake than she had been just a few minutes before. "How are you doing?"

"Just finished the night from hell."

"You too? Was it a full moon?"

Pearce chuckled. "Must've been."

"How's it going out there?"

"Not bad. Standard community hospital stuff. Busy."

"That's good."

Silence stretched until Wynter feared the connection had been broken. "Pearce?"

"You're on call again Saturday, right?"

"Yes," Wynter replied, confused. "But I—"

"I want to see you. Friday night?"

Despite the tightening in her stomach and the rapid flurry in her chest, Wynter tried to be rational. "Aren't you on call Saturday too?"

"Not until eight o'clock in the morning."

"It's too far for you to drive back here after work Friday and then get back there in the morning." Wynter closed her eyes, remembering Pearce as she'd last seen her, dressed in black, her eyes even darker. She'd wanted to kiss her but she hadn't. Hadn't wanted that final proof of their parting when Pearce said goodbye with the kiss still lingering on her lips. "I'm so glad you called."

"I miss you."

"Oh, I miss you too."

"So I'll see you Friday."

"Pearce," Wynter murmured. "I want to see you. I do. But I already told Mina and Ken I'd watch the kids—"

"I should be out of here by six, so I'll see you about eight. I'll help."

Wynter laughed, ridiculously happy. "Help what?"

"I don't know. Whatever it is you do with them. The kids."

"Janie's got a sleepover with her friends. The little ones will be in bed. Probably asleep."

Pearce's voice dropped even lower. "All the better. See you, Doc."

"See you," Wynter whispered. When she hung up, she wasn't tired any longer. She also realized that the dull ache she'd carried in the center of her chest for two days was gone.

❖

"Have a good time," Wynter said as she stood in the front foyer watching Ken and Mina bundle into their coats. Despite the fact that Mina was heavily pregnant, she was determined to attend her sister Chloe's tenth wedding anniversary party, arguing that she could just as easily sit on Chloe's couch as her own.

"I should be saying the same to you," Mina whispered as she passed. "If you don't want me waking you up in the morning, just leave a T-shirt hanging on your doorknob. In case you have overnight company."

Wynter blushed. "Don't be silly. I'm sure Pearce will be so tired by the time she gets here we'll fall asleep watching a movie. Just wake us up if you find us drooling somewhere."

"Uh-huh. We'll be quiet when we come in just the same." Mina glanced toward the street as a car pulled to the curb. "Looks like your date is here."

Ken glanced at Wynter, then craned his neck toward the street. He gave a small grunt of surprise when Pearce slid out from the driver's side. "I guess I missed something."

"That's because you're always a few weeks behind on the news." Mina put her arm around his waist and steered him onto the porch and toward the stairs. "Never mind, handsome. Let's go to the party."

"Night, Wynter," Ken called over his shoulder as Mina tugged him along. He nodded to Pearce as she passed.

Wynter heard Pearce mutter hello as she took the stairs two at a time and crossed the porch with long strides. She was in jeans, her leather jacket, and a scrub shirt. Even in the dim porch light, Wynter could make out the smudges of fatigue beneath her eyes. When Pearce stopped just at the threshold, searching Wynter's face with a question in her eyes, Wynter wrapped both arms around Pearce's shoulders and pressed her mouth to Pearce's.

Pearce gave a shuddering groan and gathered her close.

The kiss echoed with longing as much as desire, and Wynter sensed sadness and uncertainty in the way Pearce's hands moved over her back. It was as if Pearce wasn't sure she was real.

"It's all right."

"Is it?" Pearce's voice was harsh, gritty with fatigue and confusion. She rested her forehead against Wynter's and closed her eyes. "I don't know anymore."

"Then come inside and let's find out."

Wynter took Pearce's gloveless hand, finding it cold and stiff, and folded her warm fingers around it. "Have you eaten?"

"Breakfast."

"How does soup and a sandwich sound?"

"I'm not really hungry. Where are the kids?"

"They're already in bed. And you need to eat." Wynter closed the door behind them and then grasped the front of Pearce's jacket. She was concerned that Pearce seemed disoriented, and then she recognized what others often saw in her. Deadly fatigue. "Take this off."

Pearce shrugged out of the heavy leather and rolled her shoulders. The house was warm, welcoming, and for the first time all week, the tension in her neck and back eased. She grasped Wynter's hand again, needing the contact, fearing that she might disappear between one breath and the next. The week had been endless. She still didn't understand how she had come to find herself in a strange town, in a strange hospital, surrounded by strangers. She hadn't been able to sleep in a strange bed. She missed Wynter. Her only recourse had been to lose herself in the things that she knew best, and she'd prowled the emergency room until late into the night, every night, looking for something to occupy her mind and take away her loneliness.

"I'll only be a minute," Wynter said as she led Pearce to the sofa, watching her carefully. She looked so drawn, so defeated, that all Wynter wanted was to hold her. "Okay? I'll be right back."

"Okay. Sure." Pearce shook her head and smiled as she settled into the corner of the sofa. "You sure I can't help?"

Wynter laughed. "Not much skill required." She leaned down and kissed Pearce again. "God, it's good to see you."

Before Wynter could straighten, Pearce caught her around the waist and pulled her down into her lap. Wynter ended up with her legs pulled up onto the sofa and her arms around Pearce's neck. Pearce pressed her face into the curve of Wynter's shoulder, her mouth open and questing against Wynter's throat.

"Oh, baby, what?" Wynter whispered, stroking the back of Pearce's neck. She kissed her forehead. "What's wrong?"

"I don't think I can take it anymore." Pearce lifted her head, her eyes dark with misery. "I'm so fucked up. I don't want to go back."

Wynter caught her breath. She stroked Pearce's cheek. "You're tired. Did you sleep at all this week?"

"Some. A little. I don't know."

"Have you talked with your father?"

Pearce laughed, the bitter sound of hopelessness. "What can I say? That I can't take it? That I can't cut it?" She closed her eyes and rested her cheek against Wynter's shoulder. "You know what he always told me, since I was a kid?"

"What, baby?"

"God hates a coward."

Wynter was familiar with the phrase. It was another surgical mantra, another phrase designed to create confidence and conviction in the face of uncertainty. It worked for adults in the midst of a crisis, but for a child it would be an unbearable burden. "You are one of the bravest people I've ever known."

"No. That's what you are. You stood up to him."

"Pearce—"

"You *did*." Pearce tilted her head back and opened her eyes. She brushed her fingers over Wynter's mouth. "You know what I thought about all week?"

"What?" Wynter's voice was low and rough, the blood heavy in her veins as arousal coursed through her.

"The way you taste." Slowly, Pearce ran her tongue along the edge of Wynter's jaw and down her neck.

Wynter gasped.

"The way you feel." Pearce caught the delicate skin just above Wynter's collarbone in her teeth and sucked.

Wynter made a small keening sound.

"The way you tremble when you come." Pearce teased the back of Wynter's blouse from her jeans and slid her hand beneath it. She walked her fingers up Wynter's spine and fanned her fingers between her shoulder blades, holding her captive as she kissed her. Gently at first, then deeper, harder, unable to get far enough inside her to fill her own empty places. She froze when she heard Wynter cry out and jerked away, groaning. "God. Did I hurt you?"

"No. No, baby, no."

"I don't know what I'm doing."

"I do," Wynter whispered. "I'm falling in love with you." She stood, her legs trembling but her face calm and strong. She took Pearce's hand. "Come upstairs."

CHAPTER TWENTY-NINE

Wynter draped a T-shirt she grabbed from a nearby chair over the doorknob, gently closed the bedroom door, and led Pearce to the bed.

"Where are the kids?" Pearce whispered as Wynter switched on a soft night-light.

"They're down the hall. They won't wake up. Don't worry." Wynter kissed her softly. "And if they do, we'll hear them."

"What about Mina and Ken?"

"This is my old room—the guest room. Theirs is at the other end, on the far side of the kids. We're alone—more or less."

"Okay. If you're sure."

"Very." Wynter smiled and tugged Pearce's scrub shirt from her jeans. "Raise your arms." When Pearce did, she pulled the shirt off over her head along with the white cotton tank top she wore beneath. Looking down, she faltered, a fist of need tightening in the pit of her stomach. She contented herself with brushing her fingers across Pearce's chest, when what she wanted was to lower her mouth to her breasts. She forced her fingers to open the top button on Pearce's jeans.

Pearce followed Wynter's movements, her breath hitching unevenly. The briefest glance of Wynter's fingers against her bare stomach made her muscles tighten, and she was instantly wet. "Should I worry that you're undressing me like you do Ronnie?"

"Trust me," Wynter said, her voice as thick as warm honey, "there is no similarity." She hooked her fingers around the denim and sat on the edge of the bed as she pulled the jeans down. "Boots."

Thighs suddenly trembling, Pearce steadied herself with a hand on Wynter's shoulder and kicked off the boots and her jeans along with them. When Wynter leaned forward and rubbed her cheek against Pearce's lower abdomen, Pearce shivered.

"Cold?" Wynter murmured, kissing Pearce's stomach before gliding her tongue just inside the small, tight circle of her navel.

"No," Pearce said hoarsely. She threaded her fingers into Wynter's hair and locked her knees to keep from falling.

"Your skin is always so hot." Wynter played her hands up and down Pearce's back before cradling her hips in her palms. She dipped her head and traced her tongue along the trough where lean thigh joined taut abdomen, then skimmed her lips over the silky triangle between Pearce's thighs to trace the other juncture as well. "I could get drunk on the scent of you." She kissed lower, tasting the first hint of desire on the very tip of her tongue.

"Christ," Pearce moaned, tilting her hips forward as her fists tightened in Wynter's hair. "I need your mouth."

"Do you?" Wynter's question was filled with wonder and supreme satisfaction. She teased her way along the hard core of Pearce's clitoris for an instant, and then stopped. "Hmm?" She glanced up quickly, not wanting to stop, but not wanting it to end. She loved feeling Pearce grow rigid beneath her hands, hard against her lips. She loved knowing that she was the cause of Pearce's pleasure. The last time, Pearce had led and she had followed. She reached up and fanned her fingers over Pearce's breast. "Tell me what you need."

Pearce nearly sobbed as she looked down, her face tight with need. "I want to be with you. I need…to be with you."

It wasn't what Wynter had expected, and her insides twisted with how much she wanted to take away the pain she heard in Pearce's voice. She brushed her fingers up the inner slope of Pearce's thigh, then gently parted her. "I'm here." She played her tongue over swollen tissues and heard Pearce hiss in a breath. "Right here." She sucked her carefully, aware of the distant sound of labored breathing and low, guttural moans. She kept her strokes light and slow, not wanting her to come. It was too perfect. Too unbelievably special for it to be over too quickly.

"Wynter," Pearce gasped. "Let me come."

"I will," Wynter whispered, kissing her one last time. Then she stood and kissed Pearce's mouth. "Let's go to bed and I'll put you to sleep."

"You make me want you so bad."

"Good." Wynter unbuttoned her blouse and let it fall. She kissed Pearce again. "I want to make you come. I want you to want me everywhere. All the time." She unbuttoned her slacks. "I want to make you mine."

Pearce swayed, fatigue replaced by a desperate urge to lose herself in Wynter's arms. "What you said before…about loving me?"

Wynter halted in the midst of hurriedly shedding her clothes and met Pearce's gaze. "Yes."

"Does that make you happy?"

"Oh yes." Wynter caressed Pearce's cheek. "Oh yes." She pulled back the covers, slid under, and held out her hand. "Come."

Pearce followed, settling on her back with a sigh. "I missed you so much."

"Last weekend, I was afraid I'd lost you," Wynter murmured, moving over Pearce. She straddled her thigh, pressing her leg high up between Pearce's. "You're so wet. I love to do that to you."

"I love what you do to me." Pearce skimmed her mouth over Wynter's. "I need you inside me. Please, Wynter."

Wynter grew dizzy as Pearce's words shot through her like lightning streaking across a hot summer sky. She pushed up on one arm as she slipped her palm between Pearce's thighs, her fingers gliding through shimmering heat and into even hotter depths. She watched Pearce's face as she filled her, saw her eyes glaze as she pushed deeper, watched her jaws tighten down on a groan. She put her mouth lightly against Pearce's ear. "I'm going to make you come now."

"Please." Pearce closed her eyes and arched her back as the first link in the chain of her desire snapped. "Oh yeah."

"You like?" Wynter gasped, rocking along the length of Pearce's thigh as she thrust in time between her legs. "Tell me. Tell me how you feel."

"I…" Pearce gripped Wynter's arm tightly and pressed her lips to the soft skin. "I feel safe." She groaned and threw her head back, searching Wynter's face for understanding. "I feel…oh I'm gonna come…"

"I can tell," Wynter breathed wonderingly, so focused on Pearce's pleasure she forgot her own. "I love you."

I love you. Pearce's mind succumbed as fire erupted in the pit of her stomach and blazed through her, burning away the loneliness and the fear. When she stopped shaking, she slowly became aware of Wynter's arms around her, holding her close, rocking her. Whispering something. "What?" she croaked.

"Sleep now, baby. Go to sleep."

"I don't want to," Pearce muttered, but she could barely move. "Want to be with you."

"You are." Wynter kissed her forehead. "I'm not letting you go."

Pearce sighed. "Oh yeah?"

"Oh yes." Wynter laughed shakily and brushed the damp hair off Pearce's cheek. "Count on it."

"'Kay." Pearce finally let go and slept.

Wide awake, Wynter held her, content for the moment just to have her near. In the morning, Pearce would be gone. It might be a week, it might be a month, before they were together again. This time, however, she would allow herself to believe there would be a next time. Because she wanted it, wanted *her*, more than she could ever remember wanting anything, even her career. And this time, she would not allow time or distance to keep them apart. Absently, she rubbed her cheek against Pearce's hair, luxuriating in her scent. Part sweetness, part dark secrets.

Pearce stirred, and half awake, mumbled, "Sleep."

Wynter smiled. "I will."

Then quite clearly, Pearce said, "I love you."

"I'm so glad."

❖

Pearce nuzzled the back of Wynter's neck. They were curled around one another, Wynter's back tucked into the curve of Pearce's belly and thighs. Her arm was around Wynter's middle, her palm cupped beneath the soft weight of Wynter's breast. She kissed the warm skin at the edge of Wynter's hairline, running her lips back and forth over the very fine hairs, teasing them with her breath. Wynter murmured and shifted in her sleep. Pearce grinned and very delicately caught Wynter's earlobe between her teeth and tugged.

"Too early," Wynter muttered.

"For what?" Pearce teased.

Wynter reached blindly behind her, cupped her hand between Pearce's thighs, and squeezed. "That."

Pearce's breath whooshed out on a wave of surprise and instant arousal. "Fuck."

"Too early for that too." Wynter moved her hand and pushed her butt back into Pearce's crotch. "Mmm. You're so sexy."

"Now I'm so horny," Pearce complained, dancing her fingers over Wynter's nipple.

"You are *so* easy." Wynter rolled onto her back and smiled up at Pearce. She tapped her chin with her index finger. "What am I going to do with you?"

Pearce grinned and nipped at Wynter's lower lip. "I can think of about a hundred things, starting with putting your hand back where it just was."

"You'll get spoiled."

"Is that a bad thing?"

"No," Wynter replied seriously. "It isn't. I like making you happy."

Pearce kissed her. "You do. Very."

Wynter brushed her fingers through Pearce's hair. "Feeling better?"

"About being stuck out in the middle of nowhere?" Pearce flopped onto her back and settled Wynter against her side. Wynter nestled her head against Pearce's shoulder. "Not really, but I'll go back. I don't have a choice if I want to finish my residency."

"I think you should talk to your father. You're senior enough to complain about a lousy rotation like this. It's not fair at this point."

"I've been thinking about that," Pearce said, watching the shadows on the ceiling fade as light began to filter through the windows. "He's got plans for Dzubrow. I guess he figures once he gets him settled, he'll let me in on his plans for me." Pearce turned her head and looked into Wynter's eyes. "But I've got plans of my own."

"What?" Wynter asked softly, wondering at the fierce intensity in Pearce's face.

"I want to be with you. Whatever it takes."

"I don't understand."

Pearce smiled. "I'm probably getting ahead of you. I don't even know what you want—"

"Tell me what *you* want." Wynter cupped Pearce's cheek and caressed her mouth with her thumb. Pearce had always lived someone else's dream. As much as Wynter wanted her, she would not let Pearce do the same with her. "If you could have anything, do anything—what would it be?"

Pearce was silent a long time, stroking Wynter's face, her neck, her breasts. She dropped a gentle kiss into the hollow at the base of Wynter's throat. When she looked up, her face was peaceful. "I'd be with you. And Ronnie. I'd teach some, I think, and have a general surgery practice. I'd have a family—and a life."

Wynter's lips parted and she drew in a shaky breath. "I said last night that you're one of the bravest people I've ever met. I was right."

"Why?" Pearce frowned.

"It took me a long time to admit that I couldn't live the life I'd fallen into." Wynter kissed Pearce. "I know how hard it is to be honest about something that means so much. And how scary."

"Not when I'm with you."

"God, I love you."

"I'm kinda still getting used to that."

Wynter laughed. "Okay. We've got time."

"I don't want to be the chairman anywhere. I just never thought about anything else before, because that's what my father wanted me to be."

"He won't be happy about that," Wynter said.

"I know. But he's never really been happy with me anyhow." Surprisingly, Pearce found she could say it without it hurting quite so much. "The only difference now is that I *will* be happy."

"Pearce, honey—"

"I know, I'm going too fast," Pearce said hastily. "I'm sorr—"

"No." When Pearce started to draw away, Wynter threw an arm across her chest and pulled her near. "You're not going too fast. I'm crazy about you. I'm a little afraid to think about the future, because I've gotten used to living one day at a time. But I want you to be part of my life."

"Okay," Pearce said. "Okay."

"But you've got to go."

Pearce frowned. "What—"

"Look at the time."

"Fuck."

Wynter rolled on top of her and kissed her one more time, a slow, thorough kiss that promised more. Soon. The next time. Again. "If you can't come here, I'll come there."

"You've got Ronnie. I'll come here."

"I love you."

Pearce smiled. "I love you too."

Wynter sat up. It was time to do what needed to be done. "I'll make you coffee."

"That's okay. I've gotta get out of here. I'll grab a coffee on the way. Once I make rounds, I can shower at the hospital."

"Are you sure? It won't take long."

Pearce slid out of bed, grabbed her jeans, and tugged them on. "I'm okay. I slept like a log. There won't be much traffic. Don't worry."

"Call me when you get there, all right?" Wynter pulled back the covers and started to get up.

Pearce pushed her back. "You can sleep another hour or so. Do it. You'll need it later." She sat on the edge of the bed and pulled on her boots, then found her shirt.

Wynter stroked her back. "I want to walk you out."

"Stay." Pearce leaned down and kissed her. "See you soon, Doc."

"See you soon," Wynter whispered as Pearce disappeared. She listened to Pearce's footsteps in the hallway, and then as they faded as Pearce disappeared downstairs. It didn't feel right—she couldn't just let her walk away. She bolted from the bed and scrambled for her robe. Barefoot, she ran from the room and down the stairs to the front door. She pulled it open just as Pearce closed her car door and started the engine.

"Pearce!"

Pearce look back toward the house, frowned, and opened her door. "What's wrong?"

Wynter came down the stairs, mindless of the cold.

"Jesus, Wynter," Pearce exclaimed. She left the engine running and hurried toward her. "It's freezing out here. Go back inside."

"Be careful." Wynter wrapped her arms around Pearce's neck and kissed her, hard. "Just be careful."

"Hey, I'm not the one running around half naked in the middle of February." Pearce put her arm around Wynter's waist and led her back upstairs. She stepped inside the foyer with Wynter, pulled her tightly to her, and buried her face in Wynter's hair. "I wouldn't go if I didn't have to."

"I know." Wynter stroked the back of her neck, kissed her throat, her jaw, her mouth. "I just…"

"I'm not going anywhere, babe," Pearce murmured. "I'll talk to you soon, okay?"

Wynter nodded and reluctantly released her, knowing as she watched Pearce pull away that it wouldn't be soon enough. She missed her already.

CHAPTER THIRTY

An hour and a half later, Wynter slid a bowl of instant oatmeal into the microwave and set the timer. She checked the temperature of the bowl she had just heated and then placed it in front of Winston. "Use your spoon, honey."

Ronnie made impatient sounds and tried to get her hand into Winston's oatmeal. Winston ignored her.

"I think he's got the disposition of an anesthesiologist," Ken noted as he ambled into the kitchen, already in scrubs, as was Wynter. "He doesn't get bothered by people crowding his territory."

"He is pretty unflappable," Wynter agreed as she gave Ronnie her own portion of oatmeal. She looked at Ken. "Want some?"

"Sure. I've got a little time. Thanks."

"Mmm," Wynter replied absently.

"Pearce gone?"

Coloring, Wynter looked over her shoulder at him. "How did you know?"

"I kind of guessed when I saw the T-shirt."

"Oh yes," Wynter said, recalling that she'd picked it up off the hall floor after her hasty flight downstairs had knocked it off the doorknob. "Not too subtle."

Ken laughed. "I kind of felt like I was living in the frat house again."

"Nice."

"I heard her old man farmed her out. What's going on with that?"

Wynter shook her head. "I'm not sure. I don't think it really has anything to do with her."

"It still stinks."

"Yes." She passed Ken his oatmeal and then hastily ate her own. After she ran two dish towels under the warm water, she passed one to him. "You get yours, I'll get mine." As they cleaned up their respective children, she asked, "Is Mina awake?"

"Yep. She's just moving a little slow."

"Is Chloe coming over today? I'm not sure Mina is up to watching all of these kids any longer."

Ken nodded. "Chloe's going to be spending part of the day here until the baby's born, and then for a week after. She'll help keep things under control." He hefted Winston.

"I want to pay a little extra, then," Wynter said, lifting Ronnie into her arms.

"No need," Ken said as they carried the kids upstairs.

"I want to anyway," she said firmly.

Mina met them in the hallway. "Have the little darlings been fed?"

"All taken care of," Wynter pronounced. "I left the fixings out for Janie."

"Park them in there, then," Mina said, indicating the playroom. Then she looked at Ken. "Janie's still asleep. Don't wake her."

"I won't." He kissed Mina's cheek and then headed toward his daughter's room. "I just wanna see her before I go."

"How was your night?" Mina asked suggestively as she joined Wynter in the playroom and settled into the easy chair with a sigh.

"Too short," Wynter said brusquely as she dragged out Ronnie and Winston's favorite toys.

"Get any sleep?"

"Some."

"Are you all right?"

Wynter settled a hip on the arm of Mina's chair. "More or less. I miss her already, and it feels like we're constantly stealing time to be together. But it was…" She smiled. "Wonderful."

"Mmm. I'm looking forward to this story."

Wynter slid an arm around Mina's shoulder and squeezed. "Well, you're going to wait for a long time. I don't kiss and tell."

"Since when? I knew every little detail about you and Dave."

"You did not," Wynter protested. "And even so, this is different."

Mina gave her a long, serious look. "It is, isn't it?"

Wynter nodded.

"Does she feel the same way?"

Again, Wynter nodded.

"Then that's just fine." Mina patted Wynter's knee. "But I still want details."

Laughing, Wynter got up, kissed Ronnie and Winston, and started for the door. "Maybe just a few. When I have time."

"Tease," Mina called after her.

Wynter met Ken in the hall. He looked toward the playroom with a perplexed expression. "Is she talking to me?"

"No. Me," Wynter said.

"Huh. Want a ride to work?"

"I'd love one. I'll wait for you downstairs." She listened to Ken and Mina laughing together as she started down the stairs and allowed herself one brief instant of imagining what it would be like if she and Pearce shared the kind of life that her friends had. Then she chased the thought away. It wasn't that she didn't trust her feelings. She did. She trusted Pearce's too. But she didn't trust much of anything else. She'd seen too much of life's fickle cruelty to plan too far ahead.

❖

"See you later," Wynter called to Ken as she headed for the women's locker room. She hung her parka in her locker, grabbed her lab coat, and pulled it on as she took the stairs down to the ground floor. She needed another cup of coffee to really get her brain working. She was tired, but it had been worth it. Smiling to herself, she replayed the night with Pearce. Her blood ran hot as she thought about making love to her, the way it had felt to make Pearce's body writhe with pleasure. "Jesus," she breathed as the heavy ache of desire descended. "I can't think about that now."

Still smiling, she checked her watch. Pearce had been gone a little over two hours. She should be almost there by now. Wynter got a large cup of coffee and a bagel, paid, and started toward her usual table. She frowned when she saw that it was empty. She checked her watch again. She was right on time. Glancing around the cafeteria, she realized that none of the surgery residents were there for sign-out rounds. No one had been in the locker room, either. It was Saturday, which meant that only a handful of the residents were on call, but *someone* should have been in the cafeteria. Since there was no point in sitting around waiting, she started back upstairs. Just as she reached the main corridor, she saw Bruce jogging toward her.

"What's going on?" Wynter asked. "Where is everyone?"

"Downstairs in the ER," he huffed. "Pearce is there."

"She's back?" Wynter said, unable to keep the excitement from her voice.

Bruce looked at her curiously. "They medevaced her in about fifteen minutes ago. Something about a carjacking…"

Wynter stared at him, hearing the words but unable to decipher them. Her head filled with a roaring sound and the coffee cup dropped from her hand. Bruce jumped back with a surprised yelp.

"What?" Wynter cried. "What are you talking about?"

"I didn't get all the details—something about someone trying to boost her car and she tried to stop them—"

"She's hurt?" Wynter grabbed his arm hard enough to make him wince. "Is that what you're telling me? Pearce is here and she's *hurt*?"

"Dzubrow told us because her father called hi—"

"Oh my God." Wynter dropped his arm and spun away in the direction of the ER. As she started to run, Bruce called after her.

"She's on her way to CAT scan, Wynter."

Wynter veered right and pushed through the fire doors into the stairwell. A startled lab tech flattened himself against the wall as Wynter clattered by, bolting down the stairs so quickly she nearly fell several times. The hall outside the CAT scan room was jammed with residents and a few nurses. Curious onlookers. She pushed and shoved her way through, oblivious to the surprised grunts and muffled curses until she got as far as the doorway to the small cubicle adjoining the room which housed the CAT scanner. She couldn't see the desk where the tech sat in front of the monitor because the anteroom was wall-to-wall people, most of whom she recognized as surgery department heads. Neurosurgery. Plastic surgery. Cardiothoracic surgery. Ophthalmology. Wynter's heart seized. *Jesus God, what's happened to her?*

She saw Henry Dzubrow and then Ambrose Rifkin in the center of the pack. Oblivious to the disgruntled expressions from those she elbowed, she managed to reach them. Through the glass partition that comprised most of one wall, she could make out part of the person inside the scanner. Bare legs and feet. Where were her jeans? Her boots? Maybe it wasn't Pearce. Maybe it was all a mistake. It had to be.

"Make sure you get cuts all the way through the facial bones," Rifkin said, his voice cool and steady.

"Yes sir," the tech said sharply.

"Is that Pearce?" Wynter said, her throat so tight and scratchy she barely recognized her voice.

"Yes," Dzubrow replied in a strident whisper.

Part of Wynter's brain automatically assessed the situation. There was no one in the room with Pearce, which meant she was hemodynamically stable. There was no respirator, which meant she was breathing on her own. There was a single clear plastic bag of saline hanging on an IV pole with the tubing snaking inside the scanner and, presumably, to Pearce's wrist. But no blood was hanging. She wasn't hemorrhaging.

"What happened?" she asked. She would have asked why no one called her, but why would they have? No one knew. No one knew what Pearce meant to her. Right now, knowing Pearce was in that room alone, hurt, Wynter realized just how much. She wanted to get to her so badly, she feared she might scream. If she'd been thinking clearly, she would have been surprised that Ambrose Rifkin answered, but as it was, all she cared about was knowing.

"Apparently," he said smoothly, "someone tried to steal her car and she objected. There is some blunt injury to the head and chest."

Blunt injury. Someone had hit her. Wynter's stomach nearly revolted, but she forced down the swell of nausea. The room was hot under the best of circumstances, and now, with so many people jammed into it, the air was stifling. Dizzy, she put a hand down on the counter to steady herself, unable to take her eyes away from the body in the CAT scanner. "Is she awake?"

"Mildly disoriented, but responsive."

"Brain looks clear," the tech said.

"Let's let Lewis decide that," Rifkin said, turning sideways so that a tall, thin African American man could move closer to the monitor.

Wynter recognized the chief of neurosurgery. Refusing to give ground, she craned her neck to see the computer images of Pearce's cranium and brain. The fluid-filled ventricles were symmetrical and not enlarged, the gray matter showed no evidence of hemorrhage or edema, and there were no collections of blood between the brain itself and the skull. No epidural or subdural hematomas. No air in the intracranial space. She scanned the double rim of calvarial bone and saw no evidence of fractures. No serious head injury. The relief was so intense she felt weak.

"It looks fine," Lewis pronounced. "I'll wait around until they cut the spine, just to be sure her neck is clear. I'll be out in the hall. This sweatbox is getting to be a little much."

"Don't go far," Rifkin said mildly.

"I'm not moving until we're sure she's all right."

Wynter watched the machine generate image after image, as it artificially reconstructed "slices" of Pearce's skull and face, spreading them out across the computer screen like so many cards on the table. When followed in sequence, they gave a detailed survey of all the bones and soft tissue elements in their path.

Dzubrow pointed to the monitor. "Facial bones are clear too."

"No," Wynter said, stretching out a hand that was amazingly steady considering that she felt as if she were coming apart. She indicated the second row of images. "She has fractures of the right orbital wall and a blowout of the orbital floor. Right there." She was aware of Dzubrow flushing bright red beside her, but she didn't care.

"Patricia," Rifkin commanded of the chief of plastic surgery. "What do you think?"

The fifty-year-old redhead, usually jovial to the point of irreverence, was uncharacteristically solemn as she studied the films one after the other. "I agree. There's a fair amount of floor disrupted beneath the right globe."

"Scan's done," the tech announced.

Wynter didn't wait to hear anymore. She edged around Dzubrow, pushed through the inner door into the CAT scan room, and rushed to the side of the long, narrow motorized table that carried the patient in and out of the machine. "Pearce? Honey?" She heard the whir of a motor and, slowly, the platform slid out, bearing Pearce's still form. She moaned softly and fumbled for Pearce's hand. The right side of Pearce's face was misshapen and bruised, both eyelids discolored and so edematous that she couldn't open her eye. A cervical collar was Velcroed around her neck. Pearce seemed thinner, smaller, beneath the frayed white cotton hospital gown covered with tiny blue diamonds. "Oh, sweetheart."

"I'm okay, babe," Pearce said groggily, squeezing Wynter's fingers. Her voice was slurred as a result of the swelling that extended through her cheek and into the intraoral tissues. She managed a lopsided smile.

"Asked them to call you."

Wynter lifted Pearce's hand and kissed it, then cradled it against her breast. She ached to gather Pearce into her arms. "I just found out. I'm sorry I wasn't here when you got here."

"S'okay. Freakin' zoo."

Two nurses pulled a stretcher into the room. "We're going to take you up to the operating room now, Dr. Rifkin," one of them said. "We just need you to slide over onto this stretcher."

Pearce jerked and tried to sit up. "OR? Why?"

"Lie down, darling." Wynter said gently, ignoring the surprised stares from the nurses. "Let's get you out of here, and then we'll talk."

Pearce tried to turn her head but was impaired by the collar. She yanked at the closures with the hand that was tethered by the IV line. "God damn it. Can't see you."

Wynter leaned closer, into Pearce's line of vision, and gently caught her wrist, preventing her from dislodging the collar or the IV. "Don't fight. You'll hurt yourself. I'll talk to your father and then I'll talk to you. Nothing's going to happen that you don't want. I promise."

"Don't go. Please."

"I won't." Wynter brushed her fingers tenderly through Pearce's hair. "Ever."

A trickle of blood ran from a cut just above Pearce's right eyebrow into her left eye and she blinked. "Bastards tried to take my car."

"Big mistake." Wynter's smile wavered for just an instant, and then she steadied herself. She looked to one of the nurses. "Can you put a saline gauze pad on that laceration and get the blood out of her eye?"

"Sure," the one nearest said. "What about the OR?"

Pearce stiffened and Wynter squeezed her shoulder tenderly. "Let the nurses help you move onto this stretcher, honey. I'm going to talk to your father, and then I'll be right back."

"Okay," Pearce whispered weakly.

Wynter found Ambrose just outside the door, deep in conversation with the ophthalmologist and plastic surgeon. She didn't even bother to wait until he'd finished speaking.

"Pearce needs to see you. She can't go to the operating room without knowing what's wrong."

Ambrose Rifkin regarded her with surprise and interest. "I need to finish discussing the treatment plan with—"

"You need," Wynter said, her furious gaze on his, "to speak to her. She's the patient, *and* she's a doctor. Show her some respect for once in your life."

Someone coughed, and she was aware of the people around her shuffling back, but she never moved her eyes from Rifkin's face. His handsome features set angrily as he narrowed his eyes. "You forget yourself, Dr. Thompson."

"No. I don't." She moved closer so that no one else could hear. "I know exactly what I'm doing. I love Pearce. She's hurt, and I don't intend to let you hurt her anymore. Not today."

There was no sound in the hallway. No one moved. Wynter felt as if she and Ambrose Rifkin were the only two people in the world. His laser gaze raked her face, bore into her eyes and far beyond. She trembled under the silent onslaught, but she held steady until he gave an almost imperceptible nod.

"Very well." Then he turned toward the door to the CAT scan suite. "Are you coming, Dr. Thompson?" he said without turning around.

Legs shaking, Wynter followed.

CHAPTER THIRTY-ONE

Pearce heard the door open but couldn't tell who had entered because the cervical collar prevented her from lifting her head. The nurses had moved her to the stretcher but had not put the back up. All she could see was the ceiling. "Wynter?"

"She'll be along momentarily," Ambrose said. "The OR is standing by, and I want you to go straight up."

"Why?"

Wynter walked in just as Pearce asked the question and crossed quickly to her side. She leaned over and smiled. "Hi. You okay?"

"Yeah." Pearce tried to smile, but her cheek felt like a water balloon and it was difficult to move the right side of her face. She raised her hand and Wynter took it immediately. "What's the damage?"

Ambrose stepped closer to the opposite side of the stretcher. Pearce could see him now, but his expression told her little. As he had done when he first arrived in the emergency room, he scrutinized her face carefully. "Your chest CT is relatively unremarkable. There are hairline fractures of the right ninth and tenth ribs, but the lung looks good. Some pleural thickening, but no intrathoracic bleeding."

"Bastard kicked me."

Wynter fought not to let Pearce see her horror and fury. She would gladly kill the person who had hurt her. The thought of anyone even *touching* Pearce, particularly with the intent to harm, made her slightly insane.

"There are, however," Ambrose went on impassively, "displaced fractures of the right zygoma and orbital floor. These need to be corrected surgically. Today."

"Wynter," Pearce said, trying once more to turn her head and failing, "have you seen the films?"

Wynter ignored Ambrose Rifkin's surprised mutter. "Yes."

"What do you think?"

"Pearce," Ambrose said impatiently, "I've already told you—"

"Honey?" Pearce asked.

"They need to be fixed, baby," Wynter said gently. "The floor fracture especially. Your father's right. Patricia thinks so too."

Ambrose leaned closer. "If the orbital bones are not repaired and the eye drops even a few millimeters," he said stridently, "you'll likely develop double vision. That will end your career, Pearce."

"I run the risk of double vision *with* the surgery too," Pearce said. She was tired. She hurt. It was hard to think. She should be able to sort it all out, but it was so hard. She struggled to move, felt Wynter's restraining hand.

"I agree with your father and Patricia, sweetheart," Wynter said gently. "You need surgery. It will be okay."

"Will you be there?" Pearce asked.

"The whole time," Wynter kissed Pearce's forehead, then looked across the bed at Ambrose. "You're going to assist, aren't you?"

A look of surprise flashed across his patrician features and then was quickly erased. "Yes. I am."

She didn't smile but she nodded. "Good."

"Are we ready, then?" Ambrose asked.

Wynter brushed her fingers through Pearce's hair. "Yes. We are."

❖

Ordinarily it took an hour to transport a patient to the operating room, complete the preoperative and anesthesia assessments, get the operating team in place, and put the patient to sleep. In fifteen minutes, Pearce was in the operating room on the table with the chief of anesthesia standing by. Ken was there to assist. Wynter stood at the head of the operating table on the left side, her hand on Pearce's shoulder. Patricia Duvall—the plastic surgeon—and Ambrose were scrubbing just outside the room.

"Ready, Pearce?" Harry Inouye asked, a syringe full of Nembutal in one hand for the first stage of induction.

"Yeah," Pearce said. She held tightly to Wynter's hand.

Wynter leaned down and whispered, "I love you. I'll see you in just a little while."

"Love…you…too," Pearce murmured as she drifted off.

As soon as Pearce was sedated, Inouye administered another drug cocktail to paralyze her. When she stopped breathing, he quickly inserted the endotracheal tube through her vocal cords and connected it to the machine that would control her respiration during surgery. As he worked, Ken leaned over to whisper in Wynter's ear.

"You're not scrubbing?"

"I can't." Wynter stroked Pearce's cheek one last time before the nurses prepped her face for the surgery. She would not be able to touch her again until after the operation. "I just want to be her lover right now."

"I know what you mean. I can hardly look when the babies are coming."

"Thanks," Wynter murmured.

"Rifkin's going to assist?" Ken snorted. "Man, he's ice. Working on his own daughter."

"He can do it, and right now I'm glad he can. It's probably easier for him that way too."

"Huh. Maybe." Ken settled down on the metal stool in front of the anesthesia machine and began to make notes regarding Pearce's vital signs, the drugs that had been administered, and the other particulars of the procedure. He indicated another stool with the tip of his chin. "Might as well pull that over and get comfortable. We'll probably be here awhile."

"Good idea." Wynter suddenly felt shaky. She remembered she'd forgotten to eat the bagel, and the adrenaline rush of stress and fear had burned off whatever energy reserves she'd had left. Her legs trembled and she sank down abruptly.

"You okay?" Ken murmured.

"Yes." She took a deep breath as Patricia and Ambrose entered and the scrub nurse hurried toward them with sterile towels. Pearce was all that mattered now. "Fine."

For the next few minutes the room was silent as the nurses placed protective ointment in Pearce's eyes and then washed her hair and face with Betadine prep solution. When Ambrose efficiently isolated the surgical area with sterile sheets, Wynter had to edge her stool out slightly from her cubbyhole behind the ether screen to see around the barricades. She knew exactly where they would put the incisions in Pearce's eyelids to expose the underlying fractures. She knew what tools would be used to elevate the depressed bone fragments in the floor of the orbit underneath her eye, where the drill holes would be made, and where the miniature titanium plates and screws would be affixed to reposition the broken bones. She'd seen the procedure many times before and done it herself under supervision. It was technically challenging, which made it fun. The scarring would be minimal. But there was no way she could have made those incisions today. She could not have added more injury to Pearce's already battered face, even though it was necessary.

"Oh, that's good," Patricia said after a long interval of silence when the only sounds were the quiet requests for instruments, the slap of steel against flesh, and the steady whoosh of the anesthesia machine delivering oxygen to Pearce's lungs. "The floor is in two big pieces. If I can get them up without shattering them, we can get away without an implant."

"Will it be strong enough to support her eye?" Ambrose asked. "Those bones look like eggshells."

"Let's see what I can do." Patricia used a fine, blunt-tipped silver probe to gently pry the broken bone fragments back into position. "Pupils look like they're on the same level now. Once I put a plate on the lateral and infraorbital rims, they should be stable. She'll do fine."

She'll do fine. She'll do fine. The words reverberated in Wynter's head, and she closed her eyes to prevent the tears she felt quickly rise to the surface from spilling over. All she wanted was for Pearce to be well. Not to hurt. To be happy. And to be with her. Nothing had ever been clearer in her life. She wanted them to be together.

❖

It seemed to Pearce that she had only been asleep a few minutes. Her throat was dry and it burned when she swallowed. Her face throbbed and she wondered when someone would fix it. Slowly, carefully, she explored her jaw and neck with her free hand. The collar was gone. When she reached higher, strong cool fingers closed around her wrist.

"Don't touch your face, sweetheart."

"Wynter?"

"Hi," Wynter said, smiling just to hear Pearce's voice. "You're in the recovery room. Surgery went great."

Pearce frowned, although it didn't feel as if anything in her face was moving. "It's all done?"

"Uh-huh. About an hour and a half ago." Wynter petted Pearce's hair, her uninjured cheek, her neck and shoulders. She couldn't seem to stop touching her. "You're okay now."

"How did things look in there?"

Not how do I look, Wynter thought, aching to hold her. She put the side rail down just so she could be a few inches closer. "The floor was in a couple of big pieces. Patricia reduced them pretty easily. No floor implant. Just two plates."

Pearce closed her eye and sighed. "Should be okay, don't you think?"

The slight uncertainty in her voice ripped at Wynter's heart. She leaned over, kissed the corner of Pearce's mouth. "Yes. Don't worry."

After a moment, Pearce roused. "What time is it?"

"A little after six in the evening."

Pearce frowned, trying to sort out the day. She'd been driving. Stopped for coffee on the turnpike. Still dark. Not much traffic. "Is it still Saturday?"

"Mmm-hmm. Saturday night."

"Have you been here all day?"

"Uh-huh."

"Thanks. I—"

"Shh. I told you I wouldn't leave."

"Told them to call you." Pearce reached for Wynter's hand and clasped her fingers tightly. "Kept trying to tell them I wanted you. They gave me something—couldn't make them listen."

Wynter swallowed the anger, understanding for the first time how invisible their love could be to others. She wouldn't let that happen again. Lightly, she said, "I'll have to sew a label in your clothes with my name and number on it."

Pearce laughed hoarsely. "Like Ronnie?"

"Mmm. My two loves." She kissed Pearce's fingers. "I love you so much."

"Love you. Sorry about this."

"No. It's not your fault."

Pearce shifted restlessly. She was waking up more each minute as the drugs wore off. Her chest screamed with every breath. Her head pounded as if there were some very angry being inside her skull trying to get out through her eye sockets. The bed was cold and stiff, the overhead lights too bright. She wanted out of there. "When can I go home?"

"Probably tomorrow."

"Why not tonight? Nothing to do for me here."

"Do you hurt, sweetheart?" Wynter asked gently.

"Some."

"Tomorrow will be soon enough."

"Someone needs to get my car."

Wynter looked at her watch. "I'll check with the police in a bit. They probably towed it."

"Son of a bitch was trying to jimmy the door." Pearce tensed, remembering first the flash of anger, then the swift blinding pain.

Wynter stroked Pearce's neck until she felt her relax. "Not very wise of him."

"Didn't see the other one. Must have had a bat or something." The guy had come at her in the dark, just as she'd grabbed the first jerk and tossed him on the ground. Pearce winced. "Jacket took most of the sting out when he hit my ribs. Knocked me down with the face shot, though."

If he'd hit her again he would have killed her. Wynter swayed, sick with the image of terrible loss. *I've just found her. Found myself.*

"Hey, babe," Pearce murmured. "You're shaking."

"Just hungry. I forgot about lunch." Wynter shrugged and smiled. "I was a little busy."

"You sure?" Pearce squinted, trying to focus with one eye, and that one blurry from the ointment the nurses had put in it. "You look beat."

"I was worried." Wynter said softly, resting her fingertips in the center of Pearce's chest. Her heart beat strong and steady. "Now I'm not."

"I'm sorry." Pearce covered Wynter's hand with hers, ignoring the IV tubing trailing behind. "I didn't think. I just acted. I would never do anything to hurt you."

"I know. I'm okay. I just can't stand you being hurt."

"Hard head." Pearce grinned. "I'm good here. Go get something to eat."

"I will. Soon."

"Aren't you on call?"

"I traded with Dzubrow. Well, actually, your father arranged it."

"He did?" Pearce's left eyebrow twitched in surprise. "Why?"

"I was pretty surprised myself, but when the surgery was over, he said I should stay with you. I told him I intended to, although I was on call and I had some work to do." Wynter remembered the odd look that had crossed Ambrose Rifkin's face for a moment. He'd glanced at Pearce, still heavily sedated, and then back at Wynter. His eyes had been dark, impenetrable, but when he spoke, his voice was soft, almost gentle. She'd never heard him sound that way before.

"You should be here when she wakes up. I'll see that Dr. Dzubrow takes care of the vascular service until further notice."

Then he'd walked away.

"I'll try to switch the next couple of days so I can stay home with you," Wynter added.

"You don't have to do that."

Wynter studied Pearce gravely. "Yes, I do."

"If you could just pick up some groceries. I don't have anything in the apartment—"

"Oh, so that's how you think this will work." Wynter laughed and shook her head. "Do you really think I'm going to let you go home to your apartment alone? You're coming to my place."

"Your place?"

"You're going to be sitting around doing nothing for the next week until the swelling goes down. If you're at my house, Mina will be nearby in case there's anything you need."

"She's got enough to handle," Pearce protested.

"She's not going to be dressing you, darling. And I suspect that you can feed yourself." Wynter gave Pearce's hand another shake. "There's no point in arguing, because you're not going to win."

"Look, I—"

"Please," Wynter said softly. "I can't go to work and worry about you. I need to know that you're all right."

"If that's what you want," Pearce said immediately. "But I want to help with Ronnie or something. I'm not going to sit around and be a patient."

"If that's what *you* want, but not until some of the swelling has gone down." She laughed and brushed her fingers over Pearce's cheek. "And you have no idea what you just let yourself in for."

"I know," Pearce muttered.

Wynter laughed and was about to lean down and kiss Pearce again when she saw Ambrose on his way toward them. She straightened, but continued to hold Pearce's hand. He walked to the opposite side of the stretcher, his eyes going first to the monitors above the bed before flickering down to Pearce.

"Did Dr. Thompson fill you in on the results of the surgery?" he asked.

"Yes."

"I've asked Larry Elliott to examine your eyes just as soon as the edema has subsided and you can open your lids. I don't expect you'll have any problems with diplopia, but we want to be sure."

"I couldn't see well enough to tell if I had double vision earlier," Pearce said quietly.

"Patricia did an excellent job of repairing the orbit. I don't think you'll have any long-term difficulties."

"Thanks for assisting." Pearce swallowed. Her chest hurt even more, but it wasn't her ribs. "I felt…better, knowing you were there."

Ambrose's expression remained remote, but his stiff posture relaxed slightly as he fleetingly brushed his fingers over Pearce's shoulder. "You always have underestimated your importance to me." He glanced at Wynter, then back at Pearce. "I suspect that was my fault."

"I'm not going back to Harrisburg, Dad," Pearce said. She glanced at Wynter. "I've got too much to stay for here."

"There's time for that kind of thing in the future, when you've got your career firmly on track," Ambrose said.

"No." Pearce smiled, her gaze locked with Wynter's. "We've already lost enough time."

Chapter Thirty-two

Wynter let herself in the front door and stood in her living room, listening. At two in the afternoon, the house was very still, but she knew from having stopped at Mina's just a few moments before that Pearce and Ronnie were home. *Home.* Where the two most important people in her life waited. After just a week with Pearce there twenty-four hours a day while she recuperated, Wynter had begun to think of her as belonging. She draped her parka over the back of the sofa, kicked off her boots, and quietly climbed the stairs. Her bedroom door was open. She tiptoed over and peeked inside.

Pearce, in gray gym shorts and a shapeless T-shirt with a faded blue Penn logo, was propped upright at the head of the bed on three pillows, her eyes closed. Ronnie was curled up in her lap, also asleep; her coloring book, crayons, and an assortment of cars and trucks lay scattered across the beige chenille bedspread. Pearce had insisted that Ronnie not see her until the worst of the discoloration and edema had subsided, for fear of frightening her. Wynter had not been as concerned, but Pearce was unswayable. As she'd improved, Pearce had gradually taken over as much of Ronnie's care as possible to give Mina a break.

Moving carefully, Wynter stripped and slipped into an extra-large white cotton T-shirt that she sometimes slept in when alone. She'd been wearing it to bed that week, because the feel of Pearce naked against her was almost too exciting for her to bear. And Pearce was still recovering. Wynter took advantage of the opportunity to study Pearce as she approached the bed. Pearce looked better, but she was still not quite completely healed. The swelling in the right side of her face had diminished to the point that she could open her eye a few millimeters. Patricia had removed the sutures from Pearce's eyelids the day before, and Larry Elliott had examined her immediately after and pronounced her vision 100 percent normal. Although Pearce had said little after her follow-up exams, Wynter sensed her relief. Hopefully she would be able to sleep through the night soon, something she had not done since her injury. Her energy level was not what it had been, and Wynter suspected it would be another week before she was functioning normally. Sleep was just what she needed.

When Wynter lifted Ronnie from Pearce's lap, Pearce's eyes opened. "Shh," Wynter mouthed. Pearce nodded and closed her eyes again.

A few minutes later, Wynter crawled under the covers beside Pearce, wrapped an arm around her middle, and snuggled against her. "Mmm, I love nap time."

Pearce kissed Wynter's forehead. "You're home late. Tired?"

"I was ready to leave right after sign-outs at ten, and then we got a STAT consult to see one of the cardiac patients who needed an emergency CABG *and* a carotid endarterectomy. By the time that was squared away, it was almost two."

"Were you up all night?"

"Most of it."

Pearce tightened her hold and eased Wynter partially on top of her. She rubbed her neck and back. "You've got the rest of the weekend off. You'll feel better after you get some sleep."

"How are *you* doing?" Wynter lazily slipped her hand beneath Pearce's T-shirt to rub her stomach.

"Okay. Good," Pearce murmured, enjoying the soft caress. "I brought Ronnie back over here after breakfast and we played. Well, she colored and I watched cartoons."

"Has she been asleep long?"

"Not too long."

"Good," Wynter said contentedly. "She'll go another couple of hours."

"You won't, though." Pearce nuzzled Wynter's neck and circled her hand lower to the soft warm flesh left bare where the T-shirt pulled up in the back. She felt Wynter fit herself more closely to the curve of her body and shifted until her thigh nudged between Wynter's legs. Wynter was hot. Wet. Pearce smiled. "Miss me?"

Wynter scratched a nail up the center of Pearce's stomach and made her twitch. "All the time."

"It's been a long week."

"I love having you here."

Pearce's heart stuttered, then raced. "I love being here."

Wynter raised her head, her eyes dreamy. "Will you stay, then?"

"For how long?" Pearce breathed.

"Always." Wynter kissed her gently. "Always."

"I don't have very much practice at…this." Pearce waved at the room uncertainly.

"No one ever really does, until you do it." Wynter kissed Pearce's throat. "You're doing just fine. You're great with Ronnie. And I adore you."

"I'm crazy about both of you."

"That's a good start, then."

"Wynter," Pearce said so seriously that Wynter raised her head in question. "We both have to finish our residencies. You want to do a fellowship. It's going to be tricky."

"I know. Scared?"

Pearce grinned. "Hell no. I've been thinking about a lot of things this week." As she spoke, she trailed her fingers up and down Wynter's spine. "I'm not going to do a fellowship. I'm going to look for a job as soon as I get back on my feet. It's never too early to start, and I know a bunch of guys at the other medical schools in the city. I'm pretty sure I can scare up a staff position."

"If you come in at the bottom like that, you'll put yourself out of the running for a chairmanship," Wynter said quietly. "A fellowship somewhere first would be better."

"I don't want it. Besides"—Pearce rested her uninjured cheek against the top of Wynter's head—"we might have to move depending on where you get a fellowship. I'll need to be flexible."

"Sweetheart, that's not what you've planned all these years."

"No, it's not. I never planned anything. My father did all the planning." Pearce toyed with a lock of Wynter's hair, softly twining it around her finger. "This is what I want to do."

"He's not going to like it much."

Pearce shrugged. "He'll either get used to it or he won't. Either way, he can't stop me."

Wynter pushed Pearce's T-shirt high enough to expose her breasts and kissed her just above her heart. Then she rested her cheek between Pearce's breasts, cradling one in her palm. "I love you."

"I love you," Pearce sighed, shifting restlessly as Wynter's warm breath teased her nipple. "Missed you."

"Mmm, I can tell." Wynter drew her leg up over Pearce's thighs and straddled her. "Me too."

Murmuring appreciatively, Pearce stroked her fingers over Wynter's hips and between her legs, capturing her heat in the palm of her hand. "Let's see if I can put you to sleep."

Wynter rocked along Pearce's fingers, anticipating the pleasure as she tightened inside. "I won't take much."

"A little now, a little la—"

Wynter's cell phone rang, and they both froze.

"Fuck," Pearce muttered.

"Oh yes, I so agree." With a groan, Wynter rolled away, ignoring the insistent throbbing between her thighs. "Hello?"

"Hi, honey," Mina said. "Whatcha doing?"

"We were…I was just…uh…getting ready to take a nap."

"Well, Chloe will be here in five minutes to watch the kids. So, if you can do whatever you were doing in five minutes, you go right ahead. But that's all the time you've got."

"Mina, what are you talking about?" Wynter watched Pearce's eyes smolder, and her toes curled at the thought of what Pearce's talented fingers could do to her. *Soon. Please, God, soon.*

"My contractions are five minutes apart, so I thought it was time that we take a little trip."

Wynter sat bolt upright. "What? Now?"

"Can't be too soon for me," Mina said with a laugh.

"Well, don't let it be *too* soon." Wynter threw back the covers. "I'll be right there. Where's Ken?"

"He's working today. We can call him when we have an ETA on the new arrival."

"Okay. Don't do anything." Wynter closed her phone and jumped to her feet. "Baby. Baby's coming," she announced, as she began rifling through a pile of fresh laundry for clothes. She glanced over as Pearce sat up. "We'll take Ronnie next door. Chloe's coming. Can you get her?"

"Sure."

"On second thought, maybe you shouldn't carry her."

"Babe, I've been carrying her for two days." Pearce kissed Wynter, who stopped her frantic search long enough to appreciate the heat of Pearce's mouth. "I'll finish with you later."

Wynter reached around and squeezed Pearce's butt. "You bet your ass you will."

Laughing, Pearce started toward the hall and Ronnie's room.

❖

Four hours later, Wynter and Pearce tapped lightly on the door and entered Mina's room on the maternity ward. Ken sat by the side of the bed, one hand resting on the bundle that Mina cradled between her breasts. He grinned as they approached the bed.

"Congratulations," Pearce said. "He's beautiful."

Ken and Mina beamed.

"Well, that *did* go well," Wynter said, bending down to kiss Mina's cheek.

"Easy for you to say," Mina replied. "I was the one doing all the work." She glanced at Ken. "Of course, you *were* doing a lot of the breathing."

He grimaced. "Much more and I was afraid I'd hyperventilate and fall over."

"Next time, you should pay more attention in birthing class," Mina advised. "You doctors always think you know everything."

"Next time?" Ken moaned softly. "I need to recover from this time first."

Wynter gave Ken's shoulder a friendly shove. "I've heard you say you wanted four or five."

"Yeah. Uh-huh." He relaxed back in his chair. "And I heard Ronnie tell Winston just this morning that *she* was going to get a new brother or sister soon too."

"Uh-oh," Mina said as Wynter blushed and Pearce stared at a spot on the wall.

"Well," Wynter said in a rush, "we should go. Just wanted to say congratulations again." She peeked under the cover of the soft blue receiving blanket and caressed the baby's downy black hair. "He really is beautiful." She kissed Mina's cheek again and smiled at Ken. "Don't worry. We'll hold down the fort at home."

Both Mina and Ken waved goodbye. Wynter and Pearce were silent as they walked the length of the maternity floor to the elevators at the far end. Pearce pushed the *down* button and leaned against the wall.

"Did Ronnie get that idea from you? About more children?"

"That's all her idea." Wynter reached for Pearce's hand and clasped it tightly. "I hadn't really thought about it. Things weren't very good between Dave and me after Ronnie was born. Dave always said he wanted—"

"Forget about him—what about just for you? Is that what you would like?"

"Pearce, honey—I have Ronnie and—"

The elevator doors opened, but Pearce made no move to get in. She regarded Wynter intently. "Do you think we can't have kids?"

"No, I don't think that," Wynter said carefully. "I just never got the sense it was in your game plan."

"Neither were you." Pearce traced a finger along the edge of Wynter's jaw. "I'm not volunteering *personally*, but seeing as how you've already had some practice at it…"

Wynter caught Pearce's hand and curled her fingers around it, drawing their joined hands close to her heart. She took a step forward until their bodies were very nearly touching. "Would you like it, if we had one together?"

"One or two more would be good."

Wynter's expression registered shocked delight. "One. Or. Two."

Pearce grinned. "Ronnie said a brother or a sister. We could try for both."

"You do realize how crazy it will be, with both of us practicing surgeons, and kids to raise?" Wynter took one quick look over her shoulder, and seeing that the hall was empty, kissed Pearce quickly. "I love you."

"I think we can handle it," Pearce murmured. She kissed Wynter back. "Besides, you know what they say in surgery—"

Eyes laughing, hearts soaring, they said together, "No guts, no glory."

"Let's go home, darling," Wynter said, "and finish what we started this afternoon. *Then* we'll talk about the future."

"Now *that* sounds like a plan." Pearce wrapped her arm around Wynter's shoulders. "After all, we've got lots of time."

About the Author

Radclyffe has written numerous best-selling lesbian romances (*Safe Harbor* and its sequels *Beyond the Breakwater* and *Distant Shores, Silent Thunder*; *Innocent Hearts*; *Love's Melody Lost*; *Love's Tender Warriors*; *Tomorrow's Promise*; *Passion's Bright Fury*; *Love's Masquerade*; *shadowland*; and *Fated Love*), two romance/intrigue series: the Honor series (*Above All, Honor*; *Honor Bound*; *Love & Honor*; *Honor Guards*; and *Honor Reclaimed*) and the Justice series (*Shield of Justice*, the prequel *A Matter of Trust*, *In Pursuit of Justice*, *Justice in the Shadows*, and *Justice Served*), and the Erotic Interlude series: *Change of Pace* and *Stolen Moments: Erotic Interludes 2* (ed. with Stacia Seaman). She also has selections in the anthologies *Call of the Dark* and *The Perfect Valentine* (Bella Books), *Best Lesbian Erotica 2006* (Cleis), and *First-Timers* (Alyson).

She is the recipient of the 2003 and 2004 Alice B. Readers' award for her body of work and a 2005 Golden Crown Literary Society Award winner in both the romance category (*Fated Love*) and the mystery/intrigue/action category (*Justice in the Shadows*). She is also the president of Bold Strokes Books, a lesbian publishing company. In 2005, she retired from the practice of surgery to write and publish full-time. A member of the GCLS, Pink Ink, and the Romance Writers of America, she collects lesbian pulps, enjoys photographing scenes for her book covers, and shares her life with her partner, Lee, and assorted canines.

Her upcoming works include *Erotic Interludes 3: Lessons in Love*, ed. with Stacia Seaman (May 2006), *Promising Hearts* (June 2006), *Erotic Interludes 4: Extreme Passions,* ed. with Stacia Seaman (October 2006), and *Storms of Change* (October 2006).

Look for information about these works at www.boldstrokesbooks.com.

Books Available From Bold Strokes Books

Wild Abandon by Ronica Black. From their first tumultuous meeting, Dr. Chandler Brogan and Officer Sarah Monroe are drawn together by their common obsessions—sex, speed, and danger. (1-933-110-35-X)

Turn Back Time by Radclyffe. Pearce Rifkin and Wynter Thompson have nothing in common but a shared passion for surgery. They clash at every opportunity, especially when matters of the heart are suddenly at stake. (1-933-110-34-1)

Chance by Grace Lennox. At twenty-six, Chance Delaney decides her life isn't working so she swaps it for a different one. What follows is the sexy, funny, touching story of two women who, in finding themselves, also find one another. (1-933110-31-7)

The Exile and the Sorcerer by Jane Fletcher. First in the Lyremouth Chronicles. Tevi, wounded and adrift, arrives in the courtyard of a shy young sorcerer. Together they face monsters, magic, and the challenge of loving despite their differences. (1-933110-32-5)

A Matter of Trust by Radclyffe. JT Sloan is a cybersleuth who doesn't like attachments. Michael Lassiter is leaving her husband, and she needs Sloan's expertise to safeguard her company. It should just be business—but it turns into much more. (1-933110-33-3)

Sweet Creek by Lee Lynch. A celebration of the enduring nature of love, friendship, and community in the quirky, heart-warming lesbian community of Waterfall Falls. (1-933110-29-5)

The Devil Inside by Ali Vali. Derby Cain Casey, head of a New Orleans crime organization, runs the family business with guts and grit, and no one crosses her. No one, that is, until Emma Verde claims her heart and turns her world upside down. (1-933110-30-9)

Grave Silence by Rose Beecham. Detective Jude Devine's investigation of a series of ritual murders is complicated by her torrid affair with the golden girl of Southwestern forensic pathology, Dr. Mercy Westmoreland. (1-933110-25-2)

Honor Reclaimed by Radclyffe. In the aftermath of 9/11, Secret Service Agent Cameron Roberts and Blair Powell close ranks with a trusted few to find the would-be assassins who nearly claimed Blair's life. (1-933110-18-X)

Honor Bound by Radclyffe. Secret Service Agent Cameron Roberts and Blair Powell face political intrigue, a clandestine threat to Blair's safety, and the seemingly irreconcilable personal differences that force them ever farther apart. (1-933110-20-1)

Protector of the Realm: Supreme Constellations Book One by Gun Brooke. A space adventure filled with suspense and a daring intergalactic romance featuring Commodore Rae Jacelon and the stunning, but decidedly lethal, Kellen O'Dal. (1-933110-26-0)

Innocent Hearts by Radclyffe. In a wild and unforgiving land, two women learn about love, passion, and the wonders of the heart. (1-933110-21-X)

The Temple at Landfall by Jane Fletcher. An imprinter, one of Celaeno's most revered servants of the Goddess, is also a prisoner to the faith—until a Ranger frees her by claiming her heart. The Celaeno series. (1-933110-27-9)

Force of Nature by Kim Baldwin. From tornados to forest fires, the forces of nature conspire to bring Gable McCoy and Erin Richards close to danger, and closer to each other. (1-933110-23-6)

In Too Deep by Ronica Black. Undercover homicide cop Erin McKenzie tracks a femme fatale who just might be a real killer…with love and danger hot on her heels. (1-933110-17-1)

Stolen Moments: *Erotic Interludes 2* by Stacia Seaman and Radclyffe, eds. Love on the run, in the office, in the shadows…Fast, furious, and almost too hot to handle. (1-933110-16-3)

Course of Action by Gun Brooke. Actress Carolyn Black desperately wants the starring role in an upcoming film produced by Annelie Peterson. Just how far will she go for the dream part of a lifetime? (1-933110-22-8)

Rangers at Roadsend by Jane Fletcher. Sergeant Chip Coppelli has learned to spot trouble coming, and that is exactly what she sees in her new recruit, Katryn Nagata. The Celaeno series. (1-933110-28-7)

Justice Served by Radclyffe. Lieutenant Rebecca Frye and her lover, Dr. Catherine Rawlings, embark on a deadly game of hide-and-seek with an underworld kingpin who traffics in human souls. (1-933110-15-5)

Distant Shores, Silent Thunder by Radclyffe. Dr. Tory King—along with the women who love her—is forced to examine the boundaries of love, friendship, and the ties that transcend time. (1-933110-08-2)

Hunter's Pursuit by Kim Baldwin. A raging blizzard, a mountain hideaway, and a killer-for-hire set a scene for disaster—or desire—when Katarzyna Demetrious rescues a beautiful stranger. (1-933110-09-0)

The Walls of Westernfort by Jane Fletcher. All Temple Guard Natasha Ionadis wants is to serve the Goddess—until she falls in love with one of the rebels she is sworn to destroy. The Celaeno series. (1-933110-24-4)

Change Of Pace: *Erotic Interludes* by Radclyffe. Twenty-five hot-wired encounters guaranteed to spark more than just your imagination. Erotica as you've always dreamed of it. (1-933110-07-4)

Honor Guards by Radclyffe. In a wild flight for their lives, the president's daughter and those who are sworn to protect her wage a desperate struggle for survival. (1-933110-01-5)

Fated Love by Radclyffe. Amidst the chaos and drama of a busy emergency room, two women must contend not only with the fragile nature of life, but also with the irresistible forces of fate. (1-933110-05-8)

Justice in the Shadows by Radclyffe. In a shadow world of secrets and lies, Detective Sergeant Rebecca Frye and her lover, Dr. Catherine Rawlings, join forces in the elusive search for justice.
(1-933110-03-1)

shadowland by Radclyffe. In a world on the far edge of desire, two women are drawn together by power, passion, and dark pleasures. An erotic romance. (1-933110-11-2)

Love's Masquerade by Radclyffe. Plunged into the indistinguishable realms of fiction, fantasy, and hidden desires, Auden Frost is forced to question all she believes about the nature of love. (1-933110-14-7)

Love & Honor by Radclyffe. The president's daughter and her lover are faced with difficult choices as they battle a tangled web of Washington intrigue for...love and honor. (1-933110-10-4)

Beyond the Breakwater by Radclyffe. One Provincetown summer, three women learn the true meaning of love, friendship, and family. (1-933110-06-6)

Tomorrow's Promise by Radclyffe. One timeless summer, two very different women discover the power of passion to heal and the promise of hope that only love can bestow. (1-933110-12-0)

Love's Tender Warriors by Radclyffe. Two women who have accepted loneliness as a way of life learn that love is worth fighting for and a battle they cannot afford to lose. (1-933110-02-3)

Love's Melody Lost by Radclyffe. A secretive artist with a haunted past and a young woman escaping a life that has proved to be a lie find their destinies entwined. (1-933110-00-7)

Safe Harbor by Radclyffe. A mysterious newcomer, a reclusive doctor, and a troubled gay teenager learn about love, friendship, and trust during one tumultuous summer in Provincetown. (1-933110-13-9)

Above All, Honor by Radclyffe. Secret Service Agent Cameron Roberts fights her desire the one woman she can't have—Blair Powell, the daughter of the president of the United States. (1-933110-04-X)

BOLD
STROKES
BOOKS